The Singer not the Song

Theodore Lownik Library
Illinois Benedictine College
Lisle, Illinois 60532

THE SINGER
NOT
THE SONG

By

AUDREY ERSKINE LINDOP

Theodore Lownik Library
Illinois Benedictine College
Lisle, Illinois 60532
WITHDRAWN

New York
APPLETON-CENTURY-CROFTS
INC.

Copyright, 1953, By

WILLIAM HEINEMANN, LTD.

All rights reserved. This book, or parts
thereof, must not be reproduced in any
form without permission of the publisher.

*All names, characters, and events in this
book are fictional, and any resemblance
which may seem to exist to real persons
is purely coincidental.*

Library of Congress Card Number: 52–14029

PRINTED IN THE UNITED STATES OF AMERICA

48286

For Lindy,

With My Love.

48286

The Singer not the Song

Chapter 1

It would not be an easy interview. The Bishop was aware that the priest he appointed to the parish of Quantana might well be facing death. He touched a bell on his desk and said to the secretary who answered it, "I will see him in ten minutes."

Beneath the Bishop's window the crowd jostled. It seemed in perpetual danger from the impatient congested traffic. There were times when it struck the Bishop as little short of a miracle that the scene below was not transformed into one colossal and fatal collision. There were times when he gritted his teeth looking down on the shining moving mess, appalled at the recklessness of a driver determined to outdo a rival. If he opened his windows the noise fell into the room, almost solid in its deafening intensity. The Bishop, born and country bred, could never accustom himself to the noise. He kept his windows closed against it whenever he wished to concentrate. He closed them himself before his interview with the priest.

Amongst the more obvious, the parish of Quantana needed a quality upon which the Bishop found it difficult to place his finger. He was not sure that it might not be summed up simply as "common sense"—but it seemed an unimpressive virtue to ask of men who possessed so many more altruistic ones, and who might through the very nature of them be justifiably convinced that it would rank as the least important. Nevertheless, in order that he might not lose sight of its value himself, the Bishop had written a reminder upon his blotter—*Instinctive common sense,* underlined it, and sketched beside it for no particular reason a sword and a heart. He was a little ashamed of the drawing. He considered "doodling" the self-indulgence of a fidgety mind. But he was an inveterate doodler. There were several occasions upon which the Bishop had felt obliged to return to his desk upon some pretext or other, in order to remove

1

from the eyes of the arid young man who was his secretary, a series of capering pigs upon a sheet of green blotting paper.

He spent the ten minutes praying that he might make the right choice, and he prayed for the man he eventually chose.

The Bishop was a trifle uncertain of his own powers of judging character. He saw the best in everyone. He was genuinely able to make allowances where others failed to do so, and to give the benefit of the doubt however undeserving. He was not sure that it might not be cowardice. It hurt him to witness evil. He closed his eyes to it, searching for an excuse for it, trying to find some virtue to counteract it. It caused him mental pain to admit faults in his fellow men. He was an inveterate seeker of the silver lining in a character. He was not sure that it might not be construed as a venial sin, something in his own nature that sought for the easy way out. Even if his optimism was proved unwise and his trust abused, he adhered to his first impressions. His stubbornness in this direction was attributed to loyalty amongst his friends, but he himself was afraid that it might be attributable to his own ego.

In view of this he had decided to interview again each of the five men who had expressed themselves ready to go to Quantana, and endeavor to judge them afresh. It was a difficult task. The Bishop was always prejudiced in favor of anyone with whom he had had personal contact.

He had already seen four of the priests. He had been impressed by all of them. The first had a forceful personality and a "no nonsense" air about him which had quite intimidated the Bishop. But he admired it. The second had a spiritual approach to life which called forth nothing but respect. The third had small brown eyes which would have struck anyone but the Bishop as untrustworthy. He had also a cardinal for an uncle. The fourth who had been on holiday struck the Bishop as having returned from it happily out of touch with God. They were nevertheless all four of them deeply anxious to go to Quantana. Even the Cardinal's nephew, whom the Bishop suspected of mentioning his eminent uncle for reasons not unconnected with a gentle form of blackmail, could hardly be said to be doing so to his own personal advantage. The Bishop admired and respected the eagerness of the four men. He had still the fifth to interview.

He was sighing when Father Keogh was shown into the room.

The Bishop liked Father Keogh on sight. But he kept a stern

2

eye on himself. "Now I mustn't make my mind up too quickly. I must use every power of discernment." He smiled broadly at Father Keogh and made a half-hearted attempt to be hypercritical. It was not easy. Father Keogh was neither diffident nor overbearing. He was respectfully and unaffectedly at ease.

Father Keogh smiled back at his Bishop. He had all the confidence of a youth that was still close behind him, the grave maturity that his faith had given him, the wisdom and humility that his church had taught him, and the simple truths he had discovered for himself. These things had given great strength to Father Keogh. They were visible in the way he held his shoulders back and in the carriage of his head, in the depths of his untroubled eyes and above all in the calm of his unhurried voice.

The Bishop thought, "How *difficult*. It's all very well to say that it's easy to sum people up, but supposing there's nothing to sum up, supposing people are obviously admirable at first glance . . . it's all very well . . ." And the Bishop gave vent to a small sign of irritability. He banged his paper weight on an ill-spelled letter from a niece in the Sierra Grande. He looked up to see a flicker of apprehension on Father Keogh's face.

Father Keogh imagined that the Bishop was not impressed with him. He was a foreigner and he thought his chances poor. He waited anxiously while the Bishop looked down at his desk. The Bishop had a disconcerting expression. He had humorous eyes in a serious face. He was reading a report on Father Keogh. . . .

Father Keogh's academic qualifications were adequate, but not outstanding. They were not the awe-inspiring scholastic achievements of the third priest whom the Bishop had interviewed. Father Keogh's record showed that hard work in difficult circumstances could have left little time for asceticism. "Courageous, resourceful and forthright" had been written in connection with Father Keogh.

He knew the four priests who had been interviewed before him. He envied every one of them. Three were Mexicans and had therefore an immediate advantage over him. The fourth was a Spaniard whom Father Keogh had encountered during his own mission to Spain in the civil war. He was even regretting the Spanish interlude. Fraught though it was with experiences that brought him close to the everyday human need of God, and filled though it was with the everyday evidence of God's response to that need, it had deprived him of time which he might have applied to his own personal sanctification.

3

When he was appointed to a parish where vice was rampant, his favorite sister Ellen-Dora, always irreverent, wrote from Ireland, "Darling, why do they always pick you for the rough stuff? Can't they pitch someone else into the fray for a change? What do they think you are, an Aunt Sally? What's the use of a wonderful brain if they give it nothing to work on but thugs? I wish you'd never gone to Rome, I wish you'd never gone to the States. I wish you'd never become a priest!!! Don't you wish you were here to dot me one? Anyway what's wrong with the old country? We've got plenty of sinners here. Our old Poppet is getting too feeble. He drops off to sleep in the confessional. Couldn't you come and relieve him? Come back and give him a break!"

His sister's opinion of his "wonderful" brain never failed to amuse Father Keogh. He was well educated but no intellectual. He knew it and regretted it. He found it hard not to envy the regular clergy the seclusion of a monastic life which provided peace for the stimulation of the intellect. There was no time in the life of a busy parochial priest, and yet he would not have changed it. It was the life he had chosen and the life he loved. But it made him sadly conscious of his deficiencies as he stood before the Bishop. Had he not perhaps gone out of his way to volunteer for the "rough stuff"? Might it not be construed as personal vanity on his part—this desire to go wherever the faithful seemed in need of vigorous encouragement? Might it not be construed as a delight of entering into personal combat with the enemies of God for the sake of the personal conflict?

The Bishop raised his eyes from his desk. "Father Keogh, your record has shown that you are able to carry the word of God in a straightforward manner which can be very efficacious . . ."

Father Keogh had once suffered at the hands of a rector who launched into a reprimand by recounting the virtues of the victim first. He invariably ended with a formidable and emphatic, *"But,* Father So and So, it has to be admitted . . ."

Father Keogh sat waiting for the Bishop's "But."

The Bishop continued, "And if the church makes use of this particular human quality rather than your intellectual powers, you must not suppose that she is unaware of them. It must occur to many a young priest that the church might use him to her greater advantage. The first followers of our Lord were simple men, theirs was not the learned or academic approach. You might think that to carry on this tradition, those of our clergy who come themselves from

4

peasant classes would prove apt in this respect—but unfortunately this is not always the case. In these days of so-called enlightenment, one has to possess learning to interpret simplicity. One has to be clever in these days in order to be simple. It is rare indeed to find someone with the ability to keep his own superior education in the channels where it can be of most service—who has the plain approach which can carry the word of God straight into the hearts of his fellow men without being tempted to encumber it with his own brilliance."

The Bishop felt that he had explained as tactfully as possible to Father Keogh the reasons why he had decided to make use of a vigorous personality rather than erudite distinctions.

Father Keogh made no attempt to disguise his delight.

The Bishop said, "This is your first visit to Mexico, how does it strike you?"

"I think I was most impressed by the changes in the scenery, my Lord. Some of it reminded me of Ireland. It has to be a pretty good green to come up to an Irishman's standards!"

"Ah!" smiled the Bishop. "Mexico has somewhere like everywhere else, but nowhere has somewhere like Mexico!"

There was a map on his desk. He put the point of a pencil on it and drew a circle around a tiny speck in a cluster of shady mountains.

"Here we are," said the Bishop. "This is the place. It looks like a mountain eyrie, doesn't it?"

"Quantana," read Father Keogh. Then he fingered a sheaf of papers written in a close and slanting hand. "Is this Father Gomez's report, my Lord?"

"Yes," replied the Bishop. "But before you read that, I want you to read something else." He leaned over and pressed the bell. To the secretary who crossed the thick carpet without a sound, he said, "Bring me the Gomez file."

The Bishop knew that the priest was impatient with him, not intolerantly, but with the desire of a younger man to hurry the business in hand and cut short the dalliance of the old. He smiled at Father Keogh, and it was a smile that crossed his eyes before it reached his mouth. He was eating salted almonds. "I love these things," he admitted. "So I only allow myself six a day, and this I'm afraid is my sixth."

Father Keogh leaned across to push the little silver dish away. "Shall I put them out of your Lordship's reach?"

"Oh dear me, no," the Bishop said. "One must resist temptation, not remove it." And he drew the small dish back again, and sighed a little over it. Then he met Father Keogh's eyes above his folded hands.

"Your Spanish is excellent, Father. I have always attached the greatest importance to the study of language amongst the clergy. Its value cannot be overestimated. I've mastered quite a few myself."

"Your English, my Lord, is remarkable."

"Yes, well, at the moment I am engaged on a form of it which I believe will shortly become universal amongst the English-speaking races."

"Esperanto?" Father Keogh inquired.

"Slang," said the Bishop.

"Slang, my Lord?"

"Slang," said the Bishop. "It seems to be the tongue of the modern generation, and I feel that one should learn it, otherwise the older generations will find themselves in the position of foreigners in their own countries. Take, for instance," the Bishop said, "this." From a bottom drawer he produced a newspaper. It bore very extraordinary headlines—FURY WHAMS STIX.

"There you are," said the Bishop triumphantly. "What do you make out of that?"

"Not much, my Lord," Father Keogh admitted. "What's it supposed to be, Polish?" He smiled when he asked the question.

The Bishop took him seriously.

"Polish my foot. It is slang, my dear Father. I quite appreciate that you might not have grasped the fact, but these headlines refer to some cinematic entertainment entitled *Flame and Fury* which has achieved a high success at the box office in country districts. Now do you see the urgency? Do you realize the necessity to fathom this new form of speech? It's another tongue already. I keep a small book and make a note of any new word I come across. The other day I met a young American visitor who referred to his lady friend as a 'lollapaloosa.' I mean, it's just possible that one wouldn't have known what he was talking about. Ah!" he said as the secretary put the Gomez file down on his desk. He searched through it and extracted a letter. "Father Gomez was rather a special protégé of mine. I always had great faith in him, and I'm afraid I must claim it as a point in my favor. He had an exceptionally nervous disposition which gave him a somewhat unprepossessing personality. He couldn't, now let me see, what's the phrase for it . . . he couldn't say . . ."

6

"Boo to a goose?" Father Keogh supplied.

"Exactly," said the Bishop. "I believe it was always a problem to him, and although it may seem surprising that the inability to make explosive noises at feathered creatures should prove detrimental to clerical advancement, I understand that in the case of Father Gomez, this was so."

Father Keogh smiled. "But he proved his mettle in the persecution days, didn't he?"

"He did indeed," said the Bishop with enthusiasm. "He remained at his post—if post it could be called, considering such posts had been abolished. His life was in constant danger, he was frequently near starvation, he was ill, and he was badly wounded. The church has every reason to be very proud of him."

"It certainly has," said Father Keogh.

"It was not an unremarkable achievement," the Bishop confided. "As you know, in those lamentable times there were many priests shot, and any number forced to flee the country. But Father Gomez managed to avoid both extremities. There was one occasion," the Bishop smiled, "when he was compelled to dress up as a woman. I don't know how true the story is, these things get so embellished, but he must have looked rather fetching, for I hear that on this occasion he was pursued for reasons unconnected with the persecution of the church." Father Keogh chuckled. "But that is not the incident I should have told you about. There was another one. Father Gomez was celebrating the mass in the Hua caves. Somebody must have known about it, for someone informed the Comandante. The Hua ledge is a sort of terrace rock. And while the congregation made their escape from the caves, Father Gomez came out onto the ledge and drew the fire of the soldiers. They hit him twice, but it gave the rest of them time to get away. Now read this personal Quantana report."

The report bore a date only three weeks old.

Father Keogh read:

His real name is Anacleto Gonzalez Flores Comachi Alvarez. It is ironical that his mother should have called him after the martyr Anacleto Gonzalez Flores who died with such courage for the faith, but his mother was a good Catholic and she thought that such a name would prove an inspiration to him. They refer to him here as Malo, the Bad-One-of-the-Cats. I knew his family well. The father was killed before he was born.

7

The mother was a bad woman morally, but as I have said a faithful Catholic. She gave me shelter once. She is dead now. Anacleto was her only child and his mother could never control him. He grew up in times of turbulence and strife. He grew up in a State that had denounced religion and looked upon the violation of the church as patriotism. His heroes were villains and the creed he was fed upon was one of violence. He really had little chance. He was a law unto himself when the law of the State condoned sacrilege and savagery, when evil was encouraged and rewarded. I do not know his history from the time I was forced to leave the State, but one can only suppose that it left much to be desired. From time to time I heard tales of him. He was rising fast in the exploits of crime. His deeds became quite notorious. He was raiding villages and terrorizing the whole State before he was twenty-one. His minions are as merciless as himself.

He served a prison sentence in Mexico City, but it seems to have had little effect upon him.

During the last few years he has achieved complete domination in Quantana, and his influence is felt as far as Huapan, Arenales and Cerro Colorado. That I have failed to check this lamentous rise to power I cannot deny, and if I say that I have had little or no support, it is not to excuse what is inexcusable, no man of faith has an excuse for failure, but to warn my successor of what he must expect. You will have to send after me a true soldier of the church. He will need to have endurance as well as courage. The police too have little support. They are not strong and those who are not directly in Anacleto's pay, have in turn no support from the town. The people think it safer to protect Anacleto from the police than trust the police to protect them from Anacleto. They consider this last is a risk. The church (in my hands) is also powerless. He has crippled the people's faith. He has severed them from the church. If they had its protection and its solace they would not fear him, and if they no longer feared him they would have the courage to denounce him. There are many with the power to do this. But the fear of reprisals is great. Those who make a stand pay dearly for it. But those who comply are safe, so the people are law abiding according to Anacleto's law. We are, of course, far away from help in the isolation of our mountains and in the rains we are com-

pletely cut off. It is a sorry position when the people resent their priest. Although in their hearts they know right from wrong, they are afraid to strike out for the right. They are afraid to come to church. I have had as few as three to mass and not more than one for confession, and these few are taking a risk. It is as bad as the days of the persecution. They know that the church will urge them to fight against Anacleto and they believe that the church would lose that fight. They consider ME the trouble maker. I do not envy the new priest his task. As for me, I am completely unworthy of it. I dare not raise my hand against him in case I bring down his vengeance upon my flock. You will see that they deserve a stronger hand than mine.

Again, without making excuses, I must tell you that this Anacleto is not an ordinary man. He has an unworldly patience. He has a high percentage of Indian blood in him, and he has also a curious affection for cats. It is not kindness that makes him like them. He has no kindness in him. In the village they say that when the moon is full he turns into a giant white cat and roams the mountainside. It is not as superstitious and as absurd as it sounds. Anacleto has something in common with cats. He has their uncanny insights and intuitions. They are the only living creatures for which he shows any respect, and he has one other thing in common with them. He likes best to play with his victims. He seldom kills outright. This seems to be a compliment that he only pays to cats. I have seen him put an injured kitten out of its misery.

"Malo" was a word used so often in connection with him, even in his infancy, that it took the place of his proper name. He is cruel beyond ordinary cruelty. It seems to have taken the place of religion with him, or perhaps it is his faith; much as if the devil in bringing up his children taught them the same simple respect for all things evil, as our Lord taught for love and kindness. He is possessed of great personal courage, and I believe that in this lies his mastery over lesser men. It is as if he knew that in everyone else but himself he could surprise a hidden store of fear.

To give an example of Anacleto's insight, I will quote a childhood incident. It was during my fugitive days and I had returned to seek refuge in Quantana. It was then that his mother sheltered me. Anacleto was a very young child. Afraid that he might give

9

me away by childish chatter, his mother hid me from him. She fed me and let me rest on her own bed. It was during the rains and my clothes were drenched. Believing that Anacleto was safely asleep the woman put these nondescript rags to dry before a fire. Anacleto discovered them. As I have said, the mother was not a moral woman even at a time when morals were inclined to be lax, I could have been one of any number of lovers behind the locked door of her room. The child must have been used to seeing men every night, and it was indeed this fact which made me think it safe to take shelter with her. But Anacleto took a broom handle and poked my clothes well into the flames of the fire. This might have been an ordinary prank of a child brought up in such circumstances, who might have thought it amusing to put his mother's lover in an embarrassing position. But he did not destroy my shoes. He took them with their gaping soles, and their telltale marks of blood from my blistered feet, and put them side by side on the Comandante's desk. Quite remarkable sagacity in a child so young. Fortunately the mother discovered the theft before the soldiers came. She lent me some clothes of her own and I escaped as a woman. Such, then, was Anacleto at five years old. At five and twenty he ruled Quantana. Where he failed to strike against me as a child, he has succeeded as a man. I am old and I am tired, and I am powerless against him.

Father Keogh put down the report.

The Bishop said, "You must not judge the whole of the country by this one little black spot. It may well be that some of it is a hang-over from the persecution days insomuch as that Comachi, as Father Gomez tells us, was born in times of turbulence, and he may well have retained a certain enmity towards the church, but until it fell under this bandit domination Quantana was no different from any other town."

"It seems extraordinary," Father Keogh said, "that they cannot get help from outside."

"In these country places you will find the Mexican curiously unconcerned with what goes on outside his own vicinity. And then as you saw from the Gomez report, Quantana doesn't *want* help. That will prove your biggest difficulty, Father. One might say that Father Gomez has done his best—but he was not successful. He has fallen

10

into a line of least resistance. One might say that has saved him. You will not be so safe, my son."

"This Malo sounds quite a problem," Father Keogh admitted.

"This Malo sounds more than a problem," the Bishop said. "He would put the wind up me. Father Gomez has met his match. The reason I wanted to show you that report was not so much that I didn't want you to underrate Father Gomez—but because I did not want you to underrate his *match*."

Chapter 2

Three days later Father Keogh walked up a steep road that covered his boots in white dust. He carried with him his Bishop's blessing and special permission to celebrate mass before dawn and after midday.

He stood on a rocky parapet and looked down upon Quantana. It was olive-shaped, narrowing either end into a collection of straggling adobe huts. Goat tracks ran into the mountainside like deep brown veins, and the big maguey plant spread out its clumsy leaves to form an ugly hedgerow. Small stumpy acacias grew in profusion and thorny bushes spread round the mountainsides dancing black dots in the shimmering glare. From the height of the rock, little flower-decked patios sent a bright checked pattern throughout the town. A colonnaded building, faintly pink, caught the sunlight in its windows. The mountaintops jigged in the sun, tier upon tier of them, until they fell back and were lost in a hazy line. The earth was a careless golden brown. A giant cypress tree obscured most of the view of the church, but the flame tree rose to challenge it, its gaudy flower commanding attention amongst the quieter tamarindo trees.

Above the town a vulture hovered, wings flung out, cutting a triangle into the heavens as if someone had torn at the blinding blue sky impatiently and left in it a ragged black rent.

Father Keogh turned and walked down the hill. On his way he passed the Casa Grande, perched on the rock like a colossal white wedding cake.

A child was picking flowers under the old stone wall, and as Father Keogh passed her she handed him one through the gates.

"Thank you," Father Keogh said. "That was a very nice thought."

"I've got a tortoise," the child informed him.

"Have you?" he asked. "What's his name?"

"Malo," replied the child.

"Malo!" Father Keogh said, and his clearly marked eyebrows went up. "What's that in aid of, tortoises don't like cats!"

"Yes they do, my kitten rides on his back, they go for miles and miles and miles together, sometimes they go into Huapan and back."

"I think that's a bit of an exaggeration," Father Keogh smiled, "Huapan is over a hundred miles away, I don't think they'd go there *and* back."

"Oh, yes they do," she assured him earnestly, "They go further than that and back."

"Who are you?" he asked. "What's your name?"

"Dorotea Rosalia Teodora Maria-Cristina de Cortinez y Ketter. But I'm always called Locha for short."

"I'm very glad to hear it," Father Keogh said.

"Are you going to stay here?" the child inquired.

"I think so," Father Keogh said.

"Won't Malo kill you?" she asked him politely.

"I hope not," Father Keogh replied, "but why should he, he hasn't killed Father Gomez."

"Oh, well," said the child. "You see he's no need to. Father Gomez doesn't matter much."

"Do you think I shall matter more to Malo?"

"Don't know," she answered. "It's hard to tell. But Malo doesn't like priests."

"What makes you like him so much?"

The child looked shocked. "I don't *like* him. I don't know him. He isn't our kind."

"Then why do you call your tortoise after him?"

"Oh, well he's useful sometimes. He stops me from going to church." She put a foot through the trellis of the great iron gates and lifted up her weight on it.

12

"Don't you ever go?" Father Keogh asked.

"Oh, yes, Josefa's an awful silly. She often sneaks me down."

"Who is Josefa?"

"My nurse."

"What do you mean she 'sneaks' you down?—Don't you like going to church?"

"Josefa says if you don't go you drop down dead. Josefa's a terrible silly. But I think church is silly."

Father Keogh licked his lips. "What makes you think it so silly? Don't you believe in God?"

"Oh, yes, if you don't you drop down dead. It's just church that I think is silly. Our Father, Hail Mary, Our Father, Hail Mary! It's stupid," giggled the child.

Father Keogh was feeling the heat. "Are your parents good Catholics?"

"Well, mother is 'nothing' and father's 'immersed-in-his-books.' " She appeared to be quoting somebody.

"I see. And what do they think of this 'Gran-Señor-of-the-Cats'?"

"He's *not* a gran señor, he's a peon! Silly old Father Gomez says he's the devil dressed up in disguise," and the child buckled up with laughter, her chin on the side of her arm.

"Silly old Father Gomez," said Father Keogh with a touch of asperity, "sounds as if he might be right, except perhaps for the disguise. And don't you know that it's very rude to talk about people like that?"

"Goodness gracious me!" she said. "Aren't we getting cross?"

"We're on the verge of it," Father Keogh agreed with her. "You're an extremely impolite little girl. Aren't you ashamed of yourself?"

She shook her head, nibbled her arm and mumbled at him, "I wish I hadn't given you a flower now."

"Well, would you like it back?" He offered it to her and she screwed up her face, debating.

"I'm considering," she said. But she forgot it and confided importantly, "Silly old Father Gomez is the silliest man I've met. Do you know—the last time I went to confession, do you know what he made me do? He made me say ten Our Father's and six Hail Mary's and three Glory Be's."

"I should think so too," said Father Keogh. "I should make you say more than that."

"Like hell you would," she laughed.

Father Keogh asked her gently, "Do your parents know you use language like that?"

"Of course not," the child retorted. "And I don't suppose they'd care if they did."

"I'm quite sure they would," Father Keogh said. "What makes you think they wouldn't care?"

The child repeated parrot-fashion, "Mother is 'nothing' and father's 'immersed in his books.' Do you know what I did after confession? I didn't say 'Our Father'—do you know what I said instead? I knelt in the church and I said, 'Silly old Father Gomez. Silly old Father Gomez.' I said it sixteen times."

Father Keogh made a mental note to visit the parents as soon as possible. He held out the flower again. "Well?" he asked of her. "Do you want me to keep it?"

She made indecisive noises. "You aren't quite as nice as you looked."

"If you want it take it back again, but if you want me to keep it, do you know what that means? It means that we're friends and that you're on my side and not the Gran-Señor-of-the-Cats'."

The child doubled up again, laughing. "He's *not* a gran señor, he's a peon." Then she added, surprised at herself, "But I'll be sorry if he kills you."

"Thank you very much," Father Keogh said.

"You can keep the flower," she told him, was suddenly bored, said, "Adios," sprang off the gate and raced away from him. He saw her run into the arms of a fat mestizo, calling, "Josefa! Josefa! I've seen the new priest—he's not a bit like the other one."

The mestizo dropped a curtsey to Father Keogh and took the child into the house.

Father Keogh trudged on down the hill. When he entered Quantana he was still holding the flower. It was small and white and delicate. Not unlike the child who had given it to him. When he walked through Quantana he felt it his only friend.

He threaded his way through the market place. A few heads nodded greetings at him, but most of them watched him in silence. After the noise of Mexico City, he found the uncanny silence disturbing. Soft-eyed Indians sat back on their heels, dignified, patient, suspicious of him, and on the roof tops and along a high white wall that ran half around the town, the vultures perched. He passed booths offering

14

fruits and vegetables and some selling radio parts. He passed an assortment of medicines, hair oils and cooked meats, and a booth stacked with soft drinks displayed in glass jars. Chickens cooped in wickerwork baskets hung from the roofs of the booths. The Indians squatted impassively. None of them called out their wares. Their goods were arranged in precise and artistic patterns and they sat in groups according to the nature of their wares. Those who sold pottery sat together, those who sold fruits and vegetables sat together, and the heads of each group turned with a guarded interest to watch Father Keogh pass.

The violet shadows joined each other making a near-black carpet across the plaza. The bandstand looked desolate in the center of it as if no music could ever burst forth from its aging structure, and the Indian laurels struggled round it defying the sun's hard rays.

An old woman sat on her haunches beside a booth loaded with fans, lace, silver-topped combs, rosaries and nylons. There was a notice hanging down beside her for the benefit of the rare visitor: *Mother Montezera. The only true witch left. Goods bought and exchanged.* She was so old that the dust seemed to have clogged in the lines of her face making its tracery black. She smoked a cigar and nodded gently. Round her shoulders a blanket hung, punctured with holes from hot ash. The eyes in her face could have belonged to a snake which might or might not have been alive. They were deep-set and glazed and when they moved they moved so slowly that they appeared to be dragging a weight. She called out a greeting to Father Keogh. He was grateful and called one back.

He was astounded when he heard the strains of "The Lily of Laguna" rolling out. Someone many years ago had imported a barrel organ. Nobody quite knew when. A sailor had wheeled it off a ship and traded it in for liquor. Someone else had hitched it to a mule and dragged it hundreds of miles to Quantana. It had not changed hands since then. A Spanish dwarf had bought it and earned his living from it. He had no front teeth and a perpetual grin. They had a variety of names for him. Sometimes they called him the organito, sometimes el jorobado the hunchback, but more often el choco, the half-wit. Everyone liked the barrel organ. It was an ageless novelty up in Quantana. It was battered and black and had lost its design, but a name was still visible, "Liz." It retained a rattling gaiety and when the rains made its transport impossible through the clogging mud it was lodged at the end of the Avenida del Cortinez. It rolled out the

15

tunes the whole day long—"Alexander's Ragtime Band," "The Lily of Laguna," "Annie Laurie," and "Little Gray Home in the West."

Father Keogh passed an American field gun that stood a rusting relic of revolution at the corner of a street. Children crawled over the gun scratching their names upon it, filling its barrel with paper and stones. Men leaned against it arguing prices. Donkeys and mules were tethered to it. Few people remembered what part it had played in the revolution. A band of ragged children leapt off it and followed Father Keogh. Barefooted and curious, they trailed behind him, defying his efforts to induce them to talk.

He turned into a street so narrow that the shadows of houses met in the middle. It formed a black alleyway right through the town. At the end of it Father Gomez lived.

When he reached the house, the children stood round his suitcase chattering about it. He stood outside the little whitewashed building. The wash had flaked off in places, showing the mud like brown scabs on a pock-marked face. A woman was shaking a child in the doorway. The child let out a long thin wail of resentment which ceased as abruptly as his punishment. The woman had seen the priest. She was barefooted and wore a white blouse over a long dark skirt. She came forward to smile at him showing gold teeth. "Ah, there you are, Father, you've found your way. I said we should have sent someone to meet you, but then—" She broke off embarrassed, and changed the subject, but not before Father Keogh had gathered that it had not been easy to find somebody willing to meet him. "My sister's son," she said of the boy who had joined the circle round the suitcase, "is not a good child," and she went forward to pick up the suitcase.

A thin voice called out from the house. "Is that the padre, Chela?"

She called back over her shoulder, "Yes, Father." Then she made angry gestures which failed to scatter the children and led Father Keogh inside.

A slight figure shuffled into the darkness. Father Keogh was having his hand wrung before the face in front of him became clear enough to see. His eyes were still filled with the hard sunlight from the street. When they accustomed themselves to the shade, he saw a small brown face. The quick bright eyes of a mouse were buried in it. They seemed to scuttle over Father Keogh.

"My word," said Father Gomez, "I *am* glad you've come. Upon my word, I *am* glad."

He turned round swiftly and proceeded Father Keogh into a tiny

16

room where the window was barred on the street. His short hurried footsteps, half a run, reminded Father Keogh even more sharply of the sudden, rush-forward movements of a mouse. He could imagine a long thin tail following Father Gomez, sliding round the door after him as the little priest scurried into the room. He tried to remind himself that Father Gomez had remained in constant danger at a time when a priest's only crime needed to have been that he remained a priest.

Father Keogh wished that he was shorter. It was impossible not to look down physically upon Father Gomez. He could have been no taller than five feet four inches high. Father Keogh sat down as soon as possible on the old horsehair sofa.

The room was shabbily furnished. The floor was tiled and there was a pale yellow matting across it. An old-fashioned medicine cabinet with bottle-green curtains served as a bookcase, and on the top of it stood a crucifix on a heavy wooden base. A picture of Saint Anthony of Padua hung in a dingy brown frame, and under the dusty glass, Father Keogh noticed that Saint Anthony's feet were flyblown. A bureau leaned up in the corner with a giant key sticking out of its lock. On the top of it were two efficient-looking letter baskets; one bore a postcard with the printed word OUT attached to it, and the other the printed word IN. There were letters in neither basket. But there were several dead cockroaches and a chewed pencil stump. A lamp stood on the table and the whole room smelled of kerosene.

Father Gomez was making a series of furtive darts across the floor which baffled Father Keogh. He pounced on the bureau, peeped into the medicine cabinet, and then stood mouse-still, silent and thoughtful. Father Keogh found it difficult not to picture both whiskers and a tail on Father Gomez. He closed his eyes in order to picture Father Gomez out on the Hua ledge with the soldiers firing up at him. When he opened his eyes again, Father Gomez was still darting about the room.

Father Keogh asked him kindly, "Are you looking for something?"

Father Gomez replied, "Yes. Yes. My laundry list. You have to be careful of laundry here. It gets lost so easily, I've lost quite a few things lately." The look that he gave to Saint Anthony was bordering on the reproachful. "I *have* asked him," he muttered. "I was wondering if you would send the things after me if they should appear again?"

"Certainly," Father Keogh said.

17

Father Gomez rattled about in the desk. He found a small piece of paper and made a dart towards Father Keogh with it.

"Yes, here we are. With the crosses against them, those are the ones that are lost. It's just the pajama trousers missing, I have the tops . . . then four linen handkerchiefs, ones like these . . ." He held out a moist handkerchief with which he had been dabbing at his face. "It would really be very good of you, if ever they should reappear. One can't afford to lose things. Chela does the washing. She takes it down to the river sometimes. I'm afraid she's rather careless, and then of course, they *steal* things here, steal them to sell them, you know . . ." He caught sight of Father Keogh's flower. He started visibly. "What's that?"

"I don't know," Father Keogh answered, "I've just been presented with it."

"Who by?"

"A little girl, an exceptionally rude little—"

"Be careful!" Father Gomez warned, as Father Keogh put the flower to his nose. "Be careful, it might be poisoned."

"Poisoned!"

"Oh, yes, yes, you must be careful of accepting things, although of course it's chiefly food and drink. Who did you say it was gave it to you?"

"A little girl called de Cortinez."

"Oh, little Locha," Father Gomez said. "Oh, yes, well then that's all right."

"The child was anti-church and used bad language."

Father Gomez made a noise with his lips. "Yes, yes I know. They leave her too much with the servants. She absorbs all the dregs of the town. But you see the mother is . . ."

" 'Nothing' and 'father's immersed in his books,' " Father Keogh finished for him. "Well I should think it's time the mother was something and father came out of his books. I've never met such an ill-mannered child."

Father Gomez came to an abrupt standstill. "Don Pedro is quite a recluse. He is a very distinguished scholar. He went to the English Oxford in his youth, and the mother Doña Marian is an American. He once had an enormous hacienda, he was the biggest landowner for miles. Well, I must be going now."

"Going?" Father Keogh asked him. "So soon? I hoped you might have time to show me round a little."

18

"Round where?" Father Gomez asked.

"Well, just, well I thought that we might have quite a bit to discuss and—"

Father Gomez interrupted, his voice high. "I wrote to the Bishop. I sent a report. I sent the Bishop details."

"Yes, I know, but there are so many things I should like to ask you personally."

"My bus," Father Gomez replied, "I have to catch my bus. If I don't catch this one there isn't another until Wednesday noon."

Father Keogh said gently, "If you could give me a few minutes I should appreciate it greatly. I'm sure that there are things I ought to know, that only you could tell me."

"Yes, yes, I expect so . . . I . . ." The little priest sat down. His hands were unstill in his lap. He spoke in short little bursts as if he were out of breath. "Now let me see. Yes, confession, not many people wish to confess, but if they do you must hear them very early in the morning. They are frightened when Anacleto is up and about. It's mostly the four Señoras, they are always together, Señora Martinez, Señora Fereira, Señora Solano and Señora Rodriguez, they are good women, always causing trouble—now let me see, what else?"

He was quite unable to keep his little bright eyes off the clock. Father Keogh took pity on him.

"Where do you have to catch your bus?"

"From the Pass, from the top of the Hua Pass . . . only the Wednesday one starts from the town. It goes at five o'clock."

"I'll see you don't miss the bus."

"Thank you. Thank you very much. It's just that they don't know you're coming."

"They?"

"*He* doesn't know you're coming."

"You mean Malo?"

"Yes, Anacleto, he doesn't know, and if he saw us about together, well, he would know," Father Gomez finished lamely.

"Well, he'll have to know sometime," Father Keogh said cheerfully, "and I should think he knows by now. Umpteen thousand people seemed to stare at me as I came through the town."

"Yes, but Anacleto doesn't know it was me, I mean he doesn't know that I have made a report to the Bishop. He doesn't expect someone new. If he sees me about with you and I happened to miss my bus—"

19

Father Keogh asked quietly, "You're afraid he might do some harm to you?"

The little priest nodded, his eyes on his hands.

"I see," said Father Keogh. "Then of course you must not take the risk. I can manage perfectly well, and if anything comes up I can always write to you."

They heard no footsteps outside in the passage. They were taken by surprise when the door opened quietly and Malo walked into the room. Because he was whippet-thin he looked taller than his actual height. Both priests remained seated. Father Gomez sat looking at his own hands. Father Keogh sat staring at Malo. Malo returned the scrutiny in a curious all-embracing glance; up and down, straight across and into the eyes. He had judged a man's size and his wits and his worth by the time he came back to the eyes. The three looks of Malo, Quantana called them.

What Father Keogh was expecting he could not have said; perhaps the gnarled pugilism of the gangsters he had seen upon cinema hoardings, perhaps the flabby decadence he had seen on the faces of real-life gangsters, the healthless faces of the men he had seen round the docks and in foul-smelling tenement houses; or perhaps the vicious resignation he had seen on the faces of long-term prisoners. But he was not prepared for the beauty he saw in Malo. The delicate brown of his skin gave him a look of transparency. He was small-wristed and long-fingered and he held himself lightly erect. It was an impassive beauty, vital yet motionless. He made few gestures and his voice was as steady as the flickerless stare of his eyes, which were light for a Mexican's, yellow-flecked. His austere immobility made quicksilver out of Father Gomez. The bone work was high and clear in his face. It might have been modeled in bronze by a sculptor who saw no need to emphasize anything but the long thin line of the mouth and the long thin line of the narrowed eyes.

He made Father Keogh a small formal bow with his head. "I have come to apologize to you, Father. You received no welcome." He shook a reproachful head at Father Gomez. "But then how could we know you were coming, if nobody bothered to tell us?" Father Keogh sat regarding him with his head on one side and his arms folded. He was impressed by the soft tones of Malo's voice. There seemed no speed and no violence in it. "We let you walk down like a stranger, Father. What a fine welcome that was!"

Father Keogh said, "Thank you, I enjoyed the walk."

20

"The whole town would have turned out to welcome you, Father."

"Thank you," Father Keogh said, "I've no doubt I shall make its acquaintance in time."

Malo raised his shoulders. "But the pity of it, Father, no flowers, and no honors, no band!"

Father Keogh held up the blossom in his hand, "I did receive a flower."

"One flower!" Malo said. "The shame of it! We should have made such a fuss of you, shouldn't we, Father Gomez? You know, we Mexicans rather pride ourselves on our hospitality, Father. What must an Englishman think?"

"I had an English mother, but I am still an Irishman," Father Keogh said.

"For an Irlandes-Ingles your Spanish is good."

"I am an Irishman," Father Keogh said.

Malo sat down, facing the other two men. "Nevertheless, you can't think very well of us." His smile went to Father Gomez. "So old mother church is attending her garden? She's pulling the weeds out at last! She's ridding herself of her rubbish." He turned to meet Father Keogh's steady eyes. "Tell me," he asked, "what will she do with it? What does she do with rubbish when it's rotten through and through, when it's corrupt and decayed and sour and stinking? What does she do with it then? Does she burn it at the foot of her altar—does she throw it away and forget it? Or does she quietly put a bullet through it and call it a martyr? What *does* she do, my friend?"

Before Father Keogh could answer, Father Gomez spoke. He might have been speaking from his deathbed. His voice was scarcely audible, and he still kept his eyes on his hands. "Anacleto," he said, "you have driven me out. But you cannot drive out the church. It doesn't rely on men like me. Thank God it has no need to do that. It isn't made up of men like me." Beneath his lowered lids he glanced sideways at Father Keogh. Then he looked back at his hands. "The church has great strength, Anacleto. It has greater strength than you. That's something you can't understand," and Father Gomez sighed for Malo, still without raising his eyes. Then he added quietly, "You oughtn't to judge it by me."

Malo stood up. He said, "Well, since we were not privileged to make the new padre welcome, perhaps we shall be allowed to bid the old one farewell? We must give him a good send-off." He left them, soft-footed across the floor, and at the door he turned to smile at

21

them. "Quantana knows how to look after its friends, doesn't it, Father Gomez?"

When he had gone Father Gomez said sadly, "It was I who baptized him. It was on his saint's day, the thirteenth of July. I remember as if it was yesterday. We had to do it secretly. They'd have shot us all if we'd been caught."

Father Keogh answered, "I thought you were very brave with him. He put the wind up me!"

Father Gomez looked up at last, "My friend, we spend most of our lives avoiding death, and when it comes . . . it's surprising, it's quite a relief, and we cannot imagine why we have exhausted ourselves by struggling against it so long."

"Death?" said Father Keogh puzzled.

"Death," replied Father Gomez. "You'll see, I shan't escape. You heard what he said about a good send-off? I know what that means. I shan't escape."

"Rubbish!" said Father Keogh, and immediately regretted the word.

Something very like humor lit Father Gomez's eyes, "Don't worry. He was right when he called me rubbish. I am rubbish. Corrupt from head to toe . . . what did he say? Stinking, foul, decayed? That boy should know rot and decay when he sees it. He was brought up amongst it, poor lad, fed on it—it became his only plaything."

"We'll get police protection," Father Keogh said. "I'll see the Jefe myself."

"If you do that," explained Father Gomez, "you'll not be much better than a murderer yourself. If the police dare to act, in anything but a minor capacity, someone gets killed—anyone—it doesn't matter whom. I don't know how they're chosen, I've often wondered how. Do they turn up a card, or stick in a pin? I don't know, I've often wondered. But I think it goes by lettering, alphabetical order, you know." He held up a tiny brown hand and ticked off his fingers, "First Arrieta was killed and then Beltram, Carranza and Dominguez, Elizondo, and then Fernandez. It looks like alphabetical order doesn't it? Of course, it did not look like murder. Most of them met with an 'accident' but it seemed such a strange coincidence, alphabetical order like that—I often think people must have thought I was frightened because the next letter in the alphabetical order would have been 'G,' " and again something like humor kindled in Father Gomez's melancholy eyes.

"But do you mean to say that they suspected Comachi, and they let him get away with it? What on earth were the police about?"

22

"Oh, yes, they suspected Anacleto. It *was* Anacleto, or Anacleto's doing. But you see the town knows it's a hostage. It has forbidden the police to turn out. By the way, you won't drink the water? Not because of poison, you must watch alcohol for that, or coffee, but because of typhoid, only the bottled is safe. And be careful of salads. Were you injected against it?"

"Typhoid and paratyphoid? Yes."

"That's good," said Father Gomez, and stood up. "Would you hear my confession, Father?"

"Of course," said Father Keogh. "But wouldn't you rather—"

Father Gomez interrupted him, "All I can tell you, Father, is that I know that I shan't escape. An old man can feel these things." He pushed a small stool forward and knelt down on it, his joints crackling. "Why is it?" he asked Father Keogh smiling, "that the indignity of old age should strike so much worse through the knees?"

Chapter 3

At the end of the confession it was Father Keogh who felt that he could not keep his hands still. The sweat spread over his forehead and slipped down his temples, and under his mouth there was a long wet line of it.

Father Gomez still knelt before him, muttering his penance. He had only to say one Hail Mary. Father Keogh considered that he had been penalized enough. He tried not to look at the little bald head bent piously over the hands.

He had become an astute judge of character through the confessional. He had lost the early immaturity that was not unconnected with an ebullient sense of humor. He had sometimes felt the need to confess himself after absolving a penitent, when he had found himself concentrating more upon the fact that it was surprising that the whey-faced penitent should have been offered the chance of committing

23

adultery, rather than the fact that she should be made to repent of it. He had had to take in hand another inclination too. Shortly after he was ordained he found it difficult not to try and apprehend the type of sin a penitent was likely to confess. He was young and he took an eager interest in his fellow human beings. It was hard at first not to be intrigued by the insight into the human soul that the confidential confessional offered. He soon conquered that early immaturity. After that he found other things difficult. It was not always easy to ask forgiveness of a God of love for a sin against love itself.

Few people confessed to a meanness of spirit, to pettiness and small-minded tyranny or hypocrisy. Few people saw themselves clearly enough for that. They would confess to adultery and vengeance, and even to larceny and murder, but they seldom said, "Father, I befriended a man because I thought he was important not because I wanted to be his friend." They seldom said, "Father, it's not that I dislike my brother; on the contrary, we had the greatest regard for each other. It's just that he's poor now and he drinks too much, so I have to cut him dead if I meet him, for the sake of my wife and my business friends—not for their sake but because I'm so snobbish."

They seldom confessed to that. They seldom saw any wrong in it. But they found it easy to tell him, "Father, I once took a whore."

He was gently amused by those who were genuinely at a loss to imagine themselves at fault. He heard many of these, who confessed with interrogation marks, who in the same breath as accusing themselves excused themselves. Sometimes they argued with him, trying to justify themselves. "Father, I told my children they hadn't got to talk to the kids next door on account of they aren't nice kids to know—would that be counted as a lie?"

"It would if they *are* nice children," Father Keogh pointed out.

"Well, Father, it's not that the kids are bad in themselves, it's just that they don't come from—well, they're just not the kind of Catholics we're used to, Father. Before Bob had to take this job we lived in a classy apartment, why we knew everybody, and it's not our fault if things get tough and we have to live next door to people like that—I don't see why it makes it bad that we don't want to mix with them—I just wouldn't want my kids seen around with Mrs. Chevasse's kids—it's like I told you, they're just not our class of Catholic, Father—and don't you think it's just as bad for her to keep coming around and making out she's so friendly when all the time she only wants to borrow something?"

24

Father Koegh was gentle when he pointed out that he was not hearing the confession of the lady concerned.

Then there were the converts, anxious to make an impression both with piety and with sin, and the overscrupulous who felt every failing a mortal sin. It was difficult in the early days to quell a desire to deflate, difficult not to be impatient. He had never found his priesthood easy. He thought he had conquered these failings within himself. He thought he had achieved a strict impartiality through experience and age. He thought he had laid his mind open to the wisdom of God and stifled the inner self. But when he listened to Father Gomez he found that self keenly alive. He found himself fighting an anger the force of which he had not felt for many years, not against the dry little voice which seemed so determined to leave no merciless truth untold, but against the man who had forced the truths into the voice. The man who had once laid a fugitive's shoes on a comandante's desk when he was only five years old, and who at five and twenty had made it necessary for an old man to lay a succession of sins at the feet of the God he had devotedly served all his life. Father Keogh wondered if he would ever be able to feel a complete Christian forgiveness toward Anacleto Gonzalez Flores Comachi Alvarez. He prayed that he might be given the power to do so.

After the bald, emotionless confession of priest to priest, the dry little voice had whispered tonelessly, "Father, if there is anything you failed to understand, question me—you have my full permission —you are stepping into my shoes, and I want to assist you. I have not long to live." He held up a tiny brown hand to check Father Keogh's protest, and repeated, "I have not long to live. Anything I can do for you I must do for you now. Anything you would like explained I will explain—any point you wish to take up with me—take up with me. These are not ordinary circumstances, Father. You are taking over from me and a pretty inheritance I have left you. Now let me see—let me see—I told you how frightened I was for the people, not for myself, that did come later, but it wasn't so just then. I fought Anacleto hard at first, and I fought for my flock, until I became so afraid for them . . . then soon after Elizondo and Fernandez died. . . ."

Father Keogh smiled at him. "I knew that it wasn't the 'G.' "

"No, it certainly wasn't the 'G.' It's not hard to be brave for yourself, at times, but it's never easy to be brave for others. I hadn't that bravery to spare. And in my case it was sinful as well as cowardly.

25

But after the death of Fernandez I gave in. At first all I did was to stop interfering and look the other way."

"What do you mean exactly, when you say you 'looked the other way'?"

"I no longer opposed him. If he did something I did not approve of—if I made no trouble, then no one was hurt. At least that's what he always promised me."

"Did he keep the promise?"

"Yes. But he started to demand more and more of me. He began to demand my help."

"What kind of help could you give?"

"There are things that a priest can do, you see, that can help a man like that. They were small things to start with."

"What did they become?"

"Well, as I say, there are ways that a priest can help. He had not achieved absolute power then. There were many who continued to fight against him. He had to be careful still. But if I showed him friendship—"

"I see," Father Keogh said.

"Of course, in a way I was always hoping. The reason I showed Anacleto friendship in the beginning was because I was hopeful for him. Yes, my reasons were innocent once. Hope is a very bad thing if it turns itself into an excuse, and it can. It can start off all right and then you are blinded by it. I hoped I might save him. I baptized him, didn't I? I thought if I showed him friendship there might be a chance. Yes, at first it wasn't myself I was thinking about. I thought, 'This thing will not be one-sided, it gives him access to me, but it gives me access to him.' I thought I could talk to him and reason with him. He never had a friend, not even when he was a child. Not real friends, just children he bullied into befriending him, but they were always frightened of him. Well of course that's what he was doing to me, but I didn't see it then. I never thought of him as anything except 'poor little Anacleto' who once took away my shoes. I was sorry for him when he did that. It was a terrible thing in a child. So I tried to be his friend."

"I should have thought there would have been a form of hope in that."

Father Gomez's tiny head shook. "No there wasn't—no hope, no hope at all. And by that time he had an even stronger hold. I'd forgotten my good intentions . . . I was only a bullied friend. I did it

26

because I was afraid of him. I turned a blind eye to things that I should have complained of, for the sake of peace. It was not long before the rest of the town was doing the same thing. After all, they had my example. But I should have been the one to stand out. I told you he once made me give him money."

"How were you in a position to give him money?"

"Donations," said Father Gomez. "Donations to charity and public funds. There was one for a hospital. I collected it. We need one very badly here. Don Pedro de Cortinez gave handsomely to it, though I seem to remember that he was not very willing," and he tapped his elbow to show that Don Pedro was mean.

"Did you give Malo the whole of the hospital funds?"

"No—I gave him half. I put what was left to the hospital."

"How did you account for the missing half?"

"It was my private campaign. I had complete control of it. I said that I had only collected half the amount I had collected. It was easy enough to say. But I think people must have found out. You can't keep things quiet in a place like this. When I wrote to the Bishop that Anacleto had crippled the faith of the people, I left one person out. I should have told him that it was Anacleto and me between us."

Father Keogh tried to comfort him, "I hardly think that fits the case."

"Oh yes it does," Father Gomez insisted. "It entirely fits the case. Anacleto despises the church. He has never had any use for it. Most of the people do not go because they are afraid of displeasing him, but he does not actually prevent them from going, and do you know why he has not bothered to do that? Because he knows that the people have no use for me. Would you risk such powerful displeasure to come and be preached at by me? Anacleto knows that there is not the slightest danger of the chuch filling up through me. That is what he has managed to make of me, and therefore to make of them."

Father Keogh said quickly, "If the people loved God they would go to church."

"A love of God needs a good example. A love of God needs leadership. What a leadership it has had from me! So you see I ought to have told the Bishop that it was between Anacleto and me."

"Why didn't you write to the Bishop of your—difficulties sooner?"

"The Bishop has been very good to me. I think I was always hopeful that I might one day fulfill his trust—I told you how hope could become a sin. I was always hoping that I might one day be able to put things right. But from what I have told you you must be able to see that I am more to blame than any other coward or blackguard who has aided and abetted Anacleto, because I was here to protect those cowards against themselves as well as Anacleto. I am as much one of his thieving cutthroats as the villains who work for him. I am no better than Porfirio or Pablo, Lorenzo, young Vito, or old Uncle Joaquin, or that poor crippled creature, the Jeep. I am no better than the girl Maria who gives her body to him. I am worse, for she does that for love. Anacleto was right when he called me rubbish."

Chapter 4

Until it was time to catch his bus, Father Gomez retired to the bedroom he was to vacate for Father Keogh. Father Keogh insisted that he should rest. He was anxious about the little priest. He seemed exhausted by his confession and there was a faint bluish tinge to his skin. Father Gomez spent the time on his knees, with his chin supported on his clasped hands. He said prayers for Father Keogh, that a merciful Jesus might grant him extra strength and that he might never come to understand the agony of remorse. He also said prayers for Anacleto Gonzalez Flores Comachi Alvarez.

Father Keogh strolled into the patio. It was brave with flowers that grew in pots about the well, and where she had run out of pots Chela had planted jasmine and arum lilies, elephant ear and geraniums in old kerosene tins. He returned to the tiny room that smelled of kerosene.

He said prayers for Father Gomez, that a merciful Jesus might lighten the little priest's burdens, and that Father Gomez might come to know the peace of a mind at rest. He was obliged to pray first for the willingness to say a prayer for Malo-of-the-Cats. He was trying not to think of the pride in his Bishop's voice when he spoke about Father Gomez. Because he had difficulty in avoiding the thought he made a small list in his notebook:

> Tomorrow—See—
> Chief of Police
> The Presidente Municipal
> The Child on the Hill
> The Gran-Señor-of-the-Cats.

Then he told Chela the hour he wished to be called in the morning, the fruits he preferred for breakfast and the times that he would require his luncheon and his dinner. Then he added a note to his list. "See about laundry for Father G."

He slept a little afterwards, dreaming that he was a boy again in Ireland. In his dream he remembered that he had always wanted to be a soldier. He remembered that when he became a priest he thought that it was much the same thing, and in his dream he wore a muddled uniform. He wore his Roman collar and a cassock but he wore gold epaulettes and at his side a toy sword swung. He dreamed that he had an army somewhere behind him dressed as he was dressed himself. Suddenly he dreamed that he had lost the army. He was pushing his way through a crowded bar. In the corner he saw a child with pale gold hair that blew into a sharp little face and he heard a small clear voice that was saying at rhythmic intervals, "Silly old Father Gomez—silly old Father Gomez." She had her arms round the shoulders of Malo. They were laughing together, their cheeks touching. He struggled to tell her to take her arms away but he could not hear his own voice above the noise in the crowded bar. He turned to ask for silence and when he turned round again the child had gone. It was he himself who was sitting in her place and he had his arms about the shoulders of Malo. He heard himself confiding, "Silly old Father Gomez—silly old Father Gomez."

Then he said, "I must ask for forgiveness—I didn't mean to say that."

He heard Malo laughing. His shrieks rose to fury point, hysterically high.

In the yard outside Chela was killing a turkey. In Father Keogh's dream the screeches came from Malo and he tried to prevent them. He gave Malo his Roman collar. The sword that Malo gave him in exchange was real.

He could feel the heat of Malo's cheek pressed closely against his own and the bandit was asking gaily of him, "We'll give him a send-off, shall we, Father? We'll give him a good send-off."

When Father Keogh woke up the turkey was dead and he found that he had fallen asleep with his chin in his own hot hand. Father Gomez was standing beside him saying, "I'd better be off now, Father Keogh. I think I had better be off."

Father Keogh sat up. "Oh, yes, of course. I'm afraid I've been to sleep."

"You were tired, I expect," said Father Gomez kindly. "I expect you were feeling the heat."

Father Gomez might have been in an Arctic climate himself. His lips were almost blue. Father Keogh took his suitcase. "I'll come with you up the hill."

"No, no, Father, it's very kind but I shall be all right."

"Of course you'll be all right, but I'll put you on your bus." He weighed the suitcase in his hand. "Have you got everything? There doesn't seem much."

"Yes, thank you. Just except for my missing underclothes."

"Oh yes," said Father Keogh. "I have made a note about those." And as if Father Gomez had been going to the dentist he said, "It'll all be over soon."

Then he put a hand under the little priest's bony elbow and ushered him out of the house. Children were gathered outside. At the sight of Father Gomez they sped off shouting and screaming like a cloud of parakeets scattering at the report of a gun.

Father Keogh felt Father Gomez tremble. He said conversationally, "Well, I must say that what I've seen so far of our younger parishioners hasn't exactly endeared them to me." Father Gomez put the point of his tongue over his lips that might have been pressed to the neck of an ink bottle. He said vaguely, "They were good children once. Anacleto has set them a bad example. My catechism class was so big it used to overflow. Some of them stood on the steps. I used to make them take turns. First of all I . . ."

"Steady," Father Keogh said. "There's plenty of time. Don't hurry."

Father Gomez put forward an uncertain foot and followed it with the other—shifting his weight onto it, like an invalid walking for the first time after several months. "Yes, first of all I used to make the good ones go out on the steps—you know, the ones who knew their catechism best."

"Slowly," Father Keogh urged him. "There's plenty of time. Don't force yourself."

"It seemed the most sensible thing to do, because you can't hear very well from the steps, and I thought the bad ones ought to stay in front."

"Very sensible," Father Keogh said. "Put all your weight on me."

"But that didn't work well really, because they didn't like it outside on the steps. It made them feel unimportant. They used to fight for seats, and it didn't seem fair on the good ones, so in the end I made it the bad ones who went on the steps, and I used to shout as loudly as I could to make them hear, but sometimes I lost my voice."

"Very sensible," Father Keogh said. "Now look here, it's ridiculous for you to walk. You're not in a fit state. Don't tell me there isn't some form of transport. Stay here while I round someone up."

"No, no!" Father Gomez gripped his arm and his fingers bit. They seemed fleshless. "They'd hold me up. They would try to delay me. They'd make me miss my bus."

"Then I'll drive you myself," Father Keogh offered.

"No, no, thank you. They'd hold you up. They'd keep you haggling about the price for hours. They'd make me miss my bus. It will be dark soon," the little voice whined, and there was a tremulous suggestion of urgency in it.

"All right," Father Keogh soothed him. "Lean as hard as you like on me."

The children were back; small brown faces and small excited eyes, small brown fingers pointing at Father Gomez.

"You mustn't blame the children," Father Gomez said. "It isn't their fault. Anacleto pays them for spying."

Father Keogh was puzzled by the group of men who accompanied Malo. Five of them rode on mules. The sixth, a heavy sullen man, was mounted on a horse. They were gaudily dressed. The sun caught gold and silver threads round the crowns of black sombreros and upon braided jackets. It played on tight-fitting trousers where a double line of silver buttons formed horses' heads down the outer seams. They looked absurd on the legs of the little pale-faced cripple who brought up the rear. The sweat had broken through the full white shirt of the big man on the horse. Only Malo was plainly dressed. His sombrero was palm-woven, unadorned. He sat his horse casually, lightly erect.

"You seem to have inspired some sort of charro turnout," Father Keogh said.

Father Gomez sighed. "Those are not charros—I wish they were. They have no right to be dressed up as cowboys—they are—they are

31

the people I spoke to you about. They are Malo's men. . . . It's old Uncle Joaquin who rides on the horse. He's Anacleto's favorite. He used to help me in the church." Father Gomez sighed again. "That's Pablo—the fat one. They call him El Gordo—and that's El Gordito, the little fat man on his left. Yes, that's Lorenzo. It's Porfirio riding behind him. And the poor little one, the crippled one—I don't know why they should call him the Jeep—then the young one, that's Vito— El Lobo—the wolf. Not very nice names," Father Gomez said.

"They don't look a very nice bunch."

A considerable crowd was gathering. Father Keogh noticed that only the younger ones chattered amongst it. Their elders stood silent, apart. Except for the fact that he headed the retinue, Malo too, appeared silent, apart. He had no expression on his face.

Old Uncle Joaquin came riding up. He sat comfortably down in his saddle. He was thickset and heavily built. His hair belied his aging face. It was plentiful and dark. His face had the drinker's heightened color, but his features were strong and good. His eyes were a soft and a light nut-brown. They too seemed at odds with the florid face.

He lifted his hat and bowed from the saddle. "Good evening," he said. "Do you want any help?"

"No thank you," Father Keogh said. "And we could do without an escort too."

"Come, come, Father! Do you think that is very polite?"

Father Keogh was also surprised by the softness in Old Uncle's voice.

He said, "Possibly not. Nevertheless it's the truth—"

He began to steer Father Gomez through the crowd. Malo turned the head of his horse and the others followed him. The two priests walked in the center of them. The switching tails, lashing out at the flies, struck at them now and again.

Father Keogh felt Father Gomez miss a step. He caught the little priest as he stumbled and said evenly to Old Uncle, "If you insist on coming with us you can make yourself useful. Take this." And he went to hand Old Uncle Father Gomez's suitcase.

"No." The little priest's voice had tears behind it. "No, we'd never get it back. You don't understand. They're not being friendly. You don't understand them yet. If it's too heavy, I will take it."

"It's not too heavy," Father Keogh replied. He was alarmed at the color of the little priest's face. It was mauve with exertion and the

32

handkerchief with which he mopped his face had become a sodden rag. Father Keogh slid his shoulder under Father Gomez's armpit. He was half-carrying the exhausted priest. He was a little out of breath himself. "Don't worry," he said. "Don't worry about them. You're getting away for good. Get back there!" he ordered the retinue. "Give us room to walk!"

Pablo reined in. "I'm sorry, Father. 'Get back there!' " he called out in Father Keogh's deep voice. " 'Give us room to walk!' "

"Never mind," said Old Uncle. "He isn't dressed up as a woman this time, eh, Anacleto?" And he sang a single verse:

> *"Oh lady fair, what makes you flee?*
> *What makes you flee from me?"*

Father Keogh turned round. His eyes seemed exceptionally dark. Father Gomez gripped his arm.

"No," he said. "No, don't answer them. It will only be worse for yourself." His breath came out of his lips as if he were trying to force it through the neck of a bottle. The arm that lay over Father Keogh's back was soaked with sweat, and Father Keogh felt the damp from it. "Try not to worry," Father Keogh said. "They can't harm you. They're only baiting you."

Father Gomez shook his head. "It's something more than that, my friend. You'll see. I shan't escape. Anacleto makes no mistakes."

"You'll escape," Father Keogh said grimly.

Old Uncle Joaquin rose in his saddle. He stood in his stirrups and called out to the crowd, "It's a very sad day for Quantana, this. We are losing a good friend and a good man and a good priest. Don't you feel we are losing these three?"

A curious ripple ran through the crowd—half laughter, half abuse. But it struck Father Keogh as sounding reluctant. The laughter was true, the abuse seemed unwilling.

Old Uncle Joaquin stood straight in his stirrups. "I say it's a terrible loss, my friends. I say that we cannot afford to lose these things."

Malo was riding in close. Father Gomez had a hand to his heart. He winced as if he felt physical pain in it. "Anacleto, you've done so much to me—what more is there left to do?" The eyes that he turned on the rider were patient, seeking. The rest of the face was resigned.

Old Uncle Joaquin was rallying the crowd.

The crowd sent a halfhearted murmur up, as if it were uncertain of what Joaquin required it to do.

33

Father Keogh put down the suitcase. He took the bridle of Vito's mule. "Excuse me," he said. "But get off!"

The boy's mouth opened showing white teeth in a laugh that blew straight into Father Keogh's face. "Why should I? The mule is mine."

"I don't doubt it," said Father Keogh. "But I intend to borrow it. I'll pay for the privilege when I get back."

The mule kicked out at him, drawing blood with its sharp spiked shoes. He put his hands on the boy and moved him sideways. Vito regained his balance. His eyes were adder-bright. He put a quick hand to his side.

"Vito!" a voice called. "What are you thinking of? Have you no respect?" Malo trotted slowly up. "Give the Father the mule at once. It's a small enough favor to ask of you, isn't it? A great, strong boy like you."

Vito dismounted slowly and flung the bridle at Father Keogh.

Father Keogh lifted Father Gomez astride the mule and held him on. The mule stood still, its ears twitching. It resisted all Father Keogh's efforts to make it move. Father Gomez sat wet-faced, his head down.

Vito gave the animal a sharp crack across the flanks with his whip. The mule jerked forward, shooting Father Gomez flat along its neck. Father Keogh levered the little priest up again. He noticed that Father Gomez was praying. His eyes were closed, and his lips were moving. Father Keogh picked up the suitcase and put it across the animal's rump. With one hand he steadied Father Gomez and with the other he held on to the suitcase. He was aching in every muscle.

Chapter 5

Halfway up the hill Father Gomez slumped forward. Father Keogh had to let the suitcase fall before he could rescue him. It crashed on the road skidding a few feet in the dust.

A little American in a battered panama walked out of the crowd. The ragged rim of the hat seemed to jig in the dancing heat.

"Want a hand, Mac?"

Father Keogh turned round. "Thanks," he said gratefully. "If you could collect that suitcase and follow me up with it, you'd prove yourself more than a friend."

"Sure," said the little American and picked up the suitcase. He hoisted it onto his shoulder and led the mule with his free left hand.

Father Keogh's aching arms were released to support Father Gomez. He looked curiously at his unexpected ally. He had a thatch of red hair and his grin looked lonely on his face. Alcohol had turned up the corners of his eyes and given a downward droop to the edges of his mouth.

He turned to scrutinize Father Gomez. "That guy don't look too good to me."

"I know," said Father Keogh. "The sooner we get him off the better." And then he said, "I didn't expect to see a friendly face. Where have you sprung from?"

The American pulled hard at his cigarette and his eyes seemed to be absorbing the smoke. Little of it drifted past him.

"From under a stone," he answered. "Turn up any stone and if I'm not around, just leave a note. I'll get it."

"I'll do that," Father Keogh smiled. "What name do I put on the note?"

"Samuel Lewis Frankenson." He seemed to find his own name amusing. He laughed a little over it. "Didn't you ever hear of Judge Robert L. Frankenson? He doesn't like to have his kid brother around. The States ain't big enough for me and a brother like mine."

"How is it," Father Keogh asked, "that you're not afraid of this lot?" He looked back over his shoulder at Malo and the men who rode behind him.

Samuel Frankenson spat. "Oh them! I see worse than that creeping over my own walls every day. I have worse than that hatching out in my own liver right this minute." He banged his chest. "I have asthma, too. That's why I come to Mexico. That and my stuffed shirt brother. You T.T.?" He asked with sudden energy.

"No," Father Keogh replied. "Why should I be?"

"I wouldn't know, Mac. I wouldn't know why anyone's T.T. But Pussyfoot is T.T." He jerked his chin in the direction of Malo. "He don't drink and he don't smoke, and that makes them both okay

35

by me." He looked back at Malo again, his eyes creasing. "But you know, for a goddamn dirty louse, Pussyfoot packs a helluva lot of dignity."

Father Keogh turned round to look at Malo. "Yes," he admitted, "he does."

Sam said, "Well, you're welcome under my stone any time you like, Mac. Maybe we could throw a party."

"We certainly will," Father Keogh promised.

"Hey! Pussyfoot!" said Sam, as Malo rode in close again. "Shift over a little will you? And it's not that we don't like horseflesh."

Father Gomez opened his eyes. "You haven't let them take my suitcase, have you? You haven't let them take it?"

"Of course not," Father Keogh told him. "Sam is carrying it for you."

Father Gomez turned his head towards the little American. "That's kind of you, Sam," he said.

"Ain't nothing," Sam assured him. "Why don't you go back to sleep?"

Father Gomez closed his eyes, but five gunshots jerked them open. Father Keogh turned round to see Pablo fire into the air. The vultures rose dropping heavily down on the roofs again. A tremor shook Father Gomez.

"Ah, think nothing of it," Sam advised. "That's just their joints cracking. They don't get any younger neither." Then he said, "What's that?"

Old Uncle had urged his horse ahead. It struggled forward up the hill. Old Uncle unfolded a curious banner. On a couple of poles tied to represent a cross a garment was hoisted. It cut a sharp black pattern into the sky behind it.

"That," said Father Keogh, "is a black chasuble. We wear them for funerals." He spoke softly but Father Gomez heard them.

"You mustn't blame the sacristan. He's old and half blind—he's afraid of them, but he must be brave. He stayed with me." He put his sweat-soaked handkerchief up to his face and examined it, smiling a little. "I'm putting more on than I'm taking off."

Father Keogh dug into his pocket. His sister had sent him six fine white lawn handkerchiefs from Ireland. He had only two of them left. He felt a tiny pang of regret as he gave one to Father Gomez. He had the Irishman's love of good linen.

"Here you are," he said. "Have this."

36

Father Gomez took it gratefully, and mopped his streaming face.

When they passed the Casa Grande they saw the bus at the top of the hill. The bus bore a resemblance to a clumsy bottle with its narrow hood and bulging body. It also bore a name on a rusting plate: NO ME OLVIDES.

Father Keogh smiled when he saw it. "Forget me not" or, "Don't leave me behind." He said to Father Gomez, "You shan't be left behind."

Two people were waiting for it. A woman with a wickerwork basket containing three live chickens, and a man with a child in his arms.

Father Keogh struck the mule. It gave a last-minute spurt and dropped its head to nibble the burnt-up grass. Sam took the suitcase to the bus and Father Keogh lifted Father Gomez down.

"Well?" He held the tiny priest like a baby for a moment. "I thought you weren't going to escape?" He set Father Gomez gently on his feet and gave him the tender smile that had made the Bishop wonder whether Father Keogh was the right person to send to Quantana after all.

Father Gomez made no reply, but in his eyes Father Keogh saw the same expression that he had seen in the eyes of mortally wounded soldiers, a pleading resignation that was hard to reassure.

He half-carried Father Gomez to the bus. He had to lift him bodily onto the platform and into his seat. Father Gomez slumped in it but he rallied himself to ask, "Your handkerchief. . . ?"

"Keep it," Father Keogh smiled. "Keep it with my compliments."

"I'll—if there's any way I can help—I'll write you."

"Yes, yes," said Father Keogh. "But have a good holiday first."

Father Gomez strained upwards again. Father Keogh bent down to hear him. Father Gomez was still out of breath. He managed to say with difficulty, "Anacleto—needs—a—friend." Father Keogh pressed his hand. Then he blessed him and climbed down off the bus.

Sam stood in the dust with his hands in his pockets. Behind him stood the remnants of the crowd which had bothered to climb up the hill. Old Uncle held his banner high. Malo gave a mock salute to the bent figure of Father Gomez in the window of the bus. The salute was taken up from Old Uncle on horseback beside him, to Vito on foot at the end of the line. All seven of them sang out the verse:

> *"Oh lady fair, what makes you flee?*
> *What makes you flee from me?"*

37

Father Keogh stood praying for Father Gomez that he might be rested by his holiday, and for the Bishop that he might never come to hear the things about Father Gomez that he had had to hear himself that afternoon. Then he prayed to the patron saint of all secular priests. He prayed to the Curé of Ars.

The last that Father Keogh saw of Father Gomez was the top of his small bald head. He held Father Keogh's handkerchief clapped to his face as if he were weeping into it. As the bus jerked forward a hot breeze tugged at the fine white linen, lifting its corners up. Father Keogh saw it fluttering, a little white flag of defeat.

He and Sam waved the bus out of sight. Then they turned to walk down the hill. "Thank God the poor little guy got away."

"Thank God, indeed," Father Keogh said.

"Don't look now, but Pussyfoot's hot on our tail."

"I don't want to look," Father Keogh sighed. "I'll see enough of Pussyfoot."

"You said it. Where's the little guy going?"

"He's going on holiday."

"Do priests take vacations?"

"Why not?"

"You know, that's something I noticed about you, Mac. Ask you a question and you crack one back. I guess it lets you out of a helluva lot of answers."

Father Keogh told Sam, "Father Gomez is going to the coast."

"What'll he do there?"

"Paddle in the sea."

"Paddle?"

"Well, wade in it."

They both said together, "Why not?" Then they both laughed and Sam asked, "Why don't he go the whole hog and splash?"

"There's nothing to stop him," Father Keogh said.

"The poor little guy," Sam said.

They walked down the hill with the wind blowing cool from the mountainside. The sun was setting. A red and yellow sky flared up before night made its sudden descent. Bougainvillaea spilled over the terraces of the Casa Grande, and at the gates the child was waiting.

"Hallo," she called out as they passed her. "I mean, hallo *you*—not *you* of course." She indicated Father Keogh and turned a cold little face towards Sam.

"Why hallo me and not Sam?" Father Keogh asked.

"He drinks too much," explained the child, and before Father Keogh could make a stern retort she said admiringly, "Aren't you brave? They say you turned El Lobo off his mule."

"Well, they said wrong," Father Keogh told her. "Your Gran-Señor-of-the-Cats tipped him off his mule, and it isn't polite to say people drink too much. Isn't there anyone here who could teach you a few manners?"

"There you go getting cross again," grumbled the child.

"Don't you think you ought to say you're sorry to Señor Frankenson?"

The child looked with interest at the expressionless face of Sam. "You don't say you're sorry to someone like that."

"You do exactly what you're told, my child," said Father Keogh crisply. "Well—I'm waiting. So is Señor Frankenson. How long are you going to keep us?"

The child clung to the gates, leaning back from them, then she dropped her head and rested her cheek on one arm. "Sorry," she mumbled, and colored.

"Well, that's not very gracious, but it's better than nothing."

"He's holding your arm," observed the child. "Only friends hold each other's arms."

"Sam and I happen to be friends," Father Keogh explained.

"You do have funny friends."

Sam said kindly, "Go easy on her, Mac. She's only a kid."

"Oh, she knows how to be nice," Father Keogh said. "She was very nice to me today. She gave me a beautiful flower. By the way, Locha, what was it called?"

The child was about to smile at him but suddenly the smile was lost. She might have sucked it in and swallowed it, it disappeared so fast. Her mouth hung open and her eyes dilated. She said quickly, monotonously, "I didn't. I didn't. I didn't give you any flowers."

"But of course you did. Don't you remember? I pressed it in a book."

"I didn't! I didn't! I promise I didn't! It wasn't me who gave you a flower."

She loosened her grip on the gate, turned her back on them both and fled. Father Keogh looked after her, bewildered. "What a very extraordinary thing."

Sam made a grimace over his left shoulder. Malo was riding past. Sam explained to Father Keogh's puzzled eyes, "You're going to have to get used to that, Mac. Ain't nobody wants to walk out of step with Pussyfoot, not even a kid like that."

"But what harm can it do if she gives me a flower?"

"Well, it might look like it put her on your side, see? She wouldn't want Pussyfoot thinking that way. I'm telling you, Mac, it's like that all over. Even with the kids."

Malo made them a small formal bow from the shoulders and rode on down the hill. Old Uncle Joaquin rode after him. Father Keogh noticed that there were jewels on his hands. Rings glinted too on the little stunted fingers of the Jeep. The Jeep's awkward body sat back in his saddle. His stomach and chin were both thrust forward. He chewed nervously hard at the nails of one hand.

Father Keogh and Sam watched the retinue pass. Pablo, tall and fat, rode past with Lorenzo, short and fat.

"El Gordo and El Gordito!" Father Keogh sighed. "Not a distinguished pair."

"Yeah! When a guy has a special pal out here they call it his cuate—It means like you're so close you're as good as twins. It's a good thing those two have each other, nobody else would go for them."

Young Vito slackly astride his mule grinned impudently into Father Keogh's face. "You owe me for the hire of my mule, Father. A priest should pay his debts."

"I haven't forgotten," Father Keogh said.

"You will find me at the Hotel Martinez or up in Porfirio's bar."

"And you will find me at the church tomorrow morning or at my house."

Vito rode past still grinning.

"The Martinez was the best hotel in town," Sam confided, "until this lot pitched Papa Martinez out."

"You mean they get the profits from it?"

"Sure, from the bar, but it's not a hotel any more. The lot of 'em live in style up there—leastways everyone except Pussyfoot. Pussyfoot don't go for style. That broad of his, Maria, has one helluva fancy suite. I guess Pussyfoot steps in style when he visits her, but for the nights he takes off, he fixed himself a room like a monk's, beggin' your pardon, nothing but a chair and a cot nobody'd give you a thin dime for. I never did get Pussyfoot. Porfirio sleeps at his own bar."

"But why did Martinez sell out?"

"I just told you, he didn't sell. They pitched him out. That's the way they work around here. They get something on a guy so he can't squawk and then they throw him out. Papa runs the joint where I work now, the Hotel de la Costa. He's a nice little guy, but his wife's no peach."

"It seems inconceivable that a man can have his property filched off him like that and not be able to do anything about it."

"It's like I told you. They got sump'n on him."

"Wasn't he straight?"

"He was till he got in with them, but they get a guy in with them, and that means they got sump'n on him. They done that pretty well throughout the town. That's why friend Pussyfoot's King Pin around here. If the town gives him up, it practically gives itself up. They're all in it up to their necks. Catch him and they catch themselves out. Say, how about a nice little drink?"

"Sounds fine," Father Keogh said. "But I want to go into the church first."

"Better come up to my place. You don't want it getting around you're hitting the bottle."

Father Keogh laughed. "I wasn't exactly contemplating hitting it."

"Do they let you guys get plastered? I had the idea it was all tied up with hellfire and God knows what."

"Well, we're certainly not encouraged to get plastered. I think one could say it was 'frowned upon.' "

Sam grinned at him. "No, but you know what I mean, the little drop of—the little drop of what killed Auntie now and again. They wouldn't jump on you for that?"

Father Keogh smiled at him. "Well, I don't know exactly what did kill Auntie, but my Bishop is a very serious connoisseur of wine."

"Attaboy Bish!" said Sam. "He wouldn't get far on our rough stuff. Here's your stable, Mac." And he jerked a small square thumb at the church on the side of the hill.

Quantana had three churches once. The largest had been turned into a state school. The second had fallen into decay. The roof had collapsed, flowers struggled up through the rubble and scorpions hid beneath stones. The one on the side of the hill was intact.

"Are you going to come in with me, Sam?"

Sam shook his head. "I'll go my way and you go yours. That way we'll get along fine. I wouldn't know how to pray or the right guy to pray to, or what to pray about!"

41

"I thought you might like to pray for me. I think I'm going to need it."

"I'll just keep my fingers crossed, Mac."

"Thanks," Father Keogh said to him and hurried up the steps of the church.

The dust had preceded him into it. It lay a long gray carpet along the aisle and his feet left deep imprints behind him as if he were being followed by a silent-footed second self. It was dark inside the church except for the glow of the sanctuary lamp. Father Keogh lit the candles.

His were not the only footsteps in the dust. Small cloven hoofmarks had made a petal pattern all over the floor of the church. It looked as if a host of tiny devils had been scampering about. Father Keogh was still examining them, when a young goat came running out of the sacristy. They startled each other in the uneven light. The goat skidded and ran back up the aisle again. It was some while before Father Keogh was able to chase it out of the church.

All but the first front pews were thick in dust and there was a ring off the tabernacle curtain. The silence struck Father Keogh as being suspicious as if the church itself suspected sacrilege and was chary of any stranger. He noticed that the flowers on the altar were fresh and fine as if someone had cared for them tenderly. Someone had devoted considerable time to the altar decorations and someone had placed a clean duster at the end of the very front pew. It was the back of the church which expressed defeat. Vast cobwebs stretched between the pillars. A popcorn bag lay at the feet of St. Francis of Assisi. Three used bus tickets were stuck in the lip of the collection box. Along the aisle the row of dark confessionals looked dingy and cavelike behind their grilles. There were cobwebs across all except one.

Father Keogh tried not to feel that Father Gomez might have supervised the cleaning services so that they extended to the back of the church. He asked to be pardoned for having such thoughts. Father Gomez was old and worn out. In his middle age he had given battle for the church, in his declining years he had had to fight himself. It was possible that he had won. He had clung to the remnants of priesthood. He had tried to love his enemies as the Master he had chosen to follow would have loved them. He might have lacked the energy to attend to the back of the church; he might have preferred to cater only for the faithful few who occupied the front of it. He might have preferred to ignore the fact that the back of the church was itself ignored. It was excusable in an old man.

But his last thought was for the good of Anacleto Gonzalez Flores Comachi Alvarez. Father Keogh wondered what it was that had made him suppose it was Father Gomez's last thought. He wondered how hard he was going to find it, to think of the good of Anacleto Gonzalez Flores Comachi Alvarez. Harder perhaps, he suspected, than having to scrub out the church himself.

He suddenly missed Father Gomez. He was unaccountably lonely for the little man he had only just met. It saddened him that he had not done more to comfort him, and that he had grudged him a handkerchief. Then he felt that Father Gomez had somehow come back to comfort him; with a wisdom far greater than his own, with an understanding he might never possess. There was no need to feel lonely for Father Gomez. In the dilapidation of the church, in the dust in the holy water stoup, in the popcorn bag at the feet of St. Francis, in the loving flowers that stood bright on the altar, and in the little folded duster at the end of the very first pew, Father Gomez was present still. Father Gomez had not left.

Chapter 6

He looked up to see the sacristan standing in the gloom. There were hollows in his cheeks that had the circular precision of billiard balls. He was not only half blind. He was deaf. Father Keogh introduced himself at the top of a voice that went ringing round the church. The old man shook like a leaf under a strong wind. There was an apprehensive resignation deeply ingrained in his face.

Father Keogh found it hard to shout an observation and make it sound uncritical. "We need a bit of a cleanup in here, don't we?"

The sacristan shook his head. Then nodded. Then shook his head again. Father Keogh patted the ancient's bony shoulder, headed him back towards the vestry and went out on the steps to call Sam.

Sam lounged against the low wall that separated the church from the road as it curved up the hill. He came forward anxiously. "Yeah, what is it?"

"I say, Sam, it's filthy in here," Father Keogh said. "Do you think you could lend me a hand?"

"Sure," said Sam. "Won't it do in the morning?"

"No," Father Keogh answered. "I want to pray and I want to clean up first."

"Okay," said Sam, and came into the church. He caught Father Keogh's eye and removed his hat. "What about this?" He held up a cigarette between two straight fingers.

"I'm afraid not," Father Keogh smiled.

Sam edged off the lighted end against the wall and trod it underfoot. The remainder he put behind his ear. Then he put his hands on his hips and said, "Phew!"

"Yes, isn't it?" Father Keogh agreed.

"How do you aim to clear it, Mac? Blow on it?"

"No. There ought to be a broom in the sacristy. I'll go and have a look."

He walked towards the sacristy. Sam called after him, "What are the private rooms for?"

"They're confessionals," Father Keogh called back. In the sacristy he held the candle high and it sent shadows sliding along the dresser where mice had been at play. There were goats' droppings over the floor. The sacristan kept dim and solemn eyes upon him. Father Keogh gave him a reassuring smile and discovered an old broom and a rotting piece of rag. He went into the church with them, calling to Sam, "This is about all there is. I can't allow you to whistle in here, Sam. It isn't respectable in God's house. Will you sweep and I'll dust? Or would you like to dust and I'll sweep?"

Sam took the broom. "It don't matter either way, Mac, since what we both have to do is dig. Anyway I'll get started with this. Dunno how the place got like this. The little guy was pretty fussy in his way. Used to make a helluva stink about his underwear. Had a row about the laundry most every week."

"Oh my goodness, that reminds me," Father Keogh said.

"Seems they could spit on him or take a slug at him, and he'd turn the other cheek, but it sure got his goat when they pinched his drawers."

44

The dust that Father Keogh pushed off a seat fell quite heavily onto the floor. "Well, I daresay he wasn't very rich and couldn't afford to lose them."

"Rich! He and Chela came down to a handful of beans before now. I used to take 'em up food from our joint."

"I suppose that was Malo's doing."

"Yeah, that was friend Pussyfoot! I reckon that's half the reason he liked to keep the church empty. You guys shouldn't be dependent on what some old tightwad cares to drop into a church plate."

"Not everyone's tight with his wad," Father Keogh said and coughed.

Sam was a vigorous sweeper and the dust rising round him formed a fog in the aisle. He jerked his short thumb at the confessionals. "What happens to the guys with claustrophobia, when you get 'em wedged in those sinner boxes?"

"I don't know," said Father Keogh choking. "I don't think I've ever had any." He was rolling the dust off the pews and he had it in his eyes and his nose and his throat. "Or if I have they've been too polite to mention it."

"Somebody musta had it," Sam insisted. "I got it quite badly myself."

"I must say I've never seen a church used as a rubbish dump before," said Father Keogh. From under the seat he produced a soiled finger dressing, a rotting pimento and a torn magazine back advertising a scented deodorant.

"You know the little guy was sick. Chela says some mornings she couldn't get him up. Seemed like he got stiff if he laid too long, and she said he'd breathe like this—sort of hard in and hard out—like he was having to push it in and out." Sam tried to imitate Father Gomez's respiratory difficulties and choked in the dust. They could scarcely see each other through the clouds they were driving towards the doors. "I guess he was plenty sick."

"Yes, I'm afraid he was, Sam. I thought we'd never get him out of here alive."

"I'm not sure we did," Sam said.

They were gray-headed and gray-shouldered in the dim light of the candles. Sam called across the church, "Say, Mac, don't you think I could put my hat back on? I feel like I got ants in my hair."

"I'd rather you didn't, Sam."

45

"Okay, but you'll have to stand me a good shampoo."

"We'll share it," Father Keogh promised. "I've got a few ants myself."

From the doors of the church Sam called out again, "Mac? What's the birdbath for?"

"It's not a birdbath, it's a holy water stoup."

"A holy water what?"

Father Keogh came quietly up behind him. He startled Sam, making him jump.

"Holy cats! I didn't hear you creep up on me. I thought you was Pussyfoot."

"I'm terribly sorry," Father Keogh chuckled. "But you were making such a row yourself you hadn't a chance of hearing me!"

"Yeah, well, I figured I *had* to shout. I thought you was up the other end." Sam blew out his lips and patted his chest. "You start that pussy-creeping, Mac, and I'm going to have to drown my nice instincts and murder you. We can't have two guys walking around with no soles to their feet."

"Sorry, Sam. I'll goose-step in future and carry a whistle."

"Thanks, pal. That's what I don't like best about Pussyfoot. One minute you've got those eyes of his on you and the next minute he's breathing down your neck and nobody heard him slip around."

"It is uncanny, isn't it? He hardly makes a sound."

"It's all that and plenty more." Sam was still breathing hard.

"Couldn't we get hold of his boots or something? And knock a few nails in the bottom?"

"Just hang a few bells on his toes, Mac, couldja? Just so I know if he's coming or going. That's all I want to know."

He was still patting his chest and he had a spasm of coughing which alarmed Father Keogh. Father Keogh was full of remorse. "Sam, I ought to be shot. You said you had asthma. What am I thinking of—bringing you into a dust storm? It's nearly choked me, let alone you."

Sam recovered. "Oh, I'm not nearly as bad as I was. I guess this climate *does* suit it."

"Well, go out and stand in it then," said Father Keogh. "I shan't be long," and he pushed Sam down the steps. "Anyway we're really making matters worse. It's like trying to clear out the Sahara with a feather."

"How about me coming up in the morning tomorrow, early, Mac?

I'll bring up some cleaning stuff from the hotel. I got good brooms down there and some good strong soap. We can get up the water between us. We'll put such a shine on it you won't know the old dump."

"You're not coming into the 'old dump' as you call it until I've got it all cleaned up for you, and until I can persuade you to come into it for the reasons I think you would like to come in for."

"I'm going to be a long while outside."

"There must be someone I can persuade or bribe to help me clean it."

"Well, Pussyfoot kind of put the old dump out of bounds, you see. Most folks wouldn't care to risk it."

"Are you going to wait for me, Sam?"

"Sure. I don't have any girls crying their eyes out for me. It's my night off. Why not?"

He gave a mock salute, removed the cigarette end from behind his ear and relit it outside on the steps. Its glow became one with the dancing fireflies.

The first prayers that Father Keogh said in the church of Quantana were said with the dust gray upon his strong black head, making an old man of him as he stood before the High Altar; with the dust settling down again in the church behind him and with Sam coughing on the steps outside.

Chapter 7

When Father Keogh reached the church at half past six the next morning Sam had been there before him. There was a note propped up between the toes of St. Peter of Alcantara. It read:

DEAR MAC,
Recognize the old dump? I cleaned out the sinner boxes and

*I left the doors open to let the smell of the disinfectant out. You
should have smelled them before. Phew!*

SAM

*P.S. I haven't been up this early since the day I was born. They
got me up around four thirty then.*

Father Keogh removed the note from St. Peter's toes and laughed
a little at it. He wondered if the Bishop's research work into slang
would make him appreciative of the reference to confessionals as
"sinner boxes." He thought perhaps not. The church was certainly
unrecognizable. Sam had surpassed himself. Father Keogh went light-
heartedly along to the sacristy to vest. The sacristan awaited him
patiently.

The tolling of the church bell had a sharp effect upon the town
below. Father Gomez had long since ceased to ring the bell. It seldom
summoned the lapsers and it drew the attention of Malo to the attendance of the faithful few.

Father Keogh tolled it loudly. It caused a young farmer to frown
as he watered his horse at the fountain. It caused two washerwomen
to gossip about the understanding smile of the vigorous-looking new
priest.

It woke fat Porfirio, asleep by the woman he regretted marrying.
He had beaten her a week after falling in love with her. When he
first saw her he was wild to possess her. He saw her outside her father's
hut in a tiny Indian settlement and he took her straight home with
him. Her father, her uncle and her brother came to see him. He
gave them twenty pesos and still they talked, cross-legged on his tiled
floor, their cigar smoke rising. They talked of everything except the
girl he had kidnaped. He gave them another ten pesos and still they
talked, of the beans they had sown and of the new bird they had seen
on the lake. When they went he had promised to marry her and
given them another ten pesos. He never forgave her for his own
weakness. He resented paying money for an Indian girl. She was
twelve when he married her. By the time she was twenty she was
middle-aged and fat.

The bell woke Sam, newly returned to bed and fully clothed in
his back room at the Hotel de la Costa. It woke the bank manager
and the dentist.

It failed to wake the Presidente Municipal who was dreaming
that his seventh child was not his own. Up at the Casa Grande it

48

woke Josefa so that she called out to the mozo Francisco Jimenez through the thin partition of their rooms: "Paco, do you hear the bell? This marks a new time for Quantana."

It woke Señora Martinez, Señora Fereira, Señora Rodriguez and Señora Solano. It woke the Chief of Police and the doctor.

In a little adobe hut it reminded Mother Montezera that she must get on the right side of the new priest without getting on the wrong side of Malo-of-the-Cats. Small withered bodies were nailed to the walls of the hut, birds and animals, dried up with age. Herbs hung in countless bunches and a picture of the president hung between two full-length alligator skins. It was Mother Montezera's chief desire to keep on the right side of the law. Hers was the white magic of healing, she was a good bruja, an esteemed curandera, and if there were those who came to her for bad purposes they had to pay double for it. They had also to repeat extra loudly that she was a good bruja, an esteemed curandera, who never dealt in black magic. Pulque, tequila and mescal, and even a sufficient quantity of beer, were good friends to Mother Montezera. They insured a certain amount of sentiment.

"Ah! What should we do without the bruja? She has the only wise head in the town."

But sobriety brought about bitterness: "That old fool! She said to me, 'Three times a day you must brew this stuff, so that the smoke climbs up under the old one's bed'—and three times a day I brewed it. Nearly choking I was, for the smell was something it wouldn't be polite to talk about . . . but did the mother of my wife expire from it? Most certainly not, it was I who was needing the doctor!"

The bell reminded Salvadore, the manager of the cinema, that he had had no answer to his fourth letter demanding a copy of *For Whom the Bell Tolls*.

It reminded Chela that she had forgotten to warn her two cousins to make sure that the church was in good order in case the new priest should discover that they had been employed by Father Gomez, and paid out of his own pocket to clean it twice a week.

It reminded young Vito Juarez that the new priest owed him money for the hiring of his mule. It annoyed the organito who owned the barrel organ. He had spent the night with a woman who had not proved herself worthy of his money and he had gone to bed unsatisfied three-quarters of an hour before the bell tolled.

Doña Marian said to Don Pedro, "Pey honey, did you hear something?"

49

Don Pedro said, "No, go to sleep."

It roused Pablo, Lorenzo and the Jeep. It made old Uncle Joaquin heave over in heavy sleep. It brought him a secret nostalgia. In the half dreams that the bell of the church had disturbed he lay on his broad flat back and remembered a boy. The boy was vested in surplice and soutane. He wore slippers and had smooth black hair and a pale devout face. The boy was himself, aged nine. He could hear his own careful diction, piping clear as he advanced bell in hand to answer the priest in the name of the congregation. No moments in after life had ever given him that sense of importance and pride that the moments before the High Altar had given him. He frowned in his half sleep, straining his memory. Three times at the *Sanctus* he rang the bell—three times at each elevation—once at the *Hanc igitur,* and he thought but could not be certain that he rang it three times at the *Domine, non sum dignus.*

He turned over, annoyed that he could not be certain of the *Domine, non sum dignus.* But he remembered distinctly snatches from the *Judica—Et introibo ad altare Dei: ad Deum qui laetificat juventutem meam.* "There will I go up to the altar of God, the giver of triumphant happiness."

Old Uncle had never known happiness since. He turned his heavy head into the crook of his arm in an effort to force the fact far back into the recesses of his own half-dreaming mind, that it might wound him no longer with its insistent clamor for recognition. Yes, he remembered. It was many years but he remembered. That was before the flesh had thickened round his waist and become one with the stomach that protruded in front of it, before his body was heavy to shift in bed. He turned again, angry at the solid weight that had robbed him of the light movements of a boy with a bell in his hand. He had been a good server, the best, Father Gomez used to say. In Quantana they had said of him that he inspired them when he stood at the altar. He looked ethereal they said.

He was muttering out loud when Pablo called to him, "For the love of God shut up."

The church bell alarmed Maria. It woke her in a black chiffon nightdress that showed the tips of her breasts. The bell had a lifeless impressive insistence that made her think of death.

It did not disturb Malo who lay beside her.

It was half an hour before anyone came to the church. When Father Keogh went out on the steps he saw five people coming up the path.

50

The giant cypress tree plunged them into violent shade as they walked beneath its boughs. Señor Martinez, his wife, his daughter, Josefa and Locha were coming towards the church.

He greeted Josefa and smiled down at Locha. "Hallo," he said. "How are you?"

"I'm in quite good health thank you," she said. The child looked prim and wise.

Father Keogh asked them when they had last confessed. Señora Martinez and her daughter had confessed to Father Gomez on the morning before he left. Señor Martinez, Josefa and Locha had not confessed for several months. Father Keogh heard their confessions in the third confessional from the end because it smelled less strongly of disinfectant.

Señor Martinez had trouble with his memory. Father Keogh tried to assist it: Had he doubted in matters of faith? Despaired of God's mercy? Cursed himself or others? Stolen? Been deceitful? Wilfully damaged another man's goods, borne hatred or been desirous of revenge?

Señor Martinez thought he might have been guilty of all those sins. He had also eaten meat on Fridays. He had asked the devil to receive his cook, sworn at his wife under his breath, and when she asked him what he said he had lied to her. He had got drunk with Sam on three successive occasions. He had also discovered that he had overcharged a guest, and because the guest had not mentioned it, he had not mentioned it either.

Josefa remembered her sins. She had stolen five pairs of nylons, one silk petticoat and a pair of gloves from her mistress and sold them to Mother Montezera. Josefa had also charged Mother Montezera a little more than the agreed price for the goods, but she did not think that this was as sinful as it sounded, because Mother Montezera invariably cheated her over the change.

"Why aren't these thefts discovered?"

"It's when we take the things to wash, Father. Sometimes they do not come back."

"Ah!" said Father Keogh, and said it a little too loudly. Then he told Josefa that if it were possible she must restore the goods to their rightful owners.

Locha had put out her tongue at Josefa, drawn her tortoise on the flyleaf of one of her father's books, and been rude to her mother. She did not think there was anything else.

51

"I do," said Father Keogh.

The child wriggled on her hassock. "Oh, yes, and I was rude to Señor Frankenson. Well, *you* said I was rude to Señor Frankenson."

"Don't you think you were?"

"But he *does* drink too much. Everyone here knows *that*."

"Do you think it was very kind of you to rub it in? After all you weren't a very nice little girl on that occasion, but I don't seem to remember him rubbing *that* in."

"Yes—well, no. All right. I was rude to Señor Frankenson."

"And isn't there something else?"

"Oh, yes, I told a lie."

"Don't fidget," said Father Keogh. "What was that lie, my child?"

"I said I didn't-give-you-a-flower-when-I-did-give-you-a-flower." She ran the words into each other and was a little out of breath at the end of them.

"Kneel properly," Father Keogh ordered. "Was it because you were afraid of Malo-of-the-Cats? Were you afraid that he might be angry if he knew you had done something nice for me?"

"Well," Locha answered, "well, sort of, no, not quite."

Father Keogh answered patiently, "Now, which is it, my child? Either you were or you weren't afraid of him. I don't think it's a proper answer to be sort of no not quite."

"Well, it is and it isn't," Locha explained. "It's sort of half and half."

"What happens in the last half?"

"Well, I was a little afraid he'd be half as cross with you if he knew we got on so well. Do you think that puts it right?"

"I should think so," Father Keogh said. He gave her a light penance and called out after her, "Locha! I shall know if those prayers aren't said. I don't want to come in and hear, 'Silly old Father Keogh, silly old Father Keogh' going on."

When he went into the church she was tapping out a tune on the edge of the pew with her collection money. His shadow fell across her. She did not turn round. She quickly closed her eyes and folded her hands so tightly that the knuckles whitened. He heard her clear voice reciting with special care to the enunciation for his benefit, "Hail Mary full of grace . . ."

He stood smiling down at her for several seconds before he went into the sacristy to vest.

Chapter 8

When he left the church he ran into the barrel organ at the foot of the hill. It was playing "Little Gray Home in the West." He stopped to inquire of the organito, "How on earth did that get up here?" He spoke in excellent Spanish, but the organito seemed to think it a courtesy due to Father Keogh to reply to him in English. As his knowledge of the language was limited, the interview was somewhat drawn out. He beamed upon Father Keogh.

Father Keogh asked him pleasantly, "Am I going to see you in church?"

The organito flung out his hands. "I am good Catholic, but where put the music box so she is safe? Only where I see her must I go. Ah, Father, life is no more not good in Quantana, but I am good Catholic. Sure."

"Well, she wouldn't be easy to steal from you," Father Keogh pointed out.

"No, no, it is not of her stole I fear. It is the children like to play." He made a circular movement with his arm to show the turn of the handle. "All the time round and round they go, if I am not there watch catch 'em out . . . then what for people want to pay me, if the children turn round for nothing?"

"Perhaps we could arrange for you to park her outside the church where the children couldn't touch her."

"Up that hill I push her *not*."

He moved off, waving gaily to Father Keogh.

Father Keogh walked brusquely back to his house. He was greeted by the familiar smell of eggs and bacon, and a black dog. As he bent down to pat it, Chela appeared.

"Well, Chela, I expected to see you in church."

"Ah, Father, I am a good Catholic, but what would have happened to your nice English breakfast if I had been to church?"

53

When she left him to go down the dark passage that led to her kitchen, and bring back his breakfast, Father Keogh made a memo in his notebook: "See about padlock and chain for barrel organ, and pay boy for Fr. G.'s mule."

Chela carried in the breakfast. She talked as if she and Father Keogh had been in the middle of a conversation. It took him some while to accustom himself to this habit of hers. He realized in time that she must carry on continual conversations with him in her head.

"Yes, well it's right what they say about you, Father. You have taken on something here. Quantana is a bad town and the men who have power in it are bad men. Now Huapan is a nice town."

When he finished saying his grace, she laid his breakfast before him and slapped a table napkin on his knees as if he had been a child in a high chair. "Now Huapan is a nice place."

"I gather you come from Huapan," Father Keogh smiled.

"No indeed, but I like to go there. The people are fine in Huapan." She stood back to watch him while he ate. "I think to go to Huapan is a good thing to do—to go to a good place after a bad place is good for the soul."

"It's a long way to go, isn't it?"

"Yes, Father, and the roads are rough," Chela sighed. "And the bus goes only once a week from here unless you catch it when it stops at the Hua Pass from Arenales, and to do that one must walk up that hill, and then it is sometimes always full! To go there one cannot come back in a day. It is sad, that, when one has only the one day off in the week for one cannot go to Huapan."

Father Keogh hid his smile. "No, I suppose one can't."

"But then that is a bad thing for Huapan is good for the soul."

"Not as good for the soul as going to church."

"Unless of course there is some other woman to be trusted with the work you leave behind, then to go to Huapan is not hard. My sister is a fine woman to leave in a place, in fact if your Reverence saw too much of her I fear he would like her work more than mine."

Father Keogh interrupted her. "All right, Chela, when you want to visit Huapan we'll arrange it, but I still say it can't be as good for the soul as a visit to church!"

Chela departed smiling.

Chapter 9

When he set off on his visits, he was an object of acute curiosity. He went to the Presidente Municipal first, followed by a small band of children. They still refused to converse with him. If he stopped they stopped. If he hurried they hurried, but if he turned to induce them to come any nearer they retreated like nervous animals, chattering amongst themselves.

The Presidente was drinking chocolate. "Ah, Padre, I thought I might see you." He sat in a wickerwork chair on his loggia and commanded one of the best views in Quantana. At the back of his chair a parrot screeched at regular intervals in a fine imitation of the Presidente's voice, "Don Agapito! Don Agapito! Santa Madre de Dios!"

The Presidente was proud of him. "You hear him, Father? No one has taught him—no one—He has picked up these things for himself."

"I hoped I might see you in church this morning," Father Keogh smiled.

The Presidente half-narrowed his eyes. "Yes, well—yes—you'll have some chocolate? My feet you know, that hill!"

Father Keogh said, "Thank you, I would like some chocolate." And he looked down at the Presidente's feet. They were well slippered and seemed perfectly normal.

The Presidente followed his gaze. "I'm an old man," he explained with a touch of petulance. "I'm a good Catholic but I'm subject to gout."

"Oh dear," Father Keogh said. "I am sorry. Couldn't we find you a car or something? Even if it was only on Sundays—"

"There is one car to be hired in Quantana," the Presidente interrupted. "And he charges double to go up the hill and treble on Sundays."

"How does he make a living?"

"By charging double to go up that hill and treble on Sundays—and

55

also by the selling of old tires for the soling of sandals. We need not be sorry for that one."

The Presidente's feet carried him with surprising swiftness to the door. "Arcelia!" he shouted through it. "Arcelia, come here at once!"

"To take up your last point, Señor Presidente Municipal—"

"My wife makes fine chocolate, the best in Quantana. You won't taste any better than hers. Aha!"

He was exultant at the speedy appearance of his wife, but he frowned at the child in her arms. It was his seventh. The preceding six bore his every blunt feature, his thick lips and his indecisive chin. But the seventh bore him no resemblance whatsoever. On the other hand it bore a disconcerting likeness to the Señor engineer who lived next door.

The Presidente introduced his young wife. "Arcelia, this is the new padre who has succeeded Father Gomez. I'm sure we make him very welcome."

"Yes, I'm sure we do."

Father Keogh encountered the soft and merry eyes of Doña Arcelia and could find no other description for them but "saucy." He tried "gay," he tried "friendly" and he tried "humorous," but the fact remained that they were "saucy."

"He's got his hands full there all right," Father Keogh thought.

"And this," said the Presidente, "is our little Silvanito, Father. He is only six months old."

"He's a very fine baby," Father Keogh agreed. "Are you a Catholic, Doña Arcelia?"

"Yes, yes, she is a good one," the Presidente answered for her. "But then you know she has the children, and servants are not what they were in Quantana. No, no, the problem is serious. They are thieves and bad workers. It is not safe to leave children alone with them. Arcelia, Father Keogh will take a cup of chocolate. I have told him how good it is."

Doña Arcelia departed, plump and meek-faced, but not before she had given the priest a look that startled him. Father Keogh hoped that the Presidente had not noticed it, and the Presidente hoped that the priest had not noticed it. They both spoke together, smiling.

"What a wonderful—"

"Is this your first—"

"After you, Father."

"No, go ahead."

56

"I was going to ask you if this is your first acquaintance with Mexico."

"Yes, Don Agapito. It is."

"Ah, and you were going to say?"

"Oh, only what a wonderful view you have. Those mountains look quite mauve."

"Yes indeed, such colors, Father, especially after the rains. Then you will see greens brighter than anywhere else. Thank you, Arcelia. That will be all."

He took the cup of chocolate and handed it to Father Keogh himself.

Father Keogh looked out at the mountains. He was careful to remain looking out at them until he was certain the girl had gone.

The Presidente sat back smoking. "It's not often you find a good wife these days. Not often you find one obedient." Then he inhaled and said, "Well, Father, you will be wasting your time in Quantana."

"I'm not so sure of that, but then of course there are rather special circumstances here."

"Would you say your church was full this morning?"

"No, but then I was told where to look for the reason for that."

The Presidente threw his head back laughing. "Poor Anacleto! My dear Father, that's nonsense! These tales of Anacleto—people lie and they thieve and pardon me, Father, fornicate. They starve their children, they beat their wives, whatever they do you'll be sure to hear that everything's Anacleto's fault."

"You don't suggest he sets a good example?"

"Anacleto does no harm."

"He is harmful in every respect."

"He harms no one who does not harm him."

"I'm afraid I disagree."

The Presidente shrugged. "Then our point of view is different, Father. But I must ask you to reflect, Quantana is peaceful now and prosperous—"

"And sinful."

"My dear Father, it is not only the laity which has the monopoly of sin. For instance, this may distress you, Father, but the departed Father Gomez was—"

"You're using my own arguments against yourself."

" 'Wise,' was the word I was going to use. The departed Father Gomez was 'wise.' "

57

"He felt that he had been *un*wise."

"Wisdom does not necessarily mean happiness, but it can mean peace and security, not only for ourselves but for others. Whereas a misplaced conception of duty can bring havoc and destruction and generally make things worse."

"Are you a wise man, Señor Presidente Municipal?"

The Presidente spread his hands. "I am an old man and my feet are bad. I cannot get about. I have much time for quiet reflection."

Father Keogh put down his cup. "Your wife's chocolate is excellent. Congratulate her, please."

The Presidente bowed Father Keogh out. In the street he opened his notebook. He put a tick by the side of the words "See Presidente Municipal," then he balanced on one leg, rested the notebook on his raised knee and wrote in brackets beside the Presidente's name, "Watch him."

He next saw the Chief of Police. He was shown into a small bare room with whitewashed walls.

The Jefe, a big man with depressed eyes, sat behind a pinewood desk with a bottle of mescal beside him. He wore a pistol on his hip. He offered the priest some chocolate.

"No thank you, I've just been having some."

"I hear you had rather an adventurous introduction to Quantana. I'm sorry if you felt it undignified. Father Gomez must have been rather a favorite."

Father Keogh looked carefully at him. There was no hint of sarcasm, it sprang from a national courtesy and a simple desire not to hurt.

"He was certainly—'favored' last night."

"I'm extremely sorry for it," the Jefe replied.

"I suppose I didn't see you in church because you're such a good Catholic?" Father Keogh asked.

The Jefe raised his eyebrows and brought them down again. "You didn't see me in church because I am *not* a good Catholic."

Father Keogh sat forward to ask him, "I wonder if you'd tell me— to what an extent you are allowed to keep order here?"

"Allowed?" The sad eyes narrowed somewhat.

Father Keogh wondered, Have they all got that habit of Malo's? He had noticed it in young Vito Juarez, in the Presidente, and now even in the Jefe. "When I said 'allowed,' I meant of course, Malo-of-the-Cats."

"Comachi makes no trouble for me, if I make no trouble for him."

"How does that fit in with law and order?"

"Comachi makes his own laws, and in his way he keeps good order."

"By stealing people's property, collecting illegal taxes, desecrating the church, holding moral hostages, and ruling the town by an evil force?"

"The force is no longer necessary. He has his way. The people are content."

"Content?"

"They resist no more. That way they're left undisturbed. The Mexican is not as wild as he is rumored. He may have a quick-minute violence, but in his heart he's a man of peace."

"And don't you feel called upon to resist him yourselves?"

"We may feel what we please, Father, but we are not called upon."

"Suppose you used your own initiative?"

"I should come up against a stone wall. My men are underpaid. . . . One or two of them are such fine men that they could not be corrupted if they were not paid at all."

"I see," said Father Keogh.

"No one complains about Comachi—very rarely perhaps—but the complaint is soon withdrawn, and that particular individual never complains again."

"I see," Father Keogh said.

"We get no assistance, no information, and if we act on our own accord we are hindered."

"In point of fact, you're here to protect a people who refuse to allow you to protect them against an illicit ruler they have chosen themselves."

"Chosen, would not be correct. Accepted would be correct."

"A ruler who prevents them from practicing their faith."

"That's your business, Father, not mine."

"Would you call murder—your business?"

"If I was able to prove it was that."

"What about A for Arrieta, B for Beltran, C for Carranza, and very nearly G for Gomez?"

"When no one is anxious to help you prove something, Father, things are not easy to prove. When everyone is anxious to disprove something—it is impossible to prove." The Jefe sat back again and poured out a glass of mescal. "Once I thought I had something. Old

59

Don José disappeared. His body was found on the hillside in the river of small receptions, where so many young children get drowned. It's a swift river, but not very big, you never know with it. After the rains it gets ideas, but this was not after the rains. Don José could have easily saved himself. I happened to know there was trouble coming for him, Don José was always rebellious, he was one of the few who still dared. I knew there were 'taxes' owing. But—" The Jefe lifted his heavy shoulders up. "His widow swore he could never swim, and about six members of his family rallied round to swear that they had witnessed him falling in. I tried to check up on their alibis, I knew perfectly well not one of them had been near him for weeks, but their friends stood by them . . . they couldn't be moved."

"But surely they realize that if you get Malo they needn't fear him any more."

"Perhaps, but they don't care for the risk. Don José gets killed— but they say it was an accident because they don't want the same sort of accident happening to them." The Jefe smiled at Father Keogh's troubled eyes. "Yes, yes, we do know it's not good. But then, there are other things. Comachi is as careful as a woman with only a handful of beans to feed ten children. Comachi is not extravagant. And he has genius that boy. He does not want trouble again from Mexico City, he does not want Federal trouble—he will never overstep himself."

"Supposing you gave him enough rope to hang himself."

"He would not hang himself, he would hang you and me, and save what was left over for somebody else. He wouldn't waste one inch of that rope."

"There must be some way to catch him out."

"Usually all you have to do is wait," the Jefe said. "Most people get too big for themselves. If Comachi was anyone else but Comachi, I should feel that all I had to do was wait."

"Don't you think he'll ever trip up?"

The Jefe shook his head. "It would never be like that with our friend Comachi. He is wise. He's content to be running Quantana. You might think he would want to do the same thing in Huapan, or Arenales, or Cerro Colorado, but no. They're scared of him down there all right. They keep on the right side of him. Nobody likes to mention he has no business to be running Quantana, everyone's very polite. But he's not going to try to get in anywhere else like he's got in here. He's going to stick to the bird in the hand. These murders you spoke of—and I don't doubt they were murders—they were a long time ago you know, there hasn't been much trouble since."

"Supposing there was?"

"If he killed again? Well, even here we don't like killings. . . . If I could catch him red-handed, or get someone to prove it . . . we'd *get him.*" The last two words showed his ambition.

"If only we could make the people less afraid. Or less compromising, or complacent, or whatever you care to call it, don't you think then, we might have a chance?" Father Keogh asked.

"If only," the Jefe smiled.

Father Keogh stood up. "Just one thing more, in what capacity can you act if you've got all these restrictions on you?"

"As a police force?"

"Yes."

"We can deal with the petty offenses. We can pick you up if you smoke marijuana . . . or if too much pulque or mescal puts you out on your face in the street. That is, of course, if you didn't happen to have been drinking or smoking with any of his boys."

"It's rough luck on the petty offenders."

"Yes, we have a lot of time to spare for them—this town is as clean as a whistle, as far as petty offenders go. And if we didn't clean them up—Comachi would. He doesn't like disorder."

"I must watch my step," Father Keogh smiled.

"Yes, Father, you certainly must."

Outside Father Keogh wrote down in his notebook, "Chief of Police. O.K."

Chapter 10

Now," Father Keogh thought to himself, "I'd better go up that hill."

A truck thundered along the road above with a crowd of men piled into the back. Some had wound scarves round their faces to protect them from the dust, and others held their hats against it.

Father Keogh climbed the hill. He was thinking of Locha and her parents rather than Malo-of-the-Cats. A new priest had to tread warily with his parishioners at first. The laity were slow to praise a priest, deeming a job well done on their behalf, his duty and their due, but they were not so slow to blame.

Halfway up the hill Father Keogh began to sympathize with the state of the Presidente's feet. It occurred to him that his own might be in need of the services of the car that cost treble on Sundays, by the time he had been in Quantana a month.

As usual he found the child at the gate. "Hallo, Locha," he called out to her. "I'm coming to visit you."

She stood back when he opened the gate. "What for?"

"I've come to call on your mother and father."

"What for?"

"You ask a lot of questions for a rather small person."

"You're not going to tell them what I told you this morning?"

"My dear child, confession is secret. We never tell anything people confess unless they ask us to. Surely you must have known that." He held out his hand to her but she refused to take it. Her eyes looked mistrustfully at him. "Won't you take hold of my hand?"

"No."

"All right." He dropped his arm and watched her walk beside him. She walked with her head down and her arms folded. Halfway to the great wooden doors she plucked his sleeve.

"Yes, what is it?" He bent down to hear her. She held out her hand, not looking at him. He took it and held it firmly. "How's the tortoise?" he asked.

"Quite well thank you."

"Don't you think we could find him a nicer name than Malo?"

"He's not called Malo now."

"What is he called?"

"Nothing."

"What made you decide on that?"

"Nothing."

He looked down at her, smiling. "What are you sulking about?"

"Nothing."

"What a lot of nothings!"

He had to ask her to repeat it before he could hear her muttered question. "You're *sure* you won't tell mother and father about what I told you—this morning I mean?"

He gave her hand a squeeze. "That was between you and me and God this morning. Nobody else will find out."

She was silent a moment and then she asked, "What's your name—I mean your first name?"

"Michael, but my sister calls me Micky."

"Can I call my tortoise that?"

"Yes, do. I should feel very flattered."

She ran off shouting, "Micky! Micky! Micky!"

At the door he was met by the mozo, Francisco Jimenez, who took him up to Don Pedro's library.

Don Pedro sat in a dome-shaped room lined with books. He sat at a desk on which books were piled. He had a thin and emotionless face. He kept a finger on the place in his book when Father Keogh was shown into the room. Then he placed a marker in the page and stood up. He spoke in perfect English.

"Good morning, Father. How do you do?" He came forward and offered Father Keogh a chair. "May I offer you something to drink?"

"Not just for the moment, thank you."

"Not a mineral or something? You look pretty warm."

"Well, since you mention it I think I am, so perhaps I'll change my mind."

"Good." Don Pedro rang a bell.

"I've made friends with your daughter," Father Keogh said. "I think she's very sweet."

"Locha? Yes, I'm afraid she gets left on her own, poor child. But there's really no one round here she could play with. There are other children about, of course, but Locha doesn't care for them. She's a very reserved little thing."

"Is she? I found her rather chatty."

"Did you? You ought to feel honored. My wife complains that she can't get a word out of her and she hasn't much to say to me."

"I was wondering," Father Keogh began, and broke off when Francisco came into the room. He stood grinning expectantly in his white loose-fitting suit.

"A tray of soft drinks," Don Pedro ordered, and bowed his head to the priest. "You were just saying, Father?"

When Francisco went out Father Keogh continued, "I was wondering if you would give me your opinion of what's going on in this town."

"You mean the bandit grip on it? My dear Father—it's Keogh isn't it?"

63

"Yes. Is there nothing we can do with Comachi?"

"It's most reprehensible, but we are bound to submit to it. The majority have decided that for us."

"When you say 'we' do you mean to say that you yourself are bound to submit?"

"My dear Father, I am the richest man in these whereabouts. I should be the last to be allowed to escape." When he saw Father Keogh's expression his smile spread under his high thin nose. "I see you are thinking badly of me."

"I was just thinking what power this man has got."

"In my case I am left pretty well alone providing I pay my taxes to him. Anyway I can afford the taxes better than some of the poor wretches he extorts money from. They are reduced to penury because of it."

"Then surely they would be grateful if you set an example and made a stand against him?"

Don Pedro shook his head. "The opposite, Father. They would turn on me. They would never have the courage to follow any example. All that would happen is that they would resent the rich man trying to wriggle out of something which the poor man has to pay."

"What a vicious circle," Father Keogh said.

"You must remember, Father, that over ninety per cent of the population here are peasants or have been peasant bred. Superstition plays a very great part in them. Many of the surrounding villages and three quarters of Quantana earnestly believe that Comachi can use supernatural powers against them."

"Supernatural powers are not necessarily confined to evil. They can work both ways," Father Keogh said.

"I daresay. It's a question of faith, but evil remains the stronger force."

"By no means," Father Keogh said.

"Nevertheless, Comachi's accredited powers of being able to turn into a giant white cat will not be easy to compete with."

"I wasn't thinking of entering into competition with him on those lines," Father Keogh laughed.

"I hope you're not thinking of entering into competition with him at all, Father."

"I hope to lead the people back to God," said Father Keogh simply.

"I can't say I envy you your task. I am Comachi's accomplice as far as I have told you, insomuch as I pay him money which he has no

64

right to claim. If I didn't I should run the risk of the town's hostility, having my daughter kidnaped, my wife robbed and my house burned down."

"I wonder you stay here in such conditions."

Don Pedro raised his eyes. "My family have lived here for hundreds of years. This is my home. There used to be much more of it before the revolution. The property stops at the end of the wall now, and I had to buy it all back up to that point. There's nowhere else I should prefer to be. Providing we submit to his dictatorship there are no outward disturbances now. I hope you will not cause any, Father."

"I hope not too," Father Keogh said.

"Those servants," Don Pedro frowned, "they don't seem able to use what little brain God's given them. I asked for a *tray* of soft drinks, you see, so that you might be given a choice. If I had asked for one in particular it would have been here at once. This delay is due to conflict. There is no doubt a full-scale argument raging downstairs as to what should or should not be included on the tray. Excuse me." He went to the door and shouted loudly, "Paco, burro!" Then he went to the head of the stairs and shouted again.

By the time he came back Father Keogh had had time to write in his notebook, "Don Pedro—sitting on the fence."

Chapter 11

In the room above the library Doña Marian sat putting a quick red lacquer across her nails. Doña Marian was dressed with the same good taste which had decorated the room in which she sat. The hard fair hair was swept into a sideways bun. Each ear held a twist of gold. High round the throat there was a circle of pink-flushed pearls. The dress was a steel and black check. The shoes were plain, the stockings sheer, and a wine-red lipstick matched the nails.

The eyes were at odds with the rest of the face. They were blue with

65

an anxious friendliness, but the mouth denied the eyes. There were two lines either side of it so deep that they might have been scars. Behind her Josefa stood, fussing with the hard gold hair.

"Josefa, squirt me with perfume, will you?" She waved her wet nails in the air and raised her head so that the perfume sprayed her neck. "How long has he been down there with my husband?"

"Some time now, Doña Marian, but then it is that slow Paco with the drinks. 'Soft drinks on a tray,' Don Pedro orders and Paco says, 'Which drinks?' and that Pio, that one has the same brains as Paco, which are not there—so I said, 'Paco, burro! While you quarrel together the new priest dies of thirst.' Then I said, 'Put them *all* on the tray together, Paco, and let him sort them out,' and that silly Paco says, 'But all of them will not *go* on the tray.' When you think of the trouble a woman has to push a man's head into the world, to find it filled with dust must be a most unhappy thing."

"Do you think the priest will call on me?" Doña Marian asked.

"Well, Doña Marian, I should think so. To visit the lady is only polite, but then that Paco has kept him so long."

"Do you think I should let him know I'm expecting him?"

"Doña Marian, I will do that. I will catch him coming out. Oh, Doña Marian, you should see him!"

"Well, I'm going to see him, aren't I?" There was a touch of defiance in the voice.

"Yes, yes, of course. To hear him speak! It is not a voice that shouts. Even the Señorita Locha managed to sit still in church. Ah, how he says the Mass! Not mumble, mumble like the other little one. This one speaks up and yet it's soft. He has truly a wonderful sound."

"Josefa, go find me some good books. You know, the kind I leave around for my husband to see."

Josefa went out of the room, but before she shut the door she was muttering an autocratic prayer. "Now if God is good He will send him up. Yes, a good God will send up the priest. The poor lady needs to see someone just now and again. She can't live alone in her head, can she? . . . Who art in Heaven, Hallowed be Thy Name. Now where did I put those books?"

When Doña Marian's nails were dry, she powdered her nose and rouged her lips. Then she crossed her legs and drummed her long fingers on the side of the chair.

There was one discordant note in the room. There was a poor reproduction of Franz Hals' portrait of "The Fool" on the wall.

On the rare occasions when Don Pedro visited his wife's private apartment he grumbled about it. "The house is full of magnificent pictures and yet you must choose to hang up a bad print."

"I like him. He cheers me up."

It was the fact that the grin was idiotic that cheered her up. She sat staring at it when she felt disconsolate. In the vacuous smiling face with the wistful hint of melancholy there was nothing demanded of her. It held nothing of Don Pedro's haughty dreams or Locha's close-faced secrecy. The portrait was open and frank and inane. Sometimes she spoke out loud to it. "I may be dumb, but you're nuts."

It was the same in her childhood, the same in her schooldays. She grew up between two clever sisters, and she felt an idiot between them. Everyone saw that she was beautiful, everyone thought she was dumb, but nobody realized that she was sensitive.

When the Ketterenski's reached America they could speak no other language but Polish. Their son became a janitor. His son became a cook. His son became Marian's father. He called himself Joseph Ketter and he could speak no word of Polish.

Her two sisters giggled in corners. If she asked them to explain a joke to her they hugged themselves and laughed.

She grew up knowing nothing of the facts that surrounded life. She was pitched into the roaring twenties with very few warnings. Her father disapproved of cocktails, her mother told her that to smoke was unladylike. She received no other warnings.

Because she never knew what to say she overemphasized what little she had to say. When she was young there was an enthusiastic charm about it. Even so she heard, "Someone should tell that gorgeous babe to keep her pretty mouth shut."

It was easier to talk to a man than a woman. She never could understand why. She attached no importance to her physical charms. She badly wanted women friends. It was company she wanted, not admiration. It was bewildering to be a pretty girl and have no real talking friend.

She was never required to exert herself or to make a good impression with men. They found her company good. She made no attempts to lure. She had only to smile her ever friendly smile and show her teeth. She never did either for guile. It was the same smile that she gave to old ladies in wheelchairs, babies in prams or a dog that pranced past on a lead. She noticed that it was usually after dancing with them that men first suggested she should sleep with them. It

67

usually took three days. She was puzzled if it took any longer. Before she was twenty-one she met Don Pedro.

His eyes lay like two dreamy jet-black lozenges under his tranquil brows, but beneath a tiny thin moustache his mouth was firm and cold. After three days she said to him, "Aren't *you* going to ask me to sleep with you?" Don Pedro said he was, but he asked her to marry him first. She accepted him at once. When he asked her curiously whether no one else had proposed, she said, "Sure they have." When he asked her why she had not accepted them she said, "I guess I didn't want them."

When he told her that he thought that her morals left much to be desired, she put her hands to her eyes and cried. When he told her that she must know that her morals left much to be desired, she sobbed out loud. After that he put gentle questions to her.

"Didn't anyone ever tell you that to behave like that is bad?"

"I never told anybody about it."

"Do your sisters behave like that?"

"Well, Mary doesn't have any boy friends and I have never gotten very close to Sue."

He took her in his arms and wiped her eyes. He was trying not to smile. "Now, Marian, you must know right from wrong. Every young girl knows that. When did you first go out with a man? Do you know what I mean by 'out'?"

Marian shook her head.

"I mean how old were you when you first let a man make love to you?"

"We didn't go out," she said.

"Never mind where you were. What happened?"

"He asked me to take my clothes off."

"And did you?" Don Pedro inquired. Marian shook her head. "Why not?"

"I wasn't dressed right underneath."

"What happened?"

"*He* took them off," she said.

Don Pedro brushed his lips across her forehead and kissed her several times. "When we're married, Marian, how am I going to trust you?"

"Oh, I couldn't do *that* after you."

"What makes you so sure?" he asked her.

"I guess because I love you."

68

Don Pedro decided to believe her.

The Ketters were greatly excited. Marian was marrying a Spanish—Count—Prince—Duke. The title grew as it sped round the town. They were captivated by Don Pedro's icy courtesy and they were nonplused by his marrying Marian. They mostly fell back on, "Of course she *is* beautiful. She's the most beautiful girl in town."

It was her father who hit on the truth. "Sometimes a clever man doesn't want a clever woman. Sometimes he gets more peace that way."

Don Pedro wanted peace.

They went round the world on their honeymoon. At first she chattered endlessly to him. It was easy to talk to someone who loved her —someone who must have wanted something other than her body because he had married it first; someone who could not have found her a bore if he was willing to put up with her company for life; someone who had given her such solid proof, that she was something more than legs and arms and hips and breasts and thighs. Someone who must have noticed that she possessed a head. She confided happily in Don Pedro, "You know what, Pey? It seems I was waiting all along for you to come and talk to me. I guess I couldn't talk to anybody else, because all along I knew it was only you I wanted to talk to!"

She chattered so much that it took her some while to realize that he seldom answered back.

When she did notice she was anxious. "You're not getting bored with me, Pey?"

"No, my dear, of course not. I was thinking about something else."

He was frequently thinking of something else, and he suddenly ended their honeymoon.

Quantana was turbulent when they returned to it and Don Pedro forbade her to go out without him. He spent most of the day in his library and he spent a large portion of the night in it. At first she interrupted him. She burst in and out of the room. "Pey, honey, look! They sent it—my perfume's come from Paris." And she took the stopper out of the bottle and waved it beneath his nose.

"It's delicious," he told her. "What is it?"

"They call it 'Suspense.' Don't you think that's cute? They have one called 'Suspicion' too."

"Have they?" he said. "How nice."

He kept his finger on his place in his book. When she noticed the finger she began to knock before she entered the room. "Pey honey, do I disturb you?"

"No, my dear, what is it?"

"Oh, it's nothing. I just wanted to talk."

"Then come in, my dear, and talk." And he put a marker in his book and sat back with his hands folded. She could think of nothing at all to say to him.

She was willing to learn from Don Pedro but he seemed disinclined to teach her anything. She read avidly herself, anything she could lay her hands upon. She quoted long paragraphs at him, hoping to win admiration. "Why do you read that muck?" he asked her, about something that had taken her a week to puzzle out.

She paid fewer and fewer visits to the library. Then she paid none at all. They met at mealtimes, and the early hours of the morning. He would have been willing to talk at mealtimes, but she grew shy of him, frightened of boring him.

"What's that you're wearing today, my dear—'Suspicion'?"

"No, Pey, it isn't that one."

"It smells very nice. What is it?"

"They call it 'Pagan Heaven.' "

She felt a fool when she said the name and inwardly cursed its creator.

When she lay in his arms she lost her loneliness but it returned with the start of each day. There were times when she cried in his arms. "Pey honey, I get so lonely for you."

"But, my dear girl, I'm always here with you."

"I know, but I don't seem to see you."

"You can always come in to see me any time you like."

"Pey, I love you so much I get scared of you."

He kissed her and called her foolish.

The elite of Quantana called on her. They did not approve Don Pedro's choice. She smoked, and she drank, and she thought Mexican formalities "something right out of the Ark." The elite of Quantana ceased to call. Don Pedro was relieved and never once wondered what his young wife found to do with herself all day. But he found time to frown at her sometimes. "You drink and you smoke too much."

If she went away she hurried home to him. She was never unfaithful to him.

She was greatly in awe of his ancestors. She tried to make friends

70

with the portraits at first. She studied them, climbing up the stairs, standing minutes on every step. She tried to copy the way they held their hands—the proud angle they held their heads, the lifeless indifference of arrogant eyes. It was hard not to remember that great-grandfather Ketter had been a janitor and grandfather Ketter a cook. She could never make friends with the portraits, so she bought herself "The Fool."

When she found she was pregnant she prayed for a girl. When Locha was born she believed she had found a friend. She sat by the cot for hours on end sewing for the baby and chattering to it. "We're going to have such fun together. Oh, I've got things to teach you, honey. I'm not as dumb as that." And she picked the baby up and cuddled it, kissing its solemn face.

She was happy until Locha learned to read. In the beginning it was easy—the first baby words that were such a delight to teach, the bright pictures in old Polish fairy story books. At first it was all such fun, until Locha learned to read. It was fun even then for a time. She read aloud to her mother. But soon there were more important books and, "Mother, I want to hear this one myself."

Doña Marian found it "cute" to begin with. She told Don Pedro so. "Pey honey, don't you think that's cute? The kid talks about *hearing* a book."

"All books have tongues," Don Pedro said.

There were more and more books that Locha wanted to hear by herself. She started to shut herself away. At first Doña Marian interrupted her. "Locha honey, your Aunt Mary wrote from home. Don't you think this little cat your cousin Dyke Brown drew, is cute?"

Locha raised a small pale face that held Don Pedro's eyes in it. One finger marked the place in her book. When she noticed it, Doña Marian never interrupted her daughter again.

When Father Keogh came into the room he was greeted by "Pagan Heaven." He saw an aging bright young thing and he thought that it was the pleasures of a ragtime world that had stamped the hard lines on her face.

He managed to escape from her after five minutes. Against her name in his little notebook he wrote, "Gushing and *very* hard-boiled."

71

Chapter 12

He found Locha waiting to escort him out.

"How did you go down with the old folks?" she inquired politely.

"All right I hope," he told her and asked with the same politeness, "How did the new name go down with Micky?"

"He wouldn't come out of his shell this morning, I haven't been able to tell him. But so that it won't be too much for him all at once I think I'll call him Micky-Malo. Then when he gets himself used to it I can drop the Malo off."

"Ease him into it gently?" Father Keogh asked.

"Yes. Don't you think that's the wisest plan?"

"I think it's the wisest plan all round," said Father Keogh.

She looked at him curiously, her eyes thoughtful. "Do you like being a priest?"

"Yes, I do. Do you like being a little girl?"

Her nose crinkled, laughing at him. "I do think you're a funny priest."

"Oh you do, do you?" He smiled at her and waved at her through the gates.

He saw the doctor and the dentist. Against the doctor's name in his notebook he wrote "O.K." Beside the dentist's name he put a question mark. He saw the bank manager, Don Miguel, and the manager of the cinema. He interviewed several officials at the Presidencia.

He saw Domingo-of-the-Hired-Car and he saw Mother Montezera, and it seemed to him that everywhere he went he saw the barrel organ.

With the exception of the dentist they were all good Catholics and they all had good excuses. He drew a line down the center of the page in his notebook. On one side he wrote "For him" and on the other "Against him." Under "For him" he listed the names of all those who called Malo, Anacleto. Under "Against him" he listed all those who called him Malo or the Bad One. Even then he suspected that some of those who were for him were against him. He made another note. "Frightened of him—the whole lot with the exception of Sam—and possibly, the Jefe."

When he reached his house again he found the "Four Señoras" awaiting him. Chela had given them coffee, annoyed that she was unable to afford to offer them chocolate. They rose in unison when Father Keogh came into the room. He greeted Señora Martinez first because he had already made her acquaintance in church. Señora Martinez was careful to remind him that she was the only one of the four whom he had seen there. A smile sat over her thin lips that Father Keogh found hard to like.

The other three made excuses. The first had been ill for a considerable while and confined to the house, the second was forbidden by her husband to attend the church, and the third was frankly afraid of Malo. Father Keogh smiled at her. The other three turned upon her. "What must Father Keogh think of you, Aurelia?" Señora Solano demanded.

"I think Señora Rodriguez has every right to be frightened of Malo. He's a very unnerving gentleman. But I don't want to endanger anybody. All I'm hoping is that there may come a time when nobody will be endangered."

Señora Rodriguez was small and thin and grateful to him. She looked frightened of the other three.

Señora Martinez smiled again. "You mustn't think we're all so lacking in courage as little Aurelia, Father, but I'm sure we have proved that by coming here. You know, it's quite a risk."

She gave a high little laugh to show him how lightly she accepted the risk.

He knew that she needed his tolerance, if only because he felt that she did not deserve it. He wondered how she would smile at him if he were not a priest and she were not endeavoring to impress him with her piety. If he were a beggar whining at her door he wondered how the close face would look when the piety broke out of it; how the cold eyes would read without their glacier gloss of respect. He could imagine a merciless rap on the windows and the strident voice calling, "Be off!"

He had to force a respect in his own eyes when he listened to her. He said, "Well, ladies, I mustn't keep you, and I have to be off myself, but it was very good of you to come." He gave his smile to Señora Rodriguez.

73

The other three left congratulating him. "Well, Father, you see that you have friends. There are some *good* people left in Quantana."

Father Keogh found himself reciting irreverently, "One, two, three, four, five, six, seven, All good women go to Heaven."

Then he set out on foot for the poor settlement that lay back from the Huapan road. Except for a rake-thin dog who rummaged in the dirt ahead of him his own black shadow was the only other thing that moved in the narrow street.

From the high wall the vultures looked placidly down upon him, watching him pass with their bright bead eyes.

Behind the iron-barred windows along the street other eyes were watching him, some curious, some resentful, but all of them apprehensive.

Behind the barred windows they whispered about him:

"That one is going to make trouble, you'll see. Look at the way he steps out."

"What will the Bad One think?"

"The Presidente has seen him, and he said to my cousin, 'The new Ingles-Irlandes is not one to mind his own business. He has come here to stir up mud.' "

"Chela says he is always looking for trouble—small little marks he wants put on the things that he gives her to wash so that none of the things can be lost."

"It will be wise to have nothing to do with him, one can still manage that and be polite."

It took him an hour and a half to reach Tephuango and he carried an acetylene lamp with him to light his journey home. The road shot up steeply, cooling the air for a mile or two and then dropped suddenly down into heat again.

An Indian riding a burro passed by. He carried a heavy load on his own narrow back and called out a greeting in his own dialect, "Teatolao tenixo ñijno!" Father Keogh was obliged to wave a greeting back. The Indian rode ahead of him chewing a sugar cane. The feet of the burro shot stones in front of it and its tail seemed at right angles with its head as it made the steep descent. The Indian lay on its neck lost to view except for the high load he carried.

When Father Keogh reached the settlement the news of his coming had preceded him via the Indian. He was the center of an excited circle that silenced itself as Father Keogh approached. He felt like a leper coming towards it, he might have been ringing a bell to declare

74

himself unclean. The circle broke up as soon as he approached it, disappearing into straw-roofed huts. The narrow mud street was left empty except for the violent shadows of the organ cactus plant that stretched from side to side, Father Keogh, the Indian and the burro.

The Indian appeared to feel it incumbent upon himself to apologize for the inhabitants of Tephuango. He made an unrecognizable sign of the cross, raised a greasy black hat and spat by way of introduction. His black eyes remained steadily upon Father Keogh's face, his hands remained still at his sides. There seemed no movement in him. Even his voice was effortless. What he could not say in Spanish he substituted with Mexicano. He knew one English word. It was "wallop." He used it frequently to put the new priest at his ease. It added considerably to Father Keogh's confusion.

After a number of misunderstandings he finally gathered that the inhabitants of Tephuango were humiliated to feel themselves unable to extend their poor hospitality towards the stranger. They would have been willing to spread before him everything they had. Unfortunately this was not in accordance with the wishes of the Bad-One-of-the-Cats, whose soul might the devil perish. They were a poor people for what they had they could not keep, the Bad One's agent let no man escape. It was very unwise to displease the Bad One. The inhabitants felt sure that Father Keogh would understand and excuse their lack of courtesy. As if to give authority to the Indian's message they reappeared in their doorways. One or two of them nodded towards the priest. Father Keogh nodded back to them. They vanished quietly inside the huts again.

"So you will see how it is," the Indian said. "I am not from these parts myself, but I live in very great fear of him. The Bad One is everywhere having long ears and the soft tread of a cat so that a man who is not looking will not hear him and then—wallop, you never know what might happen."

He then added that the heart of his burro was guided by the devil and that it was a heart that would rather travel backwards than forwards. If Father Keogh would say a little prayer to show the animal its true path, and if Father Keogh had time to ask the protection of San Ignacio who was the patron saint of those with a hard path in front of them, and if Father Keogh could spare a silver peso at the same time, the Indian's lot would be considerably lightened. Father Keogh carried out the first two requests and spared the peso. They parted extremely good friends.

75

Father Keogh walked into the largest hut. There was no light except from the smoking fire on which a pot was boiling. It took his eyes some while to accustom themselves to the gloom. When they did so he saw that there were about eight or nine people squatting upon a reed mat that covered the dirt floor. Three children scuttled behind a woman, and an old man stood up to greet him.

"I've no wish to endanger you," Father Keogh said. "I've only come to tell you that I am your friend and that if you will let me I can help you."

There was silence inside the hut. Two geese waddled out of it into the sunlight. Father Keogh took out a cigarette and put it in the old man's hand. Then he lit his lighter. It showed up a row of clay pots and a small household altar. Father Keogh was quick to notice that it was devoid of the usual religious influences. There were flowers and there were candles, but there were no pictures of patron saints, no statuettes. There was a tiny toy coffin containing a skeleton which leapt up at the tug of a string, such as Don Timoteo sold in the market place on the day of the dead, but there was nothing else. The lighter showed up the impassive, watchful faces round him. Not a muscle in any one of them moved.

The old man rolled the cigarette backwards and forwards between his long fingers. Father Keogh took it from him, lit it himself and returned it to him. The old man regarded the smoking end, put it between his lips and sat down on the petate again. Father Keogh sat beside him.

He sensed the resentment inside the hut. It was evident that the occupants felt themselves victimized. They saw no reason why they should have been chosen to flout the Bad One's wishes. He could feel their unspoken reproach. They considered that he had abused their trust by ignoring the Indian's message. He could see it in the sideways movement of the whites of their eyes.

He spoke lightly and easily to them in Spanish. He had no way to tell if they understood him. Nobody made any sign.

"If you have burdens, share them with me. If you have troubles, bring them to me. If you do that you will be asking the help of God through me. It's not God who's deserted you, you know, it's you who've deserted Him. How can He help if you won't take His help? Can a beggar receive alms if he closes his hand against the man who is trying to put money in it? You are afraid of the Bad One. I understand that. But God would be your friend against him. The devil is

Malo's friend. You have chosen to serve Malo's friend. And what has his friendship brought you? Has it brought you contentment? Are you at peace? Can you live without fear in your hearts? Are your children well fed? Have you money to spare? What has his friendship brought you?"

It was then that he discovered they understood him. The old man leaned forward to request in soft Spanish for the services of the "little tin box that makes fire in the hand." His cigarette had gone out. Apart from that nobody spoke.

Father Keogh relit the cigarette. "Before Malo came you were serving God. Which made the best master, my friends?"

An old woman stirred in the corner, her joints cracking. Then the old man stood up. He knelt in the corner behind the old woman and dug with his hands. The earth was loose as if it were often disturbed. He brought out a bundle wrapped in a strip of blanket and laid it at Father Keogh's feet. It contained a battered statuette, four holy medallions on dirty strings, two holy pictures in passe partout frames and a little silver rosary-cross. They were snatched from him, rewrapped and reburied before Father Keogh had time to examine them.

Father Keogh stood up to go. "There is nothing to stop people practicing their faith any more. You are free to worship except for the will of this one man. As long as his will is your will, you will never be free. Help me to free you. Come to me. Tell me the bad things he does to you, tell me the money he takes. If he hurts anybody or makes any threats let me know all about it. He will never know how I've found out. If enough of you tell me you are safe. But if nobody tells me, he is safe. The Jefe is a very good man. He can save you from the Bad One if you will let him. Speak to the Jefe through me. I am not afraid of the Bad One's powers. The devil's no friend of mine."

He put ten cigarettes in the old man's hand and walked out of the hut. The sweat from the back of his knees had dried on his trouser legs by the time he had walked three yards in the sun.

On the way back to Quantana a thousand crickets chirruped at him. Great begonias grew down from the roadside, their leaves in the shape of an angel's wing, their waxy flowers oddly agleam in the fading light. There was a perfume on the cool evening air that seemed too heavy for it—as if the light wind found it hard to keep aloft and had let it fall carelessly, to lie in solid patches along the road before it was snatched up again and blown about. It was dark before he reached the town and he lit his acetylene lamp. A variety of jazzing insects followed its hard yellow light—a scorpion scurried across the road its vicious tail held up—and the small bright eyes of a startled lizard looked like darting black holes in the side of a rock as it fled from the rays of the lamp. When he passed the Presidente's house he heard the parrot shriek, "Don Agapito! Don Agapito!—Santa Madre de Dios!"

The evening parade was in progress and the lights were ablaze on the Plaza. It lay beneath the mountain road a tiny winking square. On his way through the town he passed a beggar asleep in a mud alley. Wrapped in his serape, his head alone protruding, his feet tucked under the threadbare blanket, he looked like a bundle of rotting rags. When Father Keogh raised his lamp he recognized the sacristan.

He put a hand under the old man's elbow and took him home to Chela. "Give him some food and put a mattress in front of the kitchen fire. He'll have to stay with us until we can make other arrangements for him."

"But Father, the old one has fleas."

Chapter 13

It was late in the evening before he saw Sam. He went round to the back of the Hotel de la Costa and knocked on a door that was locked.

He ached as he stood in the patio. His long walk had tired him and his arm was still sore from his vaccination. He received no reply to his knock. He rapped once again on the door. Something heavy fell down on the floor behind it. Someone swore and shouted loudly, "I've told you I'm damn well not coming out. Find some other poor sonuva-bitch."

Father Keogh called, "Sam, it's Mac."

A few minutes passed before the door opened. When it did a sour smell crept out of the room behind it and a man stood unsteadily. He screwed up his eyes in the light from the lamp. He was unshaven and his hair stood on end. He looked at Father Keogh with a soggy lack of recognition that cut him to the quick. Father Keogh said gently, "Sam, it's me. I just wanted to say thank you for cleaning out the church this morning. I couldn't get round before this."

"Whadda you want? Who are you? Whadda ya goddamn well want?"

"Just to say thank you, Sam, that's all."

The door was slammed hard in his face. Father Keogh turned sadly away.

He walked fast still in spite of his aching limbs. He walked into the Hotel Martinez. It was cool in the lounge and it smelled of perfume. Maria sat deep in a chair. She looked up over a bright magazine cover. She was smooth-limbed and deep-breasted. She had sullen lips and lazy eyes.

Father Keogh said, "Good evening. I should like to see Señor Comachi."

She shook her head. "Not here."

Her dress was cut low and Father Keogh could see the cleft between light brown breasts. Vito Juarez stood behind her. He was running his hands down towards her breasts. She said without turning, "Stop it, you. I'll tell him you fool around."

Vito looked at the priest. "You owe me some money, Holy Father." And he held out the palm of his hand. Father Keogh put a peso in it. He asked, "Where could I find Señor Comachi?"

Vito dropped the coin between Maria's breasts. She said, "Stop fooling, you."

There was still hotel furniture left in the lounge. Small tables and chromium chairs. Several cats were asleep on the cushions.

Maria pushed Vito's hand away as he felt down her breast for the coin.

"Isn't she beautiful, Father? Have you ever seen such a beautiful— neck?" Vito retrieved the coin. He threw it up in the air and caught it on the back of his hand. "Let me see now, Señor Comachi, if he isn't in church he'll be in somebody's bed, isn't that so, my Maria?" Maria hit out at him with a plump-backed hand. He dodged her and laughed, his teeth showing. "And if he's not there, in Porfirio's bar."

Father Keogh walked into the bar. Cigar smoke hung heavily under the ceiling but the bar was freshly swept. Porfirio beat his solid wife if she did not keep it clean.

79

Lorenzo and Pablo lounged at the counter dicing each other for drinks. The little Jeep sat up beside them, nervously chewing his nails. At one small table Malo sat with his head against a wall from which the plaster flaked, showing the inevitable mud behind. His eyes were narrowed, he seemed to be dreaming.

Old Uncle Joaquin sang beside him to a tune on his old guitar.

> *"Out on the mountain he lay alone,*
> *Out in the wind on the mountain,*
> *There was no one to weep save me, save me*
> *Out in the wind on the mountain."*

Porfirio blew on the side of a glass and held it, cloth in hand, towards the light. He was humming in time to the tune.

> *"For a woman cannot weep as a man can weep,*
> *Out in the wind on the mountain,*
> *The tears of a woman lightly fall,*
> *Out in the wind on the mountain."*

The whites of Old Uncle's eyes were red. He might very well have been weeping.

Porfirio saw the priest first.

"Good evening," Father Keogh said. "I have come to see Señor Comachi."

Porfirio laid a flat hand on the air as if he had been a waiter offering a dish. "In the corner we have Señor Comachi."

Malo stood up. "Good evening, Father." The arrow-straight figure looked lonely in the smoke-filled room as if nobody there had been able to keep it company. He looked almost relieved to see the priest. He pushed forward a chair for Father Keogh. There was silence through the whole bar. Father Keogh looked round.

"I'm afraid I'm intruding. There seem to be no outsiders here."

"No one's forbidden to come in. Will you drink something, Father? We can offer real pulque of Apan."

"No thank you."

Malo sat back with his head against the wall. They stared at each other several seconds judging each other's eyes. Then Father Keogh spoke. "It surprises me that you in particular should have so little respect for the church."

"Why should that surprise you, Father?"

80

"Because I think that in opposite circumstances you would have made a good priest." Laughter burst from the other men. It was broken off like the stem of a glass at a wordless command from Malo. "I did say in *opposite* circumstances," Father Keogh smiled. "Tell me something, are you content?"

"Is any man content?"

"A few, if their cause is worth while and they feel they have served it well."

"Are you content, Father?"

Father Keogh shook his head. "My cause is too great for one man to feel that he has served it well."

"I am fortunate. I have no cause."

"Then you have a dedication," Father Keogh said.

"If a man is dedicated he is led. I am led by no one."

"Everyone is led by something even if it's something in themselves. Every man loves something. Sometimes it's his country, sometimes it's his family, or a woman or his religion or beauty or power—sometimes it's only himself that he loves. But something or someone must drive him to do what he does. No man wants power for no reason."

"What love would you choose for my reason, Father, myself?"

Father Keogh shook his head. "The man who loves himself loves comfort."

"Then you cannot love yourself, Father. Religion brings no comfort."

"Sometimes a material discomfort can become a spiritual luxury. You might say that that is the highest form of comfort, unaccountable perhaps to those unfortunate enough to be untrained for it."

"You think I enjoy no comfort, Father?"

"You appear to enjoy few material ones. You've got wealth but you use it curiously—you don't drink, you don't smoke, you live very simply. I am told—it may be wrong of course—that yours is the only room in the Hotel Martinez that isn't furnished like a royal apartment. They haven't been telling me wrong, have they?"

"They haven't been telling you wrong. You're asking what drives me towards power, Father?"

"I've been a bit long-winded about it," Father Keogh admitted. "But I suppose that is what I'm asking you, yes."

Malo folded his arms but his head did not move. "You might say that it is the highest form of luxury unaccountable to those who have not been trained for it."

Father Keogh was thinking of Paradise Lost. He found himself thinking of Lucifer, the bright and brilliant angel whose company even God had missed. It was possible, Father Keogh thought, that even God might envy the devil such single-minded devotion. He was a little saddened by the feeling that while the most intrepid followers of God rarely served him without some betrayal of Him, the devil's disciples seldom betrayed him. It was easy enough to think of himself falling short of God's demands upon him and unwittingly serving the devil. But it was hard to image Malo disobeying the dictates of the devil and unwittingly serving God. It was hard to admit that Malo's loyalties were inviolate whereas his own were open to everyday lapses. It was hard not to think that God might be better served if he and Malo were able to change places. He pulled himself together and said crisply, "Well, we're back where we started, aren't we? Back to the opposite circumstances." Father Keogh stood up. "Good night."

Malo rose with him. "Good night, Father."

The laughter broke out in the bar again before Father Keogh reached the door. This time it went unchecked, but when Father Keogh turned round to look, Malo was not laughing.

Old Uncle Joaquin sang again:

> *"There was no one to weep save me, save me*
> *Out in the wind on the mountain."*

Chapter 14

The bus was back. It was Chela who brought Father Keogh the news. Through his window he could see Roberto-of-the-Bus. He was the center of a fast-growing circle that pressed eagerly about him. Quantana thrived on news. Roberto brought with him parcels from Huapan and messages from relatives and friends. But he was waving his hands about, telling a tale. He might have been miming Chela's words.

"Yes, well—you see, Father, they did not know at first. Not till they called for the tickets. They do that when it stops at the Hua Pass. They say that he must have died just there for when they shook him he made no answer. Old Don Timoteo and Doña Bernandina believed he was praying, for he still kept his hands to his face."

Through the window Roberto-of-the-Bus was pressing his face in his hands.

"Doña Bernandina addressed him once. She said, 'Father, you've dropped your handkerchief and Don Timoteo picked it up.' Then they thought the old man must be sleeping."

Roberto made his head slump forward and let it roll about.

"Then his little black book dropped down, Father, and old Don Timoteo knew he was dead. He should know a dead man when he sees one—he is the chief one in these parts to make coffins and in his spare time he is the maker of artistic fireworks. He is not fortunate either, he has for his only son that Vito, El Lobo, isn't it sad? Well, he took Father Gomez by the shoulders and he tumbled right down and made a great cut in his head."

Father Keogh could no longer see Roberto-of-the-Bus. He held his own face in his hands.

Chela said, "It was the same with my sister's husband once—only this was a train, not a bus, you see, Father, coming home from Vera Cruz. It was not so easy to tell with my sister's husband, for he was so often drunk you could take him for dead several times in a day, so it was not till they got to—what is wrong with your breakfast, Father? If it's not to your liking I'll change it."

"I'm just not hungry thank you, Chela," Father Keogh said.

When Father Keogh next appeared in church he was vested in a black chasuble. Josefa whispered to Locha, "He is going to say a Requiem for the poor little Father Gomez."

Father Keogh read the Bishop's letter carefully.

There is no doubt that his death was due to heart failure. I have been in communication with the doctor who examined the body and he gives it as his opinion that he must have been dead fifteen hours. As this is practically the length of the jour-

ney it would appear that he died before leaving Quantana, but I feel that there must be a mistake in connection with this statement. He would surely have shown some signs of his condition, which I am sure you could not have failed to detect, and that in so doing you would have prevented him from traveling in what must have obviously been a precarious state of health. I shall be glad to hear from you on this point.

There is also no doubt that his condition was largely aggravated by his devotion to duty. Had he been less conscientious he would have applied for assistance before and might possibly have been spared to us. The church cannot place too high a value upon those of her servants whose lives are spent so unstintingly in her cause. To a very great extent Father Gomez has both lived and died a martyr in his Faith. I intend to make it my duty to see that his probity and steadfastness do not lack recognition.

Father Keogh put the letter down. When he looked up he saw Sam. His hair was brushed and he was clean-shaven.

"You sore at me, Mac?" he inquired.

"No. I'm not sore at you, Sam."

"I bawled you out the other night. It didn't hit me till after you went, then I could have kicked myself. I thought, 'For Christ's sake, that was Mac!' " Sam clicked his fingers to show how suddenly the inspiration had hit him. "I thought you was Papa Martinez trying to pull me back on the job."

"I'm not sore," Father Keogh repeated.

"It's too bad about the little guy. I came up as soon as I heard."

"Thank you. It's nice of you, Sam."

"They reckon it was a heart attack, don't they?"

"Yes, they think so," Father Keogh said.

"Well, why wouldn't he have a heart attack? I nearly had one myself." Father Keogh put a hand to his eyes. Sam looked round the room and changed the subject. "Did I bawl you out bad the other night?"

"You were a little insistent that you'd rather not be disturbed." Father Keogh smiled at him. "I was worried about you too, Sam. What happens to that job of yours when you take an unofficial night off?"

"Papa Martinez may look a helluva small guy on the outside, but

84

he's a helluva big one inside—he gets good and mad at me, but well—he drinks it down."

"I am very glad for your sake."

"Yeah. And then of course Pussyfoot can go chase himself when I'm in the bar. Papa kind of likes that. It makes him feel good."

"Yes, I should think it would."

"Yeah," said Sam. "There's one thing, Mac—they say it don't hurt much—heart attacks. It's kind of over quick—and, well, it's over quick."

"I certainly hope so, Sam."

"But it's too bad he didn't get his vacation."

"He must have been dying under our very eyes, Sam. He must have been dying when the bus went off." He tried not to remember the little white fluttering flag of defeat and the fact that he had grudged it as a gift.

Sam said, "Well, so long, Mac. Take it easy around here. You don't want to flip your lid. Say, Mac, there's one thing more. If I ever bawl you out again will you come in and drink it down?"

"That's a date," Father Keogh agreed.

When Father Keogh left his house he met Malo in the street.

"Good afternoon, Father."

"Good afternoon, Señor Comachi. You must have heard that it was G for Gomez after all?"

"I don't think I quite understand you, Father."

"Perhaps I could make it simpler for you. A for Arrieta, B for Beltran, C for Carranza, D for Dominguez, E for Elizondo, F for Fernandez—and G for Gomez."

Malo stood smiling. He held up four fingers. "H—I—J—K—Father?"

Chapter 15

The news of his encounter with Malo quickly spread. The incident was somewhat embellished—" 'H. I. J. K,' he said to the priest. Right out loud like that! 'There are only four letters to go after G. In four letters' time it is your turn, Father,' and then he held four fingers up to show how quickly these letters can pass. What a way for the Bad One to talk to him! 'Four letters more and *you*,' he said. The Ingles-Irlandes will not last long."

There were sighs amongst the older ones. "It's a pity, because he's a nice priest. It's a long time since we had such a nice priest."

"I should like to have the little Candalaria baptized by him, but my Alfredo says it isn't safe."

"The Ingles-Irlandes is not like the poor little Father. He doesn't step out of the way to let the Bad One pass."

"Somebody ought to warn him that the poor little Father was wise."

Quantana watched him carefully. It was anxious to see what weapon the new priest would choose. The new priest chose his voice. Because few would come to church to hear it he used it in the streets. He used it on the Plaza and in the cantines. He went on to the stage in the cinema and he spoke at the doorway of every private house. "Are you afraid to match the power of God against the power of a single man?"

In Porfirio's bar they copied him. "Are you afraid to match the power of God against the power of a single man?" They made fun of the priest's deep voice. They made even Malo laugh.

. . . "This man Malo has no supernatural powers. He is human like anyone else. He is powerful because of the powers you give him—if you took those away, he'd be lost." . . .

The doctor, giving an anesthetic to a patient in the dentist's chair remarked, "You've got to admire his pluck."

"It isn't pluck," the dentist snapped. "It's pigheaded conceit, that's all. He ought to know about supernatural powers. Their whole faith is built up on black magic. There's more corruption in the Catholic Church than you'll even find in Anacleto's setup."

The doctor remembered that the dentist was tied to a wife whom he detested and that he could never be free of her because she was a Catholic.

. . . "If you put yourselves in league with Malo you put yourselves in league against God. The enemies of God have been destroyed through the ages, but God is eternally merciful. His arms are forever open to those who seek their protection." . . .

"There you are, Anacleto!" The Jeep giggled nervously. "You know where to go to be safe. Perhaps the arms will protect you against the priest."

"That's not so funny," Old Uncle said. "I don't like the sound of this priest."

. . . "You know what you remind me of?" Father Keogh joked with the people. "Lions who could quite well attack their trainer if only they all attacked together. But each lion sits still, afraid of him, and the trainer gets his way." . . .

Quantana listened politely to him but nobody extra came into the church. Sometimes on the edge of a crowd he was addressing, Father Keogh noticed Malo-of-the-Cats.

"I can't think what your friend Anacleto is doing," the doctor remarked to the dentist. "He's not usually so tolerant with people who disapprove of him."

"Bah!" said the dentist. "Anacleto knows he has nothing to fear from a bleating fool like that. Any time he wants to put a stop to it he will put a stop to it." And he added, his voice sharp, "What makes you call him *my* friend?"

. . . "It's yourselves you must fight against," Father Keogh told them. "You must strike first at the root of the trouble and that trouble's the fear in yourselves. If you strike against that you are halfway to winning. There's only one way to strike at it—pray," Father Keogh urged them. "Pray to dissolve your fears." . . .

"All the same old patter," the dentist sneered. "They're used to superstitious half-wits. Their church is made up of those."

"Pray!" Father Keogh urged them. "Pray whenever you have the chance. Pray in the streets, at your work, in your beds. It won't fail you," Father Keogh promised them. "You'll very soon see the results."

Now and again Father Keogh was asked inside a house. The occupants were careful to tell their neighbors that they had no alternative. "What can you do when he's standing there? You can't very well shut him out."

They were uneasy with him at first and unresponsive, but theirs was a friendly nature and his was a friendly approach. He played with their children, took an interest in their domestic problems and discussed the latest films with them. He laughed and teased and joked with them. It was not easy to shut him out. They gave him buns and made him coffee. But they always remarked to their neighbors, "What can you do when he's sitting there? It's not polite to give him nothing."

He had permission from the Bishop to make use of his medical knowledge. He attended minor injuries, gave advice on minor ailments and even doctored pets. Quantana was grateful for these attentions. The doctor was overworked and he cost money. The priest gave assistance for nothing.

"It makes you sick," the dentist said. "They'll do anything to get themselves in."

"Is he getting in?" the doctor asked.

In the bakery Doña Florencia took a quick look round and went down on her knees. She made a hurried sign of the cross and gabbled, "And take care of the Holy Father who does not know the power of his enemies and is sticking out his neck in the Name of the Father, the Son and the Holy Ghost, Amen."

Then because she heard her husband coming she scrambled up and scolded their youngest child. Her husband's income was augmented by Malo.

Father Keogh wrote to his Bishop.

I feel like a commercial traveler. If it wasn't for the fact that most Mexican doors seem to be permanently open, I might have to put my foot in some of them! So far I haven't had any active interference from the Gran-Señor-of-the-Cats. He hasn't thrown anything at me yet. No doubt it's the lull before the

storm. He's probably collecting missiles. The congregation is
still pitifully thin.

He was pleasantly surprised to see the congregation strengthened
by the Presidente. He was even more surprised to see him appear in
the confessional.

It was early in the morning and Father Keogh had not heard a car.
The Presidente must have come up the hill on his feet. Father Keogh
refrained from inquiring after them. His pleasant surprise was short-
lived. The Presidente had come to extract a confession, not to make
one.

"Now, Father, you noticed my wife?"

"A very beautiful woman," Father Keogh observed. He was a little
taken aback at the aggression in the Presidente's voice.

"Did you think she looked a good woman?"

Father Keogh answered evenly, "Have you reason to suppose that
she isn't?"

"You fellows have inside information, Father, you're trained to
look out for bad morals in people."

"Yes, but we don't use a social visit to come spying out for sins."

"Now, Father, I want the truth from you. You're the only one I
can ask in confidence. If I speak to anyone else, it's crying stinking
fish."

Father Keogh asked mildly, "Is that why you've come to confession, Señor Presidente Municipal? So that you can cry stinking fish
in private? If so, it isn't what the confessional was intended for."

"Is my wife good, or bad?"

"I'm not in the best position to judge," Father Keogh pointed out.
"You are in the best position to do that, and I asked you what made
you suspect her."

The Presidente licked his lips, "There is the question of my seventh
child, Father."

"Yes?"

"You saw it," the Presidente snapped. "Did you think it looked
like me?"

"I wasn't looking out for likenesses," Father Keogh said. "But a
child doesn't necessarily take after his parents. He can take after an
aunt or an uncle, or one of his ancestors."

"He does not take after one of his ancestors. He takes after the
Señor engineer who lives next door."

89

Father Keogh took a breath. "Have you any idea when or how many times, this adultery took place?"

"It is only eighteen months ago since this man moved next door. My child is nine months old, Father. It's not such a hard sum to work out."

There was silence until Father Keogh said, "How much do you love your wife?"

The Presidente's face was wet, and he put a handkerchief to it repeatedly, wiping off the sweat. "She is my torment, Father—my torment, and my treasure."

Father Keogh could not see the face clearly. But he winced at the pain in the voice. "Then I think I should cleanse your mind of all suspicion, Don Agapito. After all, you have no proof. You have only your fears. They might not be justified. You love your wife, and you have your wife, why not hold on to that happiness? If you mistrust her, you'll lose her, you don't want that. You'll drive yourself away from her. You'll be depriving yourself of everything you hold most dear. Why don't you cleanse your mind of all suspicion? Why don't you try to trust her?"

When the Presidente left the confessional, Father Keogh's own face felt a little wet. He was disturbed by conflicting impressions; by the sound of the pain in the Presidente's voice, and the expression he had seen in the eyes of his wife. It was hard to believe that the advice he had given was justified. He prayed that it might be so.

On Sunday a few extra people braved the church, inspired by the Presidente. The congregation, including the Presidente, had multiplied by five. Chela, the two washerwomen, and the manager of the cinema had given their support.

Father Keogh swept an anxious glance over them. They struck him as fairly attentive.

The two washerwomen kept interested eyes upon him. They had come to church for a good view of the priest.

Chela was thinking, "Well, it's his own fault if his breakfast runs into his dinnertime. How much longer will he take? Certainly the little one gabbled the mass, and he wasn't so nice to hear, but then you could start his breakfast before midday." She folded her hands and closed her eyes. She wondered whether Father Keogh would enjoy eating mole dé guajolate, and she wondered whether she might risk trying him with iguana boiled with beans. "That's providing we had the money for it. If it wasn't for the Señor Frankenson, I

90

don't know how we'd eat. What company the Father keeps! What a fine one for a priest to make his cuate! It brings a bad name to the house. And then how silly to keep that old man. As if it wasn't hard enough to feed ourselves, without that one spreading fleas in the kitchen."

Locha whispered to Josefa, "He doesn't sound a *bit* silly, does he?"

Josefa whispered back, "You know what happens to naughty girls? The Bad One comes and eats them up. The Bad One of the Cats!"

The manager of the cinema was thinking that the last time he went to church was on the occasion of his wedding. He was also thinking that Father Keogh was very good box office.

The Presidente was thinking about his wife.

Arranging the chalice at the altar Father Keogh made a special Intention, for those whose faith was endangered by fear. For those whose peace of mind was endangered by lack of trust, for those whose safety was endangered by themselves. He made a special Intention, for the whole of Quantana.

Then he gave a straightforward address. He made it purposely simple. It had taken him several hours of revision to strike the complications out. It was tempting to philosophize in words that would have impressed no one but himself; to preach for his own satisfaction. It was also difficult to avoid making simplicity sound like condescension. He spoke no differently from the way he had spoken in the street or in the doorway of a private house. He told the congregation, "Everyone of us here believes in God. We believe in Him, but how little? And how well? The more we believe the better we are able to see the unworthiness of our faith in Him— the less we believe the more we are able to see our need of faith— we seem to be caught all ways. But there isn't any need to feel caught. Our God is a God of love. He understands us. He can understand those things within us, that we can't understand ourselves. Was there ever a love like that, my children? Was there ever a love like that? We try, and we fail, and we are full of bitterness. But God who has longed for us to try, whose son is crucified again because we fail—He feels no bitterness. His is a love of hope. He urges us to try, and He mourns our failure, but on our bitterness He smiles. He urges us to try again. He sees neither the failure, nor the bitterness. He sees a man who is out of breath because he has lost his train. He sees that man use every ounce of strength to catch that train, he runs for it, perhaps he pushes people out of the way

91

for it, he might spend all the money he has on a taxi to catch it, and he loses it. What does God see that man do? He sees him sit on his suitcase and bite his nails, then he drinks tequila and moans because he has lost his train. And God sees him miss the next train, because he has drunk too much tequila. But God smiles, God smiles, and says to him, 'It isn't the only train.' Was there ever a love like that? God's love has many enemies. They are bred in lack of faith. Faith is the armor round His love. It's an armor that's easily pierced. Such ordinary things can puncture it, they hardly seem weapons at all. But they are, my children. Listen to them: slackness, and sloppiness, such ordinary things—worries, strains and difficulties, those seem more weaponlike—disappointments, too much pleasure, too little of it, and the most dangerous weapon—fear. Fear is the strongest of all God's enemies. It is powerful because it is carried within us. Think of the strength in that! If an enemy gives us a gun and tells us to shoot ourselves, what do we do? We laugh at him, or we take the gun and point it at him instead. But we don't turn it into our own hearts and pull the trigger. Yet that's what we do with his weapon of fear. We point it straight in on ourselves. Fear is a lack of trust in God. The child who loves his parents, trusts them. God is the all-protective Father. We love Him, but do we trust Him? The child who fears, runs to his parents. God is our Father, do we run to Him? Or do we run away? Faith is the only protection against fear. Fear cannot stand up against faith. Fear has no chance against faith. How can we claim the protection of faith? Pray for it, pray for it ceaselessly, pray for the habit of faith. Pray for the habit of prayer."

He then reminded the congregation that he intended to reinstate the catechism classes, and requested them not to leave litter in the grounds of the church.

He put forward a suggestion from Señora Martinez that a portion of Sunday afternoons might well be set aside for the reading aloud of pious literature. Señora Martinez would be willing to render these readings herself, and was willing for them to take place under her own roof. In consequence he was forced to put forward a suggestion from Señoras Solano, Fereira, and Rodriguez that a portion of Wednesday afternoons be dedicated to the reading of specially prepared pious literature for children. The Señoras were willing to deliver these readings in turn, and were willing for them to take place under their own roofs.

Father Keogh requested that anyone interested in these suggestions should contact the ladies concerned.

They were mundane announcements and quickly delivered. His address had been more of an uninterrupted conversation than a sermon. It had not been exacting. Yet he felt nervous and overtaxed. A sense of his own unworthiness crept up to impede his recovery. It was a feeling he was not often without. But he was aware that there were moments when it was better to expel it than allow its intrusion to monopolize him.

When his every sense should have been directed towards the supreme moment in the celebration of the Mass, for which his whole being existed, and without which he doubted if he would have been able to face existence at all, he was persecuted: by a nagging suspicion that, with the exception of Señora Rodriguez, the piety of the four Señoras was largely induced by a desire to outshine one another. He felt uncharitable and he felt ungrateful. He knew that the four Señoras were making an effort which few others were making. They deserved appreciation. Yet he could feel gratitude only towards Señora Rodriguez. How frightened she must have been!

But he should have felt nothing but the privilege in front of him. At a time when his heart and soul should have been a receptive vehicle—so that the great love he received into them, and the great love he sent out of them, should have met in a perfect unity which consumed him—he was distracted by the thought of the four Señoras and the fact that he should have informed his parishioners that he was willing to *supply* them with a litter bin, if necessary.

It was not the first time he had wished, with an aching despondency, that the Sunday morning announcements might be made at some point less near to the moment of sacrifice.

Locha waylaid him outside the church. She had a special piece of news for him. She had a new governess. "Father had an English education, so he wants me to have one too. That's why I've got Miss Finch. She says there's nowhere like Sheppet in Dorset."

"Well, I dare say she's geographically right."

He looked up to see Miss Finch waiting for her charge at the bottom of the steps. He walked down to her with the child's hand in his own.

There was a lack of distinction about Miss Finch that could almost lay claim to distinction. Her shantung suit and the stitched shantung hat had the same sallow tones as her skin. She carried a Japanese parasol such as his mother had carried in the early twenties and she wore white buckskin shoes and white gloves. Her voice and her smile had a gentle hesitancy that made her frankness sound doubly surprising.

"How do you do? I do not approve of Roman Catholicism, so I prefer that we did not discuss it."

"Quite," Father Keogh said, and was aware that the reply was inadequate.

He placed Locha's hand in the hand of Miss Finch and could not take his eyes off her parasol.

"Mr. Keogh, I find that Locha's diction is very poor for a child of her age, and as she seems to have some attachment for you, I was wondering if you would be good enough to go out of your way to stress the end syllables of your words in front of her. It would set her a good example."

"I'll try," Father Keogh promised her, and felt that he had been dismissed.

Chapter 16

It became more and more rare for Father Keogh to have a free period to himself.

He had attended twenty-eight sick calls, and fourteen appeals from the so-called dying, during his brief residence in Quantana. Eight had come from Tephuango and four from the village beyond. None of them proved to be urgent. He suspected that the people were indulging in the lost luxury of demanding the attendance of a priest. When they found that Malo appeared to have no objections they sent for Father Keogh on the slightest provocation.

He attended old men who demanded the last rites for nothing more than a mild attack of colic; children with beads in their nostrils, and women who believed their lives to be in danger from a slight accident with the cooking pot.

He made two midnight journeys by ox wagon, and one at three o'clock in the morning by the only hire car in Quantana. Domingo charged him double to go up the hill, double again because it was night, and double again because the return journey was made on a Sunday. Father Keogh managed to argue the Sunday expenses down by half because the journey commenced on a Saturday.

Nevertheless, he was not asked to be present at the one authentic death that occurred since he came to Quantana. The relatives were frightened of Malo.

One evening when he found himself with a spare hour before dinner, he told Chela not to disturb him.

"Don't you want to make the little marks beside the laundry, Father?"

"No thank you, not at the moment, Chela."

He sat down to recite his Office. There were times when he was only just able to perform this duty before midnight ran it into the task for the following day. It meant that the Office had often to be said with an eye to the passing of time, rather than an eye to the deep concentration which it was his private delight to give to it. He felt this personal forfeiture very keenly. Again it made him a little envious: of those able to discharge this devotion in contemplative serenity, or in the regulated peace of a cloistered life. He tried to regard the matter in the light of an Heroic Offering, but it was hard not to envy the regular clergy.

He had scarcely formed the first dozen words with his lips when Chela called through the door to him. Because she was afraid to interrupt him, she compromised by making her message inaudible. He had to open the door himself before he could grasp the gist of it.

"Yes, well I told them you were sleeping—but they say that the matter is urgent."

"What is it, Chela?"

"They say that it is somebody dying, Father."

Father Keogh closed his breviary and sighed. He went to the medicine cabinet and took out a bottle of bicarbonate of soda. He added six finger dressings and a laxative and put them in a brief case.

"Have you the things with you to give him the Blessed Sacrament, Father?"

"Yes. Who is it that wants me, Chela?"

"Well, it's somewhere you won't like to go to, Father . . ."

"Where is it?" Father Keogh asked.

"It is in that Porfirio's saloon."

"In Porfirio's—who is it needing me there, Chela?"

"Well, they say that it's old Uncle Joaquin. Yes, well I told that little Jeep when he came to the door, I said: 'It's no use asking,' I said, 'the padre's taking a nap.' And I said: 'We don't hear confessions just before dinner. It's not proper or right to ask the padre when he's sleeping, to come out to a man like that.' "

"You must never talk like that again, Chela. I'm available at any time anyone wants to see me."

"Yes, well there should be hours for it that's what I say. A nice time to die, before dinner."

He found the Jeep waiting outside for him. "What is it?" he asked. "An accident?"

The Jeep spoke quietly, his squeaky voice solemn. "We don't know, Father. He's very sick. He fell down on the floor—and when we put our hands to it his heart felt like a bird that was trapped in his chest. He is dying and he wants a priest, Father. Anacleto sent me up for you."

"Anacleto sent you up?"

"Anacleto says if he wants a priest he must have a priest. Old Uncle is dying, Father."

"Anacleto's gone up in my estimation," Father Keogh said.

He strode brusquely out at first, and then remembered that the Jeep was lame. He slowed down uncertainly. The Jeep grinned up at him.

"You know why they call me the Jeep?" he asked. "Because no road is too rough for me, and I can go faster than anybody, faster than Anacleto walks."

He kept up beside Father Keogh a curious, crippled, rolling movement which all but outpaced the priest.

Outside Porfirio's bar Malo was waiting. He took Father Keogh's hand and held it a moment. "It is good of you to come."

"It's my duty to come," said Father Keogh. "Have you sent for the doctor?"

Malo shook his head. "We think it's too late for the doctor, Father. He says that he wants to confess."

Father Keogh walked into the bar. He saw old Uncle Joaquin stretched out on the floor. He lay on his stomach and he was sobbing. The others stood by respectfully allowing Father Keogh to pass. They muttered, "Good evening, Father," and their voices were low and their faces grave.

Pablo and Lorenzo held him down but he struggled against them bellowing: "The priest I say, I want the priest! Holy Mother of God, I *want* the priest."

Father Keogh went down on one knee beside him. He put a hand on his heart and felt his pulse. Then he smelled his breath. "You're drunk, my friend," he told him quietly. "That's all that's the matter with you."

Someone sniggered behind him. It was Porfirio, hand to mouth. Father Keogh looked round. They stared at him, their faces grave.

Old Uncle clutched at him. His voice was blurred and his eyes were bloodshoot. His hands pulled frantically at Father Keogh. "I am dying, I have to confess. I have been a bad man but it wasn't so always. Listen, Father—I have to confess."

Father Keogh said to Malo, "You knew this man was drunk, of course."

Malo stood over them, his shoulders shrugging. His tone was injured, his eyes reproachful. "He told us he was dying, Father."

"You mean you told him he was dying." Then Father Keogh added: "Don't think you've scored off me. I don't happen to mind in the least, but it was a dangerous joke to play on a man in this condition. You'll be all right," he told Old Uncle. "Your friends were amusing themselves."

Old Uncle rolled over. He slithered forward on his stomach towards Father Keogh's feet, and gripped him round the ankles. "Stay here—there's something I have to show you. I have the right to a priest." Then he put his face in the crook of his arm, and his sobs shook his broad back. "Mother of God, I am dying—dying!"

Father Keogh looked up at Malo. He asked of him with interest: "Did he send for me off his own bat, or was that the best part of the joke?"

"It wouldn't have occurred to us, my dear Padre, that his 'passing' would be eased by your presence, but when he was so insistent we thought it would be—"

"Amusing to send for me?"

"We thought it would be right to send for you."

"It *was* right," Father Keogh said.

He bent down, put his hands under old Uncle Joaquin's armpits

97

and dragged the drunken man to the wall. When he propped him up Old Uncle's head rolled. "I have something to show you that I don't want the others to see." He made his voice intimate and beckoned the priest. "Round my neck, Father, see? I always wear it." He put a hand inside his shirt and pulled up a string. It was so long that it did not show above his neckline and the medal that hung on the end of it must have reached his waist. It was a replica of the Virgin of Guadelupe stamped onto a canvas back. It was faded and greasy and the canvas was black.

Father Keogh went to finger it but Old Uncle snatched it away. It disappeared swiftly beneath his shirt again.

Father Keogh said to him, "If you want to confess I'll hear you gladly, but that doesn't mean you're dying."

Old Uncle's tears flowed. "You're good to me, Father, yes you're good. Did you know that I was an acolyte once?" He had a little difficulty with the word and said it carefully twice through his teeth, then he put a finger against his lips. "Shush! I was beautiful, yes I was beautiful. None of these sons of bitches here know how beautiful I was. Except for Anacleto—he is not a son of a bitch. Tinkle, tinkle," Old Uncle sighed and rang an imaginary bell in his black-haired fist. "Tinkle, tinkle three times at the *Sanctus*—eh, Father? Well, Father, isn't that right?"

"Quite right," Father Keogh smiled. "Would you like to be a server again, Old Uncle? I need one badly. Would you like to?"

"Tinkle, tinkle," Old Uncle sobbed. And added: "Listen, I have to confess."

"Why not come up to the church tomorrow, it's not very private here."

Old Uncle's head shook. "I am dying, Father—it's now that I have to confess." He leaned over, supported himself on one arm, and put wet lips to the priest's left ear. His breath struck it, sickly and hot. "You know what I am? I'm a bandit."

"I do know," Father Keogh said.

"You know what these others are? They are bandits. Except for Anacleto, he is no bandit. Anacleto is someone above."

"I know," Father Keogh said.

At the end of the bar loud laughter broke. It doubled the bandits up. Vito leaned backwards, his young throat throbbing.

Lorenzo called out, "Are you blushing, Father? He'll be telling you things that a priest shouldn't know."

Pablo shouted, "Wait till you get on to his women, Father—ask him about his women."

Father Keogh saw Old Uncle's eyes roll round and a slyness creep over his face. He glanced under his lashes at Father Keogh, and he made his slurring voice childishly nonchalant. "One time a man disappeared. He knew something, see? That he shouldn't have known—I forget what it was—but he knew it. You know where he went? He went into a river."

Pablo called out to them, "What do think of the lady friends, Father? Wouldn't you like to have women like that?"

Father Keogh ignored him.

"Somebody held him down," said Old Uncle, "somebody held him down."

"Who was it?" Father Keogh asked him.

"Don José," Old Uncle said.

"Can you remember who did it, my son?"

Old Uncle's expression was crafty again. "Sure," he said carefully, "sure. I did it."

"Why are you lying?" asked Father Keogh. "I can tell it's a lie by your face."

Old Uncle clutched at him. "I say it's the truth—it is the truth—let me see, what was it I was telling you?"

"You were telling me a lie," Father Keogh said.

"That's right, that's right, I was telling the truth." His hand tugged at Father Keogh's sleeve like a plaintive insistent child's. "Father, you know what? Anacleto's young—maybe he's done some things he shouldn't, but he's young—not like me, I am old. I am the old one, Father. I haven't a son but a father should care for his own son, shouldn't he? Anacleto's been like my son. If a son sins it's the father's fault, isn't it?"

"Sometimes," Father Keogh said.

"Yes, well it's my fault—my fault, see? I am the old one, I could have stopped him. Anacleto would listen to me—so anything he's done, I've done—see, Father? It's not Anacleto, it's me. You have to absolve Anacleto, Father. I am dying, you have to absolve him—see? It's me that's done wrong, not Anacleto. I did the wrong for him—see?"

At the end of the room they were faking a confession. The Jeep was confessing to Lorenzo. He gave loud mocking sobs and screwed up his little white face. "And then, Father, you've not heard the half of it—you don't know what I did to this girl . . ." They looked round towards Malo for appreciation. But his eyes cut across them towards old Uncle Joaquin and the priest. "But it wasn't as bad as what that girl did to me, Father. Oh my! You should sample that girl."

Old Uncle's hands found Father Keogh's. They made the priest's wet. "There's something else, Father, I should have confessed. You have to absolve Anacleto—yes? But Jesus Christ, what's next?"

Father Keogh ignored the use of the Saviour's name. "Think hard, my son," he said.

"Yes, that's right, think. I have not much to think with—where did I put my head?"

Father Keogh restrained the hand that was slapping the sweating forehead. "You'll have a bad enough head without that in the morning. Was it something to do with a woman?" he asked.

"No, no, not a woman. I care for no women."

"Was it to do with Anacleto then?"

"Yes, that's right, Anacleto." He screwed up his eyes and his mouth fell open in a hideous attempt to remember.

"Was it something else that you feel you should have stopped him from doing?"

"No, no, not something he's done—it was something he's going to do. Where's my head, my head, my head?"

"Think hard," Father Keogh advised him.

"It has something to do with spelling, Father—something to do with the saying of letters, but these letters make no sort of word."

"Can you remember them?" Father Keogh asked him. "Perhaps I could work them out?"

Old Uncle held his head and recited, "H—I—J—no, yes that was right—but those letters! They do not make sense."

"H, I, J, *K?*" Father Keogh asked him.

Old Uncle nodded, his eyes dull. "Yes, Father, you have to absolve him for that. But those letters, they don't seem to spell anything, what word could such letters spell?"

"Death," Father Keogh told him.

Old Uncle wailed impatiently, "I'm penitent aren't I? I've said so haven't I? Mother of God, how many times do I have to say it? If I'm not penitent why did I send for you? It's because I am sorry—because I'm so sorry." The tears fell again and he grizzled, his head rolling, "You have to absolve me—you have to absolve me for Anacleto."

100

Father Keogh looked steadily down at him. It might be possible, he thought, that in believing himself to be dying and in sending for a priest Old Uncle could have surprised within himself a moment of sincerity. He might have revived a dormant spark of faith that could make his contrition genuine. But it was doubtful if a drunken and probably temporary repentance could be prudently regarded as sincere or that it could justify absolution.

He bent down and touched Old Uncle's shoulder, "You're not going to die—get that into your head—but if you still feel the same when you're sober tomorrow, if you still want to confess—come to see me."

Chapter 17

The next morning there was no one in church except Chela. At half past eleven three men paid Father Keogh a visit. They were Malo, Old Uncle, and Vito. They walked into his room without knocking. He was saying his rosary and he kept them waiting until he had finished.

They watched him in silence. Malo sat upright, the other two stood with their shoulders sloping.

When Father Keogh finished telling his beads he looked up at Old Uncle. "Hallo, how's the hang-over?"

"What did he tell you last night?" It was Malo who put the question.

"I'm not permitted to repeat his confession to you without his permission," Father Keogh replied.

"No?"

Father Keogh repeated, "No."

"Who are you permitted to repeat it to then? The Chief of Police perhaps?"

"Not unless he permits me to do so."

Father Keogh looked steadily back at the three of them. Old Uncle's clumsy features bore the traces of the last night's debauch. His eyes were ringed and his skin blotched. His expression was close and resentful.

"You may tell Anacleto," he said. "Anacleto and nobody else."

Father Keogh looked towards Vito.

Malo said, "Very well, Vito—go." When Vito left the room he said, "Well, Father, we are waiting."

"What did I say?" Old Uncle boomed. "What was it I told you last night?"

"That you were sorry for your sins."

Malo's soft voice inquired, "What were these sins?"

"He accused himself—in a roundabout way," Father Keogh admitted, "of having missed his opportunities of preventing *you* from sinning."

"But what did I *say*—what was it I *said?*"

"You told me that Don José was forcibly drowned. You told me that you had committed this crime yourself. You were lying," Father Keogh observed.

"Who did you think was responsible, Father?" Malo asked.

Father Keogh met his eyes. "I am not obliged to tell you my own conclusions."

"What else?" urged Old Uncle. "What else did I say?"

"You were quite a long while together, Father," Malo told him. "I should think there was something else."

"Yes, there was," said Father Keogh. "But he couldn't remember the whole of it."

"How much could he remember, Father?"

"A fragment of the alphabet."

"How curious that he should consider such a small piece of learning a sin."

Father Keogh said, "Yes."

"Which bit of it did he remember, Father?"

Father Keogh answered, "H, I, J—and—K!"

Malo turned to Old Uncle, "Well, well—you were certainly drunk, old friend!" Then he asked Father Keogh, "And you do not feel obliged to tell us what conclusion you drew from a stupid confession like that?"

"I don't think so," Father Keogh said, "except that I did not conclude that it was stupid."

"I see," said Malo. "Very well."

Father Keogh could feel Malo's eyes on his face as if they were

102

touching him feeling his resistance. "How am I to believe that this confession will go no further than myself, Father?"

"Only by accepting my word."

Malo studied him, the eyes touring the whole of his body again. He said slowly, "I accept it."

Father Keogh put Locha's dried flower in the fifty-ninth page of St. Thomas Aquinas. He closed the book and said, "As a matter of fact I'm afraid that it's one of the few occasions when I wish that a confession wasn't private."

"That I can well understand, my friend. You'll pardon the expression 'my friend.' "

"Certainly," Father Keogh said. "I should welcome it if you meant it."

Malo said, "I could mean it."

"On what terms?" Father Keogh asked.

Malo put one long leg across the other. "There are ways in which a priest—"

"Oh yes," Father Keogh interrupted him quietly. "I think I know what you're going to say—that there are ways in which a priest can be helpful to a man like you."

"Perhaps I was going to say that there are ways in which a man like me could be helpful to a priest."

"Perhaps."

"It's a pity, Father," Malo said. "We might have become cuates."

"Yes," Father Keogh agreed, and added, "By the way, there was no one in church this morning except my housekeeper. Why was that?"

"Yours is a very persuasive voice, Father. It reaches many hearts."

"If it does it's because of the message it carries."

"I felt obliged to put a stop to the message."

"So you have got a little respect for the church after all?"

"Perhaps I have a little respect for you after all, Father."

When he had gone Father Keogh sat thinking of Father Gomez. Sometimes he lay awake at nights thinking of him. He could picture the little priest on his knees by the narrow bed, in the little bare room that he had inherited from him. He must have spent many hours on his knees praying for a strength that would help him fight another day. Sometimes it was not only the memory of Father Gomez which kept Father Keogh awake at nights. Rats ran about in his room. He was glad of an opportunity to change his trend of thought. He went to the door and called down the passage to Chela, "Could we get some rat poison?"

She came in scowling. "Those men! That Old Uncle and El Lobo! What right have they to dress up like charros? What sort of cowboys are they? Rat poison? What should we do with that?"

"Poison rats."

"Yes. Well, I've said it before, and I'll say it again—what we need in this house is a python."

"A *python!*" Father Keogh said.

"Yes, Father. The big snake that will eat up the rats."

"I think I'd prefer the rats."

"A python is a good snake, Father. It will sleep on your bed and be friendly to you. It's a nice thing to have in the house."

"If it slept on my bed," Father Keogh assured her, "I should sleep underneath it. You wouldn't find us both on top."

"It is possible to become very devoted to these ones, and their faces are not unkind. It is something to come back to in a home, like the Ingles goes back to his dog. It will have quite a regard for you in time. You need have no fears about that."

"It's not its regard for me that I'm worrying about. I'm not sure I could return its affection."

"The friend of my sister's husband has just such a snake—and it was a sad thing for this poor man, for in time his wife had more love for the snake than her husband."

"He isn't by any chance trying to sell it?" Father Keogh inquired.

"Yes indeed, Father. How clever you are. Only the other day he was mentioning it to me and for you it would cost so little."

"Thank you, Chela, but I couldn't come between a man and his wife's snake. I'm afraid he'll have to keep it."

Father Keogh never discovered how many sisters Chela possessed. She seemed to have one to suit every occasion.

She called after him as he went out of the house, "Father, if you see El Choco—the one that turns the music round—will you stop him from staying outside here always? I am half mad with his noise in my head."

Father Keogh did not meet the organito but he heard the strains of "Alexander's Ragtime Band" as he climbed the hill towards the Casa Grande.

Halfway up the hill he ran into the engineer who lived next door to the Presidente. Father Keogh was surprised to feel a certain amount of personal resentment towards the good-looking young man with the winking black eyes. If he had not looked so closely at him he might never have remembered the appearance of the Presidente's seventh child with such accuracy. It bore the engineer's merry eyes and his unrepentant smile.

He exchanged a few hurried words of greeting and climbed on up the hill. He caught himself thinking that the Presidente's seventh child was fortunate in resembling the engineer and not the Presidente. He rebuked himself immediately for such an uncharitable thought.

Locha was not behind the gates as usual. She was in the school-room taking down dictation from Miss Finch.

When she heard his voice in the hall she came skipping out to greet him. "Hallo, hallo, hallo!" she sang at him.

"Hallo," said Father Keogh. "What happened to you this morning? Why didn't you come to church?"

"Oh, Josefa said it wasn't safe."

"What does she mean by not safe?"

"Malo put the word round," Locha said excitedly.

"What sort of word?"

"He said he didn't want us to go to church any more."

"But I do want you to go," said Father Keogh. "Go back to your lessons, there's a good child, I've come to speak to your mother and father."

She went backwards towards the door blowing kisses to Father Keogh. Father Keogh blew one back. She put her head round the door again. "I've dropped off the Malo, Father Keogh. He's only called Micky now."

Doña Marian was indisposed and Don Pedro sent a message to the effect that he had forbidden his daughter to attend church until further notice. They both regretted that they were otherwise engaged and unable to receive Father Keogh.

"Deadlock!" Father Keogh said.

Chapter 18

It was a "deadlock" all over the town. They avoided him with a variety of courteous excuses: They were unexpectedly busy. They were unavoidably detained. They had sudden symptoms of ill-health, which did not apparently require Father Keogh's attention. Relatives whom they not seen for years had chosen that particular inconvenient moment to call. They had to make urgent visitations to friends whom they saw every day. They would have been delighted to entertain the padre on any other occasion but on the occasion he happened to call. They were verbosely and genuinely apologetic.

But the fact remained that like Don Pedro they thought it wiser not to be connected with the church or its priest until further notice.

Father Keogh went into the bar of the Hotel de la Costa to cheer himself up by a talk with Sam.

"Hiya, Mac. What's cooking?"

"Far too much," Father Keogh sighed.

"Pussyfoot putting the skids under you?"

"He appears to have enforced a ban on churchgoing."

"He's scared of you. He didn't have to be scared of the little guy."

"Well, the 'little guy,' as you call him, at least kept a handful in church."

"Sure, but that didn't add up to much. You've been doing too damned well to suit Pussyfoot—smoke?"

"No thank you," Father Keogh said. "I'm trying to cut it down."

"It's not Lent or one of those hands-off-everything-you-like days, is it?"

"No. The reason's entirely financial."

"I reckon you ought to get danger money for sitting around in a joint like this. It's like I said—you guys shouldn't have to depend on what comes out of those little plates they cart around after the show."

106

"Well, we can't even claim all that, Sam. There are other claims made on those little plates."

"Jesus Chri—you don't say! Supposing nobody don't put nothing in them?"

"Then we don't get very fat."

"You're sure gonna lose weight around here, Mac. How do you aim to get by?"

"I couldn't if I had to depend on the benefices, but for special circumstances there are special allowances made. Even so they still don't encourage chain-smoking."

"That's too bad, Mac. Well, what'll you have? Have it on Papa Martinez."

"Have you anything soft? But not on the house of course." The dentist walked into the bar. "Good morning, Señor Campos," Father Keogh said.

The dentist ignored him and sat on a stool. "Beer," he said to Sam. Sam slammed it in front of him and went back to Father Keogh. "You know something, Mac? You want to watch out for these guys."

"Yes, they told me that themselves."

"They did? Did you go to the Jefe?"

"It wouldn't be much good if I did, would it?"

"Maybe no, maybe yes. He could keep his eyes skinned for them. It's maybe what he's looking for, a chance to catch 'em red-handed at something."

"What, make myself a bait for them?" Father Keogh sipped a Coca-Cola. "Well, you know, Sam, that's not what I'm aiming at— trying to encourage them to misbehave themselves I mean. I hope to encourage them to behave themselves. They're part of my flock as well."

"Some flock!" Sam sympathized. "Well, maybe it don't say much for him, but Pussyfoot's the best out of that bunch."

"I'm inclined to agree," said Father Keogh.

"There's one thing I kind of like about Pussyfoot. He could've set himself up as a communist, or God's gift to suckers or any one of these guys with ideals that make it worse for folks, but Pussyfoot just set up as Pussyfoot and let it go at that—and no gags about doing anybody any good but himself."

"I know," said Father Keogh. "I rather admire him for that." The dentist sipped his beer. He looked at neither of them. "Do you want anything from Huapan, Sam?"

"Why, you going to Huapan?"

"Yes. I thought I'd go down on the midweek bus."

"Well, what I want to do down there you can't do for me, Mac. I found myself some dame down there."

"I could give her your regards," said Father Keogh.

"Oh no," said Sam. "I don't go for that giving regards. It took plenty of doing to ease her into going around with a hundred and seventy pound bow-legged, red-haired jerk like me, and here you go giving her my regards. You keep away from her, Mac. You have the kind of eyes could make a girl forget she was brought up nice."

"Very well," Father Keogh said. "I'll just send you a postcard of Huapan."

"Yeah, do that, Mac. Here's mud in those hurt black eyes."

"Cheers," Father Keogh said.

When he returned home he found a note for him. It was unsigned and it was printed: YOU WILL BE UNWISE IF YOU TRAVEL BY BUS.

"Who brought this?" Father Keogh demanded of Chela.

"Maria-of-the-Gaseosa stall's third little granddaughter. But how are you to go if it isn't by bus, Father? There's not a station nearby or an airport."

"You mustn't read other people's correspondence, Chela."

"Now, Father, as if I would do such a thing. I said to the child, 'What is in it?' and she told me, that was all."

"Who gave it to her?"

"It was a man," she said. "And another man gave it to him. But that much was all I could get from her."

"But I haven't told anyone that I am going to Huapan. I only decided this morning and the only person I've mentioned it to is Sam."

"Ah! Then perhaps it was the Señor Frankenson having his little joke. It is sometimes the way with those drinking ones. It makes them play with little bricks like children do. A cousin of my sister's husband once—"

"Tell me another time, will you, Chela? I want to find out about this."

He took the note to Sam.

"If I had it in mind to tell you not to go on the bus I could have told you, couldn't I? I don't have to write you a letter."

"But I haven't told anyone else but you."

Sam clicked his fingers. "Campos, Mac! That guy's ears were flapping so hard I felt the draught right down my neck."

Father Keogh called round at the dentist's surgery. He was pounding a filling and his glasses glinted. "I know nothing about it, Padre. I don't listen to people's talk."

Father Keogh thanked him and went to the Chief of Police. "Do you think it's a practical joke?"

The Jefe shook his head. "It's a genuine warning. You must have hidden well-wishers."

"Couldn't we get hold of the child and question her? She's the Gaseosa stall's third granddaughter or something."

"You can't get a thing out of these people," answered the Jefe. "If you put a hot iron under them they wouldn't speak."

"Well, I really don't see how I could come to much harm on the bus."

"You'd be surprised," said the Jefe. "They're up to anything. I hear you've been attacking him by name from the pulpit."

"I have taken one or two cracks at him," Father Keogh admitted. "Do you have to go to Huapan?"

"Yes, I want to go to confession and it seems a good time now that everything's quiet."

"We could give you an armed escort," said the Jefe. "That might put them off if they're planning a holdup, though they haven't done that for some time. I'd be surprised if they went back to that again."

"Oh now look here," said Father Keogh. "If there's any risk of that sort of thing I won't go by bus. I don't want to endanger the other passengers."

"How will you go then?"

"I'll hire that young scoundrel who charges double every time he has to shift gears."

"All right," smiled the Jefe. "Get the price settled first, and if anything else happens let me know. I'd better hold on to this." He put the note in a file and gave the priest a mock salute. Father Keogh saluted back.

Father Keogh said to the car driver, "Now understand this, Domingo, double for the hill and after that ordinary rates for anything that goes up, down, round the corner, through water or up in the air. Savvy?"

"Yes, Father. Yes. I'm a reasonable man. What time do we start perhaps?"

Father Keogh laughed at him. "We don't start perhaps at all. We start at the appointed hour and I expect you to be punctual. Ingles

109

punctual not Mexicano punctual." He waved and Domingo grinned at him.

They left at four o'clock in the morning. Father Keogh carried a thermos of coffee and a cumbersome parcel. It was to be collected by Chela's brother-in-law at Alfredo's café on the corner of the Avenida Carranza.

He could not suppress a suspicion that the parcel was made up of his own stores—"going to my sister's husband who was visited by the sickness last fall."

Chela was an economical housekeeper but any money she saved from a particularly astute piece of bargaining she regarded as belonging to herself. Sometimes she spent it on herself and sometimes upon Father Keogh. It depended on which of them she thought the most deserving at the time. If she put an exceptionally luscious basket of strawberries before him and told him, "This one is a small gift from me," there was nothing to do but thank her. He leaned forward to order Domingo to stop at the top of the Hua Pass. He climbed out of the car and stood on the edge looking down at the platform of rock that jutted out below the Hua caves. They had circled halfway round the mountain so that Quantana was hidden from view.

He lit a cigarette and the wind buffeted him snatching the smoke away, dispersing it into shreds. The valley stretched closely green and lush beneath him and the lake shone like a fragment of splintered glass.

He kept his eyes on the Hua ledge. It was barren and stones had tumbled down onto it. It made a stark monument to the small man who had stood upon it to draw the soldiers' fire from his escaping flock. Father Keogh trod out his cigarette and prayed silently for Father Gomez. He stayed for a moment watching the clouds. Delicately tinted they joined together in a pattern of infinite beauty.

When he returned to the car Domingo kept up a running conversation to the detriment of his fellow townsmen. "Upon my word, Father, it's a terrible town we are leaving behind us. I should not live there at all if it wasn't that my family is buried there."

"Haven't you any relatives alive?"

"There is only my wife's family left alive and there you have the other good reason why I should leave Quantana."

"It's only got itself to thank for being a bad town. Other towns aren't bad."

110

"No, no indeed, Father. You don't get such badness in other towns."

"Still it's very orderly on the surface. The Jefe cracks down on the petty offenders."

"Yes, well that's so, Father. But then in the gaol in Quantana you always find fools. The rest are too smart to get caught. And then of course if it's something very bad you've done you can take it to Malo. He will see that you get no punishment."

"That's useful," Father Keogh said. "I must remember that."

He closed his eyes and slept a little. He must have been asleep for twenty minutes when he heard Domingo scream. He shot forward holding the back of the seat. "What is it? What's happened? Are you ill?"

The car raced down the mountain road careening from side to side.

"It's the wheel!" Domingo shouted. "I cannot hold the wheel!"

Father Keogh climbed over from the back. He was thrown sideways several times before he achieved the front seat. "Put on the brakes, man—put on the brakes!"

Domingo rammed in the brakes and the car crashed over a pile of stones and ran into the face of a rock.

"It's been fixed," said Domingo. "The wheel's been fixed. Mother of God, it could have killed us! We might have gone over the edge."

"I've no doubt we were meant to," Father Keogh said. He had a cut on his head and his mouth was bleeding. "Are you hurt?" he asked Domingo.

Domingo put a hand out to touch his four gold teeth. "No, no, everything seems all right. Mother of God, I thought we should be joining my family!"

They climbed out to examine the car. The hood was badly damaged, and the bolt on the steering wheel had been deliberately loosened.

"I said it was fixed!" said Domingo, triumphant. "Never could I have let such a thing go wrong with my car. And that Mateo who works for me, he could never have thought of a thing like this. Oh no, it's been fixed all right. You know something, Father? It was the little time you spent on the Hua ledge that saved us."

"Why do you say that?" Father Keogh asked.

"Well, because it isn't so dangerous just about here. But if you had not taken the little walk we should have been much further on—and then—not all the brakes in the world could have saved us. They must

111

have planned just how long it was going to last. Do you see how the bolt has been fixed? The road goes round the mountain like the arm of a woman who cuddles a child. In some places it is so narrow that I never drive without saying a prayer and down from the side of it— zoom!" He made a dive with his hand to explain the sheer drop. "Jesús María José! We'd have been over that side all right if this thing had happened up there."

"We must thank God for saving us," Father Keogh said and recited a thanksgiving prayer.

Domingo stood bareheaded with his eyes closed and made the sign of the cross. "We should also say a prayer to San Ignacio. It is he who takes care of the traveler, but a cup of coffee would be nice."

Father Keogh fetched the thermos with his handkerchief pressed to his mouth.

"Is the blood running badly, Father?"

"No, but you have the coffee, Domingo. The heat will make it worse."

Father Keogh found that his head was aching and that his hand was not steady, but Domingo appeared to have shaken off the effects of the ordeal at once. He chattered as happily as if he had been brought out on a picnic. He showed no concern for the damage done to his car. "For ten years I have been paying insurance money and never a chance until now, but now you will see I shall claim. Do not be anxious, Father," he said cheerfully. "Someone will pass and take back the news of us, and if not we have Chela's parcel. It is bound to be filled with good food. Yes, truly San Ignacio is an excellent saint. One cannot speak too highly of him."

Chapter 19

It was the midweek bus which rescued them. They had to wait four and a half hours before it appeared, its radiator boiling over like a frothing horse above the crest of the Hua Pass.

Domingo ran to greet it, determined to be first to break the news. Roberto and the passengers spilled out in an excited jumble of gestures and exclamations.

Señora Arrieta came running towards Father Keogh flapping her arms like a moor hen. "Look at your mouth, Father! Look at your mouth! Don't tell me you've pushed all your teeth in."

Father Keogh had to bare his lips at her before she was reassured. He had to submit to a conflicting variety of first-aid treatment which made his mouth bleed again and again. They pressed coffee, bottled water and tortillas upon him and their concern almost compensated him for the moments when Domingo appeared to have temporarily forgotten that his car was equipped with brakes.

Domingo was re-enacting the scene with commendable verve. He lurched violently from side to side across the road while the crowd stood back respectfully to appreciate the full significance of his performance.

Father Keogh would have preferred to travel on to Huapan but Roberto and the passengers would not hear of it. Don Timoteo said to him, "It is possible to drop dead after such a shock. I have buried many because of a shock like this."

"And then there is the car," Domingo pointed out. "Someone from the insurance must come out and see it. I shall have to go back and fetch someone."

It was not possible for the bus to turn in the narrow road, but Roberto was not in the least put out at the prospect of backing all the way down into Quantana. He did so with his head out of the window alternately commenting upon his progress and cursing the Bad-One-of-the-Cats without altering the amiable tone of his voice.

The passengers were also quite unperturbed at the interruption of their journey.

"My goodness, Father," said Señor Lopez when Father Keogh apologized to them. "What is a little time wasted? We shall get there in the end, shan't we? We have gone backwards before for less than this. We went backwards when Doña Florencia forgot to bring the baby."

Señora Arrieta insisted that Father Keogh should put his feet up. "It is not good to have the blood at the bottom of the body after a shock like this."

"I tell you what, Father," Domingo announced. "I will not charge you at all for this journey. It was not a nice drive," he said blandly.

113

"Is it not a queer thing?" asked old Don Timoteo. "That it was on the Hua Pass that I discovered the poor little Father Gomez dead? It is almost as if you were meant to follow him, Father."

The bus turned round on the Plaza, amidst considerable curiosity, and drove Father Keogh and Domingo to the door of the police station. Father Keogh was helped down as if he had broken every bone in his body.

"It was fortunate that our stomachs did not betray us," said Domingo, taking dramatic advantage of the willing hands that reached up to help him. "Neither the padre nor myself was sick, which you will agree was good behavior for stomachs with such provocation. Some people are sick for much less," he added complacently. "And it's not a nice thing on the roadside."

"So the note was a trick," said the Jefe. "We ought to have thought of that one."

"I still don't see how anyone knew I was going to Huapan."

"My dear Padre, Campos must have told them. You say there was no one else to overhear. They have an excellent Gestapo system here."

"It is plain to me, Father," Domingo said. "This Señor dentist he passed on the news. Suppose it was important or suppose it was not, it is *news*—and he is in their good books if he tells them news. Some people like to be in those good books, and then what do they do, the crafty ones? They say, 'If he goes by bus there is not much we can do to him,' so they write the little note and keep you away from the bus, and they know you will travel by me instead."

"That's about it," the Jefe agreed. "Have you any idea how they got into your place, Domingo? How they managed to get at the car?"

"Everything seemed as it should be, Jefe."

"Well, we'd better go down there and check up on the locks and we'd better keep an eye on you in future, Father."

Father Keogh went round to see Sam. The bar was empty and Sam sat reading a newspaper below an array of pin-up girls whose faces differed hardly at all from the first to the last.

"I hear they tried to bitch you, Mac."

"News does travel fast," Father Keogh smiled.

"You look as though you could use a drink today."

"Yes, I think I could today."

Sam poured out a double brandy. "Vera Cruz," he said. "Good stuff. This has to be on Papa Martinez. He'd slay me if it wasn't. I'm kind of glad you came out of it, Mac."

"Thank you, Sam. I'm not unglad myself."

"Sonsabitches!" Sam said and raised his own glass to Father Keogh.

Father Keogh said, "What I find hard to understand is the way the people treated me. They couldn't have been kinder to me, and yet they've been doing all they can to avoid me lately."

"Well, it's this way, Mac, they're kind of sweet people around here at heart. It's Pussyfoot makes them mean. They don't want to be mean but he keeps them that way. Those sonsabitches hand out trouble like they was some kind of bum Santa Claus the whole year round. Of course it don't mean they're all sweet—take Campos, he's a mean guy. There's quite a little bunch of them mean—but the rest, well it's like I told you, they don't want to see a guy like you get hurt, besides they go for you, Mac, or they would if it wasn't for Pussyfoot."

Father Keogh looked round the bar. "You couldn't be said to be doing a roaring trade, could you, Sam?"

"Nope. Been pretty quiet all morning. It's at night they come in. Those sonsabitches are too plastered themselves to notice who drinks where when it's that late."

"Why, are you boycotted too, Sam?"

"Pussyfoot likes them to drink up the bar at the Martinez. Why wouldn't he? Pussyfoot gets all the profits from it."

Father Keogh finished his brandy and went home to Chela. She was waiting to scold him and put him to bed. "Yes, yes you *will* go to bed, Father," she said to him firmly. "And you should thank the dear God that it is a bed I am able to put you in and not one of Don Timoteo's coffins. And Father! Fancy not opening that parcel up. There might have been some of those little dry gringo biscuits we ordered so specially for you."

"I bet there might," Father Keogh laughed.

Chapter 20

The Jefe let Father Keogh borrow his Buick. The fact was kept a strict secret until his actual departure. At that hour, half past five on the following morning, both he and the Jefe checked the car. Father Keogh drove himself. He refused to allow Domingo to take the risk again.

"Well," said the Jefe, "she seems all right. Bon voyage and don't forget to keep your mouth shut about the time you're starting back."

Even Chela did not know he had gone until she found his note. Mother Montezera claimed to have known the whole thing beforehand, and the rumor went round that his body had been found in a well. When it was confirmed that the body was the carcass of a goat the town could not hide its relief. It was uneasy the whole while during his absence, and Locha was unable to concentrate at all.

"If A equals 6 and B equals 5," Miss Finch's chalk squeaked on the blackboard. Inside Locha's desk Micky-Malo made a patient tour of the prospects of escape. His shell knocked the sides and his head withdrew at every obstacle he encountered.

Locha put her hand up. "Has Father Keogh gone to Huapan about Malo, Miss Finch?"

"I'm sure I've no idea, child. Don't interrupt the lesson."

"If he has won't that make Malo more angry with him?"

"If that sum is not worked out by the time I come round, Locha, I'm afraid I shall have to keep you in."

Locha set herself a problem. She tore out the last page of her copybook, with her tongue between her teeth and her eyes on Miss Finch. She tore it softly, taking her time. Then she slit it in half with her ruler. On one half she wrote:

SEÑOR ANACLETO GONZALEZ FLORES COMACHI
ALVAREZ

116

and on the other:

FATHER MICHAEL PATRICK KEOGH

She closed her eyes and shuffled the slips, putting them side by side. She asked herself a silent question, "Which one of them's going to win?" She made a stab at the slips with her pencil and opened her eyes. She had hit Señor Anacleto Gonzalez Flores Comachi Alvarez. She closed her eyes again and reshuffled the slips. The second time she hit Father Michael Patrick Keogh. But it was the third time that was important. It was the third time that answered the question. She screwed her eyes up tightly, puckered her face and reshuffled the slips several times. But before her pencil made its fatal plunge Miss Finch had caught her hand. Miss Finch had captured the slip with Malo's name upon it. She read it, crumpled it and said evenly, "You will remain indoors during the morning recess and you will write out one hundred lines 'I must not waste time in class.' "

Locha released Micky-Malo, tickled him under the chin and was rewarded by a hiss for her pains. Then she tied two pens together with her hair ribbon and began to write her lines.

Miss Finch was about to return to the schoolroom when Francisco ran in from the kitchen. His face was pale and his eyes were bulging. He spoke quickly to Josefa, waving his hands about.

"Señorita! Señorita!" Josefa cried. "The Bad One has come to the house!"

"Did you ask him what he wanted?"

"Yes, Señorita, it's you that he wants. He has a sick kitten and he has heard that the English have nice ways with such things. He will not go to the bruja, she charges too much."

"Very well," said Miss Finch. "Go down and bring him up to me."

Josefa and Francisco crossed themselves. "Señorita, Paco is afraid to be looked upon by him. They say he has the evil eye and that if it falls upon you it is quite possible to be taken with a shaking which the doctors cannot cure."

"That's just silly superstition, Josefa," said Miss Finch. "Very well, I will see him myself."

Malo was waiting in the hall. He held out the kitten. "It would be good of you to keep him for me, Señorita. If he has something wrong with him he might pass it on to the others. I have so many cats."

117

Miss Finch took the kitten. "I don't suppose anyone will mind. She's a nice little thing. How old is she?"

"He is three months and two days, Señorita."

"Oh well, she's probably outgrowing her strength and I don't suppose she gets the right sort of food out here."

"He has what I have, Señorita Finch. All my cats eat well."

From the landing Josefa and Francisco peeped, and behind them Luis the kitchen boy.

"The Inglésa is not afraid of him."

"Look how politely he speaks to her. It is easy to see he respects the Inglésa. It's a good thing for it means that he won't cast a spell on the house."

"It might be as well to have some little piece of her clothing," Francisco said. "To carry about for good luck. It's not many the Bad One respects."

"I will do what I can," promised Josefa. "But it won't be so easy. The Inglésa takes care of her clothes."

Miss Finch met Malo's eyes. They had a cold clarity that made her uncomfortable. She looked down at the kitten quickly, tickling its chin. She was sharply reminded of Malo in its upward narrowed eyes. She said, "I think perhaps I ought to go out and ask Mrs. de Cortinez if she's any objection to my keeping the kitten. After all, it is her house."

"Certainly, Señorita," Malo said, and added, "Señorita, you have the heart of fifteen men."

He smiled as Miss Finch went up the stairs.

Locha came out of the schoolroom. She carried a resentful Micky-Malo in one hand and a tuberose that she had taken from a vase on Miss Finch's desk in the other. She stood still when she saw Malo. She had expected Father Keogh. Malo came towards her, smiling at her. He held out his hand for the flower. She was tall for her age and her hair reached her shoulders.

"Thank you," said Malo. "I don't often receive a bouquet."

She put the flower behind her back. She licked her lips and stared at him. "I thought you were Father Keogh."

"Well, well, are we so alike?" She made no reply so he asked of her, "Were you bringing that rose for him?"

She said nothing, her pale green eyes upon him. Malo put a finger underneath the tortoise's chin. Micky-Malo's head withdrew. His legs waved impatiently.

118

"The priest is lucky," Malo said. "To have pretty little girls to bring him flowers." He smiled at her, the slow thin smile that spread under his eyes, making two straight lines across his face.

"You mustn't hurt the priest," she told him.

"Why not?"

She was silent a moment, then she said, "Because if you do he'll get his own back. He'll hurt you as well, that's for certain."

"What makes it so certain?" Malo asked.

"He is equipped with remarkable confidence. I wouldn't lay an even bet on either of you."

He knew that she must be quoting someone. He ruffled her hair and laughed at her. "Well done, my little parakeet."

She answered, "You don't *look* bad."

She could not take her eyes from his face, it drove every thought from her mind. She had never seen him before except in the distance. She had made her own picture of him. She had based it on a giant in her Polish fairy book. The giant's face was grotesque and overdrawn. It had become the face of Malo.

She stared at the smooth beauty that stooped to her level, at the clear skin—and the clear eyes—and the mouth that had been etched with such precision. She found herself saying, in a voice from a corner she could not have known about, "You don't look bad. You couldn't be bad."

"It is only our enemies who call us bad. Your governess, when she's cross with you, when you do your lessons wrong, what does she call you—bad?" Locha nodded. "And do you think you are bad?" She shook her head. "Well then, when I do my lessons wrong Quantana calls me bad."

She stood staring at him when he took the rose from her. It was behind his ear when he laughed at her, and went slamming the door, out of the house.

She was still staring at the door when Josefa and Francisco came running down the stairs.

"He has put the evil eye on her. She's bewitched—you can see she's bewitched. Quick!" Josefa said to Francisco. "Go to the bruja quick! Tell her the evil eye has fallen on the child! Ask for a cure, and Paco, quick!"

Francisco ran all the way to Mother Montezera. When he came back he carried an herb. It was tronadora. Locha struggled fiercely with them but at the back of the schoolroom they held her down.

119

Francisco kept a hand across her mouth while Josefa rubbed the herb into her forehead.

"Pray God we're in time," Josefa said. "Silence, child! Silence!" she ordered Locha. "Didn't I tell you the Bad One would get you? The next time he comes he will take you away."

Chapter 21

Father Keogh confessed to Father Lopez. Afterwards in the patio they drank chocolate together. There was a parcel beside Father Keogh. It contained a padlock and chain for the barrel organ.

They avoided each other's eyes until Father Lopez said, "What did you think of him?" Father Lopez had iron-gray hair and wore steel-rimmed glasses. He had a habit of biting his knuckles and his voice was dry and dull.

"I suppose it's like seeing a film that you've heard highly praised," Father Keogh said. "You expect so much."

Father Lopez nodded. "Yes."

"I heard so much about him from the Bishop."

Father Lopez helped Father Keogh out. "You thought that some of his difficulties might have been due to some of his own deficiencies, perhaps?"

Father Keogh passed his cigarette so that Father Lopez might take a light from it. "Yes," he said. "Perhaps. He scampered about the room like a little frightened mouse."

Father Lopez turned a solemn face towards him. *"That's* what it was! I knew it was something, but I could never quite think what."

"That's what it was," said Father Keogh. "Nibble nibble—twitching whiskers."

There was a note in his voice that made Father Lopez reassure him. "You were good to him. At least so we heard down here."

"Good to him?" Father Keogh said bitterly. "Yes. I was—'good'

120

to him. May God forgive me, I hadn't even the grace to suspect that he might be my superior because he was a fidget."

"You were not alone," said Father Lopez. "We were equally guilty here. There were not a few of us who privately thought ourselves better equipped to handle that particular situation than he was. But we none of us offered to do so. Our assistance was confined to discussion."

"Did he ask you to help?"

"No, he didn't. He had his own reasons, I believe. Perhaps because he didn't wish to involve us in such a difficult task, and perhaps because he didn't wish to let us know in what manner he was handling that difficult task. But in any case we couldn't have given him much material assistance. Comachi's influence is very strongly felt in Huapan. If we went to Father Gomez's aid we should have endangered him further. On the other hand if he *asked* for our aid he might well have endangered his flock. Nevertheless," said Father Lopez, "I'm afraid the position did not lessen our criticism."

"I'm paying for it now," said Father Keogh. "I know what he was up against. I see it every day, not only in the external sense but in the inner sense. I know what he must have had to fight within himself and yet—I judge him still. I think I'd give five years of my life not to have been amused by him in those first few pathetic minutes."

"It was—the scuttling," Father Lopez said. "It was that which was so like a mouse—"

"At least he had the sense to be aware of his own weaknesses. He knew himself, and he knew what he had lost in himself. He was doing his best with what was left of himself. It's not his death that has made him a martyr in my eyes. It's my attitude towards him that has made him a martyr in my eyes. I was so certain that I could do better. I tell you, I was reassured at the sight of him. Because I was sorry for him I excused myself. I was so smug—I was so condescendingly Christian towards him. It would have been more honest and more courageous to have condemned him outright. To have said to myself, 'This poor little creature has failed because he's not up to the job. I can do better than that. I'm no weakling. I'll succeed where he has failed.' But no, I hid behind a cloak of charity, I made excuses for him. I reminded myself perpetually of his fine record—and I was sorry for him. Pity," said Father Keogh, "can be a great consolation to those who give it."

"It's always better than feeling no pity," Father Lopez pointed out.

"I gave him enough sympathy to suffocate him," Father Keogh

said. "But I gave him no understanding. I've had occasion to ask myself questions since. His weakness might well have been strength. His folly might well have been wisdom. His compromise might have been courage. At least he kept a glimmer of faith alight. I went into the ring like a prizefighter and extinguished what was left. He kept a handful in church. I've had them all driven out."

"In this case," said Father Lopez, "it might not only be the handful in church that's important. It's the state of the hearts outside. There should be a church in every heart, even if it's only the tiniest corner that God can call his own."

"I have closed those tiny corners. I've made them afraid to open themselves to God. But Father Gomez knew the danger they were in. He went out of his way to protect them against it. I wasn't content to play safe. I went charging in bulletheaded and the little light that he kept burning, at who knows what cost to himself, I put out."

"You may have dimmed it," Father Lopez said, "but I doubt if you have put it out."

"My new broom swept so clean," said Father Keogh bitterly, "that I've left myself nothing to sweep. He was obliged to sin for his flock. He debased himself for their sake, he did things which he condemned himself for. It's much the same case as an honest shepherd being forced to steal food to keep his sheep alive. But it ate into his self-respect and made him despicable, not only to others but more importantly to himself. There's nothing so bitter as that. He sacrificed his honor, his pride and his faith in himself. That's quite a considerable sacrifice."

Father Lopez bit his knuckles. "In the interests of truth and your own problems, Father, one is unfortunately bound to ask oneself, to what an extent he chose to make those sacrifices or to what an extent he was unable to resist making them."

"He chose them," Father Keogh said.

"Are you troubled by the possibility of being called upon to make the same sort of sacrifices?" Father Lopez asked.

"I have no hope of being called upon," Father Keogh said. "I lack that final courage. I find myself wondering, Father, whether I ought not to go back to the Bishop, and tell him that he has sent the wrong man, and that my own confidence, my very ambition to succeed, has made me a failure, and that I consider myself unworthy of this task he has set me. But there's something else," said Father Keogh. "I wonder sometimes, whether this desire of mine to admit my deficiencies in this particular case isn't a subconscious desire to rid myself of the responsibility altogether."

"You're afraid?" said Father Lopez.

"Often," Father Keogh told him. "But particularly of failing—"

"Isn't it early days to talk of failure?"

"I don't know," said Father Keogh. "If I'm the wrong man in the job, I'm keeping the right man out and the sooner I make room for him the better."

Father Lopez spent several silent moments considering Father Keogh. Even the black hair, even the black eyes, the bent head, the whole of the tensed body, gave out a suggestion of strength. The faith was strong, the heart was strong, the spirit and the stricken conscience were strong. The self-criticism and the self-doubt and even the gentleness in Father Keogh suggested a feeling of strength.

"It can't be easy," Father Lopez thought, "to be as forcefully alive as all that and have patience with people who are only half alive."

He thought that Father Keogh showed commendable humility for one so well equipped. "He can't have a twinge of rheumatism," Father Lopez sighed. "And yet I'm sure he'd be truly sympathetic to mine."

He wondered whether he might be more useful to Father Keogh if he liked him a little less, and he thought that the church showed infinite wisdom where the services of her clergy were concerned. She was instinctively able to see which of their qualities would be of the most use to her in the particular field in which she required them. Her intuition seldom failed. Her judgment was never at fault.

He tried to prevent himself biting his knuckles. A mild old priest had once confessed that this habit had not only robbed him of the power to concentrate upon his sins, and the desire to receive the Sacrament of Penance, but filled him with a regrettable urge to rap Father Lopez over the offending knuckles with the hardest instrument he could find.

Father Lopez told Father Keogh something of his feelings about the wisdom of the church. "Sometimes we may think that she's made a mistake, but you know she very rarely has. She knows us so much better than we know ourselves. Only she can assess us correctly. What we consider our merits may well not be merits in her eyes. And what we despair over as defects she might not consider defects. Do you think we have the right to doubt her wisdom? The church is too wise to rely upon saints. She relies upon as many tiny fragments of sainthood as the best and the worst of us can find in ourselves to offer her. When

123

they are all put together it gives her a fairly high percentage of saintliness. I think that's what the church relies on," Father Lopez added, biting his knuckles. "I should find myself very surprised indeed if it turned out that she'd sent the wrong man."

Chapter 22

When Father Keogh reached Quantana the following evening Chela had news for him. "He was there in your own room, Father, and he said to me, 'Chela, you are a nice girl, Chela.' A girl, he called me, Father, and me old enough to be his mother if I'd been silly enough to marry his father. 'It would be a pity if something happened to you, Chela,' he said."

"Who are you talking about, Chela? Malo?"

"Yes, Father, and I said to him, 'What could happen to me, Señor Comachi? I am careful. I look where I'm going.' "

"Why was he threatening you, Chela?"

"Because I've been going to church."

"Oh that was it, was it? Well, what are you going to do about it?"

"Well, Father, I have a sister with little ones and the husband of my sister is not good at finding work."

"Will he lose his job if you went to church?"

"Well, being the only one going, Father, it makes me so easy to see and the Bad One has no thought for others."

"He'd take it out on your family, would he?"

"Oh yes, Father," Chela said cheerfully. "That's how the Bad One works. So I thought wouldn't it be nice if we had the Mass to ourselves just in here. The little Father sometimes said Mass in here like the times of the troubles and shootings."

"It looks as if it's that or nothing," Father Keogh said.

"It's a dreadful thing, Father," Chela told him, "that the Bad One has no manners. He has invited everyone to a great banquet tonight—everyone that's important except us."

124

Father Keogh knew that by "us" Chela was only referring to him. She always included herself when she spoke of him. It was always: "We have a Catechism Class today." "We have a funeral this afternoon." "We have a First Communion."

"The Presidente is going and the Jefe, the Señor doctor and everyone important except us."

Father Keogh patted her shoulder. "We'll have a banquet all on our own. You can cook me tostados and I promise to like it."

Chela had a second piece of news. She beamed at him. "Father, I have some washing for you."

He was surprised at the pleasure it gave her. He said, "Oh, have you? I'll check it tomorrow, Chela."

"No, Father, this is not ordinary washing. This washing isn't yours."

He went upstairs puzzled, to investigate. He went into the little bare room with the one tiny window. There was a pale straw matting across the floor and above his iron bedstead a crucifix hung.

On the bed the laundry was laid out with extra care. He recognized it at once. A small faded pajama top, flannel stiff and nearly patternless from washing, and four white handkerchiefs with a "G" in the corner.

He realized that Chela must have spent all her available spare time tracing the missing laundry. He realized that it was a considerable achievement to have recovered it and he saw in it her tribute and her atonement.

He thanked Chela for recovering the laundry and walked up the hill to the church. It was dark when he reached it and the fireflies were dancing. The dust had crept up the aisle again. Father Keogh swept it out. Then he tolled the bell. It rang hollow and dismal across Quantana. He tolled it every night. He was determined that the town should be made to hear that the church had not lost her tongue.

At first he saw no one in the candlelight. Then a small shadow fell before him. When he turned round he saw Locha. He rose from his knees to greet her.

She was carrying her tortoise and she had been crying. She held out Micky-Malo. "I heard the bell ringing so I knew you'd be here. Do you think you could bless him as quickly as you can please, because I have to have a bath and nobody knows I've come out."

"My dear child, you've no business to be out on your own. They'll be worried to death about you. What's the matter with him?"

"He's dying," sobbed Locha. "It's Malo's kitten. He's put the evil

125

eye on him. Josefa says he has. He just stays in his shell the whole day long and when he does come out he bumps into things. Do you think Malo's kitten's made him blind?"

"There's no such thing as the evil eye," said Father Keogh and took the tortoise across to the light. "Why is his head bright blue?"

"Oh well," she said. "That might be ink. I left the top of the bottle in my desk and he knocked it over once."

"And that's what's the matter with him." Father Keogh laughed. "He probably got a good mouthful of it and he bumps into everything because his eyes are all bunged up, although what he's got in them," Father Keogh said, and licked the corner of his handkerchief, "I'm sure I don't know. What else do you keep in your desk?"

"Biscuits and things," she said doubtfully.

"Then it's biscuits and things that have bunged up his eyes."

He wiped the indignant reptile's eyes and polished its head with his handkerchief. "There you are, so much for Malo's kitten. Now, you say a little prayer and then I'll take you back and you must promise me never to—What is it?"

She looked past him, her eyes wide. Then she clung to him. "I saw someone. It's Malo. He's come here to eat me. Josefa always says he will if I'm bad and I have been bad coming down here tonight."

"Josefa's no business to tell you such tales." Father Keogh took her shoulders and held her away from him. "Where did you think you saw someone?"

"Looking in at the door. I *did* see someone."

"All right. You sit here and I'll have a look round."

She sat in the pew with the tortoise beside her and he hurried down the aisle. Outside there was nothing to see except the fireflies. Crickets cheeped harshly and from the town horns conked and a jumble of music reached the church. It was the work of several radios and a band.

He flashed his torch down the path and across to the wall. It lit the flame trees and the tamarindo trees. It lit the giant cypress tree that stirred in the evening breeze, and it lit a lizard that slid round the wall, but it lit nothing else.

"There's no one here, Locha," he called to her and stood holding out his hand. She came running down the aisle. She dipped her fingers in the holy water stoup and crossed herself. She made a quick genuflection and clung to his hand, then she squeaked, "Oooh! I've forgotten Micky. I've left him in the pew."

126

"I'll fetch him," Father Keogh said.

He came back with the tortoise. "He was getting a bit hot and bothered. I think he thought we'd deserted him."

He preceded the child down the steps. He never knew exactly what happened. He had turned to the child on the steps to hand the tortoise up to her. He heard a movement that was not his own and not Locha's. He had time to cry out to her, "Go back!" Her shrieks covered the sound of a quick slice through the air which knocked him heavily up against the wall of the church. There was a sharp splitting noise and a pain in his hand that was followed by warmth. He had hit his head and was dazed for a moment, but he called out to Locha, "Stay there. It's all right." He levered himself up against the wall and found blood flowing over his hand. He heard the undergrowth crush under running feet and the beam of his torch reached the back of a man as he leapt over the wall.

He heard Locha cry out on the steps. He called back the first thing that came into his head. "Don't worry, Locha. It was just someone playing a joke." He wrapped his handkerchief tightly round his hand and trod carefully back to the porch again. Under the wall he had fallen against there was a dark object. It was the tortoise, smashed in half. Its shell was crushed right through to its stomach, but its head was still waving about. It moved slowly from side to side. Father Keogh put a quick heel on the head.

Then he went back to the porch. "Hallo," he said. "Don't be frightened. It's all over now." He kept his injured hand behind his back and smiled at Locha. With his free hand he drew her towards him. "Locha, I'm afraid I've lost Micky. I dropped him on the ground and he must have taken a walk. It's too dark to look for him now, but I'll find him in the morning." He stroked her hair and pressed her to him. "Try not to mind too much. He can look after himself, you know, and he might think it's fun to be free."

She sobbed, "I saw someone jump right out at you. Someone jumped out. I *saw* them do it."

"Yes, yes, try not to worry about it. It was just somebody playing a joke. I'm going to take you home now. You mustn't miss that bath." When he stooped to pick her up he said casually, "Wasn't I silly? When I fell over I hurt my hand. I ought to know better, oughtn't I?" She screamed when she saw the hand. He held her in one arm and comforted her. "It's all a lot of blood about nothing. You know how

127

you bleed when you cut yourself." He felt her tears against his cheek and he could feel her fingers gripping him.

"Oh couldn't you *please* be friendly with Malo? Then you wouldn't have to fight. Father Gomez didn't have to fight."

"I'll be friends with anyone who'll let me," Father Keogh said. "But I don't think he wants to be friends." He kissed her on the cheek and carried her out. "You've been a very good girl about Micky-Malo."

"He wasn't called Malo. He was only called Micky."

"Well, you've been a very good girl about Micky."

"Why are you carrying me?"

"Don't you like to be carried?"

"Yes, thank you. Will he be all right by himself all night?"

"Oh yes," said Father Keogh. "He'll have a high old time."

He put her down at the gates of the Casa Grande and took her hand. He kept her in front of him, flashing his torch. He told her about Ireland and his sister Ellen-Dora. She forgot about the tortoise and her fright.

"Was your sister a nice little girl?"

"Yes, she was, a very nice one."

"What did she look like?"

"Well, she was dark and she had gray eyes and she used to walk about without her shoes."

"Why?"

"Because she was Irish."

"Don't Irish girls wear any shoes?"

"Oh yes, but they like to take them off."

"Why?"

"Because they're Irish."

She laughed and wrinkled her nose up at him. "I do think you're a funny priest."

"Oh you do, do you?" he asked her and returned the pressure of her hand.

In the Casa Grande he told Miss Finch, "Don't be too cross with her. I rather think she saved my life." And when he went home he said to Chela, "First thing tomorrow morning before you do anything else will you go out and buy me a tortoise! I don't mind how much you pay for it as long as you get the right size. It's about—so big—no that's too big—like this," and he marked out the size with his hand.

"A fine time to be thinking about tortoises, Father," Chela grumbled. "The doctor should see this hand."

128

She held it over a basin of hot water. It was swollen and badly contused. There were no broken bones but the flesh was lacerated.

"And bring him back to me as soon as you've got him," Father Keogh said. "I want to put ink on his head."

Chapter 23

"It's my fault," said the Jefe. "I ought to have known they were up to something."

"I don't see how," said Father Keogh, "when they spent the evening right under your nose."

"I ought to have recognized that trick. It's a favorite one."

"Were they all there?" Father Keogh asked.

"They were," said the Jefe. "All under the bright lights and on their best behavior, from El Gordo to the Jeep. That's how they usually work. If it isn't a banquet it's something else to keep every one of them under the public eye. It's a joint alibi."

"Then who do you think attacked me?"

"Any number of people are so scared of them they'll do any job to save their own skins."

"Oh I see," said Father Keogh. "The banquet was arranged to keep suspicion off them."

"That's the idea," said the Jefe. "And very well it works. They know that whoever did the job won't risk his life by talking about it."

"No wonder I wasn't asked."

"You were the guest of honor outside," said the Jefe. "And anyway you didn't miss much. They're always the most dignified solemn affairs. Even Maria wears clothes. You didn't notice anyone following you up to the church?"

Father Keogh shook his head. "No. I had a good look outside with my torch but he must have been standing flush with the wall and sprang out when I went to turn round."

The Jefe poked a crushed mess on his desk. It was the remains of Micky-Malo. "It was a machete all right. It's cleaved the thing in two. You can thank your lucky stars you had this in your hand or you wouldn't have had a hand left."

"I imagine," said Father Keogh, "that he was aiming at my neck but the child screaming put him off his stroke."

"Well, you have a tortoise to thank for your neck. It was a miraculous escape."

"Miracles still happen you know." Father Keogh smiled at him.

When he went up to the Casa Grande he carried his bandaged hand in a sling and a tortoise as near the measurements of Micky-Malo as possible, in the bottom of Chela's basket. There was an ink stain on its head. Locha was waiting at the gates for him. "Did you get him? Miss Finch said I needn't do any lessons until he was found. She said I couldn't concentrate."

"Well you can concentrate now," smiled Father Keogh and lifted the tortoise out.

"Isn't he any the worse for it?"

"I don't think so," Father Keogh said.

"He usually comes out when I tickle his chin."

"Well, he's had a night out," Father Keogh reminded her. "He's probably feeling tired."

"Is your hand very bad?" she asked him and received no reply. He had noticed she wore no shoes. "My dear child, what are you thinking of? What on earth have you done with your shoes?"

"I took them off. Your sister did."

"Yes, but my dear good child, that was in Ireland, you mustn't do that out here. You'll get jiggers in your feet." He went to lift her up but his bad hand prevented him. "Quick," he said. "Hop on my back. Hold tight."

He picked up the basket and took her towards the house in a pickaback fashion.

Miss Finch met them at the door. "Oh Mr. Keogh, you shouldn't let her bother you. Locha, you're too big for that."

"She's big enough to know that she ought to wear shoes," said Father Keogh. "Now off with you! Get them on."

She ran upstairs and waved to him.

Father Keogh said to Miss Finch, "How is she? Was it much of a shock last night do you think?"

"Well, Mr. Keogh, it's hard to say. She seems to have been fright-

130

ened of this man for some while. I discovered her writing his name on a piece of paper. She must have had him on her mind. She has nightmares about him, and Josefa tells me that she quite often calls out in her sleep."

"That's not surprising," Father Keogh said. "Josefa tells her tales about him."

"Yes, but I've noticed something very strange. It always occurs after the nightmares. Mr. Keogh, whenever she's had bad dreams there's a peculiar odor about the child."

"An *odor?*" Father Keogh said.

"An *odor,*" said Miss Finch. "I simply can't account for it, but I've noticed it several times. It's most—well, it's really quite strong. Well, not to put too fine a point on it, it smells like whiskey."

"*Whiskey?*" Father Keogh said. "You're surely not suggesting *she* drinks."

"It smells more as if she's had a bath in it."

"It must be your imagination, Miss Finch. May I see the child?"

"Yes, do. I'll fetch her. You have such a good influence."

He heard Miss Finch calling, "Lo-cha! Lo-cha! Mr. Keogh would like to see you, dear. Have you washed your hands?"

Locha wore shoes and a fresh ribbon in her hair. She came round the door and said, "Me?"

"You." Father Keogh smiled at her. "Sit down, I want to talk to you."

She sat at her desk and put the tortoise on top of it. Father Keogh went across to her and sniffed her surreptitiously. He could have sworn that there was indeed a trace of whiskey in the shining hair. "What's all this about you being frightened of Malo?"

He saw her lips part quickly and close again. He saw the tip of her tongue appear and he saw that the hand which held the tortoise shook a little. She said, and her voice had the ice of Don Pedro in it, "I am not afraid of Malo."

"Then what makes you have nightmares about him?"

"I don't."

"But Josefa says you do."

"She's a silly old fool," said Locha.

"That'll do," said Father Keogh. "It's not a very nice way to talk. If you're not afraid of Malo what are you afraid of?"

She put her head down and her hair fell about her. There was no expression in her voice. "Nothing, thank you."

131

"It doesn't sound like nothing thank you to make people talk in their sleep."

"How do *you* know I talk in my sleep?" The hair fell aside and her eyes were frightened. "What do I *say* in my sleep?"

"I don't know," said Father Keogh. "But it's nothing to get worked up about."

"I'm not worked up."

He stood up and came across to her. "But you are worked up, my child." He took the tortoise and lifted the desk lid. "Have you got the top on the ink?"

"Yes."

Father Keogh put the tortoise inside the desk. Then he took Locha's hand. "Now, what's it all about? Come on, you can tell me, can't you?" She made no reply and he teased her, "Look at you, all of a shake. If you don't stop, poor Micky will be seasick."

"He's called Micky-Malo now."

"He does chop and change," said Father Keogh. "Last night he was cut down to Micky."

"He's Micky-Malo now," she said.

Father Keogh's eyes narrowed watching her. He asked her gently, "What's the matter, Locha? You can trust me. I'm your friend."

She kept her eyes on her hands when she answered him. "Why can't you be *Malo's* friend?"

He looked at her steadily several seconds but she would not meet his eyes. "Would you like me to be his friend?"

"Yes."

"Why?"

She dropped her head in her arms and her voice was unsteady. "You're *asking* for trouble—asking for it. It isn't Malo's fault, things were quite quiet until you came. He was giving no trouble and now you've stirred him up again."

He tried to lift her round to look at her but she hung in his arms with her weight against him. He gave up and she collapsed on the desk again. Her breath caught and she swallowed hard. "Why can't you let sleeping dogs lie?"

"That doesn't sound like you talking."

He could not catch her reply but he heard her repeat, "Why can't you let sleeping dogs lie? If you were friends with him he wouldn't have to be bad. It's your interference that's made him break out."

"But, Locha, he's never been anything else but bad. I really don't think I'm responsible for making him any worse."

"Yes you are. You've started an avalanche."

"Do your parents talk this in front of you? Or do you listen at doors?" he asked her softly. She was silent until he asked her, "Do you wish I'd never come here, Locha?"

"Yes, I do," she said.

"Would you like me to go away again?"

For a moment she hesitated, then she shouted, "Yes, I would! I would!"

"I'm sorry to hear that," Father Keogh said. "It makes me very sad. But you know you mustn't be afraid. The avalanche as you call it won't hurt you. The Gran-Señor-of-the-Cats isn't going to bother his head with little girls. He'll be far too busy for that. You won't be harmed in any way. I rather think that it's me whom that gentleman is going to be after. I'll take up most of his time. He'll have none to spare for you." He gave her hair a little tweak, looked down in her face and smiled.

He saw that her shoulders were jerking. "I like him. I do—I really like him. If I do why can't you?"

"I've never disliked him," Father Keogh said. "I could like him very much if he'd give me the chance."

"If he's my friend why can't he be your friend? And he truly *is* my friend."

"Well, that doesn't seem anything to cry about. If you like him so much we won't say anything nasty about him. It's a good thing to be loyal. It's one of the finest qualities. But you see I didn't know he was your friend. When I first spoke to you about him you said that he wasn't and you sounded a little bit touchy about it."

"Well, he is my friend *now*," she said. "We'd settled down into a routine and he wasn't any worse than a lot of governments because you have to pay taxes everywhere—and if you don't interfere with him—he won't interfere with you."

"More keyholes." Father Keogh smiled. "Well, I'm very glad he's found a friend like you. I think he needs one badly." He pressed her face between his hands and left.

When he went into the bar of the Hotel de la Costa Father Keogh said to Sam, "I simply don't understand it. I know the child is lying."

Sam rubbed a cloth across the bar. "She tell you what Pussyfoot said to her when he brought the kitten up?"

"No. I should have asked her that but she was so upset."

"Sounds like he put something over on her."

133

"The only explanation I can think of," Father Keogh said, "is that he frightened the poor child to death. She was so insistent that I should believe that she was devoted to him, and then she's been hearing her parents talk. She probably thinks I'm the villain of the piece. She was probably frightened to death."

"You just don't get the kid's psychology, Mac. They start pretty young, you know."

"Start what? Psychology?"

"Nope. Sex. Oh I don't say they figure it out that way, but a guy says something nice to them or he gives 'em candy and before you know it the kid's crazy about him and tells her mom and pop she's gonna be a nun."

Father Keogh laughed outright. "Don't be ridiculous, Sam. I never heard such nonsense."

He lifted his glass so that Sam could wipe the bar beneath it. Sam eyed the glass with distaste. "I have to hand it to you and Pussyfoot. It makes me sick to my stomach to see you drink that gassy stuff." And he added, "No kidding, Mac, out here a girl of eleven is halfway towards a woman. I tell you that's the way it is. That kid has a yen for Pussyfoot."

"But Sam! Before she's in her teens?"

"Women have yens before their teens. I reckon they're born in their teens. They're born knowing all about it anyway. We're the mugs that gotta find out. Next week perhaps she'll have a yen for Papa Martinez, the week after that maybe me."

"But she's frightened of him," Father Keogh said. "I tell you I know she is. You can't have a—a—yen for someone who frightens you, can you?"

"Sure. That don't make no odds. It's kinda fun to be scared, I guess."

"I've never found it so," said Father Keogh. "And as it doesn't make me sick could I have another one of these?"

Sam took down a bottle and poured the contents into a fresh glass. "You don't have to take it too serious, Mac. It's just a kind of game. This kid hears Pussyfoot's a bad smell around town and maybe momma said not to look at rude and naughty men, so the kid looks plenty. And what does she see? Pussyfoot's got what it takes. You have to hand him that."

"I'm willing to hand him anything," Father Keogh said.

"Well, it's like the bad man in pictures. If he looks good the kids'll

134

go for him. You bet your sweet life they will. So Pussyfoot gets up there and does the kind uncle act with this kid, and she thinks he's a sweet guy and momma's all wrong about him, so he sends her. But it don't last, Mac," Sam comforted.

"I'm glad," said Father Keogh. "I only hope you're right, and that next week she gets a yen for you. I should feel a little happier about that one."

"Aw, I don't have what it takes," said Sam. "Say, Mac, you have what it takes. You got plenty of it. How do you get by without women? Don't you ever feel you want to go smooching around in the dark?"

"Sam, I'm beginning to see what my Bishop means about slang. I'm afraid you've caught me out with smooching."

"Is that so?" Sam's interest was aroused. "Well, I guess it's not much in your line, but it's necking, petting, feeling your way around —like getting a girl in the back of a car and—"

"Oh I see," said Father Keogh. "No, that isn't in my line."

"Yeah. But don't you ever get ideas about women, Mac?"

"We're made the same as other men."

"What happens to it?"

"We sublimate it."

"Huh?"

"We have other sources of happiness, Sam."

"Well, I always heard that about priests but I never heard it from the horse's mouth before."

"I think you're 'getting me wrong,' as my Bishop would say. I mean we have spiritual substitutes."

"Pussyfoot don't play around none either. And it ain't that he lacks the invitations."

"Why doesn't he marry Maria?"

"Aw, he's not the marrying kind. Maybe she already has a husband. If I was the husband of that Presidente's wife I'd beat her rump until it was raw."

"Why?" Father Keogh asked.

"Haven't you seen the moo-cow eyes she's been making at Pussyfoot? Oh no, of course, you didn't go to that banquet. Well, neither did I, but Papa said if looks could get a guy into bed, she has Pussyfoot right between the sheets."

"Oh no," said Father Keogh alarmed. "Oh, surely not, Sam. Did he encourage her at all?"

"I wouldn't know. It's like I said, Pussyfoot doesn't play around

135

much, but I guess he would encourage her just to annoy the hell out of the Presidente."

"Oh, I *do* hope it comes to nothing," Father Keogh said.

Sam laughed. "Well! What's eating you, Mac? Do you have an eye on her?"

"Not that sort," Father Keogh said, and added: "Sam, does Pussyfoot come in here much?"

"No. Pussyfoot ain't exactly welcome here, I guess he must be sensitive. He's most always round at Porfirio's place. He don't seem to go for the Martinez. It's like it was too swanky for him. You'd think a guy with all that dough would want to have himself some fun with it, wouldn't you? I don't get Pussyfoot."

"I get him," Father Keogh said. "Do the others come in here?"

"Nope. Leastways that son of a bitch El Gordo comes around every quarter to get Pussyfoot's cut off of Papa Martinez. Why? You looking for company?"

"I was wondering if Papa Martinez would let me say Mass in here."

"Huh!"

"They won't come to church any more, Sam, and if they come to my house it'll look suspicious."

"Who you kiddin', Mac? You mean church stuff—prayers and things?"

"Yes, but we shouldn't say it in here, of course. I'd use one of the upstairs rooms. Some of us will have to come into the bar, though, to put them off the scent. I'll always come into the bar myself."

"Pussyfoot knows you don't drink that much."

"Well, if he sees me come in often enough he'll think I've taken to it."

"Yeah. Suppose the Bishop gets to hear of it? He's going to think you've taken to it too."

"He'll be let into the secret."

"Do you have a good boss in that Bishop, Mac?"

"He's a grand lad," Father Keogh said.

"Attaboy Bish!" said Sam.

136

Chapter 24

At eleven o'clock every morning Father Keogh went into the bar of the Hotel de la Costa. He drank Coca-Cola and played Canasta with Sam. Sometimes the dentist came in for an aperitivo. On the third morning when he discovered Father Keogh on the shiny red stool by the bar, he said beneath his breath: "Hypocritical bastards!" And never came in again.

Sam put his head on one side and clicked his tongue. "That's a real sweet guy we got there, Mac. You bet your life that's a real sweet guy."

"I'm afraid I've done you out of a customer, Sam."

"Never mind," said Sam, "now the joint's clear for your own crowd."

Every Sunday morning Father Keogh said Mass in a back bedroom on the first floor. He told his congregation: "If they find us out here, we'll go somewhere else. It might be wiser to come in smaller groups. Also, we must change our times about. If you make out a list and let me know which times will suit you best, I'll try to accommodate every group. Doña Florencia, has your husband asked any more questions?"

"Yes, Father, last Sunday he was very suspicious. But I said to him, 'I am visiting Señora Garcia, Vicente.' It was not a lie for I do see her here."

Señora Garcia rose to her feet. "It is true, Father, that Don Vicente has suspicions. On Monday when I went up for some little cakes he said, 'Señora Garcia, was it yesterday you saw my wife?' So you see, he is on the lookout."

"Doña Florencia," Father Keogh asked, "do you know in what respect your husband works for Malo?"

Doña Florencia shook her head. "No, Father, all I know is that the money comes, and I know that it's not right to work for him

137

but you cannot blame Vicente, he does it for me and the children's sake. He's a good man and he was a good Catholic once."

"It's not a question of allocating blame," said Father Keogh. "That's not the reason I'm asking you questions. I'm trying to find out who needs protection against Malo—those who are forced to work for him for one reason or another are in most need of assistance against him. Until we know who it is he gets to work for him and for what reasons, whom he bribes and whom he threatens, we are not in a position to save ourselves or anyone else from him. It's most essential that we find out whom we can trust and whom we can't, and the ones we can't trust are not necessarily the ones we should condemn. I give you my personal assurance and promise that it's not a question of collecting names for punishment. It's collecting names for help. When we know whom to help we shall know whom to pray for."

Every week he collected more names. Sometimes it was only a suspicion attached to them, sometimes a definite accusation.

Some of the names surprised him:

"That Francisco at the Casa Grande, Father, that one will carry a message for Malo. He is a poor creature and afraid to say no, but he's good at the back of his heart."

"Another one is the driver, Father, Roberto-of-the-Bus."

"And that young Mateo who helps Domingo to blow up the tires in the garage . . ."

"My Alfredo goes up to see Malo, Father, but I don't know what he does."

"And my daughter Elena-Cristina, she is maid to his woman Maria."

"The Señor dentist takes orders from him, and the Presidente has to be his friend . . ."

"Doña Maria works for him, Father, but she only carries tales."

"Hernandez from the Pulquería works for him, Father, also with carrying tales."

"And my Maximo visits him."

"Sometimes he comes to my house and he talks with my husband, but I never hear what they say."

"He sends for my eldest brother Pepe quite often."

"The Señor engineer is not friends with him, but he is a man who likes his peace."

"And the husband of my sister," Chela said. "That one is up to his neck."

138

Every week he received more prayers. On their knees in their homes they prayed for him. In quiet corners and out in the open air they prayed.

They boasted about it between themselves. "Wasn't it strange? The padre has told us our prayers will be answered, and you will believe me, Doña Filomena, for you know that I tell the truth. It was on the morning of the time of Domingo's car that I said a prayer for the padre first."

"I too prayed for him on that morning, Señora."

"Ay, but do you know when it was that I prayed for him? Well, it wasn't long afterwards that he didn't have his head cut off."

"Our prayers are most certainly heard."

"I said to Cayetano, 'Come, we will get out the holy book.' And this was the evening that the Lord put the tortoise between the devil and the padre's neck."

There was clicking of tongues and nodding of heads, and someone suggested practically: "It would be as well to go on praying for the padre for it looks as if God likes him better than Anacleto, and it would be as well to show that we agree with Him. It might also be well to save up for a fireworks castle."

It rained. Thunder burst in the sky and lightning sent a thin thread in and out of the blackening clouds. The rain fell, blotting out the mountains in a steady gray cloak, and the barrel organ stuck in the mud outside Father Keogh's window and played "The Lily of Laguna" never less than eleven times a day, and sometimes more.

"Father! El Choco! Must he always turn his handle here, I think I am going quite mad." Chela had her hands to her ears.

"He says it's the only place he gets any shelter, Chela. I don't like to turn him away."

"He will find shelter inside his grave soon, Father, if I pass him by with a knife."

She had a piece of gossip for him. "You will soon have a nice new baptism, Father. The Presidente's wife is having another little one—Why, Father—what is it? It's only her eighth! It's not so much in a very big house."

Father Keogh said, "No, of course not—when?"

"Well, Father, it will take her the ordinary time. It gets no shorter because you get used to it."

"No, but I mean—she doesn't look—I shouldn't have known unless you'd told me."

139

"You're not supposed to know, Father, and neither am I. It was one of those little secrets that leak out of a house."

"When is the baby due, Chela?"

"Well, Father, in eight or nine months' time. Doña Arcelia has not been made certain yet."

"Oh, I see," Father Keogh said.

"Upon my word, Father, you look as anxious as a real father looks at such times, only they don't start looking anxious so soon."

Father Keogh was more than anxious. He had witnessed a disturbing scene a week or two before. The Presidente's housemaid had shown him into the Presidente's private patio by mistake. Hammocks hung from the balcony that jutted out from the upper floor and the whole patio smelled sweet from the neat gardenia. Doña Arcelia and Malo were sitting by the fountain in a close embrace. Father Keogh heard the Presidente's footsteps. He called out aloud to warn the couple. Doña Arcelia struggled to free herself, but Malo refused to release her. When the Presidente came up to them he kissed her again on the lips.

Father Keogh could not bring himself to look at the Presidente's face. He could imagine the expression from the tone of the voice. "Well, Padre, so much for trust."

The Presidente had disappeared inside the house before Father Keogh had time to answer him.

He walked over to Malo and said: "You did that deliberately, didn't you? You did it to torture him."

Malo lifted his shoulders and wiped his lips. "That man is a fool with his wife."

"Nevertheless she is his wife, and you went out of your way to make a greater fool of him in front of me."

Malo said casually: "Perhaps."

Doña Arcelia clung to him. Her eyes were no longer "saucy." They glistened with something that sent a shiver of apprehension through Father Keogh. He said levelly: "You've made this woman love you, was that deliberate too?"

"She's a fool if she's fallen for me."

Doña Arcelia sobbed against him. She hammered her fist against him, alternately entreating him and threatening him. It was Father Keogh who had to rescue Malo from the insistent beating fists.

"I made her no promises," Malo said. "She knows that I have no use for her."

140

He looked coldly at Doña Arcelia. She collapsed into the arms of the priest. Father Keogh supported her, patting her back. "If you have no use for her, why do you try to take her from someone who has?"

"Father—tell him to love me—*make* him love me!"

"Nothing would make me love that one, Father. I have no use for a woman who makes fools out of men."

"Then what did you *do* it for?" Father Keogh demanded exasperated.

"It's a kindness to point out his folly."

"You went out of your way to encourage her to cause her husband suffering. In doing that you have made her suffer too. I hope you're satisfied."

"Perhaps it's my idea of a joke."

"Well, if it is it's a damned bad one," Father Keogh snapped.

He supported Doña Arcelia into the house, and put her into the arms of her maid. The Presidente was nowhere about. Malo joined him in the hall. "You are wise to have nothing to do with women, Father. They are rarely worth the joke."

"How far have you indulged this peculiar sense of humor of yours?"

"Do you mean, have I slept with her, Father?"

"Yes. I imagine that would strike you as uproariously funny."

"Then, Father, your imagination has tricked you. That would give me no sort of amusement. When a woman brings tears and her soul into bed—then, Father, it's no joke at all."

Father Keogh went to see Maria. He said to her: "You love this man. Can't you stop him making love to other women? Can't you keep him away from other people's wives?"

Maria was curled up in a chair. She opened her wide mouth showing bone-white teeth and laughed at him. "He told me how funny it was to see you—holding the weeping one tight in your arms."

"So you share his sense of humor do you?"

"Anacleto has always been faithful to me. He does not play around."

"What do you call kissing someone else's wife in front of him?"

"I call it more honest than kissing her behind his back."

"It's what he may have done behind his back that's worrying me," Father Keogh said with some heat.

"Then stop worrying, Father—like me. I know Anacleto. He would not think it worth it—a poor little sniveling fool like that— who thinks her tears will make him love her! Anacleto likes someone with fight in them, that's why Anacleto likes me. If she fought him he might think it worth it—but all women are fools with Anacleto. There's not one that he cannot make cry—except me."

"I only hope you're right," said Father Keogh.

"I am right," Maria answered easily. "He was not kissing that little fat fool on the lips, he was slapping the Presidente's face."

Father Keogh felt slightly reassured, nevertheless he realized that he would be awaiting the birth of the eighth child with as much trepidation as the Presidente himself. If it bore the slightest resemblance to Malo he would feel himself personally responsible for lulling the Presidente's suspicions.

Chapter 25

There were shadows under Father Keogh's eyes, and there were lines between his eyebrows. The rare moments when he found time for meditation or time to read were pushed later and later into the night.

On the top of the old medicine cabinet he left his books open, their places marked. Sometimes if he came into the house in a hurry, or before he went out, it was possible to snatch hungrily at a passage or two. But there was never time to reflect upon them, that was also reserved for the night.

The meditation was a more difficult matter. There were frequently sick calls during the night. Sometimes the doctor himself collected him, and sometimes a child was sent to fetch him. Sometimes it was necessary, sometimes not. He was often hours in attendance upon the dying. Usually he remained with the patient until the end or recovery released him, but if there was more than one call upon him he went from one to the other dividing his time. Sometimes he was out all night.

If there was a funeral he was allowed to conduct a simple burial service outside the church. The Requiem was said in private.

He tried by the intensity of his own prayers to make up for the deficiency of those who had not the good fortune to pray for themselves: for the deficiency of Malo, Old Uncle, and Pablo, Lorenzo, Vito, and the Jeep. There were still many prayers unsaid.

The quiet nocturnal hours of reflection and meditation were often tinged with the morning light. He did not grudge the lack of the contemplative hours. He thanked God for the privilege of spending his every minute in active service; but he sighed a little after them: sighed for the deep moments when the body felt lifeless in deathlike repose; when the thoughts crystal-clear seemed outside the head; when a problem pondered the day before was suddenly, wordlessly solved; when a great happiness akin to a great sadness filled the soul, and something that could only be heard in the song of a thousand far-off birds was said; when the heart felt cramped with the pressure of a suffocating selflessness that drained all the feeling from flesh and bones, yet substituted a disembodied peace; when a detachment lonelier than isolation held a joy more pure and a meaning more clear than any human words could find; when time had no end and no beginning but eternity was explained; when the mind sat high above the body in a world that was made of white light.

Father Keogh wrote to his Bishop:

I feel that I am letting time, or the lack of it, get the better of my own sanctification. It is suffering from serious neglect, and I am afraid that in giving way to that neglect I may be robbing my everyday activities of the spiritual power which could make them doubly effective. If this is so I am doing a disservice not only to myself, but to those who depend upon my efforts.

His Bishop wrote back:

Sometimes we have to sacrifice that which is highest in ourselves to something we feel detracts from it. Yet perhaps we should try to believe that in the rendering of this sacrifice, in our very awareness of it, we have been given the higher privilege of practicing something over and above that which we thought to be the highest in ourselves. It may be the antithesis of knowing our own limitations. If this is so, it should be the personification of spiritual advancement. It should act as a stimulus rather than a deterrent to our everyday activities.

143

*In any case, meditation, beneficial to the soul though it is,
can become an indulgence. This is a danger that should never
be overlooked.*

The day that Old Uncle walked into the Hotel de la Costa and
opened the door of the back bedroom on the third floor, Father Keogh
said: "You're more than welcome to join us, but if you've no wish
to do that will you please close the door and go out. As you see, I
am celebrating the Mass."

Old Uncle remained in the doorway. His eyes rested upon every
member of the kneeling community in turn. Then they returned to
the priest. Father Keogh was shocked when he met the eyes. He
saw a loose and relentless hatred in them that he had never seen in
Malo's. It was as if Old Uncle, the lesser disciple of hate, was more
lavish with it than Malo; as if Malo, who knew the value of it,
used it with better care. Father Keogh remembered the look in
Joaquin's eyes when he begged absolution for Malo. It was a drunken,
bewildered, but trusting look. It made the savageness which had
replaced it more hurtful and harder to understand. Old Uncle closed
the door and went out.

When the Mass was over Father Keogh raised his hands to calm
his frightened flock. "If there's someone amongst us who has failed
to keep our trust, let us say a prayer for him. You remember what
I said about prayer, that there is no stronger force? If you pray
you'll soon find out the truth of that. Pray for those you love, and
those you believe are in the power of Malo. Pray for old Uncle
Joaquin. Pray that we shall be able to save those who cannot save
themselves, and above all—pray for the freedom of prayer. Pray
that it won't be long before we are able to raise our voices openly
towards God, that it won't be long before we can use our own be-
loved church again. In peace and at liberty to worship as we please—
pray for that. Prayer is your only defense against Malo."

In Porfirio's bar they sat round in a circle. Malo sat with his hands
before him. He sat with them motionless. He looked round the table
and said, "Well, now, you've heard what Old Uncle has told us—
you have heard what he has to suggest."

There was a silence until the Jeep piped up, "If you let them go
back to the church, Anacleto, it will look as if you had to give in."

Malo said, "That's how I think it would look, my Jeepo, but Old
Uncle cannot see it that way."

144

Old Uncle banged his fist on the table. "Anacleto, I know what I'm talking about. I tell you I saw their faces—they made that room *smell* like a church. Look, Anacleto, it's like a love affair. You stop it—they want to go on with it; you give them your blessing—it's not so exciting any more."

"There's one thing," said Pablo. "Where Uncle is right. If they go to him in secret, we shall never know what he says. If he's in church we shall hear what he says."

Malo's eyes narrowed. He looked at Old Uncle. "But can we be sure that that is the reason Old Uncle would like us to send them to church?" Old Uncle was startled, his mouth hung open. The others were silenced by the tone of Malo's voice. "We must never forget that when Old Uncle was 'dying' it was not me that he asked for—he asked for the priest!"

Old Uncle's voice rose, he slobbered a little. "Anacleto, I was drunk that time—a man does not mean what he says when he drinks."

"It is then that the truth comes out, old friend."

"Anacleto, you know what I think of the church—"

"You served in it once. If you lean against a bad dye it will leave a stain on you."

"I spit on it—hate it—but I know it has power. That is why I'm afraid of the priest."

"What is it you wear round your neck, old friend? Isn't that one of the stains?"

Old Uncle swore and his hand felt his throat. He pulled up the medal that hung under his shirt and sent it swinging across the floor by the string. "Something for luck, that's all it is. Eh, Anacleto— you're not against luck?"

"I'm not against luck—but that wasn't for luck. That was a little piece of you that you couldn't give to me."

The others sat watching. They looked from Malo to old Uncle Joaquin, and back to Old Uncle again. There was a rhythmic precision in the pendulous swing of their eyes.

"Have I ever betrayed you, Anacleto? Is there anything I've ever done that could make you feel no trust in me?" Round the light the insects buzzed, and under it Old Uncle's rings flashed. "Would I tell you something I don't feel to be right?" He put his square hand to the beat of his heart. His face was heavy and hard, and his eyes burned. "Is there anyone here you could trust more than me? Mother of God, would I side with the *priest!*"

145

Malo smiled. "He has only a little piece of you, and I have all the rest." He looked down at the medallion that lay on the floor and every eye looked down with him. "But it's not always the biggest piece that has the greatest strength."

Old Uncle swayed across the room. With his heavy heel he ground the medallion into the floor. Then he lowered his voice and his mouth moved sideways. "Was there ever a time—could there be such a time that you feel that I'm not with you?"

Malo told him, and his voice was grave: "You think that you fear for me against the power of the church, but I think that you fear for the power of the church against me. The church had a grip on you once, old friend. She has not lost that grip. In that little bit left that you wear round your neck—ah, but you wear it still though you threw it away. That piece may be the padre's thumb upon you. You may be under the padre's thumb!"

Old Uncle sat forward. The sweat filled the deep lines across his forehead, and slipped steadily into his eyes. He spoke like a man in great bodily pain. "Anacleto, you've been like a son to me—Mother of God, I would kill the priest, wouldn't I?" The eyes in the heavy face lit with a viciousness that shook the whole body.

Malo put out a hand to pinch his chin as if he had been a giant baby. "Old Uncle Joaquin, I'm playing with you! I trust no man on earth except you."

The others sat back and relaxed.

"He would have taken a gun and shot the priest in the street to prove he was faithful," Pablo laughed.

Old Uncle sat back with his handkerchief. "Anacleto, the devil must live in you to make sport of me like that." He put the handkerchief up to his face and used it as a towel. "To torment me and make such a fool of me—yes, the devil must live in you. If you hurt that woman of yours like you hurt every other living thing it's a wonder she stays with you—Mother of God, what a wonder it is."

"I've no cause to hurt the woman," Malo said. "A woman is only good for one thing, and this one is good at that." Then he called out to Porfirio: "Old Uncle's mouth is dry, get him something to drink, Porfirio."

"My mouth!" said Old Uncle. "My heart dried up!"

Porfirio went behind the bar. He handed over a bottle of Vera Cruz brandy, and Vito brought glasses and a box of cigars to the table. They sat again, smoke curling round them.

146

"So you think I should let them go back to the church?" Malo asked.

Old Uncle spread out his hands. He spoke past the cigar in his mouth.

"Look, it's this way, Anacleto. Here's this priest. He tells them to pray. All the time, over and over, he tells them to pray. If they do—then he tells them, they've nothing to fear. It's their only defense against you, Anacleto. If they go to church, he says 'God will protect them against you.' Well let them go to church—God won't protect them. The priest has promised to answer their prayers for them, hasn't he? He's promised them miracles, hasn't he? All right, let us give him the chance."

"I get it," Lorenzo said.

Malo sat silent, his eyes narrowed.

Old Uncle insisted, "He's working their faith up now on promises. When those promises fail they will have no faith."

"It would be better to kill him," the Jeep piped up.

"Yes, it's better to kill him," Old Uncle said. "I love that idea. I dream of it. But how do we do it? The devil looks after him." The hand that took Old Uncle's glass from his lips was still unsteady. "Anacleto can tell me any time he likes to kill the priest, and I will kill him. But Anacleto does not tell me."

"It has to be an accident," Malo said. "Any other way's too dangerous. He's not one of those you can just stamp out. His own people have an eye on him."

"You know what I think?" Vito asked. "I think Anacleto likes this priest."

"Yes," Malo answered, "I like him."

"Let them go back to the church," Old Uncle urged. "Let them pray their damn fool hearts out. Then let them wait for the miracles—you're not afraid of them, Anacleto?"

Round the table a laugh broke out.

"I have never believed in miracles," Malo smiled.

"All right then—so what do we do then? We give him his chance and he fails."

"Could it be that he wouldn't fail?" Malo asked.

"You just said you didn't believe in those things."

"I said I didn't believe in miracles. I didn't say that I didn't believe in him."

Lorenzo wiped his nose on his sleeve. "What a mess that fool we hired to kill him made! Catch me cutting a tortoise's head off instead of a priest's!"

"There are many ways to kill a man," Malo said, "but the surest way, is to let him kill himself. It is also the safest."

Chapter 26

The next morning there was a notice on the gates of the church: MASS WILL BE SAID AT 12 P.M.

It was not put there by Father Keogh. It had nothing to do with the sacristan.

"Bless the Saints! It is the writing of the Bad One!" Chela gasped. "I have seen it before on other things."

At first the town believed it a trick. Father Keogh too mistrusted it. He paid a visit to Malo in the Hotel Martinez.

"You've come about the notice, Father?"

"Yes, I have. What's the meaning of it?"

"I thought I had made that clear. You may say Mass in your church again, Father."

"What will happen to us if I do?"

"You'll waste an hour or two, that's all."

"How am I to believe you?" Father Keogh asked.

"Only by accepting my word."

Their eyes met. "I accept it," Father Keogh said.

He took the news from house to house. The church was fuller than it had ever been before. Father Keogh was surprised to find it bedecked with paper streamers. But he was astonished when he beheld the statue of the Virgin of Guadelupe. A strip of red velvet had been hung about her feet and pinned to it there were a dozen tiny wooden tortoises.

It was Domingo who explained to him, "You see, Father, she cared for you—didn't she just? It was she who put the little tortoise between you and the machete no doubt about it. Clever wasn't it? But then, no one is wiser than she is—of course they should be in silver of course they should, but then the miracle came so fast we couldn't cope with it so they had to be in wood. See them, Father?" He put a straight finger under three of the small images and flipped them upwards. "They are to show her we know just how clever she was."

Father Keogh said to the congregation, "You've prayed and your prayers were answered. They have forced him to open the church."

Locha did not appear in church. Father Keogh went up to call on Don Pedro. He found Don Pedro at home to him and Doña Marian no longer indisposed.

"Well, Father?" Don Pedro greeted him. "I hear you've had some narrow escapes."

"Are you going to allow the child to come to church again?" Father Keogh asked.

"Certainly, Father. Why not?"

"I was wondering if I might touch your generosity, Don Pedro. We badly need a hospital. Would you make a donation again?"

"I am not the rich man I was," complained Don Pedro. "If you rely on my subscription only, the place will remain half-built."

"I was thinking of asking for other subscriptions."

"It's not a rich town," Don Pedro said. "I don't know where you're going to find them."

"I was thinking of asking Malo."

Locha came into the room. She was followed by a tall boy with a closely cropped head. He had only a shy smile for Father Keogh.

"Father, this is Locha's cousin Dyke Brown," introduced Doña Marian. "Dyke, what have you to say to the padre?"

Dyke held out a hand with his eyes on the floor. He mumbled, "It's nice to know you, sir."

"And Locha?" Father Keogh inquired. "What have you got to say to the padre?"

She had nothing to say. She too kept her eyes on the ground.

Don Pedro interrupted. "It's useless to ask Comachi."

"There's nothing like trying," Father Keogh smiled.

Locha looked up. "He gives money if he's asked for it nicely. Francisco told me so."

"Then I shall ask him as nicely as I know how," said Father Keogh. "Well, Don Pedro, are you going to be left behind?"

Don Pedro pointed across to his daughter. "The day she gets married I'll give it."

"For heaven's sake!" Doña Marian wailed. "Do we have to wait till then?"

Father Keogh put his hand under Locha's chin. "Never mind," he smiled. "We'll be sure of our hospital if she keeps that pretty face."

She turned and ran out of the room. Dyke Brown followed her, a slow sleepy grin on his face.

Doña Marian smoothed her dress. The hips that she stroked were rounded and slim and above her belt her breasts stood out. She smelled of Pagan Heaven. "Well, Father, if we keep my husband from those old books of his we'll never be forgiven. Would you care to have a chat with me?"

"It's most kind of you, Doña Marian, but really I ought to be going."

"Oh come now, Father, relax a little."

"No, really it's awfully good of you but I wonder if I might have a word with Francisco before I go?"

"Sure, sure," she said ringing the bell. "Is it private?"

"If you don't object."

"Why no, of course not. Go ahead." And she preceded her husband out of the room, her legs long in sheer, mesh stockings.

Don Pedro turned back from the door, "Ask Francisco for anything you want, Father."

"Thank you so much, but there's nothing."

He heard Doña Marian say to her husband, "Do you care to come up and have a chat with me, Pey?"

"My dear girl, I haven't the time."

"I'm kinda scared of Finchy. She seems to know so much. Well, I guess I'll go find those kids again. It gets pretty lonesome upstairs."

Francisco put a grin round the door. "Were you wanting some drinks on a tray, Father?"

"No, Francisco. I wanted to talk to you. Do you often take a message for Malo?" The grin disappeared and the boy stood still. "You're not the only one," Father Keogh assured him. "Do you want to take messages for him?"

Francisco shook his head. "No, but I don't carry many, Father. It's only now and then."

"I don't want you to have any trouble from him, but before you deliver a message do you think you could bring it to me?"

Francisco considered, his tongue in his cheek. "It's not that I like to help him, Father, but there are times when he catches or sends for me and then it's not wise to say no."

150

"I don't want you to say no. I want you to deliver the messages as usual but let me read them first. I'll take very good care that he doesn't find out, and, Paco, I'll *pay* you too."

The grin returned. "Very well, Father. Certainly. Yes. I am a good Catholic. I'll bring you the messages."

On his way out Father Keogh met Miss Finch. "Good morning, Miss Finch."

"Good morning, Mr. Keogh."

"How's the weather in Sheppet?"

"Well, I've not heard for some time, Mr. Keogh, but—" She broke off amazed and stared at him. "What a very extraordinary thing!"

He followed her gaze to his black serge coat. "What is it? Oh, do you mean this?" He held up the coat and examined a tiny square which had been cut out of it. "Yes, isn't it odd? I've been wondering about it myself. My housekeeper tells me it's rats but it looks much too even for rats and there's a bit gone out of my dressing gown just the same size, and a piece from the hem of my overcoat."

Miss Finch bent down to examine the square. "I hope you'll excuse my being so personal but I couldn't help remarking on it. You see I've noticed exactly the same thing in my own clothes."

"What, little bits cut out?"

"Yes, and I'm certain they *are* cut out although Josefa also says it's rats. When did you notice yours first?"

"Well, I'm sure they were all right yesterday."

"I first noticed mine some weeks ago. I puzzled and puzzled about it. No one else seems to suffer from it in the house and I can only suspect Josefa as she's in and out of my room all day."

"Well, Chela's in and out of mine, but what on earth could they do with little bits like that?"

"I'm quite at a loss, Mr. Keogh, but if you should happen to solve the mystery perhaps you'd be good enough to let me know. It's a little disturbing, isn't it?"

"If it gets any worse," he smiled at her, "it will be very disturbing indeed. We shall have to get into chain mail."

He saw Locha peeping out at him from behind the terrace wall. He called to her but she bobbed out of sight again. He went over and looked down at the shining head that crouched behind the wall. He smiled at her and said, "There's absolutely no law against a person having two friends, you know." She scrambled to her feet and ran away from him.

Chapter 27

In Porfirio's bar there was a second conference.

"Well, Old Uncle," Malo said, "do you know what I saw in the market today? On Mother Montezera's booth?" Old Uncle shook his head. "I saw dozens of small black pieces of cloth not more than the size of a peso selling at two pesos each."

"But what is the meaning, Anacleto? What are the pieces for?"

"They are to be worn about the person, Old Uncle. Round the neck, against the heart, in the pocket—to protect the faithful from people like me."

"What good can cloth do?" Vito asked. "What sort of protection is that?"

"It is *holy* cloth, ignorant one," Malo answered him. "It is cut from the clothes of the priest, and as I think he would be naked by now if all those bits had come from him, I do not doubt that Mother Montezera has chopped up her best black petticoat. That old woman deserves to get rich."

Old Uncle's face fell. "They wear bits of his clothes for luck, Anacleto? They think so highly of him?"

"They think so highly of him! I think that the only person who would smile as much as I do is the priest."

"But why, Anacleto, what has done this?"

"I let them go back to church, didn't I? He was asking them to pray just for that, so you see I have answered their prayers for him. He has given them their miracle."

"I always said we should kill him," the Jeep piped up.

"We have tried that twice, my Jeeponito." Malo pointed out. "And we've failed twice. We cannot afford to miss a third time."

Old Uncle beat the base of his glass on the long wooden table. "At last he has said it! At last, at last!" He turned round on Malo,

152

his eyes alight. "Anacleto, you'll let me be the one to do it? You know I will not fail."

"None of us will do it," Malo said.

Consternation broke out round the table.

"But, Anacleto, accidents go wrong with the priest."

"The devil looks after him," the Jeep complained.

"If we kill him outright he will win," Malo said.

"Anacleto," Old Uncle said. "I know your ways. It gives you no pleasure to kill outright, but you cannot afford to play with this one. This one could be dangerous. A cat can play with a mouse, but a man is not wise if he plays with a tiger. It is better to shoot him outright."

"The people who sent him here know that he's risking his life. They are watching from Mexico City and even from Rome. If we shot him outright he would win."

"How does a dead man win?" It was Pablo who wanted to know.

"If he knew he would win by dying, he would die," Malo said. "I know this priest. He would win, because if we murdered him he would be a martyr and we should pay the price. He would be willing to die to get rid of us. I tell you, I know this priest."

"And I tell you you love him," Vito spat, and something like jealousy showed in his eyes.

"If I love him it's just as well," said Malo. "I might underrate him otherwise. It's a good thing to know the value of someone you're going to destroy."

"And how will we destroy him?" Pablo asked. "If we're not allowed to kill him. Or does somebody answer *our* prayers?"

"He has a kind heart," Malo told them all and leaned forward on folded arms. "You know what he did when that tortoise died? He bought the child another one." He smiled at each disgusted face and waited to hear the comments.

"Now, isn't that sweet?" the Jeep inquired. "It makes you want to kiss him."

"A kind heart can also be a weak heart. It shows he's a man as well as a priest. Don't you think that's what it shows?" They looked at each other, alarm growing. "He doesn't enjoy hurting others. Rather than cause a hurt to someone else he will put ink on a tortoise's head."

Old Uncle asked with no trace of a smile in his voice, "Anacleto, how does *your* head feel?"

"It feels fine, Old Uncle. Fine."

"That is good, for it doesn't sound fine."

"No? Then get your own heads clear, my little goats. Someone who is so afraid of hurting others that his first thought when his own life has been in danger is to buy another tortoise for a child, what does that make him?"

"Nuts," said the Jeep promptly.

"Perhaps so. But what else?"

They were silent until he answered for them. "Someone who prefers to hurt himself before other people."

"You already told us that."

"And you still don't see how that can serve us?" They shook their heads in unison. "We teach him the alphabet," Malo said.

At seven o'clock in the morning Father Keogh received a note. Francisco brought it round to him.

"Come in, Francisco," Father Keogh said. "I'm not going to let you regret this."

"Ah well, Father," Francisco confessed, "I shouldn't take money for this message. He told me to bring it to you."

Father Keogh opened the note. It had only one letter printed inside it, and the letter that was printed was "H."

At eight o'clock in the morning a body was discovered at the foot of the mountain where the road turned round to climb the Hua Pass.

The body lay with the boulders and stones that had shot down the mountainside after it, with a broken neck and an upturned face. The name of the body was Silvanito Elizondo Hernandez.

Father Keogh saw the Chief of Police.

"My dear Father, you can't arrest people for murder on a letter of the alphabet."

"But I tell you he threatened me with it once, and I've told you what Father Gomez said. They worked it out in alphabetical order. Surely you're going to investigate."

"I *have* investigated it. There is nothing to suggest foul play. This is a man who works at the Pulquería. He could have been drunk, and out in the dark—it's easy to slip on those paths. We've had several necks broken before. The only thing that's odd is that he lived on the other side of the mountain. He didn't appear to have been going home. But then many men don't go home."

"This one wasn't going home because he was lured out here and thrown down the mountainside. I happen to know that he worked for Malo."

"Then why should he be killed?"

"For no other reason than that his name began with H." Father Keogh waved the note at the Jefe. "I tell you it's all started up again. This," Father Keogh said tapping the note, "is an invitation to me to get out while the going is good. They've had a couple of cracks at me and they didn't come off, for which miracles I have only God to thank, but if my interpretation is right it means that they are going to see if I've got enough courage to stand by and watch innocent people done to death on my behalf."

"And have you?" the Jefe inquired.

"I doubt it," Father Keogh said. "It takes a lot."

"More courage than if they took another crack at 'K'?"

"I came here expecting trouble. If I get it, it's nothing more than I expected. This isn't a new line of approach for them. It worked on Father Gomez. Besides, it's exactly the form of torturing that would appeal to Malo."

"I don't doubt for a moment that it's the work of Comachi. All I say is that you can't prove it on a single letter in a note. All we can do is to keep a close watch on everyone whose name begins with I."

"How many of those are there?" Father Keogh asked.

"Not many, thank God," said the Jefe. "Our only chance is to catch them red-handed. Now you can see what we're up against."

"I certainly can," said Father Keogh.

"And perhaps what Father Gomez was up against?"

"Yes, I can see that too."

"Well," said the Jefe, "I'll keep my eyes skinned."

Father Keogh thanked him and walked down the Avenida de Cortinez and into the Hotel Martinez.

Father Keogh had no idea of what he was going to say to Malo. He knew that to appeal would be useless and yet he knew that he must make the attempt.

Malo walked into the room. "How may I be of use to you, Father?"

Father Keogh pursed his lips and smiled. "That was the question I've just been putting to myself and I'm afraid I couldn't answer it."

"Oh well, sit down, Father. Let us both try. Chocolate?"

"No thank you." A cat jumped onto Malo's lap. He tickled it under the ear.

"You must have given shelter to every cat in the neighborhood, haven't you?"

"Pretty well," Malo smiled. "Cigarette?"

155

"Thank you," Father Keogh said, and took one from Malo's case. "I thought you didn't smoke yourself."

"These are just for my guests."

"That's noble," said Father Keogh. "I'm trying to cut it down."

"Yes? You have much difficulty?"

"Chiefly when I'm worried."

"And you're having such difficulty now?"

Father Keogh held up the cigarette. "This is my fourth this morning."

"Is that a lot?"

"It is when your ration's six."

"No one is to come into the lounge until I say so," Malo told a servant.

"I admire your discipline," Father Keogh said. "Nothing stops Chela popping in and out."

"She is a woman," said Malo. "Nothing can discipline women. I never have women to work for me."

Father Keogh said, "By the way, would you give a donation to my hospital fund?"

"Certainly," Malo said.

"Thank you so much. We need one badly. I believe Father Gomez made an effort once but it appears to have been dissipated."

"As you see the hospital stands half-built. Now, Father, that was not what you came here to see me about."

"No, it wasn't, but I'm afraid I am having a little difficulty in explaining. I know what it is, of course, but I'm not sure how to make you see it."

Father Keogh put his hand in his pocket. On the table he put a piece of paper. It was the crumpled letter "H."

Malo fingered it, raising his eyebrows. "I'm afraid you have me here, Father."

"It was put on my table this morning just before Hernandez was found."

"You must forgive my stupidity, Father."

"It does seem odd that so many deaths should occur in alphabetical order."

"Have such deaths occurred?"

"A for Arrieta, B for Beltran, C for Carrenza, I can't quite recall the rest, but you know them," Father Keogh said. "And G for Gomez of course. 'H' is the right letter to follow that."

"There are many deaths in Quantana, Father. People cannot live for ever. There have been deaths since you came here, I believe. Did they all follow this alphabetical order? That old woman you buried on Tuesday, what letter began her name?"

"Well," said Father Keogh, "that was 'S.' "

"Yes, Sanchez," Malo said. "That doesn't seem to have followed 'G.' "

"I'm not talking of natural deaths."

"What sort of deaths are you speaking of, then?"

"They appear to be—accidents."

In Father Keogh's eyes there was no accusation, only a sadness that might have been pity. In his voice there was only gentleness.

"These accidents trouble you, Father?"

Father Keogh sighed heavily. "Yes."

"You are too sentimental, friend."

Father Keogh lit one of his own cigarettes. He said as the smoke drifted past Malo, "Father Gomez and I shared one thing in common in our approach towards you."

"I can think of nothing that you could have in common with Father Gomez."

"He never wished for your personal downfall."

"He was sentimental," Malo said.

"It is our duty to save, not destroy. It was for that reason and that reason only that he wished to be your friend."

"You cannot offer such friendship?"

"I haven't the courage to offer it on such terms."

"I said there was nothing in common between you and the little Gomez."

Father Keogh put the letter "H" in his pocket. "Death is only a tragedy if it's unnecessary and undeserved."

There was silence until Malo answered: "It seems to me your case is simple, Father. You have only to make up your mind. It's the same in almost any battle. Either you retreat and admit that you're beaten, or you fight to the bitter end and watch innocent victims fall."

"It's a little more difficult than that."

"You've no doubt that the cause is worth it, I suppose?"

"None at all," Father Keogh replied.

"Well, then, my poor friend, I admire you but I do not envy you. You create complications yourself. You see, I never suffer from any. I put nobody's good before my own."

157

"That sounds even more disturbing," Father Keogh said.

"Well, I offered my help but you wouldn't accept it."

"Did you expect me to?" Father Keogh inquired.

"No," Malo said, "I did not, my friend." He shook his head and smiled.

Chapter 28

Victorino Ibarra, a child of eleven, was found dead on the side of the road. He had been run over. The only suspicious circumstances attached to his death were the fact that he was found several miles from his home, and that his name began with I. His mother had last seen him in the corral, and had never known him to stray before.

The Jefe checked up on every car and cart which had entered or left Quantana. But the rains made the tire marks impossible to identify and no one had witnessed the accident. The Jefe and Father Keogh were forced to give up the inquiry.

The town knew it was not an accident. It made no spoken comment to Father Keogh, but he felt a question in the uneasy silence. They continued to pray when he urged them. The church found no new recruits, but it lost none. Yet in the air he sensed a time limit. Nothing was said and nothing hinted, but there was something in the bent heads, the anxious watchful eyes, that warned him he had not long. It was as if he had built a dam of faith across their fear, but as if their fear was rising daily and at any hour their faith might break. They were willing to give it a chance, they were willing to test their trust in him, but they could not give him long. Their children, their husbands, their friends, were in danger again. He felt it outside in the air, in the quiet of the church when they knelt before him, and when he met them in the street. He could easily read his time limit in their patient warning eyes.

He felt a desperate man himself. He invited the Jefe to dine.

"Comachi gave you an alternative," the Jefe pointed out.

"Yes. 'Retreat,' " Father Keogh replied.

"Well, it is an alternative," said the Jefe. "It's you I'm thinking of, Father, as well. I find it hard to forget that there's only one letter before they get to 'K' again."

"It's that one letter in between that I can never forget," Father Keogh said.

"I don't envy you your responsibility, Father."

"If I go, someone else has to take on my task, and a pretty inheritance that would be. We can't leave the community priestless."

"To retreat doesn't actually mean that you have to leave the town. You could always accept Comachi's 'help.' "

"If I stay I'm risking physical lives. If I go I'm risking spiritual ones. If I 'retreat' I'm turning my back on everything I've told them to rely upon. I'll be in danger of destroying their faith. I can't tell them that all I've said is wrong and that it's less risky to trust Malo than put their faith in God. Don't you see, if I show defeat myself I might just as well tell them that?"

"Then you'll have to settle for Comachi's alternative and watch the innocent victims fall."

Father Keogh put his hands to his head.

"Well, Father," said the Jefe, "we're back where I started— To catch him red-handed's our only chance. Let's hope 'J' will provide us with that."

Father Keogh smiled up at him. "Callousness doesn't suit you, Jefe."

The Jefe banged his fist on the table. "Look, Father, we serve different Gods. I don't admire yours. It seems to me he's a bad policeman. Every crime you can think of goes on under his nose. If he's so all-powerful why doesn't he do something about it? He doesn't lack proof, and he doesn't lack witnesses. He's got enough evidence. A merciless liquidation is carried out under my eyes—I know who's responsible and I can't touch him. I haven't any angels on my side, and I'm not all-powerful. I have no witnesses, no evidence, and no proof. All I want is that proof—that's my God, see? Comachi isn't going to give it me, nobody else is going to give it me. If 'J' can provide it, that's okay by me."

"Only prayer could provide you with proof."

"Okay," said the Jefe. "I'll pray for 'J.' "

Father Keogh exhorted the people to pray again. He told them that

159

it is often the final weary effort that can bring about a victory. He warned them of the dangers of defeat that lay in doubt. He told them that at such a time their faith might be undergoing a deliberate test, that God had many ways of judging their sincerity.

They were co-operative. They prayed. But in their eyes he saw that his time was nearly up.

He kept himself brusquely cheerful. Only with Sam he relaxed. He spent much time with Sam. Sometimes Sam was sober, more often he was not. When he was not Father Keogh sat with him. In the small back room at the Hotel de la Costa where the air was unfresh and mosquitoes jigged in and out of the smoke, Sam lay on his back on the little iron bedstead. Sometimes he sang, sometimes he swore. Sometimes he told long, disjointed stories. They were often unintelligible, often crude, but from them Father Keogh learned something of Sam.

"Never heard of my brother? Sweet jumping Jesus, he would be pleased. He thinks everybody's heard of him. So does his wife. Jeez! What a dame! I guess she'd have helped him run me out of town. My asthma saved the three of our faces. 'What happened to that brother of yours?' they say to him—and you know they sorta cough through their noses before they say it. 'Oh, Sam has asthma,' he tells them. 'We sent him to Mexico. It's a fine place for chests.' "

There were stories of women, too, and there was a repetitive attempt to make Father Keogh drink. "Aw, come on, Mac—have yourself some fun." And sometimes he said into a silence: "Nag! Nag! Nag!"

"I'm not nagging, Sam," Father Keogh said.

"Like hell you're not nagging! Like hell you're not! Just sitting around reading that little black book with a face like a goddamn— A guy can nag without nagging, can't he? It's a hell of a way to nag."

Father Keogh closed his breviary. "Would you rather I left you, Sam?"

"No, stick around. Stick around and nag." And then there were tears, with Sam's head in his arms, or his fingers threshing in and out of his thick red hair. Father Keogh held him sometimes, and Sam cried, loud and angry sobs against him. "A son of a bitch of a canting priest! I guess I love you, Mac. Who'd have thought I'd've gone for a dog collar. Hey—Mac, didja hear that? I love you, Mac."

"Yes, I heard it. I love you too, Sam."

There were times when he was sober. "Well, I reckon if Pussyfoot ain't run out of town by all this praying, he has a right to stay here."

"Have you said a prayer for me, Sam?"

"Nope. I keep my fingers crossed."

"Don't you believe in God?"

"Sure. Somebody had to put us here—but what I can't figure out is how a guy with a reputation all that good could be *mean* enough to put us here."

But there were times when he was drunk again. "Say, Mac! Your life belt's slipped." And he collapsed on the table, laughter shaking him. "See what I mean? It's a joke—see, Mac? That back-to-front collar round your neck's a life belt slipped up from your belly. Get it?"

"It's not a bad name for it," Father Keogh smiled.

He always found comfort in Sam.

Francisco brought a message to Father Keogh. Father Keogh wrote it down and took it to the Chief of Police.

" 'The Peaceful Farm,' " read the Jefe. "Nothing more, nothing less than that. Let me see . . . it's about fifteen miles west of Los Diagos. As you know, Diagos is only a settlement, but this man Morel that the message is addressed to, is the local no-good. He's a mestizo and whether he's a half-wit or not when he's sober I wouldn't know—I've never seen him sober."

"Who lives at the farm?"

"Only the farmer and his wife. It's a tumbledown shack of a place."

"What are they called?"

"Jaime."

" 'J'!" Father Keogh exclaimed.

"Exactly," the Jefe grinned. "Well, thanks to your staff work on Francisco they may have a chance."

"But it gives no date—we don't know what he plans to do, or when!"

"No, but by keeping a constant watch on Morel and the Jaimes themselves, we might get some idea. I shouldn't be surprised if Morel wasn't our friend with the machete who made the attack on you."

"What makes you think that?"

"It's the kind of man Comachi would find most useful, a drunken half-wit who wouldn't make a good witness even if he did have the nerve to talk. He's also the kind of man who might have muffed the job and killed a tortoise."

"Yes, very possibly," Father Keogh said.

161

"Will you give me a list of the people you think you can trust, Father, and I'll give you one, and we'll see how they fit."

They exchanged lists poring over them.

"Now," said the Jefe, "there is something a little difficult. Jaime himself can't be trusted."

"Jaime! But surely—"

"As I told you, the farm is no more than a shack. I think he sows beans, and he has one or two citrus trees, but poverty is no doubt his master, and therefore—Comachi."

"But isn't it curious that he should pick on his own supporters?"

"It's not unwise, if only because it leads people to ask that very question. As you yourself pointed out, Hernandez was one of his supporters."

"Oh yes," said Father Keogh, "so he was."

"Our major difficulty is this—if we warn the man, it's ten to one he'll warn Comachi. After all, we don't know this message alludes to murder, that's purely our own surmise. It might allude to any number of things. All it says is 'The Peaceful Farm,' and all we know is that Francisco was commissioned to run it out to Morel."

"Yes, but surely we dare not risk not warning him? It might cost the man his life!"

"It might indeed, Father. On the other hand if we warn him, we might be risking other lives by throwing away the chance to catch Comachi red-handed. The good of the many, eh, Father?"

"It seems so coldblooded," Father Keogh sighed.

Later he discussed it with Sam.

"Seems like it's setting a weasel to catch a fox," Sam said. "And knowing the fox, and knowing the weasel, I don't give a darn. This Jaime's a louse."

Chapter 29

On the Corner of Executions where four citizens had stood against the wall in the revolution while a line of soldiers fired at them, Father Keogh met the doctor. The doctor looked tired and dispirited. Father Keogh said to him, "You ought to let me help you more, Don Manuel, you look absolutely worn out."

"My dear Padre, you do quite enough."

"But I could do more. As a matter of fact I was coming up to chat about it. That shop by the jai-alai court has been empty for months and months. Couldn't I take it over, and turn it into a secondary surgery? I have a rudimentary medical knowledge, and you could keep me under supervision." It was pleasant to be able to divert the thoughts from the dilapidated farm on the hill. "I could deal with minor maladies and injuries. It would take a bit of the burden off you. Anything doubtful I'd send up to you, of course."

"It sounds a good idea, Father—could you get hold of the shop?"

"I think I could rent it. I believe it belongs to Señor Sanchez."

"That's fine," said the doctor. "Would Malo stop you?"

"Not if I treated cats as well," Father Keogh smiled.

"I've just had a call to the Casa Grande."

"Oh? Who's been ill up there?" Father Keogh asked; his voice was anxious.

"The child's been running a temperature. She's off her food and has bad nightmares. She was always a nervy child."

"What is giving her nightmares?"

"Josefa, I should think. She keeps babbling about the evil eye or something. They're a superstitious lot."

The doctor was moving on. Father Keogh stopped him.

"I suppose—I know it's a ridiculous suggestion, and I'm not very well up in this sort of thing—but I'm told that even children of that age are given to conceiving violent passions for people. If she had, could it make her ill?"

"Who could she have developed a passion for? She never sees anybody outside the Casa Grande!"

"I believe Malo has made an impression on her."

"I'm not surprised. I caught Josefa threatening her that he would kidnap her if she didn't take her medicine."

"I didn't mean that sort of impression. I meant that she'd taken a fancy to him."

"Nonsense," the doctor said. "What on earth gave you that idea?"

"Well, I must say I thought it was rubbish at the time," said Father Keogh.

"If you listen to people in this place, my dear Father, you'll be a prey to white cats, vengeful spirits, and heaven knows what. If that unfortunate child suffers from nightmares, it's not surprising. D'you know the cure for the espanto?"

Father Keogh replied that he did not.

"I got it out of the child herself," said the doctor. "She told me they'd been giving her the special cure for the nightmare caused by fright. I'm not surprised that the cure increased the fright."

"What is it? I hope they didn't make her eat anything—"

"Oh, no, she sits in front of a bowl of flowers, bougainvillaea blossoms or something, but they must be red, and while she's concentrating on them, Francisco spits a mouthful of alcohol onto the back of her neck and Josefa claps a red rag over her head."

"Alcohol!" Father Keogh said. "It wouldn't be whiskey by any chance?"

"I don't know what type," said the doctor. "All I know is, that when I put a patient on iron tablets I'm quite likely to find them discarded for a snakeskin tied round the head, or a concoction of God knows what attached to the soles of the feet, and then of course the lack of recovery is put down to the little pills which are having their revenge for being disregarded."

"It doesn't make it easy," Father Keogh agreed. "Doctor, I was wondering if I might suggest that that child should come down and help me in my surgery. You know, she could wash out medicine bottles, I could teach her quite a bit about herbs, and in time I could teach her what little I know about medicine myself."

"It'll do her good," the doctor said.

He waved and hurried off.

164

When Father Keogh returned to his house Francisco was waiting. He had brought a second message. It was addressed to Morel and read, "Tell Jaime to expect visit early hours Thursday morning. Tell him unwise to resist and to see that he is alone." It was signed, "Anacleto Gonzalez Flores Comachi Alvarez."

"Well, at least there's a signature," smiled the Jefe. "Has Francisco taken it out to Morel?"

"He took it straight on after he brought it to me," Father Keogh said.

"Good. Then we'll see that Jaime isn't alone and we'll make it unwise for Comachi to resist. We'd better stand by for a shoot-up."

"It's likely to come to that, is it?" Father Keogh asked.

"Yes. It looks as if your Gran Señor is going to do the job himself this time and when he finds us there we may have to exchange a few courtesies."

"Very well," said Father Keogh. "But we'd better be up there well before time if we're going to give the man a chance."

"We?" asked the Jefe.

"We," Father Keogh replied.

"Very well," said the Jefe. "Tonight after dark I'll have a strong squad sent up. You and I will follow. We will remain in and about the farm until dawn."

"That won't give Jaime a chance to warn Malo, will it?"

"He'll be a prisoner and so will his wife," said the Jefe. "Nobody leaves the farm. Now, Father, if you're coming and—I should prefer that you didn't—"

"You want no interference." Father Keogh smiled. "I hope you're not intending to sacrifice the man."

"We shall do our utmost to save him, but if we are too previous we shall have no evidence."

"It's better to save a life than get evidence of a murder."

"I am not arguing, Father. Evidence of intended murder will suit me fine. Now perhaps it would be better if we were not seen to be conferring too often. I'll collect you tonight on my way."

It was just before midnight when the Chief of Police picked him up. The moon sat solemn in the ink-blue sky and the wind was cold out on the mountains. The Peaceful Farm lay, a small decaying building, eerie in its silhouetted loneliness under the moon.

"I'm sorry, Father," said the Jefe. "We shall have to walk. We'll have to leave the car here."

165

They left the car in the crook of a road that was heavily sheltered by trees. The walking was rough and the rain began to fall. They made a stealthy approach to the farm.

From behind an ox wagon six men appeared. They were armed and the Jefe held a brief conference with them. When he came back to Father Keogh, he handed him a gun.

"You may have to defend yourself, Father," he said. "Do you know how to use it?"

"Yes, but I don't think I'll have it, thank you. You've certainly arranged a good reception for them."

"I've been waiting for this," the Jefe said. "I've spread the men out. Come along."

They walked unannounced to the farm. Inside a woman sat, rocking herself in a chair, her eyes frightened black holes in her head. Two policemen lolled against the wall and one was smoking a corn-leaf cigarette. He put it out when he saw the Jefe.

At the table the farmer sat, glum-faced and silent. Round the light of a kerosene lamp insects buzzed and hit the walls and there was a stale smell of smoke in the room.

It caused a sharp little stab of happiness to Father Keogh when he saw how glad the woman was to see a priest. He crossed to her, taking her hand. "Try not to worry, Señora Jaime."

She sat gripping his hand, with her fingers like claws in his palm.

The Jefe sat opposite the farmer. He explained that no blame would be attached to him for his connection with Malo.

The farmer broke into sudden abusive speech. "Fool of a man, who asked you here? When Señor Anacleto finds out he will think it was me who sent for you. Then surely my life is in danger."

"What message did Morel bring you?"

"Only that Señor Anacleto would come here this night for my signature. The Señor is wanting my farm."

"Why should he want a place like this?"

"How can I tell what he wants? The Señor would not talk to me. It is a poor farm. I am lame and my woman's no good. The taxes have not been paid. If I do not pay them he wants the farm."

"What happens to you?"

"He will have work for me."

"What sort of work?"

"How do I know? The Señor does not talk to me. I am lame and my woman is old and no good."

166

"Why does he choose to interview you in the middle of the night?"

"How do I know why he chooses?"

"We believe that he is coming to kill you," the Jefe replied. "And if you give him the slightest hint that there is anyone here but yourself and your woman I shall shoot you myself."

"Dear saints! He will think I have sent for you."

The Jefe stood up. "Sit here and wait for him. The woman can go to her bed."

Father Keogh felt the woman shake. He helped her out of the chair which rocked behind her, and assisted her out of the room.

"All right," said the Jefe. "Get behind."

They crowded into the tiny recess that led off the one main room, leaving the farmer alone with his lamp.

At a quarter to two they heard horsemen. The farmer raised his sullen head and Father Keogh heard the faint click of three automatic safety catches. They heard a clear voice call out, "Halt!"

"They've all turned out," whispered the Jefe. Father Keogh turned his head and looked through the small barred window.

They made a black line in the moonlight. The Jeep's rings sent out tiny points of light like fireflies playing round his hands. Malo's face and his hands were pale blurs in the moonlight. He sat his horse lightly so that even Vito looked heavy beside him.

He dismounted alone and walked into the house. He carried a paper in his hand but he was not armed. He put the paper before the farmer and said, "Very well, Jaime. Sign."

The farmer looked up, and then looked down again. Malo tossed him a pen and said, "Sign."

Jaime wrote, the nib near his fingers in his big clumsy hand. Malo picked the paper up and addressed the small recess. "Can you breathe in there?" he asked politely. To the silence that followed he said, "It's a strange time to be out of your beds." Then he picked up the lamp leaving the farmer slouched in darkness and held it high in the little recess. It shone on the Jefe and Father Keogh and the two men with leveled automatics.

Outside there were voices. Old Uncle was shouting, "We came here on business, pig dogs."

Malo turned, and looked out through the doorway. "Your men are armed, Jefe. Mine are not. May I ask why they are being arrested?"

The Jefe stood up and moved into the room. Father Keogh followed him. The two men pushed forward. Their automatics looked snakelike in shadow form across the peeling wall.

"What do you want with this man?"

"I am taking the farm over," Malo said.

"Why do you choose to do business at this time of night? And why have you turned out in full force to collect his signature?"

"I do business at any hour to suit myself and I prefer to ride in company. Is there some law against that?"

Father Keogh picked up the document. It was an authentic deed of sale but at the bottom of it Jaime had not signed his name. He had written, "Policia."

"Well, shall we go back in company?" Malo asked. "Or did you come on foot?"

Outside the police held the heads of the bandits' horses. The Jefe made a signal to let them go. They wheeled round and rode across the rough grass. Malo put a foot in his stirrup and sat down in the saddle. He raised his hat before he cantered off.

When the Jefe slowed down his car at the Hua Pass the bandits trotted onto the road in front of him.

"They've taken a short cut," he said.

They preceded the car at a leisurely pace into Quantana paying no attention to the repeated hooting of the Jefe's horn.

Father Keogh lit a cigarette. "Well, what do you make of this? The man was expecting him to come out about the farm and apparently he did go out about the farm."

"I don't understand it yet," said the Jefe.

They understood when they reached Quantana. Francisco Jimenez was dead.

Chapter 30

The Jefe pushed forward a bottle of mescal.

Father Keogh shook his head. "I don't think I'll ever forgive myself. I never thought of him by his second name. I always said Francisco or Paco. I never remembered the 'J.'"

"Isn't that how I said they worked?" answered the Jefe. "Always a cast-iron alibi, every devil-spawned one of them, and what better alibi than a police ambush?"

"Do you think they changed plans at the very last minute? Surely Jaime's warning came too late."

"It was a blind all the time," said the Jefe. "I'd like to kick myself right round Tierra del Fuego and right back home again."

"You think the farm was legitimate business then?"

"The farm was a put-up job to get us out of town and to get themselves out of town at the same time. He knew you were intercepting Francisco's messages and he played us for suckers, that's all."

"How do you think he found out?"

"I wouldn't put it past Francisco telling Comachi himself."

"Oh surely not, Jefe. He was scared out of his wits of Malo."

"So scared that he probably thought he'd play safe. He got paid by Comachi for taking the messages, paid by you for intercepting them, and paid by Comachi again for intercepting the interception! As you say, he was scared out of his wits, and they weren't the most reliable part of him."

"It must have happened between two and three this morning then."

"Certainly. Just when Comachi and his merry boys were under the nose of the Jefe himself. I'm beginning to see how that God of yours feels." The Jefe spat and crushed out the stub of a cigar which had smoked so low that it burned his fingertips.

"Does anyone know why Francisco went out so late?"

"Josefa heard the bell ring about two o'clock at the Casa Grande. She heard Francisco go down to open it and she heard him go out. Some phony message from Comachi no doubt, though who brought it and who sent it we've no hope of finding out. He should have carried a tortoise, Father. This job wasn't mucked. Morel must have been sober this time."

"You think it was Morel again?"

"I shouldn't be surprised. It was another machete job. I cannot prove it though. His wife, his daughter and three separate neighbors all swore that he never left the house last night. Oh, by the way, Father, this was found on Francisco's body."

On the desk he put a tiny black square of cloth. Father Keogh put out a slow hand to pick it up. The Jefe looked away while he fingered it. There was no hiding Father Keogh's relief. "I've never possessed

169

a garment made of this sort of stuff in my life. It was no souvenir of me."

The Jefe took back the square. "No? Well, it's a relic of Mother Montezera then. She can't have an underskirt left."

Father Keogh left the Jefe pouring himself a great goblet of wine. He said good-by with the cup against his teeth.

Father Keogh had to visit Francisco's mother and there were arrangements to make for his funeral. He could not hurry up the street and when he met Doña Florencia he found it hard to meet her eyes. He was afraid of what he might read in them, but he was not prepared for her whispered, "Oh Father, you'll have to get out." She hurried past him before he could answer her.

When he reached his house he found Sam waiting for him. There were three bottles of beer on the table and two glasses from the bar of the Hotel de la Costa.

Father Keogh asked of him, "What did you think I drank out of, Sam? Didn't you think I possessed any glasses?"

"I wouldn't know, Mac. A guy who guzzles all that coke might have drunk out of any old thing." He poured out a glass of beer and passed it to Father Keogh. "Sit down, Mac, make yourself at home." Father Keogh sat. "Mud in your eye," said Sam.

"Mud in yours," Father Keogh replied.

"You look like you didn't sleep in weeks."

"I don't feel too bright," Father Keogh admitted.

"If you're smart, you'll take a powder."

"I can't afford to."

"You can't afford *not* to." Father Keogh raised his eyes. "Ever figure out how to spell your own name?"

"Spell it?" Father Keogh inquired.

"Ever recollect that it starts off with K?"

Father Keogh dropped his eyes to his glass. "Oh yes," he said. "We've got back to 'K.' It's nice of you, Sam, but I can't go away."

"You nearly got me praying, Mac."

"That might be worth it," Father Keogh smiled.

"I have my fingers crossed so tight I can't hold a bottle in my right hand any more."

"Sam, I feel I'm personally responsible for Francisco's death."

"You get the hell out of here, Mac. Never mind Francisco. He already got the hell out."

"It was my fault for making him bring those messages to me."

170

"If it hadn't been him it would've been somebody else. Pussyfoot ain't particular."

"It's so appalling to know that he's responsible and not have any proof."

"Yeah? We're kind of used to that feeling around here. Can't you go play life belts some place else?"

"His mother's widowed and he was her only son."

"You know what that Chela's doing? Packing for you!"

"Then she must *un*pack," Father Keogh said.

"Wanna give a nice little guy like me a bad case of the shakes? Don't they have any priests with a name starting Zee? Even Pussyfoot can't work that fast."

"The Jefe's pretty upset," Father Keogh said.

"Yeah? Too bad, ain't it? Well, I guess I thought the church didn't go for suicide, but you're committing hari-kari right this minute."

Father Keogh smiled and shook his head. He was looking down at his hands when Sam passed him and ruffled his hair. "So long, Mac."

Chapter 31

In Porfirio's bar there was a cat on Malo's knees.

Malo asked, "Have you no heads on your shoulders at all? How often must I tell you? The time has passed when a man can shoot a priest—if that man wants to live. There are other ways to kill a priest. Have you no patience?"

Vito spoke, his voice shaking. "Anacleto, this priest is dangerous. You have no idea of the power he has."

Pablo supported him. "Anacleto, if there was a fight in this town now most people would fight for the priest."

"It's true," said the Jeep, "they go on praying! They know you have no use for praying. They are laying their bets on the priest."

"Not for much longer," Malo said. "He can only promise them hell in the next life. I can give them hell in this."

"It's not hell that he promises them, Anacleto—it's heaven," Old Uncle said.

Old Uncle's face was red and so were the rims of his eyes, and the little threads that ran across his eyeballs. Before him a bottle of tequila stood, only a quarter full.

"Look, Anacleto," Pablo begged, "he doesn't have nine lives—let's have another try at him."

Their excitement grew, inspired by former triumphs:

"Look, we don't have to shoot him, Anacleto. Arrieta—you remember what happened to him?"

"Arrieta fell into his own fire," Lorenzo said. "Will I ever forget those screams? You might have been killing six geese."

"And Carranza," squeaked the Jeep. "You hit him on the head, and you leave him to lie by a pile of stones. Then you send his horse home without him, even a horseman like Carranza can be thrown."

"Then there's the road," said Vito. "Cars run along it."

"And the mountainside," sighed the Jeep. "Treacherous for anyone drunk or sober, much more for an Ingles priest."

"And then Beltran! Poor Beltran! He was drunk and gets into a fight in the dark—well, you never know what may happen."

"The priest does such a lot of work at night. He is always about. These sick calls—they take him right out to Tephuango. . . . Well, somebody could be sick. . . ?"

Old Uncle's eyes narrowed. "The devil looks after this priest."

Vito laughed out loud, his young throat throbbing. Old Uncle looked tenderly at him. "It is good to hear that boy's laugh. He laughs because Old Uncle is drunk again. He is glad because Old Uncle is drunk again. To himself he is thinking, 'This makes it good for me. It makes Anacleto angry with him. It makes the old one's head go wrong. It makes his speech a fool's. Anacleto will not trust him long. Anacleto will turn Old Uncle out, and then he will turn to me.' "

There was a silence until Malo said: "You talk like a fool tonight, old friend."

Old Uncle shook his head and kept his eyes on Vito's lowered lids. The boy's face had flushed and his mouth was sulky. "I had no such thoughts," he said.

"Yes, Vito, you had such thoughts, and I am very glad of them. It means you are jealous for Anacleto, and jealousy makes a good friend."

172

Vito muttered, "Keep your mouth shut! It's not good to see an old man drunk."

"Anacleto is the sun and the moon to that one," Pablo laughed. "You shouldn't have teased him, Old Uncle. The young are very tender in any kind of love."

"And the old are very wise in it," Old Uncle said.

Malo said: "Since when have any of you been wiser than me? If you leave the priest to me, I'll get him. If I get him—nobody else is hurt except him. Whenever you left things to me before did anyone else get hurt?" On the table Malo rolled dice. The cat crouched down, its head low, its tail twitching at the tip, its whole body still and its eyes on the dice. "Do you see, Old Uncle," Malo asked, "what patience this little cat has—and how quietly she waits? Do you see how she watches? That is because she has to see which way her prey is going to jump. When she knows that she will know which way to jump herself. Until then she will not move."

Malo put a finger behind one of the dice and jerked it sideways. The cat moved nothing but its eyes.

"You see?" Pablo said. "She has sat still so long that she hasn't the power to jump."

"A cat is a good judge, Old Uncle," Malo said. "You have something to learn from this one." He moved the dice again. The cat remained crouched in the same position.

"Well, Anacleto?" Pablo asked.

Malo flicked the dice. The cat sprang. It landed with all four paws on the dice.

Old Uncle Joaquin stood up. He poured the rest of the tequila down his throat and wiped a powerful hand across his mouth. Then he turned towards Malo. His eyes were wet and his voice was soft. "Young Vito, you have your wish."

"Sit down!" Malo ordered. "You're drunk."

Old Uncle remained standing. "I'm going to say to you, Anacleto, something I thought I should never live to say."

A wariness sat round the table as alive as the cat that had returned to sit on Malo's lap, its tail gently flogging the edge.

"What is it you have to say, old friend?"

Old Uncle leaned towards him, his hands on the table. "I am leaving you, Anacleto," he said.

Vito drew in his breath. Porfirio's mouth hung open. Lorenzo and Pablo sat staring at him. The Jeep bit through the tip of his thumbnail.

173

"After so long?" Malo asked.

"After so long," Old Uncle said.

Malo's hands lay motionless gripping the cat. The cat turned round and bit at him. "So the little piece won, Old Uncle? The little piece that belonged to the priest." Old Uncle pulled his shirt open. His neck and his chest and his stomach were bare. "I always said that it hung there still, although it was thrown away."

"He's drunk, Anacleto—pay no attention to him," Pablo said.

Malo gave him a look that silenced him.

Old Uncle answered Malo. "In a way, Anacleto, you're right." He turned to Vito again. "Well, Vito, a man must be worth his sun and moon."

Malo stood up. "Old Uncle, I'm going to put you to bed. It won't be the first time." He put an arm round the big man's shoulders.

Old Uncle flung it off. He walked with aggressive steadiness towards the door. From it he turned and said: "Remember, Vito, a man must be worth his sun and moon."

He went out of the bar with Malo calling after him: "Come back, old friend, come back!" Then he suddenly slapped his hand on the table top so that the cat jumped off and spat. "All of you—quick! Go after him—all of you! Bring him back! Do you know what that old fool has gone to do? He has gone to give his life for me. He has gone to kill the priest."

There was no sign of Old Uncle outside on the Plaza. Vito and Porfirio ran down the Avenida del Cortinez. Pablo and Lorenzo went down the Calle Jacinto. The Jeep sped along the mud alley. Vito and Porfirio caught Old Uncle up. He stood still while they took his arms.

"Yes, I am going to visit the priest. I have a favor to ask him, that's all." Then he swung up his arms and knocked Porfirio out. Vito he gripped by the shoulders so that the boy sang out in pain. "Listen my young bandido, Anacleto is something more than the sun and moon. If you love him after me, my young galante, see that you love him well." Then he put his knee in Vito's stomach and kicked his chin as he twisted on the ground.

Malo went straight to the priest's house. Chela opened the door, saw his gun, and dropped in a faint at his feet. Malo stepped over her. He found Father Keogh finishing his dinner.

Father Keogh put down his book and looked at Malo's gun. "Hallo, is this what is known as 'it'?"

Malo put the gun on the table. He said: "This is no time for joking. Has old Uncle Joaquin been here?"

174

"Not that I know of. I'll ask Chela—Why?"

"Chela is stretched on the floor."

Father Keogh sprang up. "What have you done to her?"

"Nothing. She did not like the look of me."

Father Keogh made a movement towards the door. Malo picked up the gun. "Stay here! Old Uncle may have entered the house—I'll bring the woman in." He backed out of the door and returned with Chela in his arms. "Where shall I put the fool?"

Father Keogh pushed up the horsehair sofa. Malo dropped Chela's stocky body onto it. Father Keogh went to the medicine cabinet.

"You've no business to frighten a woman like that. Why couldn't you keep your gun behind your back?"

Malo laughed. "Father, you are the most remarkable of men. The devil has sent you to tempt me."

"Well, I'm blessed," Father Keogh said. He found a bottle of smelling salts, but before he reached Chela she had revived.

"Father—the Bad One!"

"Yes, I know, it's all right," Father Keogh said, and he turned to Malo. "Can she take herself to bed?"

"Let the idiot woman take herself where she pleases, as long as she leaves us in peace. But you are to stay in this room."

Chela scuttled past them and they heard her hard steps on the stairs.

"Now then," Father Keogh said. "Just what is this all about?"

"Old Uncle is coming to kill you."

"Oughtn't that to worry me more than you?"

"If he kills you, he kills himself."

Father Keogh smiled. "I see."

"I am staying here with you until Old Uncle comes."

Father Keogh said: "I know that it isn't *really* funny—but this strikes me as rather amusing. The last person in the world that I expected to come to my rescue, was you."

"I have come to Old Uncle's rescue."

"Yes, I know, but it's still a little amusing to have you sitting here with a gun in my defense." Father Keogh's mouth was working. "Whenever I found anything inordinately funny my sister used to tell me to think of our old dog's grave. She thought that would sober me up."

"Think of it now," Malo said.

"Is he armed?"

175

"Of course."

"There's a bolt on the door."

"He would shoot it off."

"Oh dear," Father Keogh said.

Malo turned round on him angrily. Father Keogh held a handkerchief to his mouth. His shoulders were shaking.

"I fail to understand the joke, my friend."

Father Keogh said: "Yes, you really must forgive me—it's just—well, you sitting there as my bodyguard. I know it's not really funny—I must pull myself together." He put his handkerchief up to his mouth again.

"I'm glad you can laugh, my friend."

"Yes. Oh dear, oh dear . . . Is that door open?"

"I have left it open."

"Why?"

"So that he will not have to shoot off the bolt."

Father Keogh collapsed again. He recovered himself under Malo's disapproving gaze. "Look here, when he does turn up, what are we going to do with him?"

"If you are not laughing too much, my friend, I will put myself between you."

Father Keogh looked at him. He emerged from his handkerchief without a smile on his face. "You mustn't do that in case he shoots you."

"He will not shoot me."

"Oh good. May I offer you any form of refreshment? I mean, do you think you'll be here long?"

"Thank you, I want no refreshment."

"I'm afraid the Jefe will never forgive either of us. We're depriving him of evidence."

"You would do better to think of your old dog's grave again. Your eyes are still laughing, my friend."

Father Keogh stood up. "There are more sobering thoughts than that. Not the least of them being that this must be the first time you've ever stood out against murder." He moved a chair forward for Malo. "D'you play Canasta?"

"I play nothing," Malo said.

"No, perhaps not. D'you mind if I read?"

"Not at all."

Father Keogh picked up the *Summa Theologica* of Saint Thomas

Aquinas. He asked politely: "I suppose you're certain he's heading for me?"

"Certain."

Father Keogh opened his book, but could not restrain a last glance towards Malo. He was sitting on the hard chair with his eyes on the door, his gun in his long thin fingers half lightly between his knees. He was tense at every sound.

"Chela," Father Keogh reassured him. "Inclined to be heavy-footed."

Once when a street dog howled and Malo stood up with his gun leveled, Father Keogh asked: "If he's drunk, mightn't his condition overcome his ambition? He might be flat on his face somewhere."

"If he was, one of my men would have picked him up and reported to me. Or the Jefe would have put him in gaol."

"In gaol! I thought the Jefe had orders to keep his hands off your friends."

"Not Old Uncle. I do not like him to be seen lying about."

Father Keogh went back to St. Thomas Aquinas. . . .

The moon hung yellow outside the window, and all the street noises had stopped. At first they thought that the creakings were rats. Then they realized they were footsteps, deliberate but uncertain. Father Keogh raised his eyebrows. Malo nodded. Father Keogh put down his book. They both stood up. Malo moved backwards until his body covered the priest's. He kept his gun on the door. The cautious footsteps took their time. It seemed minutes before the door pushed slowly open. Old Uncle nearly filled the space. He appeared to be carrying no gun. He smiled when he saw Malo.

"You're a fool, old friend," Malo said to him. "I've told you what harm it will do to me if you try to kill the priest."

Father Keogh made an effort to come forward. Malo pushed him back roughly.

"So, Anacleto, you love this priest so much you are willing to put yourself between him and me."

Malo said: "You're coming home, my fine old fool."

Old Uncle walked steadily towards the point of Malo's gun.

"Is there still room for an altar server, Father?"

Father Keogh answered, "Yes."

Old Uncle held out a hand to Malo. "Will you shake me by the hand, Anacleto? Come! Surely you will not refuse to tell such an old friend good-by."

177

As he held out his hand he opened it. In the palm a medallion lay. It was dented and split from Old Uncle's heel. It was not for more than a few seconds that Malo looked down at it. He had just time to say, "So I was right about the little piece that—" when Old Uncle's left hand whipped round in a hook that sent Malo violently backwards, to lie unconscious at the feet of the priest.

When Father Keogh bent down to attend him, Old Uncle lunged.

There was a strength in him that a whole night of drinking had kindled into a last flare-up of a youth that had long since been dwindled away by drinking. The blows that fell on Father Keogh had the power of granite behind them, and the hands that he was trying to force away from his throat had a strength in them that was almost impossible to resist.

Chela appeared in the doorway. She screamed, and went running out of the house. They heard her raucous cries for help.

Father Keogh had Old Uncle's big fleshy hands about his throat. They rolled across the floor. They were grappling at the feet of St. Anthony of Padua when Malo opened his eyes. He shook himself, got to his feet, and made a panther spring upon them. He shouted:

"Father, get hold of his arms!"

After that, there was no sound except the thuds of their bodies against the furniture; the overturning of chairs, and the crash of the glass from St. Anthony's frame as it slid to the floor.

They had Old Uncle pinned between them, one arm each, when the Jefe came in with six men. Neither Father Keogh, Old Uncle, nor Malo had breath to speak.

"Red-handed," the Jefe grinned.

Two men forced Malo onto his feet, and whipped his hands behind his back. It took three more to pull Old Uncle up. The Jefe himself helped the priest.

"Are you hurt, Father?"

Father Keogh shook his head. One eye was swollen and his lip was cut. Malo was also bleeding from the mouth. When Father Keogh found his breath he said:

"Jefe, this wasn't Comachi's fault, he came down here to protect me."

"Whose gun is this?" the Jefe asked.

"Mine," Malo told him. "You know it's mine."

The Jefe gave the gun a kiss. "Evidence." He smiled. Then he said

178

to his men. "All right, take them away, and shoot if they try to resist."

Malo was marched towards the door. Old Uncle had to be dragged.

Father Keogh insisted, his voice urgent: "Jefe, you can't arrest Comachi. On this occasion it wouldn't be just."

"No?" said the Jefe.

"On this occasion—certainly not. He came here to *prevent* my death."

"I'm afraid it's your word against what I have seen for myself, Father. After all, I find you struggling for your life against him—"

"Not against *him*. Against Old Uncle. Comachi was fighting *for* me."

"That's not what it looked like to me, Father. I can only rely on my eyes. Chela has sworn that he came here with a gun—with *this* gun, Father."

"Charge Old Uncle, by all means. He came here to kill me, but Comachi saved my life."

"Well, well," said the Jefe, "he owes us a few."

"Yes, I know, I don't say he did it for my sake, I shouldn't be such a fool. He did it for his own and Old Uncle's sake, but in the interests of justice—"

"He will do quite a nice little stretch. For attempted murder you do quite a *nice* little stretch."

"But I tell you—"

"The woman Chela makes one witness. Myself and six men make seven more. It's your word and Comachi's against ours. I don't think Comachi's will carry much weight—as for you, the ordeal has confused you."

Father Keogh took the Jefe by the shoulders. "Jefe, you really must believe me. The man wasn't responsible this time. To arrest him for this is unjust."

The Jefe threw Malo's gun in the air. When he caught it he winked at Father Keogh, and the voice he was using was a bad imitation of Sam's. "Well, ain't that just too bad, Mac—ain't that just too bad!"

Chapter 32

Malo and Old Uncle were lodged in the gaol pending a charge of attempted murder. Nothing Father Keogh could do or say altered the Jefe's conception of the case.

On the following night Porfirio, Pablo, Lorenzo, the Jeep and Vito blasted the southern wall. It left the north side in which Malo and Old Uncle were imprisoned open to attack. The Jefe sent every available man into the fray and the rest of the town joined in.

At first when he heard the explosion Father Keogh could not collect his senses. He heard the violent blast that shook the house and a volley of rifle shots. Chela came running into his room in her nightdress, her hair down her back in an Indian pigtail. She carried a candle and shouted at him, "It's the Bad One, Father, he's broken out! Mother in Heaven, we'll all be killed!"

Father Keogh leaped out of bed. "Go round to your sister's house, Chela, at once!"

He dressed and ran up to the Plaza. The lights were all on in the town. It was almost impossible to shout above the noise. A shot whined past him cracking open a plaster wall behind his head and tiles clattered down from the roof. The ground was wet underfoot and the rain beat against him in a steady slanting stream. A mule slipped in the mud and rolled down on its rider. Father Keogh could not reach the man.

He was astonished to find himself greeted as if he were a long-awaited guest at a carnival. Men found time to embrace him and women clutched and kissed his hands. They seemed to regard the whole upheaval as a matter of personal congratulation to himself. He was bewildered at the odd mixture of gaiety that prevailed amongst the crowd. He marveled at the strange effervescence of these people; that they who had crouched for so long in the shadow of a fear of just such a turmoil should apparently welcome it in the spirit of a fiesta.

180

"Well, Father, this is a night for us, isn't it?"

"Upon my word, Father, you've worked hard for this."

"And we worked alongside you, didn't we, Father? Didn't you say that our prayers would be answered?"

He was completely nonplused. Buffeted, bruised and embraced, he fought his way towards the smoking gaol. It was some time before he gathered that the town had taken it upon itself to fight the supporters of Malo within itself.

He grabbed a man by the shoulders and shouted a question into his face. "Where is the Jefe?"

The man pointed. "He's up by the fighting, Father. They are shooting Old Uncle and the Bad One out."

Father Keogh pushed his way through to the Jefe. Now and again a cheer ran through the crowd like a ripple of wind through the grass.

"They have him! They have him!"

"Which one?"

"El Gordo." And a complacent comment that might have been within Father Keogh's own eardrum it sounded so close: "Bless the Saints, that *is* good."

He saw that the two front walls of the gaol had been blasted away and that one colonnade stood in half. Small puffs of smoke dissolved in the rain. Behind a jagged shelf that the wall made he saw the Jefe crouched in front of a group of men who fired into the steaming gaol.

Father Keogh reached his side and shouted, "Anyone injured up here?"

"One of my men got your boy friend."

"Malo?" Father Keogh asked.

"No, the big fellow. Old Uncle Joaquin."

Father Keogh screwed up his eyes and peered towards the gaol. A heavy figure lay stretched by the steps. He started to run towards it.

The Jefe caught his sleeve. "Don't be a fool, Father. You can't get through this."

Father Keogh freed his arm. A young policeman knelt behind the wall with his gun at his shoulder. The Jefe called out to him, "Cover the priest."

The policeman ran doubled up under the wall to where Father Keogh crouched. "Keep them busy if you can while I get across. I want to reach that man," said Father Keogh, and he pointed to the figure that lay by the steps.

Father Keogh edged his way round the wall. The young policeman

181

covered him, firing before them. In the half-shattered doorway of the gaol Father Keogh saw three figures. At first he could not distinguish them until Malo's light form became clear. Lorenzo and Vito were both on one knee firing at Malo's side.

Father Keogh reached Old Uncle. Bullets crossed over their heads. Old Uncle was shot through the stomach. Father Keogh realized that the dark mess that slid over his side were his bowels. Father Keogh raised his head. "Old Uncle—say an act of contrition. Say it after me." Old Uncle's eyes were raised to his face. They were oddly alive in the lights from the town. The rest of his body felt already dead. Father Keogh had never seen the whites of Old Uncle's eyes untinged by red before. "Say an act of contrition after me. Old Uncle, this time you *are* dying." Father Keogh's voice was gentle and his hand stroked the big man's head. He looked down into the eyes and saw that it was hatred that was keeping them alive. There was something else alive in them. It was fear. Father Keogh spoke to that. "You are a very brave man, Old Uncle, but you are frightened to die. I can see that. I know the reason. You are frightened of dying without absolution. Don't deny your heart. What good can it do Anacleto if you die in darkness against your faith? Don't deny God for Anacleto. Don't deny Him this last time. Don't make that final sacrifice. Die in peace. Die as you wish to die. Die in your faith."

Old Uncle's lips opened. They made a black hole in his face. He said, and it was no more than a whisper, "You will not escape Anacleto."

Father Keogh sat holding him several minutes after he was dead. He hoped that the conditional absolution which he whispered might benefit Old Uncle. He prayed that the God to whose mercy he had recommended the soul of Old Uncle—an infinite mercy, beyond the human understanding of it—might accept as a "good reference" the prayers of one who had realized that an old man had died against the directions of his own heart, rather than betray the earthly loyalties to which he felt he was bound. The Jefe crawled up to him. "Good," he said, "that's one struck off the list."

The lights were still on when the day broke. They shone faintly, faded by the sun, forgotten in the confusion that still blocked the streets.

There were a hundred and twenty minor, twenty-eight major, and three fatal casualties. Two of the last were police officers. Old Uncle was responsible for one of them, Lorenzo for the second.

In the Town Hall, Malo, Vito, Pablo, fat Porfirio and the Jeep were under guard.

Outside the Town Hall the crowd serenaded the priest.

Father Keogh and the Jefe shared a mug of coffee out of a thermos. Chela had brought it to them battling her way through the crowd. "A pathway if you please. I have to take this to the priest—Ruffian! Kiss me, would you? See what I say to your wife!"

"How does it feel to be the victor, Father?" asked the Jefe.

"I was going to ask you," smiled the priest. They were mud-spattered, damp, and their clothes were torn.

"No, I think this is your achievement, Father. There's no one who doesn't feel that."

"Call it God's achievement," Father Keogh said.

"Call it whose you like, but the fact remains that it is you who undermined his control. You've been working away at his hold on the place. A year ago they wouldn't have put up a fight like this."

"They certainly put up a fight."

"I was right to have put him in the gaol, eh, Father? If he'd been outside it those fools would never have blown it up."

"Yes, you've got your evidence."

"And you've had your prayers answered. If I was told a thousand times last night I must have been told a million times, 'The padre told us to pray and we did pray, and look at the fine results.' It started several little side fights, Father. Each one put in a claim for his own prayers."

"How has Malo taken it?"

"Comachi will never change. Isn't it odd that after every weapon we've tried against him he should be finally beaten by words?"

"By prayers," Father Keogh corrected him.

"He couldn't have realized the importance of your work against him. Only Old Uncle appears to have known that."

Father Keogh's eyes lowered. "Old Uncle knew better. He knew it was God's work."

"Oh, I don't say that Comachi underrated you personally. I think he recognized a pretty formidable foe in you. After all, he had two cracks at you. But he could never have realized to what an extent you were chipping away his influence."

"May I see him?" Father Keogh asked.

"If you like," said the Jefe. "I am sending them down under double guard to Huapan. It's the happiest day of my life."

183

Malo sat handcuffed in a whitewashed room. He had nothing to say to the priest. Father Keogh drew a chair up towards him. Two guards were armed at the door. Outside the town was singing, "She ees my leely of Laguna—she ees my leely and my rose."

It was Father Keogh himself who first taught the words to the organito. The town, in his honor, had gained a sketchy knowledge of them and serenaded him en masse, accompanied by an unrecognizable rhythm of dozens of guitars. The town was highly delighted with its tribute to him, regardless of the fact that the words were hardly applicable to his sex or his calling. It considered "She ees no girl for seeing down to dream" particularly apt. It gave itself several encores.

Father Keogh spoke quietly. He told Malo that no soul was ever lost to God, and that God could be found in every man; no soul was ever left unprotected once it found that God within itself. He told Malo that no man was ever lost if there was one friend left to trust him. He offered to be that friend. Malo made no reply to him. He had nothing to say to the voice which had beaten him.

Father Keogh was shocked by his expression. He had never seen it before on Malo's face. It was as if Malo had inherited the look in Old Uncle's dying eyes.

Chapter 33

The trial took place in Huapan. Father Keogh gave evidence on Malo's behalf. He recited the details of Old Uncle's attack and insisted that upon that one occasion Malo was innocent. The Jefe, Chela, and six policemen swore the opposite.

Lorenzo was sentenced to twenty years imprisonment. Malo's lawyer was unable to reduce the term, but Malo's own sentence, Pablo's, Vito's, Porfirio's and the Jeep's, he managed to reduce to five years. Maria found work in Huapan. She wished to live close to the gaol.

Quantana held a three-day fiesta to celebrate "the Day of the Holy Father's Winning." The band played all day. On the Plaza there was a fireworks castle. It was a magnificent construction. All the artistry of Don Timoteo had gone into the making of it. It stood nearly a hundred feet high and it was made in sections representing flowers, saints, crosses, and on the left-hand side an image of Father Keogh. Each section was timed to go off separately. It took twenty minutes before the figure of Father Keogh exploded into the air.

Father Keogh himself was baffled by the tribute. "How on earth did they do it?" he asked the Jefe. "They couldn't have run it up over-night."

The Jefe laughed at him. "Father, they must have had more faith in you than you had in yourself. You may be sure they prepared this months ago. They must have thought it on the cards that you would succeed, and saved up to be on the safe side."

Father Keogh was in danger of physical collapse. There were banquets, receptions, national dances and a rodeo. He was allowed no moment's rest. They crowded outside his house and stamped and clapped. They threw fresh flowers at him, and onto his door and the bars of his windows they tied bunches of tin flowers, garish and bright. An Indian delivered an English phrase on behalf of Tephuango, "For he issa jolla goot fella hooray." They dragged him to dances and luncheons and dinners. The Presidente shook his hand. It was an occasion of double celebration for him. His wife had given birth to a son. It bore the Presidente's weak eyes, blunt nose and indecisive chin. Father Keogh found time to go down on his knees to give thanks for these facts.

Only the dentist made no amends. Father Keogh went up to the Casa Grande and was congratulated by Don Pedro, gushed at by Doña Marian and warned by Miss Finch, "Do keep an eye on your clothes, Mr. Keogh. I feel they will be in even greater demand after this."

He was uneasy about meeting the child. He was ashamed of the feeling and asked to see her. "Is she better?" he asked Miss Finch.

"Oh, quite restored," answered Miss Finch, and he heard her calling, "Lo-cha!"

He sat in the schoolroom waiting for her. She closed the door carefully behind her and stood waiting to be addressed.

"Hallo," he said. "I hear you're better."

"Oh yes, I am, thank you."

185

"Feel well enough to come and help me in that surgery I'm going to open?"

"Yes please."

"That's good," said Father Keogh. And then, "I suppose you've heard about all this."

"How long have you sent him to prison for?"

Father Keogh defended himself. "Well, it wasn't exactly me that sent him to prison, you know—well, in a way I suppose it was—I certainly think he ought to be in prison—as a matter of fact I think he deserved much more—"

"How long has he gone to prison for?"

"Five years," Father Keogh said.

"*Five* years!"

"Yes. You see in a way he was lucky to get off with that. As I say, he deserved a good deal more." He was just preparing a short lecture in his mind upon the doubtful benefits to be derived by very young girls on falling in love with bandits of notoriously poor reputation, when he felt her arms about his neck. She hugged him and kissed his cheek. "*Five* years!" she sang. "Five years!"

"I don't think," said Father Keogh, "that I shall ever make you out."

"If he's in gaol—he'll be safe!"

At the thanksgiving service which he held on the following Sunday the congregation flowed down the steps.

He was twice as busy after the fall of Malo's regime. He found it necessary to set his alarm for four o'clock in the morning in order to recite his Office, and the books on the top of the medicine cabinet had the same markers in the same page for weeks on end.

It became a custom to dine at the Casa Grande once a week. He looked forward with quiet enthusiasm to his discussions with Don Pedro. He enjoyed the conversations with Miss Finch, but he dreaded Doña Marian. When he went up to the Casa Grande she tried to monopolize him.

Her brittle laugh made him wince mentally. He felt himself a prey to her. Whenever they met she increased her efforts to secure his interest, and he suspected that she only paid attention to her daughter for his benefit.

"Honey, do you have enough on? It's cold tonight."

"Yes thank you, mother."

"Did you write your cousin Dyke today?"

"Not yet, mother."

"Pey, do you think a little sherry would hurt your daughter? Would you like a glass, honey? Just so you don't look left out of things."

"I don't like it, thank you, mother."

Father Keogh wrote to his sister Ellen-Dora:

> . . . she shows a heavily maternal interest in the child when there's an audience but you can see by the child's response to her that she hasn't been used to such attentions. She lives in a selfish little luxurious world of her own and seems entirely content to devote her life to her own person. It's for the sake of the child I resent it so much.

Ellen-Dora wrote back:

> You seem to have taken a fancy to the brat.

His conscience nagged him incessantly about his intolerance towards Doña Marian. He regretted the letter he had written to Ellen-Dora. He felt much as he might have felt had he betrayed a confessional confidence. He felt himself treacherous for laying bare the faults of one human being before another; as if he had taken a mean advantage by placing her character on paper.

At considerable cost to himself he tried to make amends. He allowed her to monopolize him. This meant cutting short the pleasures of conversation with Don Pedro, spending less time with Miss Finch, and paying less attention to Locha. It was difficult not to resent Doña Marian for this self-imposed penance of her company. Doña Marian blossomed under it. He had so convinced her that his interest was genuine that she took frank advantage of it. "I don't know what I'd do without you, Father."

He was forced to read letters from relatives of whom he had heard interminable tales, advise on trivial business matters, check bills and explain bank statements. All the small things with which Don Pedro never bothered, fell to Father Keogh. There were times when his spirit weakened, but when such phrases as "You know I never had a real friend until I met you, Father" made retreat impossible.

Because she was unwilling to discuss her daughter or her husband with him in any respect other than flattering to herself he failed to understand her. Her loyalty towards them forbade discussion of them. She had no wish to harp on former neglects and hurts. If she

187

talked about them at all it was to shield them against him. "You know, Father, Pey might seem like a cold fish, but he's crazy about me at heart." Or, "Locha's not the demonstrative kind but you know what she told me once when she was just a little kid? She said, 'Mother, I'm glad you look so pretty.' Don't you think that's cute?"

It was always the same when she spoke of them: Don Pedro's early but treasured compliments and the few little endearments of Locha's baby days.

Father Keogh was obliged to confess to Father Lopez that at a moment when he should have striven towards Christian tolerance he had only one thought in his head: "This unbearable woman thinks of no one but herself."

He found her conversation trivial and egocentric. There was no way for him to know that never before had anyone encouraged Doña Marian to talk of the small things that mattered to herself.

He suspected that she was reveling in his companionship in the mistaken belief that she had achieved a conquest late in life. There was no way for him to know that she believed she had conquered that elusive thing, friendship, at last.

He hardly saw Locha at all at the Casa Grande. But she came down to his surgery for an hour in the afternoons. Josefa escorted her and collected her and it was the only place in which Father Keogh ever heard her laugh. He taught her all he knew and she proved an apt and enthusiastic pupil.

They shared anxieties and jokes and when he had time for it he realized that she was growing up. But he rarely had the time.

He did notice that she was appearing at the weekly dinner parties, pale and slim, and as fragile as a shell.

"Do you have an eye for a pretty dress, Father? Don't you think that one's cute?"

"I think it's lovely," Father Keogh said, and he turned an appreciative smile on her. She spoke very little at dinner parties.

Doña Marian spoke for and about her and in front of her.

"Wouldn't you think she'd like to show off a pretty dress like that outside a one-horse place like Quantana, Father? My sister wrote asking her to go to the States for six months. She'd really have fun there and lots of beaux."

"Don't take away my assistant," Father Keogh joked. "I don't know how I'd get on without her."

"Did you write your aunt about the visit, honey?"

"Yes, mother. I told her I didn't want to go."

"Can you beat that?" Doña Marian said.

In the surgery the next day Locha was waiting excitedly for him. "Well?" he smiled. "Beaten me to it." She appeared to be expecting something. "Anyone been in yet?" She shook her head. "Don't tell me Doña Florencia's headache's gone?"

"Oh no, she'll be back with it later."

He looked closely at the small smile round her mouth. "What's the matter? Have you been up to something?"

"Can't you see what's different?" He looked round the room and failed to notice any change. "What's new about Saint Anthony?"

Father Keogh walked across to the picture. Saint Anthony's feet were no longer flyblown. He no longer possessed any feet. They had been scrubbed to a sodden mass of pulp. Father Keogh's eyes widened and his mouth opened. Locha skipped to his side.

"My dear good child, what have you done to him?"

"Cleaned him up," she said gaily. "I've been meaning to do it for ages, but you've always been about."

Father Keogh licked his lips. "It's—sweet of you," he said. "I'm sure he'd be very pleased about it. Do you think perhaps we should have left the glass off a bit longer to give him a chance to dry off?"

"Oh no, it'll dry in time. He just looks as if he's stepping out of a cloud."

"Yes, doesn't he?" Father Keogh agreed.

The tone of his voice made her anxious. "You do think it's an improvement, don't you? You wouldn't rather he was covered in fly marks?"

"Oh no, no. Of course not. It's much more dignified like this." But he failed to reassure her. There were tears in her eyes. "My dear," he said, "it really was extremely kind of you. I've been meaning to have a go at him myself, but what with one thing and the other—" He gave a quick squeeze to her hand. She snatched it from his grasp and put both her arms round his neck. She clung to him, rubbing her cheek against his. Her lips were parted, and under the gentle moving pressure he felt the warm tears spread.

He said, "Locha, Locha, I've told you I'm pleased." He tried to release himself to reassure her but she only clung more closely to him. He noticed that there were two different perfumes about her. One came from her skin and one from her hair. They were both delicate but both distinct. "My dear sweet child, what more can I say?"

She held herself slightly away from him and in her breath he felt the perfumes mixed. Her eyes were searching his. She asked him sharply, "Did you really like my dress last night?"

He was startled at the question. "Of course I did. I said so, didn't I? I shouldn't have said something I didn't mean."

"What color was it?"

He flung his mind back to the candlelit table and the fragile little figure in the shadows, but all he recalled were the shadows and that Locha had made a pleasing picture amongst them. Her image obstinately refused to clarify itself. He answered her desperately, "White."

She slowly shook her head at him. She held his face a few seconds between her hands and then almost collided with Chela as she ran towards the door. Over her shoulder she said to him, "You don't have to agree with *everything* mother says."

He was still standing with a puzzled frown on his face when Chela said to him, "Father, that grocer! That Saturnino! That shop of his! Wouldn't you think he would like to make a living, but no, he's too lazy to order the things that you want him to sell."

Father Keogh interrupted her, "Chela, can you put Saint Anthony in a more prominent position, and if the Señorita asks you about him, can you possibly think of some way of saying his appearance is improved without actually telling a lie?"

Chela went to look at the picture. "Mother in Heaven! What's happened to his feet?"

"I'm afraid they're a dead loss," Father Keogh sighed.

Chela turned round to look at him. "And Mother in Heaven, what's happened to you?"

Father Keogh surveyed himself. There was a white stain on his shoulder. "What is it?" he asked.

"Powder," she said.

"Powder?"

Chela patted her cheek. "Powder off somebody's face." She began brushing it off with the flat of her hand.

"Surely she's too young to use face powder?" Father Keogh asked.

"The Señorita is growing up, Father." She picked three pale golden hairs off him and dropped them on the floor one at a time.

"She was very upset," Father Keogh said. "And I made it worse. I couldn't remember what dress she was wearing."

"You see," Chela told him. "She *is* growing up."

190

"I suppose so," Father Keogh said. "But I think the poor child gets put in the shade at the Casa Grande. I should have remembered her dress. It must be very hurtful not to be noticed at that age."

Chela repeated sternly, "She is not such a young one now, Father. I tell you, she is growing up."

Father Keogh gave his shoulder a final vigorous rub. Then he looked at Saint Anthony's missing feet and smiled at the sodden mess. "Today she seemed most *un*-grown up."

Domingo drove Father Keogh to Huapan once a week free of charge. He went to confession and once a month he visited the gaol.

Porfirio, Vito, Pablo and the Jeep refused to see him. Malo allowed him to visit him—but he never spoke.

They sat opposite each other under the bare bulb in the small cell, their shadows head to head on the wall. Malo sat upright, his legs crossed and his arms folded. During the interviews he seldom removed his eyes from Father Keogh's face. He had been adopted by the prison cat. It was nearly always to be found on his lap.

Father Keogh found a way to defeat the silence. He answered for Malo himself and he became so accustomed to it that he lost the habit of trying to extract an answer. He argued for Malo against himself and then tried to flaw the argument. Nevertheless there were moments when he nearly enraged the bandit into violent speech.

On every occasion he offered his friendship. Father Keogh said, "Well, what are your plans? Yes, of course you have plans. Don't tell me that someone like you who has all this time on his hands hasn't made plans. Oh I know what they are. To avenge yourself on me and to get back your former status. There will be no possible chance of your regaining your influence. It's broken once and for all. It was never a welcome influence, you see. Your power was an imposition and it was resented. You had no voluntary supporters in Quantana outside your own immediate organization. You can never get up again. There is no one who would benefit if you came back. You have no cause, you see, however misguided, to which the mistaken might still adhere. You had only a snowball of fear which gathered strength as you rolled it, but that's melted now. You gave no cause for loyalty. If you come back to Quantana I personally have no fears that you'll gain a single foothold. Your future depends on your state of mind. You may love Quantana, you were born there and most people love their homes. If you wish to return to it on those grounds I should welcome you, but if you wish to return to it on the possibility of reinstating yourself in your old position you are doomed before you start. I don't want you to face defeat when you come out of here. I don't want you embittered by failure. I want you to succeed in your new life and I want it to *be* a new life—devoid of vengeance and devoid of ambitions that can only bring you down again. That's why I'm talking like this and why I shall continue to talk like this while there's still a tongue left in my head. I can think of no way you can get your own back on me except by refusing my help. Incidentally, I'm looking after your cats."

To a gaoler who asked him in wonderment, "Will you never say a word to the priest?" Malo replied, "The day I speak to him again is the day I can tell him I have him beat."

Chapter 34

Malo never spoke to him, not once in the whole five years. It was three weeks before the prison sentence terminated that he finally broke the silence.

"Well, well, well," said Father Keogh. "It's a long time since I heard your voice. May I ask what has broken the spell?"

"I have something to say to you," Malo said.

Father Keogh sat back in his chair. "I must say I'm rather relieved. It's been a bit one-sided, hasn't it?" He accepted a cigarette from Malo and smiled at him over the smoke. "It was having an odd effect on me. I found myself chattering away to people without giving them time for an answer. It worked quite well with the four Señoras."

The five years had made little difference to Malo. They had added no lines to his face. It had still an impossible motionless beauty.

"I have enjoyed your visits, Father."

"I'm very glad to hear it," Father Keogh said. "There were moments when I felt unwelcome."

"Tell me something, Father. Do you feel there is very much difference between your hold on Quantana and mine?"

"I have no hold on it personally."

"You don't think that over the years the Catholic Church has achieved dominance through a snowball of fear? I threatened with guns—you threaten with purgatory and hell—I blackmailed them for peace—you blackmail them for heaven. You don't think we have something in common?"

Father Keogh said equably, "No."

"I find that curious," Malo said. "I've watched your church at work."

"You're forgetting one essential," said Father Keogh. "Our motive is different from yours. We work for charity, love and kindness. Do you really think we have something in common?"

"I've detested your church ever since I can remember—ever since I was so high in fact." He held his hand four feet from the prison floor to denote his height.

Father Keogh held out his hand and corrected him. He held it lower down. "No—so high! Father Gomez said you could hardly see over the Comandante's desk when you went to deliver his shoes."

"Ah yes—Father Gomez. He told you about that? Well, and how about Father Gomez?"

"You lowered him in his own estimation," Father Keogh said. "You lowered him in yours. I've no doubt his God will recognize his worth. I think you can give Father Gomez that he never deserted his God."

"I've hated your church because of its *tryanny!* You think that a strange thing for me? I despise it because it hides behind the names of charity, love and kindness. It grinds the souls of the millions under the jackboot of hypocrisy with its threats of spiritual extinction, its pistol points at hell. And it does it in the name of God. It terrorizes the poor, it soaks the rich, it rules entirely by fear. It is a militant political power. It is concerned only with its numbers—even its rules of procreation are enforced to keep up its strength. It is mercenary, it is ruthless, it has a history soaked in blood. It says of itself as Hitler said: 'Give me the children and I can rule the world.' It gathers to itself the humble-minded. It feeds his ignorance and it crushes him beneath its weight. He dares not disbelieve."

"Some quite brilliant minds have embraced the faith," Father Keogh pointed out.

193

"It is a monster of spiritual dictatorship. It has no charity. It sees neither to left nor to right. It sees only itself. It is bigoted to a criminal extent. It would rather have the faith of a murdering madman than the opposition of a saint. It has no love, for its love can be bought by money. It has no kindness, for it is willing to destroy. It serves as a lucky charm to the ignorant, as a reprieve for the wicked, and for the few brilliant as an escape from a truth they dare not face. Nevertheless I could be willing to accept such a faith and such a church."

"I gather," said Father Keogh, "that you would be coming in under the heading of 'reprieve.' "

"I would be willing to come into it because of you."

"And under what heading," Father Keogh asked him, "do you suppose I am in it? I'm afraid we must strike the brilliant out, so that leaves me with the reprieve or the lucky charm."

Malo stood up and walked about. "I don't know, my friend, that's what I should want to find out. I admire no women, Father, and very few men."

"You don't think that's a little 'bigoted'?"

"You are one of the men I admire. We two are much alike. I could kill you, you could also kill me. Oh, it would have to be right with your conscience first—but then that is your church."

"On the contrary," Father Keogh said, "our Faith is made up of every individual conscience. It is from those multimillion consciences that the church derives her power."

"In that rotten, money-grabbing spiritual tryanny there is something which has appealed to a man like you—I am willing to find out what that is if only you would show me. In that you have discovered my weakness, Father. In that is your chance to beat me. You have the same faults as I have, Father. You are arrogant in this faith of yours. You cannot believe it will not win. That makes you a fool— and it turns me into a fool for admiring you for it. Yours is a curious calling, Father. It puts you at the mercy of anyone who cares to take advantage of it."

"You'd have to begin by discarding one or two prejudices."

"I am willing to start where you tell me. In three weeks' time we are leaving the gaol. Pablo is going back to Yucatan, but the rest of us intend to return to Quantana."

Father Keogh asked, "Is that wise?"

194

Malo held one thin hand before him. He examined his carefully cleaned nails. "You think we shall not be welcome, Father?"

"You'll be damned unwelcome."

"You have promised to be my friend."

"Would I make up for a town full of enemies?"

"Yes."

Father Keogh stubbed out his cigarette. "You think that because I'm a priest I won't or I can't refuse you protection. You're right, because I don't wish to. You want to come back to Quantana, take advantage of my hard-won influence there, and in time restore yourself to your former position at my expense, isn't that it?"

"It's up to you," Malo said. "If you can convince me, then the answer could be—'No.'"

"I am bound to accept your challenge as genuine for your sake, not for mine. You see, I believe that if you're given the chance and you make the best of it, you cannot fail to benefit."

Chapter 35

Father Keogh received a petition from the town. It requested him to use his influence to prevent the bandits' returning to Quantana. With the exception of the dentist the whole town had signed. Father Keogh saw Don Pedro's stiff signature, Sam's forceful scrawl, and the crosses that the Indios had made beside their printed names. The Jefe and the Presidente had also signed. And he saw the calm, neat writing of Beatrice Victoria Finch. Beside the name of Mother Montezera there was a cabbalistic sign. "What's that?" Father Keogh inquired.

"It's a warning, Father," Chela told him. "The bruja sees trouble again."

Huapan, quick to pass on gossip, had sent the news that Father Keogh had approved of Malo's return. All day long he received visits of protest, from Papa Martinez to the organito.

Porfirio's wife shed tears before him. "He will beat me and drink all the money I've made while he was in prison, Father. People came into the bar when he was away, but they will not come in again. We shall need the money, I have it hidden away in a box which is buried."

Father Keogh reminded her that she owed Porfirio loyalty as his wife, and suggested that she dig up the box and lodge it with him.

He also reminded Vito's father that he had a parental as well as a Christian duty towards his son. The old man shook his head repeatedly. "I have no son. My wife has no son."

Señora Martinez, Señora Solano, Señora Fereira, and Señora Rodriguez paid him a call. Three Indios from Tephuango greeted him with a joint: "For he issa jolla goot feller." And then begged him in rapid Spanish to solicit the aid of the Almighty to visit Malo and his accomplices with sudden death upon leaving the gaol. The manager of the cinema, still without a copy of *For Whom the Bell Tolls*, said that his wife had been unable to sleep for a week upon hearing the news. Domingo and Mateo gesticulated to such an extent that Father Keogh was obliged to keep a hand round the base of his flower vase.

"Rotten fruit gets no better for storing."

"The road will be unsafe to travel again, Father. Bless the Saints! You know how it was the day we went over the cliff."

"Well, we didn't actually go over the cliff," Father Keogh pointed out.

"Yes, but another time I might not keep my head so well," Domingo said.

Doña Florencia went down on her knees.

"Get up! Get up!" said Father Keogh. "It isn't as easy as all that. You can't stop people coming back to their homes."

"It was the same with my sister in Chihuahua, Father," Chela said.

"Yes, I'm sure it was," Father Keogh said quickly.

Sam put his doleful face round the door. "Be quicker to borrow my cutthroat razor, wouldn't it, Mac?"

Then Father Keogh received a note. Someone had typed it on bright pink paper. It was signed "A well wisher," and it read:

A.B.C.D.E.F.G.H.I.J. . . . the next letter is still "K." Is it safe?

Miss Finch paid a call at his house. She was leaving Quantana. "Mr. Keogh, something is troubling me. I thought I might speak to you about it. I know how fond you are of Locha."

196

"Anything I could do for either of you will always be a pleasure, Miss Finch."

"You saw perhaps that I had attached my signature to this document asking you to use your influence to keep Mr. Comachi and his followers out of the town."

"Yes, I noticed," Father Keogh said.

"I had a particular reason for signing, Mr. Keogh."

"Oh?"

"For some time I have suspected Locha of having an unhealthy interest in this Comachi man."

Father Keogh was silent, then he said: "Miss Finch, when they're very young—girls do form attachments to colorful personalities. But now that she's—"

Miss Finch interrupted him. "When she was quite a child I found her writing his name on a piece of paper—that may seem nothing in itself, but it's a pointer. As you know, the man was on her mind to such an extent that she suffered from nightmares about him."

"I think Josefa used to frighten her with him."

"Yes, indeed, and the cures for the fright were much worse. Had I known about them I should have put a stop to them of course, but it's occurred to me lately that Locha was not frightened *of* Mr. Comachi, but *for* him."

"What's made you think that, Miss Finch?"

"Well, it concerns these nightmares again. She always dreamed that it was *you* who had harmed the man. She used to sit up in bed and say, 'Why can't he let sleeping dogs lie?' Such a quaint phrase for a child to use."

"She used to overhear her parents talk. It made her think I was the troublemaker."

"I thought nothing about it at the time. But since the news of his return she's been sleeping very badly again, and she's been behaving most strangely."

"Oh? I hadn't noticed any difference in her."

"No—well, she's occupied when she comes down to help you in the surgery of course. That's the best possible thing for her. But when she's at home, she's not herself at all. She's all on edge and very difficult. She shuts herself up for hours on end and writes."

"Are you sure it has something to do with Malo coming back?"

"Quite certain of it. When Josefa broke the news she said—you must excuse me, Mr. Keogh—she said, 'Oh, my God! I hope Father Keogh won't bait him again.' "

"I see," said Father Keogh. He lit a cigarette. "Must you leave Locha just now?"

"I'm afraid so. My sister's been widowed and needs me."

"Locha's losing a very good friend, Miss Finch. . . . And, so am I." He held out a hand and she shook it warmly.

"You will do what you can, Mr. Keogh?"

"You may rest assured that I'll do everything I can, Miss Finch."

"I'm sure you will. Good-by, and, Mr. Keogh—look after yourself."

Father Keogh went up to the Chief of Police. "Well, Jefe, I seem to be held responsible for the murderer's return to the scene of his crime."

The Jefe grinned at him. "They think you're a miracle worker, Father."

"We can't actually turn them out, can we?"

"Not unless they make a nuisance of themselves again."

"Well, there you are," said Father Keogh. "I haven't the power to keep them out even if I wanted to."

"I gather you promised them a welcome."

"I did nothing of the sort. It's my duty to do my best for them. I have a duty to these people's souls."

"You've promised to befriend Comachi, haven't you?"

"It's part of my job to befriend him."

"Rather you than me," the Jefe said. "Comachi will never change."

The following Sunday Father Keogh preached on forgiveness. There was not a rustle amongst the congregation. Old Señor Dominguez remained awake. Doña Arcelia forbore to fidget with her rosary. There were not the coughs, whispers, clearing of throats, and the occasional crying of children which had so often irritated him in the past. The congregation kept their eyes upon him in a close concentration which made him nervous. He would have welcomed the old disturbances. Once he had had to demand of Chela: "Chela, *who* brings a rattle to church?"

"Well, I think that its Doña Florencia, Father. It's to keep the baby quiet."

He found himself missing the rattle.

He spoke severely to them, his deep voice alive in the silent church. "The Jefe will tell you what I have to tell you, there's no way of keeping these men out. Their sentences have been served, and they will shortly be discharged from gaol free men. They have paid for their crimes in the eyes of earthly justice. It is not up to us to extend their punishment. It is up to us to follow the instructions of our Lord—to love and forgive our enemies, it is what He would have done, it is what He would wish us to do. We must set these men a good example. We must give them no chance to feel that there is no hope in salvation. These men are our responsibility. If we behave as they behaved what are they left to think? How are they to repent of their sins if they find themselves sinned against? We must show them the value of love and kindness, and what better way to prove it to them than by giving them a living example from which they can benefit themselves? When they see the difference that these virtues can make to their own lives, don't you think that they're going to appreciate them? What better way to teach them the words of Christ, than to show them the ways of Christ? And," Father Keogh added, forcibly clearing his throat, "if anyone resorts to any form of revenge, they will be acting against my wishes. I am holding myself responsible for the treatment these men receive, and I have every confidence they will receive good treatment. If they do not—you will be betraying my trust."

He supposed that it must be his own imagination, but he thought that the Lord's Prayer was recited with even more piety than usual. The congregation was meek when it filed out of the church.

Then he discovered that there was not so much as a single centavo in the collection plate.

"There you are, Father," Chela grumbled. "You've driven us back to beans again."

Chapter 36

When Doña Marian passed her daughter's door she thought she heard sounds of sobbing. She opened the door and looked into the room. It was dark except for the big lamp on the old Spanish bureau. In its red glow Locha's head rested on her arms.

Doña Marian ran across to her. "Why, baby—what's the matter? Tell momma all about it."

Locha shook her off. "I don't want to talk to you, mother, please."

"But, darling, that's what your mother's for. What made you unhappy, baby, tell me—maybe I can help."

"*You* couldn't possibly help." It was not meant as an insult; it was stated as a fact.

Doña Marian had shed many tears in her life, she recognized the signs. "Oh, my! You've fallen in love."

Locha asked. "Is that a crime?"

"It's only a crime if it hurts so much."

"What's it supposed to do—make you happy?"

"Why, sure!" Doña Marian smiled. "That is, if you've picked the right fellow." She was stroking her daughter's hair. The head moved abruptly away from her hand.

"I'm afraid I have *not* picked 'the right fellow.'" The American intonation was harshly exaggerated.

"Is he married?" Doña Marian asked.

"Oh, mother—please don't pry!"

"Is he married?" Doña Marian asked.

"No, he's not. He's not. He's not."

"Then why isn't he the right fellow?" She over-Anglicized the words.

"Because he's just not the right choice. You wouldn't approve of it." Locha sat up and faced Doña Marian, making ugly square lines with her mouth. "Father wouldn't approve of it—no one would approve of it. Even I don't approve of it. Is that enough for you, please?"

Doña Marian shook her head. "You're my little girl. You're unhappy, and I want to know why. You didn't tell me anything I could make head or tail of."

"Oh, you'd only think it 'cute.'"

Doña Marian continued steadily: "If something's not right, maybe I could put it right. You know you're very young, and I'm very old."

"Yes, I was waiting for that one."

"Don't you think you'll forget this man?"

Locha answered: "No."

"Then what are you going to do about it?"

"Nothing."

"That doesn't sound very satisfactory."

"It isn't—look, mother, I really don't want to hurt you, but if you stay here much longer—I shall."

"I guess I can take it," Doña Marian said.

"You wouldn't approve—you couldn't understand—so what's the good?"

"Oh, I'm not all that dumb, if you give me a chance."

"I didn't say you were dumb, mother. I said you couldn't understand."

"It comes to the same thing," Doña Marian said. "Won't you give me that chance?"

Locha opened a drawer. Out of it she took a writing pad. She put it into her mother's hands.

"For heaven's sake!" Doña Marian said. "What's this? Letters?"

"Sort of. They never get posted of course—but I find them a comfort to write. Silly, isn't it?" Doña Marian started to read. Locha interrupted her, uncomfortably. "Those references to you, mother— I'm sorry, perhaps I haven't always been fair to you—but—"

Her mother paid no attention. She was reading intently, her lips forming part of the words. When she put down the pad, her eyes were open wide on her daughter.

"Well?" Locha asked her. "How much do you disapprove?"

Doña Marian wetted her lips. "Why, honey, I just can't believe it of you. If this is who I think it is—"

"I said it wasn't a very desirable choice."

"But—but it can't be true," Doña Marian insisted. "You just couldn't fall for a man like that."

"I fell for him a long time ago, mother. Though I don't think I realized it then."

"But, darling, this is just asking for every kind of trouble there ever was." Doña Marian's hands were shaking, and the paper crackled between them. "Why, what kind of happiness do you think you're going to get out of a thing like this?"

"I thought I explained that I expected none."

"Why you must be crazy—you know what he is!"

"Naturally, but it doesn't always help."

"He doesn't know?" Doña Marian asked anxiously.

"You've read the letters. Not yet. I thought I might tell him some day, if only to see what he says."

Doña Marian stood up. "No! I won't let you do that to yourself! If I have to keep you under lock and key, I won't let you do that to yourself! Why, a man like that would crucify you—" She ignored her daughter's puzzled frown. "He'd take you for the biggest ride you'd ever known. Oh! He'd make you think it was a great big romance like you get on the movies—the handsome bandit, and the nobleman's daughter—but that's only in movies. In real life it stinks. Why, he'd murder you, honey. How *could* you love him? You have good blood in your veins. You're a de Cortinez. This guy's the scum of the earth and he acts like it. He's a killer, and he never did one decent thing in the whole of his life."

Doña Marian was flushed from her protest, and one of the sleek curls had shaken loose. When Locha put her head in the crook of her arm, the whole of her body was shaking. It was some moments before Doña Marian realized that she was laughing instead of crying. Doña Marian stood staring in outraged silence. Then she snapped: "Be still, there's no need to get hysterical!"

Locha made an effort to control herself and failed. "Oh, mother," she laughed, "poor mother."

Doña Marian shouted: "See here, it's not me that's gone crazy, it's you. Maybe I don't have grand Spanish blood in my veins, and I was never born a de Cortinez, but you're my daughter as well as your father's, and no daughter of mine is going to run around after the local thug. I'm not going to see you ruin your life."

"How will you stop me chasing Malo, mother?" Locha's voice was unsteady and her eyes still wet.

"I'm going right down to talk to the priest."

Locha was silent. She was in control of herself when she asked coldly: "You'd welcome any excuse to do that, wouldn't you, mother?"

"Father Keogh's a very good friend of mine," Doña Marian replied. "There isn't anything I couldn't talk over with him."

"So I've noticed."

They held each other's eyes a moment. Doña Marian dropped her voice. "Look, honey, you're my little girl and I love you very much but it hurts me to have you look at me that way. Father Keogh's a very intelligent man, and if he doesn't think so badly of me I can't figure out why you should."

"Do you know what Father Keogh thinks about you, mother?"

"Well, he'd hardly spend so much time with me if he didn't have a fairly good opinion of me. Don't tell me you grudge me a friend."

"You've worked hard enough for his friendship."

"How do you mean?" Doña Marian asked.

"It's not only me who's noticed it—you treat him as if he belonged to you, and I shouldn't imagine he likes it."

202

"He never gave me that impression."

"I don't suppose so, he's well brought up."

"I think you just want to hurt me because you're hurt inside yourself."

"It's got nothing to do with my inside. The whole world can see you're making a fool of yourself."

"The whole world didn't mention it."

"Oh mother, you *surely* can't think he's interested! Do you imagine he cares about all the silly things you talk to him about? Do you imagine it matters to *him* what Aunt Somebody or other writes in her letters, or the mistakes that you make in your banking account? Do you think he *likes* your kind of music, or listening to the details of your new spring outfit?"

"Perhaps if I could talk it over with you now and again I wouldn't have to bother Father Keogh."

"He sits there unable to bear it sometimes, but you just go gushing on and on and on."

"I never saw him look like he couldn't bear it."

"Well, I have, and it makes me so *ashamed* of you." She put her head back in her arms again. "There, I said I'd be bound to hurt you if you didn't go away."

Doña Marian smoothed her dress. "Well, I still think Father Keogh is a very good friend of mine, and that we do have a thing or two in common, and until he tells me different I'm going to keep right on thinking that." She held out the letters to Locha. "I wouldn't write any more of these if I was you, I'd use the time growing up."

Locha made no attempt to take them. "Show them to your boy friend, mother—for once you'll have something worth talking about."

Doña Marian kept the letters and walked out of the room.

That night Josefa had the two of them to comfort.

203

Chapter 37

Josefa went up to her room. From beneath her mattress she extracted a brown paper parcel. Round her head she wound a cotton shawl. In the cool night breeze its fringe sent a flutter of color round her face. In the back of the shawl so that it rested lightly upon her neck, she stowed the parcel.

At the door the merry-eyed Luis called after her, "Well, Josefa, and what have you stored in your rebozo tonight? Is it nylons or gloves, or what, Josefa?"

Josefa asked the devil to pay special attention to the soul of Luis and in the same breath asked the good God to forgive her. "But he deserves it that one does, most certainly he does." The moon laid a cold cloth across the mountaintops as Josefa jogged down the hill.

Mother Montezera was up when Josefa reached the little adobe house. Wrapped in a blanket she sat, cigar in mouth, and was not surprised to see Josefa. The witch found it expedient to keep late hours. Those wishing to solicit her aid in black magic always called at night.

Josefa was deferential. "I am your attentive and faithful servant who kisses your hand." She looked into the dead snake eyes and waited. The eyes remained fixed upon her. Josefa delivered her story. "The daughter of my heart has still the evil eye on her. I have seen it in the letters that made her mother cry. Her mother is foolish and left them about. The Bad One has cast a spell on the Señorita's heart. She speaks of him even in her dreams. Am I right in what I'm thinking, mother?" Josefa asked.

"You are right," Mother Montezera replied.

Josefa clasped her hands. "Is it bad?"

"It is bad."

"Is it worse than I think?"

"It is worse than you think."

Josefa crossed herself. "Will sorrow be born of it?"

"Sorrow will be born."

"Will it bring about death?"

"It will bring about death."

Josefa wept. "Mother, you must cast a spell for me. It's the daughter of my heart that's in peril. Oh dear, oh dear, oh dear!" And from the neck of her dress she brought out a tiny red bag. On the table she slapped down two pesos.

The eyes of the witch did not move, but the voice rasped out unemotionally, "Two pesos is not enough. Sorrow and death is difficult—five pesos."

"Five?" Josefa wailed. "The holy Virgin herself could tell you I'm poor."

"Sorrow and death are not easy, my daughter. It's a difficult spell to cast."

"Once before I paid five pesos for your cure that did not work. What good is the tronadora to rub on the forehead if it does not cast out the evil eye? When the Bad One first bewitched the child I paid five pesos out—you can see how it worked for she's still bewitched. Two," Josefa snapped.

"Five," replied the witch.

Josefa wailed again, "But, mother, the child of my heart is in danger."

"Five," replied Mother Montezera, and added by way of inducement, "Two for the spell and three for the meeting."

"What meeting?" Josefa asked.

"Am I a bird where I sit?" demanded Mother Montezera. "Can I fly as I am to the mountainside? This Malo turns into a cat at night, and roams the mountaintops. Can I meet him as I am? To parley with him I must change into a bird, and a bird is not safe with a cat—five pesos!"

"Two."

"Five—and four pairs of nylons," conceded Mother Montezera.

"Four pairs!" Josefa gasped. "Ave Maria Purissima!—would you see me in gaol? Where do you think I shall find four pairs? I tell you the Señorita has brains in her head, and as for her mother there are eyes in her toes. 'This pair is no good,' I said to them. 'This one has a bad little hole.' And what do they answer? 'Let me see.' And then there's a mender in Huapan now, may the devil take care of her soul, and she makes good the runs. 'Send it to Huapan,' they say to me.

I tell you it's no longer easy, mother. And where is my share on the last lot?"

"Five pesos, three pairs, and no share on the last lot."

Josefa blew out her lips. "What sort of spell will you cast?"

"The destruction of unhappy love."

Josefa was deeply impressed. "Well then, three pesos, four pairs of nylons, and no share on the last lot."

The witch agreed amiably. "Done."

Then the eyelids fell over the lifeless eyes with the click of a china doll's. Mother Montezera moved ten colored stones on the skin beside her to a curious rhythmic pattern. "After me say these words, my daughter—'The daughter of my heart's blood . . .'"

Josefa licked her lips. "The daughter of my heart's blood . . ."

"Is in mortal danger from unhappy love . . ."

"Is in mortal danger from unhappy love . . ."

"With the tongue of a bird . . ."

"With the tongue of a bird . . ."

"That has died in full song . . ."

"That has died in full song . . ."

"With the liver of a sacrifice killed in the act of love . . ."

"With the liver of a sacrifice killed in the act of love . . ."

". . . I dispel this evil."

"I dispel this evil."

"Turn around, please," requested the witch. Josefa turned round. "Now daughter, on the wall before you a mirror hangs catching the moonlight. Does it twist in the light? Does it send many fires?"

Josefa stared at it until the tears came into her eyes. "Yes, mother, it sends many fires."

"Look hard at this mirror, my daughter, for as I work the spell you will see and hear many strange things."

Josefa heard a considerable thumping. Suspicious of treachery she tried to see Mother Montezera, but the witch's reflection was not in sight. Her voice drifted on, eerie in the little dark room.

"Do you hear the song of a bird starting up with the sunrise? What do you hear in the song, my daughter? Hope and love and light? Do you hear the singer fall . . . ? Do you hear the last note of his song, my daughter? That was the note that we saved from his death. You can turn around now," said the witch. She handed Josefa a package. "The liver of a live sacrifice, and the tongue of a bird that has died in full song. Put it in any kind of liquid, coffee is best but soup will do.

206

It's the tongue that's expensive," she added, and held out her hand for the money.

Josefa counted out three pesos. Then she bobbed a little curtsey. "I am your attentive and faithful servant who kisses your hand." She unwound her rebozo, took out the parcel and placed three pairs of nylons in the witch's lap.

"When will the fourth pair come, my daughter?"

"Tomorrow, mother."

"The spell does not work until full payment is made."

Josefa hurried home, the potion secreted in her dress. It was made of crushed-up aniseed.

Chapter 38

The following morning Locha ran away.

For Father Keogh she left a note. She said that she had gone to the States to take up nursing and she requested that he would persuade Doña Marian not to go in search of her.

Father Keogh went up to the Casa Grande.

Don Pedro kept his finger in his book. "She's with my wife's people, she should be all right. In any case she's old enough to look after herself."

Father Keogh went up to see Doña Marian. She received him with her handkerchief to her nose and her eyes red. "Oh Father, thank God you came. I guess I can't bear it alone." She let the tears fall unchecked, and he watched them, wishing he felt more moved. "How could she have done this to me—this last cruel thing!"

Father Keogh said gently but pointedly, "I think we should think of *her*."

Doña Marian raised her eyes again. She smelled of whiskey. "She spoke to me the way no mother ought to hear her daughter speak. She said things I—"

"It was inconsiderate of her to leave home without telling you, but

207

Don Pedro tells me she'll be living with relatives, and nursing's a good career."

"If I thought she was just going to nurse I'd think she had some crazy idea of fun, but I'd be content for her."

"What do you think she's gone to do?"

"She's gone to wait for him."

"Wait for whom?"

Doña Marian's voice was flat. "She's in love with Malo, Father. She told me so last night."

Father Keogh sat down. He spoke evenly but he could feel his color leave his face. He thought stupidly: "I wonder why the color drains the face? I wonder where it goes?" He said to Doña Marian: "I find that a little hard to believe. How serious d'you think it might be?"

Doña Marian passed him the letters. She chipped at her nails while he read through the pad. He read in the stilted writing that was so like Don Pedro's:

> I love him. I've always loved him, and nothing and no one can help. I know he isn't meant for me, and I know I'm not allowed to love him. "Convention" has placed us apart. There are a thousand barriers that could never be broken down. Think of the scandal! Think what people would say! It doesn't bear thinking about. Sometimes I touch my own hand with my eyes closed because I must never touch him. I touch it and stroke it and put my lips against it. Sometimes I think I must be mad. I can't think when I loved him first, but I was certainly still a child. It might have been the very first time I ever saw him, but I don't think so. I think it was when I first realized that I was afraid for him. He's no business to lead the life he leads, and look so unsuitable for it. It's not fair. There should be some form of protection against it. What does it matter what he is, if he looks like that.

Father Keogh glanced up, and found Doña Marian's eyes upon him. She looked down again, chipping her nails. He read on:

> I must be a very bad girl. I would give everything I have to spend one single hour in his arms—one hour to be near him, and feel his breath, to be able to touch him in the way that I want to touch him with all my love and longing. I think I would even die for that. I miss him so—stupid isn't it to miss someone

*you've never really been as close to as all that, but I feel I belong
in those arms, I feel it's my right to be in them. Why not, when
I love him so much? Oh God, I'm so lonely outside them.*

Father Keogh looked up again. He said tenderly: "This letter's
pathetically young."

Doña Marian answered. "It gets younger yet— read on."

Father Keogh turned a page:

*Oh Malo, why must you come back? I think I could bear it
if only you'd stay away, but now it will all be the same again—
all the same terrible fears—my dreams have crept into the daytime now. He'll never change, how could he? He's made like
that. He won't make an effort to save himself—he'll run the
same risks and he'll do the same things, and nothing will warn
him and nothing will stop him. Some day it's bound to take its
toll of him. I wonder if he knows my feelings? Once I thought
he did. I wish I had someone to talk to about it, but there's only
Micky-Malo. Mother would make it seem worse hell, father
wouldn't be interested, and I can imagine the sort of reception
I could expect for a confidence like that from him! I can't stay
to watch it all happen again. You can't stay to watch someone
who—rightly or wrongly—you love so much that you can
hardly see him without wanting to fling yourself against him and
beg him——beg him!—beg him!—for what? That one hour?—
you can't stay and watch him putting his head into a noose. And
he will do that—he would always do that—he simply can't alter
himself. Sometimes I wish I was very very very old—or dead.*

Father Keogh put down the pad. Doña Marian still chipped her
nails. "Makes you feel kind of good, doesn't it? 'Mother would make
it seem worse hell'!"

"We must thank God that she's run away."

"What's to stop Malo from following her?"

"He said he was coming back here."

"It's easy enough to say."

"Surely she's too sensible to have anything to do with him permanently."

"Look, Father, she doesn't have only Pey in her, she has a bit of
me. If she's crazy for someone she'll stay crazy. I know the way she
ticks."

Father Keogh stood up and walked to the window. Below him Quantana spread. The hand that took his cigarette to his mouth was unsteady. He found himself trying to breathe a fragrance that was not part of the heavy perfume that lay in the room. He found himself drawing in his breath as if he were trying to force into his lungs a delicate pastel fragrance that had lingered on his shoulder for over a week.

"What did you say to her, Doña Marian?"

"Oh, I guess I made everything worse." She spoke bitterly and her answer inflamed him. "I said I'd report her to you."

"Report!" Father Keogh said. "That was making an ogre out of me. Didn't you offer her any advice?"

"Sure." She was puzzled by his tone. She frowned at it.

"What did she have to say?"

"She said I was making a fool of myself."

Father Keogh had to struggle with his voice. He succeeded in making it gentle. "Doña Marian, I can't disguise the fact that when I came here first, I thought Locha was very neglected."

"We have never been very close. She has all her father's reserve."

"Reserve isn't natural in a child. If a child is reserved it is forced into it. You couldn't expect her to battle her way into your busy life."

"I don't have so much to do."

"But it takes up your time. If a child finds a parent has no time for it, it is bound to fall back on itself."

Doña Marian kept her eyes on him. Her cigarette was burning very close to her fingernails.

"Oh, I know it's not always easy, Doña Marian, other interests crowd in, and however trivial they may actually be they're still of the utmost importance to ourselves. I'm not blaming you, Doña Marian." The more forcibly he chose his words, the more gently he used them. "I think I understand. A beautiful woman is used to being the center of attention, but you accuse Locha of doing 'this last cruel thing' to you. I ask you, was it cruel to run away from a home where she knew she could find no help?" Doña Marian stubbed her cigarette out. There was a little brown stain on one nail. "And in this last test when she needed you most—you admit that you shelved the responsibility once again. You said you'd 'report her' to me. Didn't it occur to you that if she failed to find understanding in you, she might despair of discovering it anywhere else?"

Doña Marian made no attempt to answer his question. She said: "I

210

guess the kid was right. You'll have to pardon me, Father, you must have found me quite a bore."

Father Keogh went down to see Sam.

"What's eating you, Mac? You look like somebody just told you you didn't have a father or something."

Father Keogh sat up at the bar. "You were quite right, Sam."

"Yeah? Well, don't take it that bad, Mac, everybody had a father some place, even if it don't quite do to call him dad out loud."

"I meant about the yen."

"Huh?"

"Locha and her yen—only you said that the next week it would be somebody else. In that you were unfortunately mistaken."

Sam banged a bottle of Coca-Cola in front of Father Keogh.

"I think I'd like something stronger, Sam."

"Hang on to that life belt, Mac! Or did you grow up at last?" He put a bottle of Vera Cruz brandy on the bar. "You don't say that kid's still hot for Pussyfoot."

"Apparently," Father Keogh said.

"Some women just don't deserve a nice clean-living sober guy like me."

"You've been better lately, haven't you, Sam?"

"Yeah! Well, I was sick to my stomach, see—I couldn't touch the stuff—but I'm right back in my old form again now."

"I'm sorry to hear it," Father Keogh said. "I was hoping you might have stayed off."

Sam gave him his lonely grin. "Was it you wrote A.A. about me?" Father Keogh nodded. "Good old Mac! I had a letter asking could they do something for me. I wrote back a fancy 'no thanks'—say, how come that kid takes a powder the minute Pussyfoot shows up? That don't sound like she's hot for him. It sounds like she's scared."

"Her mother's afraid they intend to meet. I'm worried to death," said Father Keogh, "I don't know what to do for the best."

"You're kind of crazy about that kid yourself, aren't you, Mac?"

"Good gracious no," Father Keogh said. "I'm certainly exceedingly fond of her—I feel I've brought her up, and she isn't a kid any longer."

"If she's thinking of hitting the hay with Pussyfoot, she never was no kid." Father Keogh stood up. "Hey, Mac—you didn't finish your drink."

"I don't feel I want it now, Sam."

Sam finished the brandy in one gulp. "Seems like everybody's nuts around here." Before Father Keogh reached the door he called out, "Talking of hitting the hay, where's Pussyfoot going to lay that handsome head of his? Or did you forget that Papa Martinez got back his hotel, and Pussyfoot don't own nothing around here no more?"

"Oh, he'll find somewhere," Father Keogh said.

"Yeah? Who's going to give that louse bug-room?"

Father Keogh waved to him and blinked in the bright sunlight outside the bar. He was thinking of neither Sam nor Malo, he had remembered something. He had remembered the color of Locha's dress.

Chapter 39

They came back at eleven o'clock in the morning. They came in a car from Huapan. They drove straight to Porfirio's bar.

At half past one Malo presented himself to Father Keogh. He put his suitcase on the floor and sat down. Father Keogh was eating his lunch.

"Don't tell me you've come for religious instruction already."

"I've come for accommodation." Father Keogh pushed his plate aside. "I'm not troubling you for nothing. I can't get in anywhere else."

"Have you any money?"

"Not much. Most of it went on the trial, Father. I needed good lawyers to see that there were no more trumped-up charges against me —they might have thought up one that was fatal!—and then we did not want to spend our lives in prison—well, you know what can happen to money when you have to smooth your path. No, I have not much left—and what I have will not buy me somewhere to sleep."

"Have you been to the Jefe?"

"Yes."

"Well?"

"He suggested I leave the town."

212

"Where are the others going to sleep?"

"Porfirio's."

"Why isn't there room for you?"

"Because they didn't build it large enough. Maria has gone there too. She's sharing a bed with Porfirio's wife. Porfirio's wife has turned into a great lady, Father. She does not care for a man like me and a woman like Maria to share the same bed in her house. And like that, you see, it keeps Porfirio out of bed with her. There was a time when he could have beaten her, but I understand no longer. It has something to do with money." He lifted his eyes to the priest.

Father Keogh asked him carefully, "Then you are still anxious to stay in Quantana?"

Chela burst into the room. "Father, what are you thinking of? You must never allow him here."

"Chela," Father Keogh said. "I thought we'd reached a gentleman's agreement by which you would no longer listen at doors."

"This is something so bad I could hear in the kitchen."

Malo said to Father Keogh, "I believed that there was a tradition amongst your calling, Father, to shelter the homeless and lost."

"There is," Father Keogh told him. "But I am afraid I have no room."

"And if we had we wouldn't give it to you," Chela spat.

"I know this house," Malo reminded them. "I had an old friend who lived here once. You remember Father Gomez? There is room for a bed in the kitchen."

"My kitchen!" Chela screamed. "I would rather see it filled up with crocodiles."

"You wouldn't be very comfortable," Father Keogh pointed out.

"I'm not asking for comfort. I'm asking for a bed. I will bring a mattress from Porfirio's and put it in the kitchen. I shan't trouble you during the day."

Chela turned on Father Keogh.

"Chela," he warned her, before she could speak. "I don't think I want to hear anything about one of your sisters."

"Listen, Father, I haven't a sister as foolish as this. If I had she would be dead, for she'd be too foolish to breathe. Here is our chance to get rid of him, Father. Now you can send him away. Didn't you tell them in church there was no way to do it? Talk, talk, talk and your dinner burning—well, now you have a way, if you turn him out he has nowhere to go—he will have to leave the place."

"Where would you go if you left Quantana?" Father Keogh asked him.

Malo said casually, "Maybe the States."

"There you are, Father," Chela crowed, "he can't sleep in the kitchen, it's not nice for the food. Let him go off to the States."

Father Keogh asked him carefully, "Why would you choose the States?"

Malo spread out his hands. "Where else if you want to leave Mexico?"

"You have no special friends there?"

"I have no friends at all, Father—that is, unless I can still count on you."

"You can still count on me."

"You remember our bargain then?"

"I remember *your* bargain."

"And does it still hold good?"

"If you keep your side of it."

"My side is up to you. I thought we understood that."

"Very well," said Father Keogh, "you may put a mattress in the kitchen. But I want you to spend as little time as possible here. You'll have to fend for yourself as best you can, I won't have you bothering Chela."

"I will not bother Chela."

Chela went wailing out of the house. "Dear God, the Father's brains have left him! Mother in Heaven, we'll all be killed."

Chapter 40

Few people went into Porfirio's bar except the occasional stranger who had not been warned, and the tourists who came out of curiosity.

When the tourists went out they drank down their disgust.

"Still," said Porfirio, "it brings in the money."

"Money!" the Jeep said. "That's all you think about."

"And why wouldn't I?" Porfirio demanded. "Do you think of it for me? Does Vito? Does Anacleto?"

Porfirio overcharged the tourists, and now and again induced his wife to part with a portion of her savings. But that was becoming increasingly difficult. She never complained but her eye was sour. Sometimes he challenged it when his own were bloodshot. "Well, woman— what do you expect? Can a man make himself money in prison?"

"There need never have been any prison."

It was hard to remember that he was no longer in a position to beat her. He spluttered at her. She blinked when the moisture hit her cheek. She was owl-faced and dull-eyed, and she hated him.

"The Bad One is finished," she said.

"Finished?" he spat at her. "Finished, old fool?" And because he half believed her, he laid about him. She stood beyond his reach.

"He would do better to do like the priest says, and go. He's as good as a dead man here."

"The priest!" laughed Porfirio. "Ah, yes now—the priest. It's a good thing he says that, it shows he's afraid. That shows we're not dead."

He lurched forward to strike her, but the table edge hit into his stomach. He grunted and put a hand up to his face. She had gone when he opened his eyes again. He made a grimace at the thought of her stuffy black figure, and the thin black hair that parted to show a yellow scalp. He could smell the heavy odor of sour perspiration that preceded her into a room and remained behind. He hated her. He feared that she might have been right about Malo.

It was the same with young Vito. Sometimes he met his father. Usually the old man passed by the boy, but sometimes he broke his rule.

"Well, Vito, your mother is sick with a fever."

"Too bad," Vito said, and he narrowed his eyes. It always enraged his father.

"Listen, young half-wit, you're wasting your time. What's the good of staying with him?" When he roused no reply Don Timoteo said: "Listen, Vito, I have two hundred pesos—two hundred, saved up in a box that your mother has hidden. I said to her, 'It would be better if we put so much money in careful hands.' I wanted her to put it into the Banco de Comercio, where I have such a good friend in Don Miguel, 'but no,' she said, 'if the Bad One is ever in power again what

215

good is a banco for hiding your money?' Your mother is silly like that. She does not remember that those days are passed. So she hides it herself. But she would show me the place, I know she would. And, Vito, that money's for you—You take it, and get somewhere fresh. Take it to make a new life for yourself." The old man was pleading but the pleading soon stopped when he looked at the boy's narrowed eyes. "You're no son of your mother, and no son of mine. The devil himself must have crept in between us that night. Well, then, go on then—be with him, stay with him, rot by his side! He's a dead man, he's finished!"

Vito watched the old man walk away and hated him. How if his father were right?

There was no one to mind about the Jeep.

They had nothing to do but quarrel or bolster each other up. They argued backwards and forwards amongst themselves.

Porfirio's wife paid scanty attention to the bar. Cockroaches lay dead under the benches, and insects in small heaps round the lights. The dust crept unchecked across the floor, glasses left sticky rings along the table tops, and on the walls there were patches from greasy heads. There was a smell that crept in from the patio that savored of goats and pigs.

Her money was kept by Father Keogh. If Porfirio asked her for any she took the request to the priest. Sometimes she came back with half the amount he had asked her for, but if he had made an attempt to beat her she came back with no money, and Father Keogh.

The others made fun of him for it.

"What fat man is afraid of his wife?" Vito asked of the Jeep. And the Jeep answered puzzled: "Is there a fat man afraid of his wife?"

Porfirio's eyes bulged. He shouted at them: "Listen, what sort of a place d'you think I'm running here? Twenty pesos you owe me, and you—twenty-five! Can I feed you for nothing? And how about drink?"

"It's your money, isn't it?" Vito inquired. "Why not get it back from the priest?"

"It *was* my money," Porfirio fumed. "That old fool of mine made it a *gift* to the priest. 'Father,' she tells him, 'this money I *give* you. But my husband squanders every cent he has on his friends, so you will have to be very good to me out of it.' "

"She is not such an old fool," said the Jeep.

"She *is* an old fool!" Porfirio screamed. "It is the priest who has lent her these brains."

216

"Well, it's a fine thing," Vito answered, "if we are to sit here and starve to death."

"You are *not* starving!" Porfirio roared at him. "You are living on me, on my flesh!" And he pummeled his heavy chest.

"We will pay what we owe you, greedy one," answered the Jeep, and he grinned hard behind his cigar smoke.

"It's a fine thing," Vito repeated mildly, "if we are to sit here and starve to death while Anacleto talks church with the priest."

"He should think of us more," said the Jeep, and his weak voice was petulant. "When people stand by you, you ought to think of them."

"What sort of revenge is it?" Vito demanded. "To sit nose to nose with a priest, and argue church matters. Can arguments injure the priest?"

At the foot of the stairs Maria stood. They took no notice of her.

"Old Uncle is better dead. He could never stand by and watch this."

"Why should it be worse for Old Uncle to watch?" Vito asked.

"Still jealous?" the Jeep inquired. Then he sighed and informed them, "I have a nice aunt in Oaxoca, she was always fond of me."

"My father would pay me to go," Vito said.

"And as for me," Porfirio said, "I could sell up this hellhole and make a new life."

"Then someone should tell him."

"Yes, somebody should."

Maria listened sullenly. "He'll be great again," she said.

If they heard her they paid no attention.

"Ah," said Porfirio, "it makes a man vomit, when you remember how he was."

"He'll be great again," Maria said.

Porfirio slapped a bottle of pulque across the bar. "Well, and whose fault is it, might one inquire? It's nobody's fault but Anacleto's. Half the night they are talking, those two, Chela says. Anacleto's gone out of his head."

"He'll have his revenge," Maria said. "He's promised to have it, hasn't he? Did you ever hear him make a promise he did not keep?"

"A fine way to keep it," Vito sneered. "Chat, chat, chat, half the night with a priest."

Maria's lazy anger flared. "Cowards!" she said to them. "Growling like bears, not one of you speaks to his face."

217

"Yes, well, we just said it was time to remind him. The Jeep was just saying it's time."

"Me?" squeaked the Jeep. "All I said was . . ."

"What are you frightened of?" Maria inquired. "That he will get back—or that he won't get back? Which are you frightened of most?"

They all shouted at once, and were silent at once. They had seen Malo come into the bar.

He stood with his arms at his sides, and looked from one to the other. Nobody cared to speak. It was Maria who said at last: "I have told them you'll have your revenge. Oh yes, they have plenty to say to you as long as you turn your back. You are wasting your time here, you are wasting theirs, you've gone soft in the head, you are 'in' with the priest."

"It's all very well for you, Anacleto," Porfirio whined. "But I have to feed these pigs."

Malo walked past them and went up the stairs, Maria turned and followed him.

Vito went out of the bar. He went straight to his father's house. He said: "Father, I'm going away." His father wept. His mother wept. They kissed him and gave him the money.

Vito went back to the bar again. He put the two hundred pesos in front of Porfirio. "There you are, greedy one, there is your pay. Now let's hear no more out of you for a bit."

Chapter 41

Father Keogh felt weary throughout every bone in his body. Since Malo's return he had spent the busiest three months of his life in Quantana. But in the everyday race against lack of time, he found many minutes to wonder about Locha. He had received no letter from her. Neither had Doña Marian. Don Pedro had received one postcard. "All well. Hope you are. Give my love to Fr. Keogh."

He rarely dined at the Casa Grande. First one and then another duty

218

had deprived him of Thursday evenings. He found himself glad to have Thursday evenings filled. He no longer found in Don Pedro an intellectual stimulus. He saw in him a man who acquired knowledge greedily and selfishly with no desire to impart it, or to create from it, who sought to please no one but himself, and who had not lifted a finger from the page of his book to prevent his only child from leaving home.

He felt ill at ease with Doña Marian. To Ellen-Dora he wrote, "I was obliged to tell her a few home truths. I fear she didn't like them much."

Ellen-Dora wrote back, "Are you sure they were truths? She sounds somewhat 'hard done by' to me. It's the brat and the father I don't like the sound of—they both seem impossible prigs. I'm afraid I'm on 'mum's' side! If I had a husband and daughter like that I'd shoot the pair of them."

Doña Marian was brightly courteous to him, and avoided him whenever possible.

Father Keogh said to Sam, "You'd think she'd be lonely spending so much time on her own."

"She has a glass and a bottle, hasn't she? That's when three's company, Mac."

The Bishop paid his five-yearly visit to the diocese. He received only one form of complaint in connection with Father Keogh. The town protested en bloc against his harboring of Malo. Some called him foolish, and some saintly. But there was not one who did not genuinely fear for him. There was also no one who did not genuinely object to Malo's appearance at Mass.

Chela explained to the Bishop, "To see that one kneeling in church, my Lord, is like seeing the devil let into heaven. Heaven is somewhere for nice people. There is hell for the other sort."

The Bishop was also afraid for Father Keogh. His short acquaintance with Malo unnerved him. He blew his nose into a spotless handkerchief, and made no pretenses. "That young man puts the wind up me. He seems to have a very high opinion of you though. I gather you're a loss to the underworld. My dear Father," he said when Father Keogh laughed, "forgive me if I appear to be flippant, but I get the impression of a snake charmer. It seems to me that the minute the music stops, that young man will strike."

"I must keep the music going," Father Keogh smiled.

The Bishop looked closely at him. "Father, I appreciate what you are trying to do. I admire your courage, and in the circumstances I grant you that it is extremely difficult to see what else you could have done. But are you sure of your own reasons?"

"I believe," said Father Keogh simply, "that *any* risk is worth the salvation of this man's soul."

"Are you certain that you're not in danger of entering into combat for the sake of it? Not pitting your strength against a personal foe? It would be very understandable and a great temptation. You're very young, you're enjoying this fight."

"Shouldn't we glory in fighting the devil?"

"Not in order to achieve a personal victory. There are times when our faith is so much a part of us that it can be confused with our own confidence, when it might be a greater service to God to sacrifice that conquest."

"Does your Lordship think that this is one of those cases?"

The Bishop took a bag from his pocket. It was filled with salted almonds. He put three on the table in front of him. "The devil has many disguises. He can hide in our own beliefs—and dress up as our own conscience. Not the least of those disguises is justifiable confidence. If it were not justifiable it would be no disguise. If the devil appeared as pride, or as a human love of power and personal achievement, we should see straight through him." The Bishop smiled. "I am merely warning you that there are motives within ourselves that we may not be aware of—providing we possess the qualities of integrity which you possess."

"Your Lordship, it's true I might have made it awkward for Comachi if I hadn't taken him into my house. But of course it's not a bad thing to have him under my nose, and besides—he has expressed himself willing to embrace the faith if I am able to convince him of it. He attends Mass regularly, he reads all the pious literature I can give him. He pays the deepest attention to any instruction, and I give him plenty, what more can I demand of him?"

"But is he benefiting by it?"

"That's difficult to say, my Lord. As yet he's not convinced. But so far he's caused no trouble to me, or to anyone else. So I suppose one might hope that he is."

"But he has also expressed himself equally willing to take advantage of you if you fail. Of using it as a weapon against you. And that means against the rest of the community which is also entitled to your consideration and protection."

"In his own words, your Lordship, it's 'up to me.' "

"Do you think you will succeed, Father?"

"I do, my Lord."

"Why?" Father Keogh's eyes widened. The Bishop repeated, "Why?"

"Because Comachi is willing to listen and I believe that anyone who listens cannot fail to be convinced."

"Is that due to confidence in your faith, or confidence in yourself?"

"It is confidence in my faith."

"I believe you," the Bishop said. "But if you failed, Father, the blow to a man of your worth would be so much more bitter if you discovered your motives to be other than what you supposed them to be. I was simply trying to spare you that, and give you a chance to retreat."

Father Keogh could not conceal his astonishment. "Is your Lordship suggesting that it might be my duty to retreat?"

The Bishop met his eyes. "You remember Father Gomez?"

"Often," Father Keogh said.

"Father Gomez may well have been ignoble. But he knew nobility. He forfeited it. He scourged and chastised himself because of it. He died a broken man because of it. He condemned himself to purgatory because of it. He brought that condemnation on himself because he put the welfare of others before his own—even in his afterlife. Could that not be construed as a sacrifice?"

"I couldn't compete with a courage like that."

"Whichever way you look at courage, it remains courage. The church has need of men like you. You have a great future in her service. You have accomplished your mission here—you have been entirely successful. Isn't this the time to go elsewhere and apply those qualities afresh?"

"That is hardly for me to decide, my Lord."

The Bishop smiled. "No, perhaps not."

Chapter 42

Except for their discussions Father Keogh need not have known that Malo was in the house. The mattress was stowed away by half past six in the morning, and Chela was usually well behind her bolted and barricaded door before his return at night.

He made no noise and was scrupulously tidy. The only complaint which Chela could find to make about him was in connection with the stray cats who followed him back to the house; a small undisciplined and bedraggled army which lacked everything but dignity.

The cats never remained in the house without him. They slept round the dying fire at night; when he left for Porfirio's bar in the morning they stretched their limbs, washed themselves, ate the breakfast which Father Keogh insisted that Chela should leave for them, and walked sedately after Malo. At nighttime they followed him back, but they were always several minutes after him.

"Where's your escort?" Father Keogh asked.

"Ah, Father, a cat is like a woman. She will not openly follow a man. She will start off in another direction, and turn up in the same place as him."

Father Keogh waited up for Malo at nights. He challenged himself to hear the footsteps. He set himself the task every night, but he never heard Malo come in.

When Malo entered the room he looked up at the ceiling. "Is the old one protected against me yet?"

Father Keogh chuckled. "Judging from the row that went on, I should think she's put every piece of furniture that she could find against her door."

Malo sat down. "It was bad again in the bar tonight. I went for a walk on the mountain."

Father Keogh was sympathetic. "Tourists? They even come up to the church."

222

"They wanted to see the place where old Uncle Joaquin died."

The lamp burned between them, and the room smelled of kerosene. One of the old green curtains that covered the medicine cabinet had faded into a dull yellow. The big crucifix cut a stark black shadow into the whitewashed wall. The tiled floor felt cold underfoot at night, and there were dead beetles round the rim of the lamp.

They sat opposite each other, their arms on the table. Father Keogh poured Malo out a cup of chocolate.

"You could tell me something, Father. . . . That night Old Uncle died, you were there when he breathed his last, how did he die?"

"He was brave but unrepentant, I'm afraid."

"I thought perhaps at the very end he might have gone back to this." Malo dropped something onto the table. It was the medallion Old Uncle had stamped upon.

Father Keogh shook his head. Malo put the medallion back into his pocket. Father Keogh never failed to be impressed by the beauty of Malo. He was fascinated by the expressionless Indian face, and sometimes before he slept at night, he saw the straight features behind his own closed lids. Sometimes it was impossible to believe that such a face could be connected with evil.

They were disturbed by a heavy rumbling noise upstairs. They both raised their eyes to the ceiling.

"Here comes the checkup," Father Keogh smiled.

"Why does she block herself in to begin with when she knows that she has to come down again?" Malo demanded irritably.

"She feels it's her duty to see that I'm safe," Father Keogh replied.

They heard Chela's feet on the stairs. They looked at each other, their eyes amused. Then the door opened inch by inch. Father Keogh called out, "It's all right, Chela, I'm still alive."

Chela complained through the crack, "If a man wants to die then there's no one can stop him."

The door closed behind her and she climbed the stairs. They heard the furniture dragged to the door again.

"Poor Chela." Father Keogh sighed. "We've run her out of sisters. More chocolate? Oh, I'm sorry there doesn't appear to be any."

"We could ask for some fresh," Malo said.

"What, and go through that racket again?" Father Keogh raised his eyes to the ceiling. "I'd rather make it myself."

"I will get it," Malo said. "I make the best chocolate in Mexico."

"Everyone claims to do that."

When Malo returned with the chocolate, Father Keogh asked: "Is your escort in?"

"Asleep by the fire," Malo said. "Well, can anyone challenge my claim?"

Father Keogh tasted the chocolate. He smiled and said: "Frankly, Chela can."

"That is loyalty speaking," Malo said. "We were speaking of loyalty just now, Old Uncle was thinking of me?"

"He was assuring me that you would have your revenge however long it took you."

"It's possible," Malo said. "If the opportunity presents itself."

"You know sometimes," Father Keogh confessed, "I find it quite uncanny sitting here with you."

"You would hardly be human otherwise."

"The other night I dreamt that you were a skeleton. You had a prayer book in your hand, and nothing would make you give it up. Your fingers were clenched round it. I was trying to prize them open, but I couldn't. I had no strength."

"Why were you trying to take it from me?"

"I don't know. It's silly, isn't it, when I spend my time forcing it on you."

"Perhaps it's what you really feel. It's the prayer book and not the skeleton that might mean the symbol of death."

Father Keogh put the base of his palm to his forehead and thumped it several times. "It does seem a little nightmarish. We sit here drinking Chela's chocolate—"

"We sit here drinking *my* chocolate—"

"We sit here drinking *your* chocolate—"

"You see," Malo told him triumphantly, "you could not tell the difference. It was only loyalty speaking."

"Well, whosoever it was," said Father Keogh, "we sit here drinking it. We sit here apparently at peace with one another and yet if the opportunity presents itself you wouldn't hesitate to kill me. It makes you hard to understand."

"That's because you suffer from the halo habit, friend. It is something you are taught to strive towards for yourself and for other people. But a halo has no place on the head of a bad man. It can never be made to fit."

"That still doesn't account," Father Keogh argued, "for your love of inflicting pain."

"It is the final celebration of power within oneself. If you cannot understand that you are still judging me by the wrong standards. You are judging me by your own. You should judge me by mine."

"But yours are the wrong ones, Anacleto."

"Father, what is the best in your life? You are a Mass priest. I understand the Mass now you've explained it to me."

"The ignorant call it mumbo jumbo, that's why I had to make it clear."

Malo said, "I follow every sign that you make. I know why every movement is made."

"You make me quite nervous," Father Keogh complained. "What with Doña Florencia's rattle and old Benito's cough it's a wonder I get through it at all."

"You told me you were *always* nervous."

"It's a nerve-racking experience," Father Keogh said, "for those who put their soul into it. I don't doubt there are people who rattle through it purely as part of a job, but I should think there are very few. It would have no meaning for them. The priesthood offers a poor career to people who approach it like that. They could do much better much quicker in almost any other profession on earth."

"The moment when you take the wine—that for you is something so full of pleasure and so full of pain, that it's something you cannot describe?"

"I am taking the body and blood of Christ into my mouth. There is no description for a feeling like that."

"There is no description for the feeling that I have when I celebrate power within myself."

"You are comparing sadism with a moment of spiritual ecstasy, Anacleto."

"I am comparing two moments of ecstasy, my friend."

In the big room where the windows were closed against the noise of the traffic the Bishop was drafting a lengthy letter to ask the advice of the extremely aged and patriarchal Bishop who, many years before, had ordained him to the priesthood.

> . . . *and Your Lordship will appreciate that a man of Father Keogh's considerable worth has no alternative but to accept this line of duty. Indeed it is not possible to present him with an alternative in view of the circumstances. That they are likely to*

endanger his personal safety influences him not in the least. But rightly or wrongly I am gravely concerned for him and for the consequences for which he might find himself held responsible. I endeavored to present him with a possibility within the limits of his conscience, of withdrawing from his responsibilities. In the very nature of the case this was all I found myself able to do. But such is his sincerity and his devotion to duty that he is unable to grasp a loophole even within himself. This human failing does not in any way detract from but rather enhances his integrity, for while it may possibly fall into the category of over-confidence it has nothing to do with conceit.

Had he not accomplished his mission with such obvious success and were not his services so obviously valuable I should not be venturing to ask of your lordship whether you do not feel with me that some measure should be found that would legitimately relieve him of a post which places him in this problematical position . . .

The ancient Bishop was bedridden. His right hand was painfully arthritic. Nevertheless he wrote back shakily with it:

Agree with you. Feel he should be transferred. Suggest you effect it as soon as possible.

Chapter 43

It was Malo who told Father Keogh that Locha was back. At the time Malo was engaged upon carving an image of a tiny wooden war god. He broke the news in a roundabout way. He did not look up from his work.

"That de Cortinez girl was in love with you. She was in love with you even when she was a child. You could see that without any eyes."

Father Keogh answered evenly, "I am very flattered if you think so but I'm not blind and it wasn't apparent to me."

"You're not made to look out for those things and besides you're a man of modesty. You are the last person that you would suspect."

"If she was in love at such a tender age," Father Keogh said, "I am afraid it was not with me."

"They tell me she's come home."

"What!" Father Keogh put down his cup.

"It was news in the bar last night. You see, she cannot keep away." Father Keogh sat back in his chair. "You are looking as if it was bad news, my friend."

"Am I?" Father Keogh pushed back his chair and stood up. "I didn't mean to look anything of the sort."

"They say she's come home to be married."

Father Keogh was taken off his guard. He sat down and said urgently, "Married?" He was hardly able to ask the next question. His eyes and his voice were alarmed. "Whom has she come home to marry?"

Malo laughed. "Well, Father, it does distress you. Did you think she was marrying me?"

Father Keogh snapped, "I asked you a question. Please answer it."

Malo told him, "I can't. I don't know, but it's someone she met in the States."

He kept his eyes on Father Keogh silently traveling his face.

Father Keogh picked up his black gloves and walked out. He went up to the Casa Grande. The heat struck him fiercely on the hill. His mouth was dry and he longed for the gray mists of Wicklow.

Doña Marian was changing a gramophone needle when Josefa showed him into the room.

She turned and flashed her teeth at him. "Why, hallo there, Father. You just missed the kid. I guess she went down to see you."

Father Keogh was still out of breath. "She—she hasn't come back to see him?"

Doña Marian turned round and laughed. "Why, Father, you look downright scared. No—I guess that's all over and done with. She's fallen for her cousin Dyke Brown."

"Dyke—oh, the boy I met here once. Does she really seem in love?"

"Oh sure. I never saw her so gay. For the first time it seems to me like at last she's acting really young. He's a doctor, they have a lot in common."

"You must be very pleased. It's certainly wonderful news."

"It certainly is, Father."

"Well, I must be getting back," he said. "I don't want to miss her again."

"So long," Doña Marian called.

He hurried down the hill but at the foot he met Señora Martinez. It was impossible to get away under fifteen minutes.

Malo was still at work on the war god when Locha arrived at the house.

She knocked at the door and called out gaily, "Father, may I come in?"

Malo made no reply but she heard him move inside the room.

She pushed the door open, her face alight. "I couldn't wait—" When she saw Malo she stood still. He continued to chip at the image. Then he looked up and smiled. "What a hurry you're in to see each other. Sit down, Señorita. He won't be long."

She remained standing. He went on working. For a second or two she looked at him; then she looked about the room: at the old medicine cabinet and the crucifix and at Saint Anthony restored to his original position. Her lips were open and her eyes were soft. There were tears in them when she looked round.

"You've grown very beautiful, Señorita." She made no reply. "You'll make a beautiful bride. It will be an interesting wedding this one—to see a young lady go up to the altar to be married not *to* the man she loves but *by* him. Yes, it will be an interesting wedding." He sensed that her body stiffened. "When will it be, Señorita?"

"I have come to discuss it with Father Keogh."

"You had better make it soon or it will never take place at all."

She wore a crisp blue dress and her hair was waved flat at her temples. Her ankles and wrists were overslim, her waist was nipped in and her breasts protruded. She had made a square box of her mouth. Her eyelashes stiffened with thick mascara gave her eyes a startled look. Her nails gleamed and she smelled of a sophisticated perfume.

"Will you tell Father Keogh I couldn't wait?"

"No, because you will wait."

She half sat again eyeing the door.

Still he did not look at her. "How happy will you be, Señorita?"

She said, "Why are you living here?"

228

"Because no one else would have me."

"You could have put a mattress on the floor at Porfirio's."

"Porfirio's wife would not let me. She is a very important lady now. How happy will you make your husband, Señorita?"

"I am devoted to my cousin—I'm—" She raised her head. "I'm in love with him."

"Perhaps—until you came into this room again."

"We have a very slight acquaintance, Señor Comachi. I don't see how you can judge me or my feelings."

"They are visible, Señorita. You looked at this room as you would like to look at him, and besides we have not a slight acquaintance. I have known you since you were a child. Your feelings were visible then."

"I'm afraid your notorious intuition has led you astray this time."

He turned round and looked at her full in the face. She lowered her eyes before him. When she raised them he was chipping at the image again.

She was unable to take her eyes off him. Bent forward, his lashes pressing two dark crescents onto the overhigh cheekbones, his profile showed none of the insolence, none of the ruthless impassivity that was visible full face. She thought that she had never seen a more taut or more severe beauty. He was like a high note she had once heard on a violin. She had forgotten the violinist but she had remembered the note all her life. She watched Malo's hands at work. Every movement was quick but studied, as if he even put his gestures to the most effective use. She asked softly, "Have you forgiven Father Keogh now?"

"Was it I who had something to forgive?"

"No, it wasn't, but sometimes that makes no difference."

Malo put a hand into his pocket. Onto the table he dropped a rosary. It made a tiny rattling noise before it lay finally quiet.

Locha said, "Yes, I was told about that. But somehow I couldn't believe it."

"Well, perhaps you are right."

"Are you going to try?" He nodded. She asked him, "Why?"

"Why not? If it satisfies him it could satisfy me."

"How could the same things appeal to you?"

"It might be that his choice is better than mine. I shall not know if I do not find out."

229

"You won't—you won't hurt him again?"

He said, "There! He's finished—Huitzilopochtli!—" And he held out the small wooden war god. "Would you like him?"

He leaned over and dropped the little figure into her hand.

She turned it over. "You've made it very cleverly. Don't you want to give it to—"

"Maria?" He shook his head.

"Why not?"

"Because Maria already has one. No girl is in need of two war gods."

She stood up with her fingers closed about the image. "Well, thank you very much—I think after all I'd better not wait."

She kept her eyes down when she walked to the door. When she reached it she found he was standing in front of her.

When she tried to go past him he pulled her against him. He had seen Father Keogh pass the window.

"Father Keogh and I are much alike. Why not kiss me if you cannot kiss him?"

She fought against him at first but he held her arms and his mouth gave her lips no escape. She was thin and she felt his every bone against her. It was a merciless kiss. It deprived her of resistance and when it was over she felt exhausted as if he had physically beaten her. There was no color left on her lips. There was the faintest suggestion round his.

He said, "Well, do you think you would find us much different?"

Father Keogh came into the room. Locha took three steps backwards. Malo leaned on the point of his shoulder against the wall. His whole body could lean without lounging.

Father Keogh looked quickly from one to the other. He took Locha's hands and smiled at her. "My dear child, I'm so happy to hear this good news."

"How kind of you," she said. He did not recognize the voice. It was too quick and too bright and too breathless.

He drew her by the hands towards a chair and sat opposite her. "Come and tell me about it. I remember him of course. I thought him very charming. When do you want to be married?"

"Mother sent me down to ask about that."

"Well, I daresay I can help there." He gave her a smile but his eyes strayed. They strayed to the figure she held in her hand and they strayed to Malo's lips.

230

"Well, perhaps when you think you can manage it you'll let my mother know."

She was out of the room and passing the window before he could make a reply. He turned slowly round towards Malo.

Neither of them spoke.

Chapter 44

Father Keogh was the first to hear the gossip. Señora Fereira, Señora Martinez, Señora Solano, and Señora Rodriguez called upon him.

They sat in a polite little circle in his tiny room, and sipped the chocolate Chela had made.

"Father, perhaps you have not heard . . ."

"I've heard," Father Keogh interrupted. "And I think that we oughtn't to encourage such talk."

"We are not encouraging it, Father." Señora Martinez's metal sharp voice was reproving. "We are trying to do the opposite, that's why we've come to you."

"It's a terrible scandal, Father," Señora Solano said. "Wherever she goes he follows her. You might think she'd remain at home."

"When she comes to church he hangs about, and there is no other word for it, Father—he is definitely making sheep's eyes at her."

"You must have got very close to him, Señora Martinez, to see what kind they were."

"There was no need to go close to him, Father."

"He smiles at her in the most impertinent manner," Señora Fereira told him. "He stands in the doorway of Porfirio's bar, and those other brutes join him and leer at her."

"Well, they've probably taken a fancy to her. After all, she's a pretty girl."

"Creatures like that should keep their fancies where they belong," said Señora Fereira. "And they do not belong amongst people above them. The girl's encouragement lets down the whole of womanhood."

Father Keogh asked: "Does she encourage him?"

"I just told you she did, Father," Señora Fereira interrupted crisply.

"I was just wondering what Señora Rodriguez thought."

Señora Fereira replied stiffly, "Aurelia cannot see further than her own nose, and then she only sees what it pleases her to see."

"Well, what did it please you to see, Señora Rodriguez?"

"You have it on my authority, Father, that she definitely leads him on," Señora Solano broke in.

"There you are!" said Señora Fereira.

"On the contrary," Father Keogh smiled. "You were saying, Señora Rodriguez?"

"She's completely fascinated by him, Father," said Señora Martinez. "She seems unable to help herself."

"There's a perfectly good way to help herself," Señora Fereira snapped.

"He had the effrontery to address her in the street."

"Do you know what he said to her, Señora Martinez?"

"Of course. He asked her whether her wedding was going to take place after all."

"That doesn't sound very impertinent."

"Is it any of his business?"

"Possibly not, but then an interest in a local wedding isn't necessarily confined to the aristocracy, Señora Martinez."

"The girl has set herself out to challenge the man's attraction for her," Señora Martinez explained. "We thought it our duty to warn you, Father."

They rose with a dignified unity and went in single file out of the house.

Señora Rodriguez slipped back. "I don't think she *wants* to encourage him, Father, I don't think she *can* help herself."

"I see," said Father Keogh gravely. "Thank you, Señora Rodriguez."

He went up to Porfirio's bar. He was told that Malo was upstairs, and he ignored the winks and the rolling of eyes that followed the information.

He took the steps two at a time and knocked at the door. Maria's voice called out, "Come in." Father Keogh went into the room.

Maria lay on the bed, and Malo was beside her. His hand rested

232

lightly on her hip. She put her hands behind her head, thrusting her deep breasts forward. Her eyes on the priest were insolent.

"Well, Father, I did not expect to see you in a lady's bedroom," Malo said.

"Does Porfirio's wife know you're in it?"

"Oh, yes, Father, she is not so sensitive in the daytime. It is at night that she feels it is wrong. Is there something I can do for you, Father?"

Father Keogh said—and it was the first time he had ever addressed Malo sharply—he nearly lost his temper: "I've had about enough of this, you know that if there are any complaints about you, you won't be allowed to remain here. I've done my best, I can't do any more, and there have been complaints. You, Señorita," he said to Maria. "Haven't you any influence over him? Do you approve of his making eyes at an innocent girl all day?" And to Malo: "If you cause Señorita de Cortinez the slightest annoyance, I shall inform the Chief of Police that you are making a nuisance of yourself." He turned and walked out of the room. He heard their laughter as soon as he closed the door.

It had ceased by the time he reached the bar.

Upstairs in the bedroom Maria caught Malo's hand. She was frightened for his sake. Her soft voice was sharp. "You've angered him now. I've never heard him so angry before. What good do you think that will do you? Why don't we leave this place? He has the power to hurt you, but what harm can you do him? That scum downstairs . . . they are right, you can't hurt him."

"Eyes," he said, "eyes! Aren't there eyes in your head?" His voice was cold. "This is the time to be happy, you fool! This isn't the time to weep."

She gripped him. "All this church stuff? Is that how you'll get your revenge?"

"It could be," Malo said.

She lay back again smiling, her eyes soft. "Supposing he makes you 'believe'?"

He sat up on the bed beside her. He put a finger over the curve of her elbow. He let the finger stray, and he sat smiling at her, showing his teeth. She turned over and raised herself into his arms. She eased herself slowly up his body until she found his lips. She pushed her own between them, and when she leaned away from him she said: "If you went for this girl, I should kill her." She pressed the sharp points of her nails in his cheeks. "Do you hear? I would kill her," she said.

He pulled her towards him, then pressed her backwards. . . .

233

Downstairs in the bar Porfirio raised both his eyes to the ceiling. He lowered them hunching his shoulders, and opened out his hands. The Jeep pushed his tiny shoulders back, and blew out pallid cheeks. Vito held up his glass. The other two followed, and the three of them drank a toast to the ceiling above.

Chapter 45

At night Locha lay trying to recapture Malo's smile. She could remember the others—Porfirio's, Vito's, and the Jeep's, but she could never remember his.

She could see them wriggle across the ceiling. They made a weird procession, a queer little earth worm retinue; just the smiles detached from the faces, closed lips that might have been fleshy pink slugs. Malo's was always missing, and the others appeared to be lost without it, claiming its leadership, squirming like grubs in search of it.

The next day she slid him a look when she passed him by. She held his eyes and stared back defiantly at him. She thought: "I must try to remember it." But at night she forgot it again. They paraded before her, the folded lips without an anchorage, Porfirio's a lecherous sliding grin, Vito's a thin sneer of derision, and the little tortured crawling thing that foretold that the Jeep was amused.

Josefa sat up with her, scolding. "Why do you look at him if it takes away your sleep? Why don't we go in the automobile? He couldn't make eyes at that."

"It gives the town something to gossip about."

"A fine way for a young bride to talk."

"I am not a bride yet," Locha answered her crisply. "Kindly don't marry me off before you've got to, it makes me feel immoral—by the way, I've lost some nylons."

Josefa hurried on. "You think it's only me that talks like this, but listen—" and she ticked off the names on her coffee-brown fingers, "Señora Martinez, Señora Fereira, Señora Solano, and Señora—"

"Those four are always tittle-tattling," Locha said.

"And this time they have something that's worth it. For a name like yours to be linked with a man like that. Even the Father's Chela," Josefa said, "even *she* said to me, 'Have you seen how the Bad One makes bold eyes at the Señorita?' Imagine how I was ashamed! Coming from someone like that!" Josefa moved heavily round the room. She opened an old oak drawer, and counted the stockings within. "You have all your nylons here."

"Have I, darling? I thought some were missing."

"Those were too bad to mend, Señorita," Josefa snapped, and hurried on. "Don't think I haven't noticed—you're more like my own child, aren't you? When was it you last took holy communion? I'll tell you—" She counted backwards. "It wasn't since the day you got back. And when was it you went to confession last? Well, you haven't been since you got back."

"I'm a 'lapser,' " Locha said.

"I don't understand that kind of talk, I don't know what it means, but what I do know is that you don't dare to go to confession. A nice thing! You can't face the padre, that's what it is. And I know why you can't. You would have to confess to the Bad One, wouldn't you?"

"Josefa, you are a dream!"

"Oh yes, I'm a dream, I'm a dream am I? Americano talk! It's a pity they let you go away, you haven't come back the same."

Locha put her hands behind her head. "Josefa, have you ever loved anybody?"

"Bless the saints! Have I loved anybody? Aren't you more my own child than your mother's child?"

"No, I mean a man."

"Well, yes, there was a German once."

"How long ago was it? When?"

"A fe mia! I forget, I was young."

"Then you couldn't have loved him very much."

"Oh yes, I loved him," Josefa said. "But I pushed him right out of my mind, of course."

"Why 'of course'?"

"Because he was not meant for me."

"What was the matter with him? Was he mad or married?"

"He was something to do with a bank." Josefa was indignant when Locha laughed. "It's a very fine position, he was the Señor First Accountant."

235

"Josefa, I am sure he was, darling, I'm not making fun of you—really I'm not. It's just—well, it's just that it must be so nice to know that someone's not meant for you—and well—know that someone's not meant for you." She became serious at Josefa's face. "All I mean is, that sometimes the more people aren't meant for us, the more we want them, and it isn't everybody who has the strength to put them out of their minds."

"Señorita, I shall speak to the priest."

"Yes, honey—do. Do speak to the priest. And tell him everything I said, but tell him especially—tell him especially what I've just said, tell him, 'The more someone isn't meant for us, the more we want them.' Josefa, did you sleep with your German?"

"Bless the saints!"

"It's all right, Josefa, I see that you did. You were lucky."

"Señorita! Señorita!" Josefa stood up.

"Sit down. You lay in his arms, didn't you? You felt his breath. Even if it was only for a few hours now and again—even if he's forgotten, you haven't—you lay in his arms and you felt his breath. You were lucky, Josefa."

Josefa went out of the room. From the door she turned back and said to Locha, "Most definitely I speak to the priest."

Chapter 46

The next morning Father Keogh went up to see Locha. She was in the heavy Spanish bedroom writing wedding invitations. On the bureau a dutiful portrait of Dyke Brown stood, and under it the little war god.

Father Keogh looked steadily at her. "That doesn't strike me as being a suitable expression for a bride."

"What would you like instead?"

"A happier one perhaps." She forced a deliberate smile at him. "That won't do either," he said. There was a heavy scent attached to her. She pushed a box of cigarettes towards him. He took one and lit it, and said: "How much do you love that young man?"

"Which one?" She picked up the war god and showed it to him. He tipped his cigarette towards Dyke Brown's photograph. "Oh, that one! He's charming," she said.

Father Keogh studied her face. It was paler and thinner, and she did not meet his eyes. But it was none of these things that worried him. It was a faint resemblance to something he disapproved. Then he recognized it. There was a look of Doña Marian, powder thin across her face, and a promise of something "hard-boiled."

"When you came back your mother said you were in love with this boy. What's happened to change all that?"

"Has something changed it?"

"Obviously. You're not happy about it now." He suddenly leaned forward and sniffed at her. "You used not to use that perfume."

"It's Pagan Heaven—don't you like it? Mother's always swamped in it."

Father Keogh sat back and said: "Yes."

"You're growing most observant, Father. You used not to be like that."

He thought how strange it was that a girl who had spent all her life in her mother's company should only have acquired her mother's voice after three months' absence.

He said simply: "Locha, I've loved you ever since you were a child. You were my very special little friend, and I hope you're still my friend." She made no reply and he told her gently, "One of the things I should like most in the world is to feel quite assured of your happiness."

She asked him: "Would you like a drink?"

"No, thank you very much."

"I hope you don't mind if I do." She leaned over and rang a bell. When Josefa answered it she ordered herself a large Old Fashioned. "Oh, please don't look so shocked, Father, after all I am grown up."

"That's growing up with a bang, isn't it?"

"What's wrong with a bang? As long as you hear it you know you're alive." Then she said: "I'm sorry, Father, but I just can't take priestly advice at this moment." Josefa brought the drink, and Locha saluted Father Keogh with it. "Now, what are you staring at?"

"Nothing. I just thought how young you were, and how like your mother you've become." He sat forward, his hands between his knees.

237

"Poor mother," Locha said. "She once told me she grew old in this place by herself. I'm beginning to see she was right."

"She needn't have been by herself."

"She's lonely, lonely, lonely, Father—the closer she is to the people she loves. I ought to know, it's happened to me." She held out her glass. "Come on, be human—have a sip—drink to the bride's good health."

Father Keogh took a sip. Then he looked down at his hands. "Locha, that day you were in my room you had been kissing him, hadn't you?"

She asked him politely, "Señor Comachi? Yes, I'm afraid I had. To be accurate, he'd been kissing me, but I dare say it's the same in the end."

"But why—why—why—?" Father Keogh thumped a fist in his palm.

"I don't know, I should think it's biological. At a certain point you don't know who's kissing who."

"I didn't mean that. I meant how could you kiss him knowing what he is?"

"Well, Father, I'll tell you—I don't know how." She leaned forward, her glass loose in her hand. She spoke with confidential sophistication which sat very clumsily over her youth. "Unless, if you're really interested, and you know you ought to be—it'll give you a wider outlook—unless it's something to do with desire."

"But surely someone like you couldn't—"

She interrupted. "If you've been longing for someone—if you've been longing, or in love, for a very long time—it's—surprising—what—can—happen—to—you." She sang the last part of the sentence, and tipped up her drink in a rush. "Shall I be gay and have another one?"

"You've had enough. You must realize that you wouldn't have a hope of happiness with Malo."

"Now in that conclusion, Father, you and I are just like that—!" And she put one finger over another and flicked them both under his nose.

He leaned over and pulled the bell.

Locha said: "Don't tell me I drove you to drink too, Father!"

"You need some black coffee," he said.

"Oh tut! tut! On one Old Fashioned! Well, I haven't a very good head, but I hope to acquire one in time—mother just wallops them down."

"As you realize you'd have no future with Malo, what do you intend to do?"

"Marry my cousin Dyke Brown. Oh, don't worry, I really am fond of him."

"I hope so for his sake," Father Keogh said.

"Yes you would—you think of *everybody*. But listen, before the coffee comes, I might not get it out after that—I'm really a *very* bad girl. I gave up morals long ago before I found out what they meant."

"How very, very young of you."

"I only ever wanted one thing—to be close to the man I love. If I could do that I wouldn't mind what happened to me. I wouldn't mind living in sin, or in poverty, or as a social outcast, or in hell, as long as I was living with him."

"But you're *marrying* your cousin Dyke Brown."

"Oh yes, but then you see I haven't any choice. Because I don't think Malo would have me, would he? He isn't the marrying sort."

Father Keogh stood up. "When you're feeling better, Locha—"

"When I'm more sober, you mean."

He smiled at her. "If you'd like to talk to me seriously about it, you know I shall always be there."

"I might come for your help if I thought I should get it."

"Any obstacles I put in your way would only be there to protect you."

"They'd still be obstacles," she said.

When he reached home, Sam was waiting for him. There were two glasses and a bottle of beer on the table.

Father Keogh smiled. "Sam, you must be psychic. You always turn up when I need you."

"Oh, I don't have to be psychic, Mac. This town's a walkie-talkie. I heard you went up to the girl."

Father Keogh sat down. "Yes, I did."

Sam poured him out a glass of beer. "How was the little bitch?"

"Tight," Father Keogh replied.

"You don't say? Right in the footsteps of dear old mom."

"Yes, possibly," Father Keogh said. "Will you excuse me a moment, Sam? I want to write a note."

He sat at the bureau and wrote to Doña Marian.

If I do my utmost to speed up this wedding my end, can you push it forward yours?

Chapter 47

Three weeks before the day of the wedding Father Keogh received Locha and Dyke Brown at the church, together with the friends and witnesses who had come to swear under oath before an image of Christ that the couple were free to marry one another.

Outside on the church steps Father Keogh shook hands with Dyke Brown. His slow smile, his cropped head and the eyes that he kept fixed on the ground were higher up than when Father Keogh first remembered them but were otherwise unchanged. He had lost none of the shyness which made him look half-asleep.

He called Father Keogh "Pardre" and agreed with everything he said in a solemn voice which made Father Keogh smile. It was obvious that the young house surgeon had had small contact with the church and he seemed to be under the impression that a fitting expression to be assumed before a cleric was one of funereal respect. He doused his smile whenever he caught Father Keogh's eye and straightened his shoulders as if he were a schoolboy about to receive a reprimand from his headmaster.

He seemed also to be under the impression that it would be impolite to show any signs of affection towards his future bride in front of a priest. He stood several paces apart from Locha and stared either at her feet or the top of her head when he felt Father Keogh's eyes upon him. But it was the looks that he gave her when he thought himself unobserved which endeared him most to Father Keogh. They were shy, proud looks, filled with a steady devotion that warmed Father Keogh's heart.

Locha herself was ill at ease and smiled too often. She dispensed the courtesy in a manner which reminded Father Keogh of the way she handed out bottles of medicine in the surgery to people in whose malady she had long since ceased to believe, polite, uncritical, but meaningless.

"Doña Florencia's headache!" Father Keogh thought. "That's how she's smiling at me. I wish there were some way to help the child."

Doña Marian put her arms round her nephew's shoulders and turned him towards Father Keogh. "Father, could you tell this great baby here, that we don't have human sacrifices at Mexican weddings and that if we did it wouldn't be him."

His agitation and confusion over the ceremony attached to a Mexican wedding drew from Dyke Brown a heartfelt admission that he would be "darn good and glad" when it was all over.

"I just wouldn't want to make a mess of it," he said miserably.

"There's nothing for you to make a mess of," Father Keogh assured him. "As long as I don't make a mess of it, you won't!"

"What about those bits of silver—supposing I dropped them?"

"You won't drop them," Father Keogh said.

Dyke's forehead puckered and his smile was apologetic. "I guess I must sound like the all-time dope but I was never so scared in all my life—it's bad enough with just top hats and carnations and things but when it comes to—"

Locha interrupted him sharply, "Dyke, what a fuss! It's perfectly simple." He turned troubled eyes upon her.

Father Keogh said quickly, "Look here, if you're really worried about it, why don't you come home with me and we'll run through it together?"

"Do that, honey," Doña Marian urged her nephew.

Don Pedro smiled his thin smile. "There is nothing uncommon about a nervous bridegroom, Dyke."

Doña Marian rounded on him. "Why, Pey—at our wedding it was *me* that was scared, you acted like you'd been a bridegroom all your life."

Father Keogh was quick to see that the idea of being closeted with a priest in his own house was alarming to the young American. He said, "Or look here, why don't we drop into Sam's bar and discuss it over a drink?"

Dyke's slow smile reappeared. He turned to Locha. "Coming, honey?"

She shook her head.

In Sam's bar Father Keogh ordered a Coca-Cola and said to Dyke, "Don't feel you have to drink this stuff because of me. I'm on the

241

wagon as a good example to Sam. Sam, this is Doctor Brown, he's got stage fright."

Sam took down a bottle of brandy and banged it on the bar before Dyke. "You got further than I ever got, pal. I never got around to popping the question."

Dyke tipped back his glass and grinned at him. "The way I feel right now, you're lucky."

"Nonsense!" Father Keogh laughed. "It's not as bad as that."

Sam jerked a thumb at him. "Ain't it all right? 'It's not as bad as that,' he says. What's he know about it? All he has to do is to stand up there and say, 'Dust into dust' or whatever it is."

"It's certainly not that," Father Keogh said. He was relieved to hear Dyke's laugh. The young doctor was drinking rapidly and he turned round confidentially, his shyness on the wane.

"It's this way, Pardre—I feel that it's like you have to go through so many weddings before you can get married around here—there was this thing today—and then the day before the wedding—"

"That's just for confession and communion," Father Keogh explained. "Your godparents accompany you then."

"I don't get all these godparents—I didn't know you could have so many."

"Now, let's take the wedding day first." Father Keogh moved their glasses together to represent the bridal group.

"Hey! Mac!" Sam called out. "You pass mine back, Mac, I didn't get invited!"

Dyke looked up earnestly. "You didn't? Well, now see here, I'll put that right."

"Now!" said Father Keogh. "Here's Locha—here's you—and here's me." He picked up the glasses and replaced them heavily down upon the bar. "Now, for the wedding, the godparents—don't look so worried, they're not your responsibility."

Sam interrupted, "I bet you never thought you'd be married by a glass of coke, pal."

Father Keogh said, "Sam, will you kindly not hold up the ceremony."

"I don't know who's marrying who now," Dyke smiled. "You have me all confused again."

"The coke's hitching the brandy to the brandy, pal."

"Where was I?" Father Keogh said. "Oh, yes. Explaining godparents, now for the wedding there are three special sets of them."

242

He ticked off on his fingers, "Padrinos de ramo, they buy the bouquet, padrinos de lazo, they supply the white silk cord, the bible and the rosary, padrinos de arras, they're the ones who give the thirteen pieces of silver and the three wedding rings."

Dyke said, "What'll you have, Sam?"

"Oh, just a couple of godfathers." Sam poured himself a brandy.

"Now look," Father Keogh said to Dyke, "I meet you at the door of the church, and that's where I perform the ceremony. I bless the three rings, two for Locha, one for you. Then you take the silver and let it slip from your hands into Locha's. That means that you'll give her all your future earnings and that you hope they'll be plentiful."

"Poor sucker!" Sam interjected.

"And all this is at the church door?" Dyke asked.

"Sure," said Sam. "They don't take any risks around here, they kind of make sure of you at the first opportunity! Then you and the little woman take a hold of Mac's cape or whatever he calls it, and march up the aisle behind him, ain't that so, Mac? Oh, don't let it worry you, pal, Mac'll get you up the aisle, won't you, Mac?"

Father Keogh said, "Then you kneel together during the Mass that follows, with the silk cord round both your shoulders to indicate your union. That's all! It's not very terrible, is it?"

It was Sam who saw Malo first. He looked up and said softly, "Hey! Pussyfoot—we don't have any coke left. Mac, here, drank us out."

Dyke Brown disentangled his long legs from the stool of the bar and walked slowly towards Malo. "You son of a dirty bitch!"

The violence in the soft voice which had been up until then nothing but an increasingly thickening blur so took Father Keogh by surprise that for a moment he remained seated, staring at Dyke's broad back.

Sam called out a warning, "You have to be careful what you say to our Pussyfoot, pal. Our Pussyfoot was raised nice. He don't like bad language."

Malo said, "The Señor Doctor has my sympathy. It must be very disheartening to find that your bride has transferred her affections. But to be frank with you, Señor Doctor, I must tell you that I feel you never received them in the first place. They have merely returned to the original, isn't that so, Father?"

Father Keogh was only just in time to prevent Dyke's big fist from striking Malo's expressionless face. He said, "That won't get you anywhere, Dyke."

Malo walked back to the door. From it he said, "I gather your friend hasn't been helping to drink the bar out of coke, Father."

Father Keogh released Dyke's arm when Malo stepped into the street. "Dyke, that man's thoroughly dangerous, for goodness' sake don't get involved with him."

Sam echoed, "Yeah! Don't tangle with Pussyfoot, pal."

Dyke's face was wet. "The son of a dirty bitch! If he hangs around Locha just one time more, I'm going to grind that goddamn face of his so hard into the sidewalk it's going to look like somebody dropped jello on it."

Father Keogh steered him back to the bar and asked uneasily, "When does he hang about Locha?"

Dyke mopped his face. His eyes were shy again. The funereal expression was not far off. "Pardre, you're going to have to forgive me. I guess I shouldn't have shot my mouth off like that in front of you."

Father Keogh said, "That's all right."

Dyke rubbed his big palms together, spreading the sweat. "Pardre, I guess I had too much liquor. When I'm on duty I lay off the stuff, and I guess when I do hit it it kind of hits me back. But—well, Pardre, it's maybe foolish talk, but Josefa says this Malo put the evil eye on Locha. She says she knows Locha's crazy about Malo and that—well—she *always* was crazy about him right from a kid."

Father Keogh and Sam caught each other's eyes. Father Keogh lit a cigarette and Sam unfolded a toothpick, vigorously attacking his front teeth.

Father Keogh inhaled and smiled. "Dyke, I believe that Locha has a very sincere affection for you, and if you're going to believe everything Josefa says, you'll have to believe that Malo also has the power to turn into a giant white cat."

"I'm not so sure he doesn't," said Sam.

"There's no such thing as the evil eye," Father Keogh said. "Not even in Quantana."

"Yeah, but Pardre, Locha's just not the same girl any more and I have the feeling it has something to do with this *louse*."

Sam clicked his fingers. "Mac, didn't I tell you I seen Pussyfoot someplace before?"

Father Keogh said gently, "You'll be married in three weeks' time, Dyke, and you and Locha will be safely in the States."

Dyke looked up and Father Keogh hoped that it was sweat that was moistening the eyes. "A helluva lot can happen in three weeks—

244

you'll have to pardon me, Pardre, I'm not myself tonight, but I have to go back to the States. I can't leave the hospital that long—and she's, well, it's not just the wedding that's eating me up, my nerves are shot. I tell you there've been times in these last few days when I thought she hated me, and every night this louse is hanging around the house."

Father Keogh asked sharply, "Hanging round the *house?*"

"Yeah, he plays that damned guitar thing and sings to it."

Sam burst out, "Pussyfoot! *Singing?* Say, Mac, did you teach that guy hymns when he bunked with you?"

Father Keogh asked carefully, "What does Locha say about it?"

"I have the feeling she likes him around. Uncle Pey was all for having somebody go tell him to get the hell out of it the other night, but Locha said he wasn't doing anybody any harm. Aunt Marian was good and mad at her for that. She said to remember this guy never did a decent thing in the whole of his life and he never did anything without it did somebody harm."

"What had Locha to say to that?"

"Well—Oh! I know Aunt Marian's Aunt Marian, Pardre, and she—well—she's Aunt Marian, but the kid didn't need to hurt her that much. It wasn't so much what she said, it was sort of how she said it and the way she looked. I never saw Locha look that way before."

"How *did* she look?" Father Keogh asked.

"Kind of stuck-up and spiteful. I didn't get it, but Aunt Marian sure did. I thought she was going to burst out crying right then. Locha only said she thought this guy had more understanding in his little finger than some people have in the whole of their heads. But I tell you, it was how she said it."

Father Keogh said, "Yes, I see."

"Uncle Pey asked her how the hell she'd gotten so close to the guy's little finger, and Locha said you didn't have to get close—he could see things five miles off that other folks couldn't see going on under their own noses. I tell you, she goes for this guy. She said maybe he had a 'mother's intuition.' I guess it was a gag, she laughed when she said it, but it killed Aunt Marian. She just got up and left the table. I tell you, Pardre, the kid's all burned up inside and I want you to believe that the reason it knocks the hell out of me is for her sake most. I'd give my right hand to see her happy. And then I can't stand to see her hurt Aunt Marian. She thinks the world of

245

that kid." When Father Keogh was silent Dyke raised his eyes. Father Keogh was lighting a cigarette. Dyke said, "Why, Pardre, Aunt Marian's the kind of woman makes you remember you have a date someplace else that you never had—but she sure thinks the world of that kid."

Father Keogh replied, "I'm glad." Then he said, "Look, Dyke, three weeks go past pretty quickly, not such an awful lot can happen between now and then."

Sam broke in, "And me and Mac'll keep Pussyfoot busy. Mac'll teach him hymns, and I'll drown him in coke."

When Father Keogh and Dyke left the bar, Dyke slipped back. "Say, Sam," he said, "I didn't forget that wedding invitation—and look—Sam, would you keep my telephone number? Would you call me—reverse the charges of course, would you call me if anything happened and you thought I could maybe do something about it by being around? I'd get here if I had to jump the distance. I guess I'm the all-time dope. Would you do that, Sam?"

Sam said, "Sure" and stowed the slip of paper behind a bottle on the shelf.

Dyke added, "That's one hell of a nice guy, that Pardre."

Sam answered nonchalantly, "Mac? Yep. He's okay."

Chapter 48

Five days before the wedding Malo wrote to Locha.

SEÑORITA,

Have you been able to forgive me that kiss? If you knew what it meant to me I think you would. Those four old tongue-waggers are right (I have heard what they say, that I have no business to cast my eyes upon someone like you). But there is no understanding in those withered old hearts and no pity. In yours, young and soft and sad, there are all these things and I make my appeal to them.

The same thoughts which keep you awake at night keep me from sleep—yes—I know that you lie awake! My heart knows understanding, or did you think I had none? Perhaps it was you who discovered it for me—perhaps you brought it to life in that kiss?

Señorita, you must be certain that you have nothing in common with me. But everything you suffer for him, I feel for you. I know that when I tell you this you will understand how much we share. Remember that I, too, am a victim of hopeless love. I have no more chance with you than you have with your priest, but I do beg of you one favor. Consider this marriage well. Would it be fair to your bridegroom? You have too kind a heart not to consider others. If you marry this unlucky young man you will be using him as a bandage for your own wounds. Will either of you find happiness through that? Believe me, Señorita, I only ask this favor of you because I fear for your happiness.

If you feel that you are unable to face this marriage, I will help you. Use me in any way you please. I will get you out of the town if you wish.

Consider again, Señorita, you will have to walk towards the man you love—and he will marry you to someone else. Could you bear that? It is that which I wish to spare you—that is all I can hope from my love—that I am able to save you from a lifetime of wretchedness. Even if it is at the very last moment do not deny me this chance—at the very last moment you will find that I am by you and that I am willing to help. You need have no fear that my assistance would compromise you, or that I should claim any form of repayment. I should be content in the role of a rescuer. It may seem a strange one for me, but if you doubt me, Señorita, take up a mirror. Have a good look at yourself. What do you see there, Señorita? If it is only beauty you are blind as well as modest. You are looking at something which can change the heart of a man like me.

There was a postscript to the letter.

If Father Keogh cannot see how you feel—remember that he is not only a "good man" but a modest one—he would suspect

*you of loving everyone else in the world (even me!) before him-
self. Remember also that he went into a school at nine years
old which turns little boys into priests! So how could he understand?*

Malo laid the letter on the table and read it out in Porfirio's bar.

"Now," he said, "I am not good with my pen—but Maria has
helped me to write this—it is the kind of letter she is certain that any
young girl would be pleased to receive. This bit about the mirror—I
am told is touching and flattering, what do you think?"

Porfirio's eyes bulged and Vito stared at him, a mixture of petulance
and mistrust on his face.

The Jeep chewed his thumbnail and demanded, "I think it means
your senses have left you, Anacleto. It is something Old Uncle always feared."

"I am in my right mind," Malo assured them. "Because you have
dull wits does not mean that I have."

"Dull wits!" They all said it, stung into resentment.

"A nice thing to call those who work for you—stick by you—"
Porfirio spluttered.

Malo asked them, "If your wits are not duller than mine, why are
you paid by me and not me by you?"

"*Paid* by you!" Porfirio wailed. "Not so much as a peso!" Indigna-
tion overcame caution as he met Malo's narrowed eyes. "It is I who
pay money out."

"You!" Vito shouted at him. "You pay out money! All my father's
savings you've had off me—and a fine return you've given for it—
that wife of yours cooks like a louse. I have a right to a better showing."

Malo interrupted. "You are none of you entitled to anything. Not
one of you has a thought worth paying for. If you had, you could see
beyond your noses."

"I cannot see what good a letter like that does," snapped the Jeep.

Malo said slowly, "If that girl gets married, I have lost the only
chance I have left to beat the priest. This is an important time for us,
my half-wits, it's now that we win or lose. If luck's on my side, and
she should be, she's deserted me long enough—that girl will change
her mind."

"You flatter yourself, Anacleto," said Vito. "If you think she will
forget her priest and turn her affections to you."

"I do not want her affections, Vito, and this letter is to make her *remember* her priest. There will be more letters before the wedding —with my brains and Maria's feelings, I think we should make her find it hard to forget him."

"And how will that help you?" the Jeep inquired acidly.

"That won't make our fortunes again," said Porfirio.

"All it will do," Vito told him, "is to give an already high and mighty girl an even greater swollen head."

"I have told you what I hope it will do," Malo repeated. "It will stop me from losing my last chance to bring down the priest. I can get him no other way now."

"I don't see how you can get him this way," persisted the Jeep.

Malo smiled at him. "Your nose is a long way from your face, Jeeponito. It's not surprising that you cannot see past it."

"All he will lose is the wedding fees. That will not kill him," the Jeep complained.

"I am not trying to kill him. I wish to be rid of him without harm to ourselves."

"So you write love letters!" Vito sneered.

Malo said, "Yes. I must write them for him since he cannot write them himself."

"You think he *loves* her?" squeaked the Jeep.

"I think his heart is very soft towards her."

"So what?" Vito asked.

"Well, it should not be so hard to imagine," Malo said. "After all, it has happened before, and it could happen again. It's surprising how a favorite can fall from grace. It is worse if the favorite's a priest. When it is found that he has a heart and desires, like an ordinary man—or that he has ordinary human weaknesses, and if he puts any of these before his duty, people have no mercy upon him. They make no allowances and show no forgiveness. People who have gone out of their way to catch his smile and ask his blessing on their babies' heads are the first to tear him down. You may be too young to remember, Vito, when Father Gomez walked proudly about the town, and men lifted their hats and women dropped curtseys to him—and everyone listened when the good Father spoke—but you are not too young to remember what happened. It's quite understandable," Malo added. "You feel a fool to have whispered your sins and begged forgiveness from someone who has sinned more than yourself."

Porfirio suggested, "Supposing you are wrong and he does not care for her?"

"I am not wrong," Malo said.

"Then supposing the girl does not read the letters?" the Jeep inquired.

"Have you seen the looks she has given me?" Malo asked. "If you have not the rest of the town has—she will not only read them, she will look at her face in the glass. Young girls are easily flattered and a good man's heart is easily turned into his own enemy. Perhaps it is well you are all such fools. It has given me good experience of them."

Locha was trying on her wedding dress when she received the letter.

Josefa fussed about the hem, "It is too long in the front here, your mother was taller. Señorita, stand upright or how can I see?" She looked up and saw that Locha was reading the letter. "Well, I hope that's not from somebody else we've left out. I said to Doña Marian, 'How funny it is that when there's a wedding everybody writes to say you have always been friends.' It is the same with a funeral—Señorita, what are you doing? First on one foot and then on the other, how can I tell with the hem?"

Locha said, "Josefa, will you bring me my little mirror?"

"What can you do with a little one? That will not show you your feet—wait till I've pinned it, then look in the big one. It was just that your mother was taller, you see, there had to be a small piece put in for her, but for you it has had to come out."

"It's not my feet I want to see."

Josefa fetched the mirror grumbling, "Do not move or you'll put it all out." She spoke through the pins in her mouth.

Locha took the mirror up slowly towards her face. She looked at it carefully. There was a trace of excitement in her voice. "Josefa, do you think I'm pretty?"

"Yes, well you'll do," Josefa said. "There are uglier girls about."

"I was quite a success in the States. Do you know there were at least a dozen men who could have remembered the color of my dress?"

She folded Malo's letter and put it into a special drawer. It lay next to a holy picture. On the back Father Keogh had written, "For Locha, a happy Christmas."

The parchment-colored wedding dress had covered many a de Cortinez bride. It was well over a hundred years old. It made a stiff little figure of Locha in the cool dark room, against the heavy hangings. The yellowing lace echoed a faint suggestion of the gold in her own pale hair. The slippers that peeped out from the frills had heart-shaped diamond buckles upon them, and the mantilla threw a train that was four yards long. Josefa put an ivory-backed prayer book in her hand, and stood aside to admire the effect.

There was a knock at the door. "May we come in?"

"Yes, mother," Locha called.

Doña Marian came into the room with Father Keogh.

"Hallo, dress rehearsal," he smiled.

"Oh! Honey, you look lovely! Doesn't she look lovely, Father? My pretty little girl!" Doña Marian went forward to kiss her with tears in her eyes.

"I don't think I've ever seen a more beautiful bride," Father Keogh said.

Josefa beamed. "It's unlucky to see the bride before the wedding, Father, so the good Señorita Finch always said."

"Oh, it doesn't matter as long as I'm not the bridegroom," Father Keogh laughed.

"Josefa, doesn't it want lifting a little bit there?" Doña Marian pointed out a dipping frill, and then fitted her hands round her daughter's waist. "Gosh, Father, I was married in this dress, and I thought *I* was slim—but just look at this!"

Locha pushed the hands away. "Please don't prod me, mother. I'm not up for sale in the market place."

Father Keogh grinned at her. "You fetched a good price today."

"Wait till you hear it, Locha honey! What do you think? The padre came to remind your father he promised to give a donation to help rebuild the hospital on the day you got married."

Father Keogh's eyes were gay. "He couldn't very well get out of it. I put him on the spot, as my Bishop would say."

"He's going to give three thousand pesos. It'll make him mad for weeks."

"So you'll be a benefactress as well as a bride," Father Keogh told her.

Locha's voice was quiet. "Were you afraid you might miss the money, Father Keogh, if you didn't speed the wedding up? One hears tales of the church being mercenary."

"Now, honey, that's not very nice."

Father Keogh asked her gently, "Doesn't it make you happy to think that you'll be helping us rebuild the hospital?"

"Have you been paid yet?" Locha asked. "Or do you have to wait for the golden day?"

251

Father Keogh made one last attempt at a joke. "Perhaps we were unwise to settle for cash on delivery—we ought to have made it payment in advance."

Locha raised her small white prayer book and struck him across the face.

There was a stifling silence inside the room, until Josefa screamed.

Then Doña Marian spoke. "Why, Father, she must have gone crazy. I can't think what's gotten into her. When she first came back she seemed okay."

Father Keogh went forward and took Locha's hands. She made no attempt to move away, she stood entirely still before him. He said: "Locha, if that made you feel better I'm glad you did it. But if it didn't help, come to me, we might think up another way." He pressed her hands and walked out of the room.

Doña Marian led Locha towards the bed. The girl walked as if she possessed neither sight, nor hearing, nor feeling. Doña Marian said: "She's as cold as ice. Josefa—go get her a cup of hot chocolate."

Josefa hurried out. She passed on the order to Pio, and went to her bedroom. From beneath her own mattress she pulled out a parcel she stowed in her rebozo. She made a painful half run down the hill, and she had not regained her breath by the time she stood sweating beneath the snakelike scrutiny of Mother Montezera. "Mother, the spell was not strong enough."

"My daughter, how is that?"

"The unhappy love is not destroyed. It makes her do terrible things."

"You mixed the potion right?"

Josefa nodded at her. "Mother, we need a stronger spell."

"A stronger spell has a stronger price."

Josefa put the parcel on a bamboo table.

Mother Montezera asked: "How many pairs?"

"One dozen."

"My daughter! Won't such an amount be missed?"

"Yes, it's the trousseau, it will be missed."

"Is that wise, my daughter?"

"They can send me to gaol, mother, I shall not care. I will say nothing of where they went—this must be a *bad* spell, mother. It has to be a bad one that works." And onto the bamboo table she counted out her savings.

Mother Montezera picked them up. "Very well. We shall cast another spell—to bring *death* to the one that she loves."

Chapter 49

On the day before the wedding Father Keogh shook hands with the godparents on the steps of the church, and was relieved to note that the funereal expression was absent from Dyke Brown's face. He was also glad to feel the reassuring warmth of Dyke Brown's handshake.

But his own eyes were anxious when they looked at Locha. She stood very straight with her arm through Dyke's, a small polite smile on her lips. Her cool little voice had just been confessing to Father Keogh, accusing herself of inconsideration towards her fiancé, ingratitude towards her mother, and ill-temper towards her servants. It also stated that she was aware that her love for another man had caused her fiancé unhappiness. She was truly sorry for the fact and hoped to find it possible to make it up to him.

When they left the church Malo was passing. He carried a tortoiseshell kitten. He stood back to allow Locha to walk towards the de Cortinez car. Father Keogh hoped that he was the only one to have overheard his remark to her, "Even at the very last moment it isn't too late." He walked straight across the path of Father Keogh and Dyke Brown so that they were obliged to step backwards to avoid colliding with him. He looked at neither of them. Father Keogh laid a restraining hand upon Dyke's arm. Nobody mentioned the incident.

Doña Marian chattering to relatives climbed with them into the car. Father Keogh also hoped that he was the only one to have observed the fact that Locha's head turned sharply to watch Malo up the street.

He had placed the kitten on its feet and was encouraging it to follow him, calling and clicking his fingers. It started after him in fluffy spurts of indecision. Then it sat, opened a tiny pink mouth, mewed defiantly and set about washing itself with vigor. Malo returned to it laughing and picked it up. He went off with it held against his shoulder, talking to it.

Father Keogh made a deliberate point of watching Malo himself. He said cheerfully to Dyke, "I've always been fascinated by kittens. If I had one in the house I should spend all my time playing with it."

Dyke did not turn to him. His eyes were on Locha. But he patted Father Keogh's shoulder. "Yeah. Cute, aren't they? See you tomorrow, Pardre."

The town was in festival spirits. It declared the wedding day a holiday. Don Pedro had given a handsome if unwilling contribution to the fireworks display.

In the great vaultlike hall at the Casa Grande the wedding breakfast was laid for a hundred people. Included amongst them by the persistence of Dyke Brown was Sam. The Casa Grande was full of relations. There was not a single de Cortinez present. Don Pedro was the last.

The button-faced Ketters made merry inside the old walls. Doña Marian had never heard the Casa Grande alive with loud voices and laughter before. She glanced apprehensively at the portraits climbing up the wall. But the cheerful Ketters swamped them. Small Ketters climbed the balustrade and came sliding down the banisters. Adolescent Ketters ate candy in corners and squealed in delight at antiques. Elderly Ketters puffed at pipes and thought nothing of dining in their bedroom slippers. Doña Marian defied the portraits.

The streets near the church were hung across with paper streamers. Into each colorful strip images of saints had been perforated. Nearly every saintly namesake of the de Cortinez family had been represented.

In the bridal car Locha sat tight-lipped. Because she could not keep her hands still Josefa held them.

Doña Marian said before she left, "For heaven's sake, honey, put some rouge on your cheeks."

The crowd was packed tightly round the church. There was an archway of flowers at the entrance. Malo moved towards her as she stepped out of the car and the excited spectators fell back a little. It was considered unlucky to be touched by Malo. It was only for a few moments that they stood together, but a sudden silence fell down on the watching crowd. He said nothing to her but she seemed unable to take her eyes from his face. A whisper broke out round them then.

254

"He is putting the evil eye upon her!"

"Jesús María José! He is cursing the bride!"

It was Josefa who eventually put a hand in the back of the bride.

Father Keogh stood at the door of the church. Behind him it smelled close and oversweet like a heavily scented flower shop. His eyes and his hair looked extra dark against his white cotta. He was smiling as he waited.

Locha walked slowly up to him. The bridal party matched her pace. She looked china-frail in the stiff folds of lace. Within two feet of him she stopped. For a few paralyzing seconds she stared at him. She was entirely colorless. Father Keogh believed she was going to faint. He moved forward anxiously and Dyke Brown turned towards her. She caught up her train and wound it round her arm. The small satin slippers caught the sun in their diamond buckles as she ran back down the path.

The impulse that had forced her to escape had left her with no thought in her head but that to hear Father Keogh bind her in matrimony to Dyke Brown was not bearable. She was shocked into wondering whether she had said the words aloud which had shouted inside her head as she stared at Father Keogh. She stood, lost, at the gates of the church. She had no idea what she intended to do. She was oblivious of the gaping crowd.

Malo appeared at her side. He opened the door of the bridal car and pulled the chauffeur out. Malo was in the driving seat and Locha was beside him, before the crowd had time to catch its breath and Father Keogh hurried down the steps, and Dyke Brown came running after her.

Malo drove towards the Hua Pass. "We shall have to go out of our way a little to shake these people off. Then I'll take you to Porfirio's bar. If you go home there'll be terrible scenes. I want to spare you that. I will go up to the Casa Grande and make one of the servants hand over your clothes. Then I will drive you to Huapan. After that you must look after yourself."

Locha sat nursing her bouquet. She was trembling. "Señor Comachi, I couldn't thank you. I shouldn't know how to do it."

"Then spare us both the attempt, Señorita."

"But there is something I want to tell you—I—your letters—I think they saved my life. And they—they made me forget everything I've heard about you and everything I've ever felt." She was nervously destroying her bouquet.

They heard a car changing gear on the hill. Malo looked back. "Your bridegroom has not given up yet." He turned sharply right and sped down the Los Diagos road.

Locha's voice was unsteady. "I'm—I'm trying to tell you how it helped me to know that somebody understood—right up until your first letter I didn't realize—I mean I still thought the same of you— but then, I do so want you to know it helped, Señor Comachi."

"I am very grateful, Señorita."

"Those letters seemed to turn you into a friend—my *only* friend— Do you know it was as much as I could do sometimes not to run out to you when I heard you outside? I was longing to talk to you. There's never been *anyone* I could talk to about it before. I've had it all shut up inside me so long. I've kept your letters, Señor Comachi—I just couldn't throw them away. I didn't feel quite so lonely when I thought about them, and when I was at my unhappiest I read them again and again."

The car that was following them passed the sharp right fork to Los Diagos and drove on towards the Peaceful Farm.

Malo said, "No good could have come from that wedding, Señorita."

"I know. You made me see that. But right up to the last moment I thought I ought to try and go through with it. I'm so terribly, terribly fond of Dyke, I believed I could make him happy and that seemed worth it, and then everything's so hopeless in the—the other direction —but you and your letters made me feel it was wrong."

"Yes," Malo told her, "it would have been wrong."

She plucked viciously at her bouquet and her voice was tight and tearful. "But today I didn't love—you know who—I *hated* him."

"It can be much the same emotion, Señorita."

"He looked so smug and self-satisfied waiting for us. He didn't *care,* he didn't *care*—he was *smiling*—he looked so pleased with himself. I wanted to shout when I got to him—I'm not sure that I didn't . . . 'Don't look so pleased—I am sinning, *sinning*—I don't love this man—I love *you.*'"

"You have robbed the four Señoras of something they would have liked to hear."

"Priests are supposed to have understanding, aren't they? Well, *this* one hasn't got any." She was tugging at the ribbon that bound her bouquet. "He hasn't got any at *all*. He was just waiting for me, waiting for me—as if it didn't matter."

256

Malo told her, "He cannot be blamed, poor man. You have gone out of your way to make him think it did not matter. After all, he is not a witch."

"Priests are not the right people to care for the soul."

"Oh?" Malo asked her. "Who else would bother?"

"They are absolutely removed from *life*."

"They are lucky," Malo said.

"They are bigoted, narrow, and smug. *Smug,*" she repeated and turned to him, her eyes were fierce. "You have *no* idea how smug he looked. *He* thinks he looked handsome but—"

"I doubt if he thought that."

"But he didn't, he just looked smug, smug, *smug!* Oh! I *hate* him," she sobbed. "I love him so much. I wish I could die."

"That is due to your age—only the old have no wish for death."

She had loosened the bow off the big bouquet and some of the blossoms had fallen free. They lay in her lap and on the floor of the car.

"It is wrong. It's all wrong. Why can't they marry? Some priests can."

"Perhaps that is why there are so many Catholic ones."

"Please don't laugh, Señor Comachi. I'm *very* unhappy."

"Only because you are young."

"But in your letters, you said you understood. They say you can understand things . . . that you can see in the dark, like a cat."

"Youth is not hard to understand. One does not have to be a cat to see through that."

When they reached the bar Malo put a hand beneath her elbow and guided her to the foot of the stairs. Porfirio and the Jeep watched. Neither of them spoke. The Jeep slid off a stool and followed them. Malo closed the door in his face.

In the tiny bedroom above the stairs Porfirio's wife was half undressed. Malo gripped her fleshy shoulders and propelled her towards the door. "Get out, old witch, and do not come back. This is my room now."

She wailed at him, "But, S'ñor Anacleto, where shall I sleep? I cannot go back to Porfirio."

"Sleep with the priest," he told her curtly. "You shall have my mattress there."

He took Locha to the bed and sat her on it.

"Señorita, that priest of yours will be coming here soon."

257

She looked up frightened. "I can't possibly see him. I couldn't face him."

"You will face him," Malo said.

Her eyes were frightened, her voice appealing. "Señor Comachi, you've been so good—couldn't you please try to spare me that? You must know how I feel."

Malo said, "Listen, my poor little lovesick fool, I've no wish to hurt your priest—for my sake not for his— So don't force me." She sat back from him, her eyes on his face. "Señorita, one of us must go and it has to be him. If I can drive him out through you—that's fine. I have told you, it's risky to hurt him." He said it quietly—there was no hint of violence.

"Drive him out through *me?*"

She stared blankly at him. His voice was still soft and he had not lost his smile. He sounded as he had sounded in the car, gently amused. But there was something about his eyes. She lowered her head when she recognized it and it looked as if she ducked. They were the eyes she had seen in the dreams which woke her screaming in the night to be set upon by Josefa and Francisco with whiskey and bougainvillaea blossoms. They had nothing to do with the smile below them or the precisely drawn beauty of the pointed face. They were alone— as she dreamed of them, coming towards her with a nightmare isolation that responded to no human appeal. And yet they held no insanity. They were not the bulging horror-eyes of the giants in her Polish fairy books. She was not aware that it was for that very reason they frightened her more. There was nothing in them to account for the terror they brought. They were deadly, and brutally, patiently sane. They belonged to ruthless business deals, to a series of little vital cheats—where every decision is aimed at a downfall—to a steady, everyday, precise world where a murder is done through paper and ink and the body is never discovered.

She put her hands to her eyes.

He took them away. "All you have to do is to tell him you love me, that it's your own wish to stay here with me. It matters to him more than you think, Señorita—I saw how he looked when I kissed you. He will not want to watch you here, day after day, apparently living with me. He will have to go, and for all I care you may go with him. I tell you, it will not be long." She scrambled away from him flat to the wall. He leaned over and held her wrist. "I have no interest in you —don't be too hard on yourself, most girls would have looked in the

258

mirror after letters like mine—young girls are not famous for brains, and when they are flattered, they've no brains at all."

She said, "No. Oh! Please, no—I thought you meant them—I thought they were real—I used to touch them and think they were friends. Please, please, Señor Comachi—no."

Malo put a hand in his pocket. On the bed he threw a gun. "All you have to do is to make him believe that you want to stay here. He does not know his feelings yet, but it won't take me long to show him." Then he asked, with interest, "Did you think I could really admire you? Someone who would rather suffer all her life than tell a priest that she loves him in case he might look shocked?"

She pleaded, "He wouldn't believe that I loved you. He'd think I was mad."

"We have made our fascination for each other very plain, so gossip tells me, and then you did run straight from the church into my arms." He picked up the gun and sat down at a little bamboo table. His left hand lay innocent upon it, but beneath it his right hand held the gun. His voice was reasonable and even appealing: "Señorita, you know that I have no choice. Now which would you prefer, to see him alive or to give evidence against me after he is dead? It depends upon how much you love him, of course."

The mantilla had slipped from her head dragging the hair back. It made her face look sharp.

In the bar below a noise broke out. They heard the voice of Don Pedro, Doña Marian and Dyke Brown. But above them all they heard the priest's.

They heard Porfirio say, "I am sorry, but these were my strict instructions. The Señorita will see no one but the padre."

They heard Father Keogh's footsteps on the stairs.

Beneath the table Malo's right hand made a movement.

The dust had streaked Father Keogh's clothes. He paid no attention to Malo. He walked straight across to Locha.

She spoke before he reached her. "I love him. I want to stay with him." Her voice was unconvincing, petulant and sharp like a child's.

"You must have gone out of your mind, my child. You need protection against yourself." Father Keogh's voice was even but his eyes took her courage away.

She repeated stonily, "I love him. I want to stay with him."

"Come away with me now. Go home with your mother. Give yourself twenty-four hours to think."

She saw Malo's hand make a second movement.

Father Keogh's voice was no longer even. "You won't have a friend in the world, Locha. You'll disgrace yourself and your parents, but worst of all you'll destroy every hope of happiness."

Malo asked, "Can you not see that she loves me, Father?"

Father Keogh said, "Won't you come back with me, Locha? I implore you to give yourself time to think."

Locha answered, "I've made up my mind."

Father Keogh said, "Very well." He left her standing in her wedding dress with the dirt from the bar round its hem. He did not look at either of them and when he climbed down the stairs again he could find nothing to say to Don Pedro or the crowd that was awaiting him.

Chapter 50

When Father Keogh went out, Malo raised the gun. He pointed it at Locha's head and pulled the trigger back. It gave a feeble click. The gun was unloaded. He asked her, "If all I had to do to get rid of my enemies was to put a bullet into them, don't you think I might have shot that priest of yours before?" Then he laughed. "I forgot, Señorita, when we are young and in love we have nothing to think with, otherwise we should not be in love."

She stood up. She managed to find Don Pedro's voice. It was ice cold, and clear, "You have not been as clever as you think, Señor Comachi. My Father will not leave it at this. The Jefe will come here at any minute."

"You are right," Malo told her, "the Jefe will."

"I shall tell him exactly what's happened and I'm afraid I wouldn't mind if you shot him right through the head. I don't happen to love him at all."

"That is understandable, Señorita. He is not an attractive man. When he comes, you must say what you please. You are free to walk out with him—but if you do, that priest can count his hours."

Locha came back from the door. "If you didn't dare kill him before you wouldn't do it now."

Malo put the gun in his hip pocket. "My dear child, I do not happen to be in love, I have something left to think with— It would be too great a risk if I killed him outright but— Consider, Señorita. I have spent many months with Father Keogh lately. We know each other's habits. For instance I know that every time he is called out to Tephuango he pays a tribute to Father Gomez. He goes down on his knees to pray at the place where that little priest died. He feels that the spirit of Father Gomez saved his life at the Hua Pass. At any time Father Keogh might receive a sick call from Tephuango. At any time he will be making this tribute. Those mountain roads are treacherous —certainly he has had one or two lucky escapes, but no man's luck can last forever. Even mine deserted me. Any man could meet his death in a fall from the Hua ledge—especially if he was absorbed in prayer."

"When the Jefe comes I shall tell him to warn Father Keogh. I don't care what you do to me."

Malo told her, "If I fail in one way, you must know I'll find another. You could not warn him of something before I had done it, and I cannot be arrested until I do it. Wouldn't it be better to help me drive him out? You need not be afraid of me. I shall not touch you. I have no interest in you. I do not like little fair girls with proud Spanish blood in them—I like soft full women who know how to use love, with good Mexican blood in their veins. You may be quite sure, Señorita, you'll receive no attentions from me."

Locha said coldly, "I'm afraid you can't make a fool of me twice. I don't believe in your threats any more."

Malo continued patiently, "Señorita, after he came to see you here, the priest received a message. Someone was sick in Tephuango. It's not a healthy spot. He has gone out there now. On the way back he will be praying for Father Gomez. He has not gone alone, Domingo drove him, but as you know, the ledge cannot be seen from the road and Domingo is not a religious boy. I do not think he will get out and pray. Domingo is more likely to sit in the car and smoke. But Vito will be praying. Vito is up there now. The Jeep will be listening when you talk to the Jefe. It depends on what he hears. If he hears you say that you need no assistance Father Keogh will come back alive. But if he hears you warn the Jefe—well, if the Jeep does not cancel Vito's orders he will know what he has to do." When Locha was silent Malo

261

continued, "The Jefe is not here yet and Father Keogh will soon be coming back. It is a question of time, Señorita. The Jefe cannot arrest me on your word alone, and if he did, it would not help Father Keogh. If the Jeep does not tell him otherwise, Vito knows what to do. The gun that you will tell the Jefe I threatened you with is not even loaded —he will have to go up to the Hua Pass to prove that your other fears are true. Do you want to furnish him with proof? By that time Vito will have got away, and while the Jefe is investigating, I shall get away. Certainly it involves a risk . . . but I wonder you force me to take it. Wouldn't it be better to do as I ask and stay here with me for a short while?"

She relived her nightmare looking at him. They were always the same. He crept up soft-footed behind the priest, it was only she who heard him come. He raised an arm but she could never see the weapon he held in it or what it was that struck the priest. She heard a sharp slice through the air and she dreamed of a tortoise, banging about in her desk. Then she raised a pencil like a dagger high in the air and tried to stab a slip of paper with it. There were names on the paper that did not make sense, "Anacleto Patrick Gonzalez Keogh." She said them aloud in her sleep. A hand shot out to stop her when she went to plunge the pencil down. It was Malo's and his fingers hurt her wrist. Then she knew that if she struck with the pencil she might find Father Keogh dead but if she did not have the courage to bring it down she might lose her one chance to save him. She was in an agony of indecision. She could not remain for the rest of her life with her hand in Malo's suspended above her own head. It was always there that she woke up and screamed.

There was a commotion in the bar downstairs. They heard the Jefe's voice. Malo glanced up at Locha. He told her quietly, "Señorita, if you think I'm tricking you, ask the Jefe himself where the priest has gone."

The Jefe came up the stairs. Behind him came three policemen and behind came the Jeep.

Locha went forward to meet him. She asked, "Jefe, where is Father Keogh, please?"

"He went out to Tephuango. Someone is dying or sick. Señorita de Cortinez—"

"Did you see him go out yourself?"

"Yes, Domingo drove him. Señorita de Cortinez, your father has asked me—"

262

Locha raised her voice. "Jefe, I need no assistance, thank you. I came here of my own accord. I wish to remain here with Señor Comachi. Tell my father that."

The Jefe said, "Rather you than me."

The Jeep stood aside to let him go down the stairs. He grinned up at Malo. "The deal's off, Anacleto?"

Malo replied, "The deal's off."

The Jeep went downstairs. "That Vito has had his long journey for nothing then. It will do him no harm, he is fat."

In the bar downstairs Vito sat with his feet up. He said to the Jeep, "What happens when the holy father finds out his long journey's for nothing?"

"It won't hurt him," the Jeep said. "He should have more exercise. My God, that young girl is a fool."

"It is easy to be fooled when you fall in love," Porfirio sighed, and he sent an angry look after the heavy figure of his wife as she shuffled towards her kitchen.

Chapter 51

On Sunday morning Father Keogh's heart leapt. For a second it leapt with hope. Then it plunged into a depth of apprehension and depression that he had never known before.

As he made his entrance from the sacristy four people came into the church. For a moment Father Keogh faltered, his eyes on the late-comers, the congregation turned to stare at them as if it possessed one head. The church was filled with whispers.

The late-comers genuflected and filed into their seats. They were Porfirio, Vito, Maria and the Jeep.

Father Keogh was forced to make a superhuman effort to ignore their presence but his eyes were individuals. They operated as if they were in no way controlled by himself. Time and time again they

263

strayed to the back of the church. They saw nothing to cause them anxiety. The four who knelt differed in no way from the rest of the congregation, except for the fact that they were more attentive. They were neither overpious nor derisive. They might have been churchgoers the whole of their lives and they were apparently unaware of the sensation they were causing.

They appeared at benediction on the following Tuesday and at Holy Communion two days later. All four of them came to receive the Sacrament of Penance. They wished to amend their ways. To each one of them Father Keogh said the same thing, "I am obliged to doubt that your penitence is genuine. If and when I am able to think otherwise, I will absolve you of your sins."

He was white-faced and heavy-eyed and he had no sleep for three nights.

The Jefe asked, "I am ignorant in church matters, Father. Can the 'management' reserve the right to refuse to serve undesirable customers?"

Father Keogh said, "I can't forbid people to come to church because I don't like the look of them. They're creating no disturbance."

When they met Father Keogh in the street, the three men raised their hats, and Maria dropped a curtsey. There was no sarcasm attached to the gesture; it was not exaggerated, and it was not burlesqued. It differed in no way from the courtesies he received from the rest of the town.

Malo presented himself at the Casa Grande and demanded Locha's clothes. At first she refused to send for them, but she was reduced to the discarded Sunday best of Porfirio's wife and the armpits smelled sour. She wrote a note to her mother at Malo's dictation and he returned with a suitcase which Josefa had reluctantly packed.

There was no hope of adding a message to the note. She was never left alone and the door was always locked. If Malo was out Porfirio, Vito, the Jeep or Maria sat with her. She dreaded Maria and Vito most.

Porfirio kept up a continuous complaint about his wife, or an attempt to embarrass Locha with the effect of the scandal upon the town: "Your name is like a swear word in nice circles now. Nobody likes to mention it—but in the streets and everywhere else it is mentioned all right!" and Porfirio whistled to show her the impact. "You should hear what they say! And I do not know how true it is, but I hear you have killed your Father, no one has seen him about."

The Jeep chewed his thumbnail and went out of his way to frighten her: "Upon my word it will be bad if the priest does not pack up and go—we might have you here for life, but of course, Señorita, that would not happen. Anacleto would never stand for that. He would take you away somewhere, and your body would never be found—we got rid of someone else like that. . . . It's not hard where the country gets wild . . . we could not find his grave ourselves if we looked for it now," said the Jeep. "I believe Anacleto will mention this thought to the priest. It might hurry him up."

She could ignore both Porfirio and the Jeep, but it was harder with Maria and Vito.

Vito pestered her, putting his hands on the back of her neck and sliding them down towards her breasts. When she pushed them away he grinned at her. "What, all these airs and graces still? Do you think such things still fit? What will they say at the Casa Grande? I think you would be no more welcome there than we should now—they will think you have slept with Anacleto, they'll be sure you have sinned." When she made no reply he continued to bait her: "I'm a good boy, Señorita, I confess all the things that I do to you!" Vito folded his hands and made his voice devout, " 'And then, Father, I have an eye for Anacleto's new little mistress from the Casa Grande, you know who I mean? I cannot keep my hands off her, what shall I do? The other day I touched her breast, I thought she looked pleased so I touched it again. (Isn't it strange for a girl so well brought up? But then you can never tell with looks.) If Anacleto found us at it—oh! my word, Father, he is jealous of his bed rights, I think he would kill us both.' " Locha turned her back upon him and stared at the flaking wall. "Yes, the priest has a terrible time. He really looks worried, poor man. Our Porfirio, too, has bad feelings towards you—could you believe that? Fat Porfirio! 'Father,' he says, and you know it sounds true, he can make such a solemn, sad voice, 'I'm tired of my wife. She is like an old turkey—all thin in the neck and all fat in the body, and she makes a turkey's noises too— When I am drunk I think of the fair Señorita, and when I'm asleep I dream that I lie with her . . . this is not good, Father, for one day I might wake up and get drunk and take her—and then Anacleto would do us both harm.' " When Locha put her hands over her ears Vito continued, raising his voice, "And then, Señorita, Maria's sins! My word, they must shake the poor priest. Maria also can hardly keep her hands off you—but it is not for quite the same reasons. She is filled with great longings to kill you, Señorita, she says they are terrible, making her sweat. It is because of her love for Anacleto, you see, and because you have taken him away. Over and over again these feelings sweep her like a sickness that makes you go mad in the head. She says she is frightened, for one day she will do it, and she begs the priest to help her, to save her. Oh! you should hear how hard she begs. Her soul is not her own, she says, the devil is eating her heart away, and she cannot think straight in her head. He told her she ought to leave the town to get out of the way of temptation and she said she thought his voice shook. And Jeepo!" laughed Vito, "our poor little Jeepo! Do you know what he has to confess?— that Anacleto has set him to spy on us. He is to tell him if you play around with me or Porfirio. Well, the Jeep says how scared he is—if Anacleto found out he would kill us of course, and the Jeep does not want that on his poor little soul. On the other hand he is a good boy now like me, he goes to church, and he does not want to tell Anacleto an outright lie. What shall he do? It's a terrible problem for someone who's trying to be good. Do you know what the priest told him? To go to the Jefe! If Anacleto makes threats he's to go to the Jefe! He tells that to all of us . . . you see we confess to a terrible thing between us. Maria is different, she *wishes* to kill you, but if anything happened to Anacleto or if he was put into prison, we should rather take you with us, Señorita, but Anacleto forbids us to do that. If anything took him away he would make one of us kill you. He would rather see you dead than anyone else touch you, Anacleto is jealous— and we are all afraid that we might be the one to be chosen. We do not want to sin and yet we are frightened of Anacleto. What if he came out of prison and found that we had not obeyed him? Oh, my word, we *are* frightened—we could not disobey him. You know how it is with Anacleto—so we ask the priest what we should do. 'Go to the Jefe—tell the Jefe' is all that poor creature can say. He must not give away our confessions. He cannot tell the Jefe himself." Vito rolled back on the bed and shouted with laughter. Then he sat up and said soberly, "There's a fine priest for you, Señorita! He refused us absolution! He will not ask God to forgive us our sins because he cannot forgive them himself—that's it all right. He does not want to hear our confessions again if you please, until he can believe we are truly penitent—he thinks himself too grand for poor sinners like us. He does not care about our salvation. There's a bad priest for you! It's because he cannot bear to hear the things we do to you—it makes him jealous—that's the reason. Eh, Señorita, what a fine priest!"

Maria's big teeth showed when she threw back her head. "Mother of God, those love letters! How we laughed!—we laughed and laughed. I said, 'Oh! but of course, she's a vain little fool—this bit will catch her, and this bit will! Such a grand house and such a grand family— "I have no right to cast my eyes upon someone like you"—that bit will get her!' " Then Maria stopped laughing and was suddenly vicious. "Such a grand family and such a grand house! When the people were starving that family ate! When the people were homeless that family was housed! That house was built from the bones and the blood of the people who were not good enough to go inside it. The revolution was not for nothing, Señorita, against rich people like you and against a rich church. A fine lot, a good lot, the rich and their priests! A rich man had more chance of reaching heaven, he could afford to buy a Mass for his soul. The priest sells his God and the rich people buy him and they pay a high price for that God.

"Mother in Heaven, when I said I would kill you, you should have heard your priest—his voice shook. Oh! Yes, he believed me. Why not? I believe it myself."

The whole town was waiting. There was a silent, deadly apprehension that found tongue in Chela's voice. "Father, these ones have never been to church before. What are they doing there now?"

On his way back from the Wednesday catechism class, Father Keogh was bumped into by Malo. He knocked Father Keogh's breviary out of his hand. He bent swiftly and picked up the little black book. He opened it, and he read aloud from it blasphemous words, and a lascivious rhyme. He said: "Well, well, Father, no wonder you bury your nose in it." Then he gave the book back, and walked on. There were loud expostulations from the bus queue which had witnessed the scene. Father Keogh hurried home.

There was a picture of the Virgin of Guadelupe attached to his door. There was a photograph stuck over the original face. It was a photograph of Locha cut out from a paper that had announced her forthcoming marriage.

It seemed to Father Keogh that wherever he went he met Malo face to face. Malo stood still until Father Keogh was forced to give way. He stepped off the narrow pavement and allowed Malo to pass.

Then one morning Chela screamed. Father Keogh ran up the stairs. There was an effigy propped up on his bed. It was made out of sackcloth and stuffed with straw to the succulent shape of a girl. It had a grotesquely painted face and long tresses of primrose-colored straw.

267

It had swollen breasts and swollen hips. Its whole appearance was foully obscene. It was arrayed in Locha's wedding dress and its clumsy hands were bound in prayer. The two satin slippers were sewn on its feet. There was a notice attached to it: "She's my lady love—she is my dove, my baby love. . . . She is my lily and my rose."

There was no service in the church which was not attended by Porfirio, Vito, Maria and the Jeep. They continued to be unostentatiously polite and were never seen about with Malo.

The Jefe said: "Listen, Father—it's the old alibi in reverse. Up to now Comachi has always got somebody else to take the rap. Suddenly he comes out in the open. Everyone goes to church and repents except him. Everyone's in the clear except Comachi. Suddenly he does his own dirty work—why?"

Father Keogh sent for Malo. There were lines round his eyes, and his voice was weary. "I don't pretend to know what you're doing, but I know that whatever it is it's not to my advantage. All I can tell you is that if you continue these childish persecutions, I shall be obliged to charge you with annoying me personally and get the Jefe to lock you up."

Malo answered: "Do. Put me in gaol. Have Porfirio, the Jeep, or Maria caused any disturbances?"

Father Keogh answered: "No."

"You have no reason to lock them up, Father?"

Father Keogh answered: "You know perfectly well that I haven't."

"That's a pity," Malo said. "If anything happens to me I should worry about the Señorita. Women are merciless creatures, Father, and Maria hates the girl—and then, Porfirio, Vito and the Jeep—they are not to be trusted. If I was not there to protect her, do you think she would be safe?"

Father Keogh answered slowly, "You're threatening me of course."

Malo said: "How could I do that, Father? My liberty entirely depends on your good nature, you could put me in gaol again any time you like."

"But if I do you're threatening me?"

"Come, come, Father. I said they were not to be trusted, that is all."

Father Keogh went to see the Jefe.

"So it *is* the alibi in reverse," said the Jefe. "Now we know what he's doing. Comachi sees to it that he's the only one we could get something on. But he also sees to it that you're the only one who could get something on him. And he's counting on you being scared. Well,

Father, how scared are you? What's so special about this fool of a girl? She made her own bed, let her lie on it. She chose Comachi's company, she isn't kept there by force."

Father Keogh pleaded with him. "Surely, after what I've told you, Jefe, you could put the whole lot in gaol?"

The Jefe's voice was impatient. "My dear Father, you have not told me anything. A man informs you that one woman hates another and that three men are not to be trusted, and you think I can lock them all up?"

Father Keogh said, "Jefe, couldn't you take my word for it? I happen to know a little more than I am able to tell you. I am certain the girl is in danger."

"Can you prove it?"

Father Keogh answered, "No."

The Jefe's voice was patient. "Father, you and I do not seem to be able to get together. You are a man of religion. Right is right and wrong is wrong, but in law we have to prove it. I need *proof,* Father. Proof! Proof! Proof! And your word is not proof. I cannot arrest a bunch of men and a woman because of a veiled threat that you might have misunderstood, but I can and I shall be delighted to arrest Comachi any time you like for causing you personal annoyance. I have plenty of proof of that."

· Father Keogh said: "Jefe, I've had an opportunity of getting to · know Comachi. I haven't lived under the same roof with him for nothing. I know that he wouldn't stop at anything."

"Then you intend to put up with these demonstrations rather than make a charge against him?"

"Let me try another way first. After all, it only adds up to a series of bad practical jokes. If I ignore them he might get tired of them."

"It sounds like the thin edge of the wedge to me, Father. I don't care for this business at all."

269

Chapter 52

In Porfirio's wife Locha thought she might have found a friend. But Porfirio's wife was afraid again.

"Señorita, my husband will beat me."

"But you've only to go to the priest."

"The Bad One is fighting the priest again. This time the padre might lose."

Locha had hidden the diamond buckles off her shoes, and gave them to Porfirio's wife. "Take this note to the Chief of Police."

She had written:

I am being kept here by force. Comachi has threatened me with Father Keogh's death if I try to escape. I cannot possibly make the attempt. Before you try to rescue me see that the priest is completely protected. Please arrest Comachi first.

Malo came in with the note. He smiled pleasantly at her, his voice was gentle, as he tore it up. "You should never trust someone like Porfirio's wife—what a pity you lost your buckles." Then he said, "You have a visitor, I should advise you to keep good control of yourself. It would be a pity to spoil everything now. Your priest is on the run."

Josefa dared not visit her, Dyke Brown had gone back to the States, and Don Pedro possessed no daughter. It was Doña Marian's heels that clacked over the floor of the bar. Vito showed her up the stairs.

Malo remained in the room. For Doña Marian he might have had no existence. The interview was short. Doña Marian sat down on the edge of the bed. She waved her big ringed hands about, and the room held a sudden eddy of Pagan Heaven. "Now see here, honey, I don't give a damn for the whys and wherefores, the padre had some idea

270

that there's something behind this. He just can't believe that a girl like you could do a thing like this. Well, I don't believe it either. But I guess maybe somebody just dropped you on your head when you were a baby, and didn't have the nerve to tell me about it. You don't have a father any more, but you do have a mother. Now what do you say you and I go someplace nice in the States, and set up house together? We could have no end of fun."

"Mother, would you really leave father for my sake?"

"Look, honey, it has to be that way—you know what your father is. It's all that old de Cortinez stuff."

Locha leaned over and kissed Doña Marian's cheek. "I know just what that would mean to you, mother. So thank you very much. But I'm quite content to stay here."

Doña Marian made one last attempt. She did not look at Malo, she said to Locha, "Honey, you think this man loves you? Well, suppose I were to tell you he threatened Father Keogh he'd kill you if anything happened to him. Do you think that sounds like love?"

"The Señorita would not believe you, Doña Marian," Malo pointed out. "I think you trust me—Señorita?"

Locha answered: "Yes."

Doña Marian stalked past Malo. She went straight to Father Keogh's house. He was anxiously awaiting her. She flung herself into a chair and dropped her hat on his table. "Father, do you have a drink?"

"Not in the house I'm afraid, Doña Marian, but we could go along to Sam's."

"No," she said, "skip it! It's quite okay, I guess it isn't good for me." She passed both her hands over her face.

Father Keogh asked with difficulty, "How was your offer received?"

Doña Marian made a downward movement with her thumb. "My daughter is 'quite content.' "

Father Keogh sat wearily back. When Doña Marian rose to go, he took her hand. He held it extra long. He found it hard to speak. "You would have had to cut yourself off from your husband, and your home —that would have been a very great sacrifice—I—I—" He could find no way to tell her that he had never thought her capable of making any sacrifice.

Doña Marian flashed her teeth at him. "Why, Father, for heaven's sake!"

The practical jokes increased. They became a daily persecution.

271

The humiliations were petty and often absurd, and they were directed at no one else but Father Keogh. Vito, Porfirio, the Jeep, and Maria continued to play no part in them. Malo alone remained responsible. The more childish and trivial the campaign became the more sinister it appeared. Malo lost no dignity, but it was becoming an increasingly difficult struggle for Father Keogh to retain any semblance of it himself.

Malo followed him everywhere he went. Once when he refused to move out of Father Keogh's way, the Jefe sent two policemen out. One of them asked: "Is this man annoying you, Padre?"

Father Keogh said: "No, let him go."

When Malo came swiftly round the corner, and again sent Father Keogh's breviary skidding along in the dust, Domingo, Mateo, Roberto-of-the-bus, and old Don Timoteo made an angry movement towards him. Father Keogh was obliged to forbid them to touch him. The Plaza was full of angry murmurs.

When a two-foot notice appeared on Father Keogh's door: "A priest should not put the love of woman before his love of God," a crowd gathered outside it shouting for Malo's arrest. Father Keogh destroyed the notice and preached in church upon turning the other cheek. He was aware that the congregation was not receptive. With the exception of Maria, Porfirio, Vito, and the Jeep, they were apprehensive. He could feel their anxiety as if they had placed it physically between his hands. He spoke reassuringly to them and was aware that they left the church without being reassured.

There was no denying Malo's confidence. The Jeep was sent out to round up men who would not dare to remain his enemies if he ever gained the power to have friends again. Porfirio's bar began to fill. The company was no longer pleasant late at nights, and it kept the tourists out.

The town was alive with uneasy whispers. There were only small signs but they were disturbing. For the first time since his return to Quantana the Presidente acknowledged Malo in the street. Mother Montezera offered him her services for the treatment of a sick kitten, and Porfirio's wife demanded her money box back from the priest.

The dentist ordered an aperitivo in the bar of the Hotel Martinez. Malo was with him. Sam refused to serve them. The dentist complained to the management. Papa Martinez came into the bar, he smiled at the dentist, avoiding Malo's eye, and said to Sam in a whisper: "Serve them, we do not want trouble."

272

Sam whistled: "Well, well, well, so that's the way the wind's blowing. What'll you have, Pussyfoot—a coke?"

The town was becoming divided amongst itself. There were those who gave Malo quick, ashamed smiles when they met him; and those who said loudly within his hearing, "He will go one too far with the priest."

Most of them had a dozen excuses for why Father Keogh should make no move; but some of them voiced their doubts: "This is how it began with the little Father."

"Ah, no, this one has his reasons—you will see. This time he'll really get him."

"He is biding his time, it's his duty to turn the other cheek."

"He had a long talk with the Jefe. You'll see, those two are cooking something up."

"But I tell you this was how it began with the little Father."

"This one is different. He isn't like that."

The majority had absolute confidence in him. What he did once he would do again, if the necessity arose. He had given them a faith in God; but in the privacy of homes and amongst one another, even the most steadfast sometimes wondered.

It was Chela who put the town's question to him: "Why do you stop the Jefe from locking him up? You are not the little Father, you need not put up with these things. Is it true that it has something to do with the girl?"

Father Keogh received a note from the Chief of Police. "I wish to see you. I am surprised you have not wished to see me."

Father Keogh went up to the station. The Jefe said, "Now, Father, this has gone too far. I insist that you make a charge against Comachi at once. No one can do it except you."

Father Keogh sat down. "Jefe, you know what I'm frightened of. Comachi would keep his word."

"Let him keep it," the Jefe said. "I'm sorry, Father, but I do not share your admiration for this girl. If she refuses to leave Comachi— let him slit her throat. The sooner he does it, the sooner I get my proof, and the happier I shall be."

Father Keogh's voice was defensive. "I feel I have a duty towards that child, Jefe. Nothing will convince me she isn't in danger."

The Jefe sat forward, his voice was urgent. "The whole of Quantana's in danger. You have a much greater duty towards that. You were sent here to save this town—you saved it. You gave it faith in you—are you going to take that faith away?"

"Comachi isn't harming anyone but me."

"If he finds he can kick you around, it won't be long before he thinks he can kick the rest of us around. Have you thought what would happen if you were to lose your influence?"

"Why should I lose it?"

"Comachi would happen," the Jefe said. "Have you thought what the people would say if they found out you were putting the good of one girl before theirs?"

Father Keogh stood up. "Jefe, listen to me—she could be *any* girl. Any girl in the same ghastly mess."

The Jefe said: "Okay, Father, you think it's a mess, she doesn't. You dislike him—she loves him. It's her business, it isn't yours. But Quantana *is* your business. You may have swept it clean, but there is always some dirt that escapes the broom. Comachi is going to find friends again—someone too scared to say 'no' in case he makes the grade. Someone who sits on the fence, and someone who just gets tied up with him because he gets something on them. That's how he got up in the first place. That's how he'll do it again. If people see you putting up with these insults they're going to think you've lost your power against him, or your God's lost His power. They're going to think there's something to these insults—images put on your bed, filthy accusations pinned up on your walls—*that's* how you could lose your influence— that's how you will lose it. What kind of an example are you setting them if you let him have it all his own way? They had that example from Father Gomez, and you know what happened to them then. You and I went through this once before, Father —only then it was everyone else who was too scared to act against Comachi except you and me. Now it's only you. We're right back where we started, Father." The Jefe's eyes were too bright and his voice was not steady. It was the first time Father Keogh had ever seen the Jefe personally afraid. "You're in danger of exploiting the moral weakness of this town—you're in danger of giving it a chance to slip back. Human nature can move in that direction so fast it doesn't need pushing by you—and all for the sake of one goddamn *girl*." The Jefe used the last word as the swear word. He sat back, lit up a cigar, and asked gently: "You never told me what's so special about her."

"I did tell you, Jefe. I said it wouldn't make any difference who she was or what she was if—"

The Jefe interrupted. "Then I must tell you what is special about her. You're in love with her—that's what's so special."

Chapter 53

The Jefe's accusation astonished him. He was able to reply with mild amusement that he thought himself too old, among other things, to become involved with affairs of the heart.

He even repeated the story to Sam expecting that Sam would laugh. But Sam's answer sent him home doubting an affection which had hitherto caused him no more suspicion than his love for Ellen-Dora.

"I suppose you'd know it when you saw it, would you, Mac?"

Father Keogh argued against himself, and for himself, inside his own head until it reeled. There were times when he convinced himself that he would be as worried on behalf of any other young girl of his acquaintance who had thrown in her lot with Malo. But the Jefe's accusation returned to torment him, and he wondered whether he really were in danger of putting one girl's welfare before the rest of the town's.

From the cramped quarters of his tiny room his light shone out most of the night. He spent many long hours on his knees. But there were times when he even suspected prayer of becoming an indulgence: when his brain felt red-hot with self-doubt; when he scarcely knew whether he was praying for relief or for guidance. He was physically exhausted from the mental attempt to shut himself out of his own mind so that he could throw it open to the wisdom of God. But the channels which should have cleared to receive were blocked by his own interpretation. His thoughts clashed like cymbals inside his own head, drowning the God voice out. He was deafened by his own persistent clamoring. Never before had he felt so completely aware of himself. Every nerve that should have been quiet was aflame. He felt every muscle. He felt every bone. Even the hairs that grew on his head felt alive as if they too were conspiring against him to prove that he was flesh. His whole body refused to accept the extinction of self. It felt like an anchor attached to his spirit. He hated the body that fettered

275

him, he longed to destroy it, and the angry violence of his enmity towards his own flesh removed it even further from the image of God in which it had been cast. He failed to achieve that inexplicable nothingness that can bring with it the answer to everything, the emptiness that contains the only fullness. He failed to achieve that contemplative quiet that can lead to a quiet beyond all quietness, where silence is loud in tongue. He tried every material method he knew. He thought of himself as a pool of hot wax that was free to receive the impression of a seal, but there were too many imprints on the wax already, and the mark of the mighty seal was lost. He thought of himself as an ice-still lake where no wind can disturb the surface. He thought of a stone that might drop into it, and of the movement that stone might send across the water. But there were other currents at work beneath and there was no way to tell what had caused the movement. The lake was convulsively choppy. He suspected himself of reciting his favorite prayers as if they were old friends to be touched for money. There was no moment in his life when he had ever felt more lost. He might have been shipwrecked, adrift on a raft, instead of a man on his own knees beside his own bed. He might have been at the mercy of the elements instead of cornered by his own mind in his own room.

There were moments when he felt less alone. Those were the moments when he felt Father Gomez. How many times must he have knelt on this same spot, by this same bed, in the same devouring doubt. Father Keogh remembered that Father Gomez had suffered from very few doubts— ". . . I no longer opposed him. If I made no trouble then no one got hurt . . . there are things that a priest can do, you see, that can help a man like that . . ." The memory of the little thin voice sounded merciless in Father Keogh's ears. ". . . the reason I showed Anacleto friendship in the beginning was because I was hopeful for him—yes, my reasons were innocent once —I turned a blind eye to the things that I should have complained of . . . It wasn't long before the rest of the town was doing the same thing, after all, they had only my example. I should have been the one to stand out, but at first—yes, at first, it wasn't myself I was thinking about . . ."

Father Keogh ached when he rose from his knees. Again he remembered Father Gomez: "Why is it that the indignity of old age strikes so very much worse through the knees?"

Father Keogh was thirty years younger than the man he remembered, but he felt an old man in those early hours.

That morning he hired Domingo to drive him to Huapan. He visited Father Lopez.

After one or two relapses Father Lopez had finally cured himself of biting his knuckles. During his conversation with Father Keogh there were moments when he found himself in danger of slipping back. He removed his hand from its tempting position close to his lips. But his apprehension was short-lived and his voice was relieved: "Powder and perfume, my dear Father, are everyday symbols of feminine allure, but because we become conscious of them and perhaps even pleasantly affected by them does not necessarily mean that we have succumbed to their influence. I think that the same thing applies to your suddenly remembering the color of her dress. You had probably been subconsciously trying to do so for some while. It is irksome not to be able to bring something to mind, especially when one has hurt someone in connection with it. No, no, Father, from everything you've told me, and you seem to have examined yourself very thoroughly, I am quite satisfied that your affection for this girl has not altered since you found her so greatly in need of your care. I think we need not fear that you are in the slightest danger of being fond of her in any way that you should not. It is to that same child in her that you are trying to extend your care and protection now." He was glad that he had not given way to the temptation of biting his knuckles. It would have been doubly unfortunate for a moment's anxiety which had proved unnecessary so soon. "Is she fond of you?" he asked.

"I don't know. I think she used to be."

"Have you told her how hard she is making things for you? Does she know about all these indecencies that have been directed against you?"

"I don't know. I haven't seen her since the day it happened. It's something I rather dread."

"Well, I should try to overcome that. I should tell her the responsibilities she's putting upon you. She must have some influence with this man. Presumably there is some form of attachment between them to make them go to these lengths. She should make him leave the town."

"She seems completely in his power."

"But surely if she has any affection or gratitude towards you, Father, she could be made to see that she's doing you a great disservice in staying here. If not the Jefe is right. She deserves your consideration less than the people her selfishness might endanger."

277

"She isn't happy with him, Father. One doesn't need eyes to see that."

"But how can that be if she refuses protection against him? No, no, Father, if she persists in putting her own interests before the welfare of other people, and if you believe that the Jefe may also be right when he says that you are in danger of exploiting the moral weaknesses of the town, then it seems to me that your duty is clear. Towards this one girl it should end. And if Comachi continues to make a nuisance of himself to you—you must charge him and get him under lock and key again."

Father Keogh was unable to rid himself of the unworthy suspicion that Father Lopez had given him the Jefe's advice in more gentle terms: "Let him slit her throat."

Chapter 54

As soon as he reached Quantana Father Keogh went up to the church. He had arranged to hear confessions and there were five penitents awaiting him. In the cool of the fragrant church four of them knelt together, the fifth sat five pews behind, with a straight back. They were Señora Martinez, Señora Solano, Señora Fereira, Señora Rodriguez—and Malo.

Father Keogh stood still and his heart thumped. His mouth was dry and his clothes still clung to him from the heat of the long grueling journey. The windows of the car had been closed against the white clouds of dust that billowed against it, so that Domingo and Father Keogh were incased in a boxlike heat inside, until the backs of their knees sent the sweat through their trousers to dampen the seats, and Domingo's brown hands were moist holding the wheel.

The four women turned round to look at Father Keogh. They made signs towards Malo. He remained facing the altar although he must have heard Father Keogh's step. For a moment Father Keogh felt faint, then he nodded to the women and hurried towards the sacristy. A bottle of water and an unturned glass stood on the dresser, and he drank two glasses quickly. The stone floor of the sacristy struck cold after the dancing heat outside, and Father Keogh shivered. There was a wine stain on the dresser and the flies walked over its fading flavor. Father Keogh washed his hands and his face, stood still for a moment to steady himself, and then went into the third confessional from the end. He was childishly loyal to it because it had housed his first penitent in Quantana on the morning that Sam had scrubbed the church.

His mouth was still dry in spite of the water and he hardly knew whether to be relieved or sorry when the first penitent proved to be Señora Martinez. He supposed that there must have been moments when he had felt more afraid. It seemed absurd that there could not have been, but he failed to recall them. Certainly the moment when Malo walked into his house with a gun on the night of Old Uncle's attack had not been included in them. He experienced none of the cold depressive fear then, that he felt as he waited in the close confessional. He had a knifelike apprehension of Malo as he sat in the church. He tried to convince himself that it might be God's final triumph, a miracle that had brought Malo to true penitence. There were times in their months of discussions together when he had believed Malo to be wavering; when it seemed hard to believe that such a clear inquisitive and intuitive mind could fail to benefit. It might be that the mind had only just conquered its inheritance of doubt and come to accept at last. But it was impossible not to remember the confessions of Porfirio, Maria, Vito, and the Jeep, and to know with an aching certainty that it was no miracle sitting straight-backed in the church outside, but some final unbeatable devilment.

For a second or two he leaned back and closed his eyes, to wonder how it had first come about that he himself had been fettered by Malo's power. It was not easy to concentrate upon the small self-denunciations of Señora Martinez, which were even then not untinged with self-righteousness. It was difficult not to wonder whether Malo would be next, or whether he would wait until last—aware of the effect it would have upon the priest. He waited until last. It was almost a relief to see the bronzed outline of that smooth face through the grille; almost as the hangman might appear as a dreaded release to the condemned man who has been haunted by him for so many merciless marching days.

Father Keogh said evenly, "Anacleto, you once told me that my calling was a curious one because it lays itself open to anyone unscrupulous enough to take advantage of it."

"I did not use the word 'unscrupulous.' "

"But there are limits to the advantages that can be taken. If you are really repentant, which I'm compelled to doubt, I suggest that the best way for you to make amends is to go and confess to the Jefe."

It was an attempt, but he knew its futility as he spoke it. There was no advantage too great to be taken of his calling while that calling still refused to admit that there was no such thing as a soul beyond redemption.

Malo said, and there was sympathy in his voice which was not easy to bear, "You do not believe that, poor friend. You are obliged to struggle for my salvation. Even while you try to save others from me you must try to save me from myself. You know that the Jefe could not do that . . . you will not refuse to hear my sins while there is a chance to save me from them, and you are right, because there is a chance."

Father Keogh said wearily, "Haven't I heard that before?"

Malo said, "Yes, and your answer was this, that every man has God within him, even if that man is not aware of it himself. In those months that we spent and talked together you gave me thoughts of God as another limb, which the unpracticed do not know how to use. But for those who can use it—what power it must have. It seemed to me that a man with the use of that limb could dispense with his own."

Father Keogh's eyes turned towards Malo. He heard another voice in the confessional, "Hope is a sin if it becomes an excuse," and looking at Malo's shadowed face he wondered deeply at the power it possessed. While inspiring no trust it could still inspire hope. Father Gomez had hoped to the end—"Anacleto needs a friend"—Father Keogh knew that he too would never give up hope and that he would welcome it as an excuse. What extraordinary complications of power must be concealed behind a face that could mirror a man's doom and yet not destroy his hopes.

Malo said, "Father, in those talks together, there were times when you nearly won. I thought that in what you are, there is something so much greater than what I could ever be. But where you failed, my valiant friend, was that you could show me nothing I preferred to be. Oh, yes, your church has miracles. She has people like you which she does not deserve—she remains her greedy thankless self and takes credit for people like you, that in itself is a miracle. Because you do not see through it."

280

Father Keogh said heavily, "I am unworthy of the church."

"I said it was a miracle—of propaganda if nothing else. I tell you, Father, you could have had a convert in me perhaps, if your beliefs were worthy of what they have made of you. But you as the outcome of them are a tower of strength and the things that gave you that strength are pitiful."

Father Keogh said, "Faith is not pitiful."

Malo said, "Father—I said you could help me. And in a way I am trying to help you. You have not been to the Jefe and locked me up because you're afraid of what would become of that girl. I have caused you annoyance and you have turned the other cheek. I'm afraid I must cause you still further annoyance. It will be impossible for you to remain here, Father, and keep the respect and the faith of your flock. You are beginning to lose it already—there are angry murmurs concerning yourself and the girl. You know that because you have heard them, and I know it because I have caused them. I have seen it happen before—and believe me," his voice had an odd sincerity, "I should not like to think of it happening again. Not to you—I should not like to see you go creeping about grateful for any smile that came your way, trying not to notice that nobody takes off his hat any more. Father, I should not like to see that. But if you stay here, by the time I am through with you—we shall not be able to avoid it. They will not forgive you much longer for putting her interests first. For the things you will suffer from my hands, Father, any sane man, or a man who is not in love, would lock me up. Remember this is not a new line for me, I have had great experience in it."

Father Keogh's eyes were closed, his voice was quiet, when he said, "Go on, Anacleto."

Malo continued, "I am willing to help you. You may take the girl with you if you get out of Quantana."

Father Keogh's eyes opened. Then he closed them again and asked, "How could I do that when you know perfectly well she refuses to leave you?"

Malo said gently, "Now, Father, here come my sins—There is nothing in the world she would like more than to leave me. I am holding her to me by force. That girl is in love with you, friend, not me—and by all the saints, how strongly that poor little creature loves! She nearly found my sympathy—she certainly found my respect." Father Keogh's eyes opened. He turned towards Malo and his tongue touched his lips. "I told you that once before, Father, but you

281

seemed to think of it in the light of a joke. You were too conceited to believe it—you thought it was priestly modesty, but it was nothing but human conceit. The faithful should not have carnal thoughts about their priests—if they do, it means that their priests become men and not priests. If they do, it means their church slips up—and nobody ever admits that. It is dangerous. But, Father, you and the church have slipped up together somewhere—that girl thinks of you as a man. Your priesthood could not have impressed itself, or perhaps it was missing sometimes? She has had no attentions from me. She awoke my respect but never my interest."

There was no expression on Father Keogh's face. He looked as he looked when he thought of Ireland. He might not have heard Malo speak. But he took in his breath at the next words. They were said softly and reasonably.

"If you take her away, you must marry her. It is not such an un-heard-of thing. Plenty of priests have been forced to marry. If you did not do that—how could I trust you, my friend? You could take her to safety and turn round and come back. You would have enough courage for that. You cannot marry her here—because there is no other priest and too many people who might object—I do not feel I can trust you to marry in Huapan—so I've worked it out like this. You must tell me if you know of a better way. You must send for Father Lopez. He is a fool and if you make it sound urgent he will not refuse. I suggest that he conduct the ceremony halfway to Huapan —by the San Ignacio stone which so many knees have worn away to give thanks that the worst part of the journey is over. Oh, I know it's not usual, but you must persuade him. The Jeep and Porfirio will accompany you, and it's surprising what difficulties can be overcome at the point of a gun. I think you will find that he will not argue long. Do you feel ill?"

Father Keogh's head was resting against the dark wood of the confessional. He opened his eyes and said, "No."

"Do not take it too greatly to heart, my friend. There is nothing a good Catholic cannot get out of. The marriage might not be valid as far as the church is concerned but it will serve my purpose here. My purpose is to disgrace you in the eyes of your flock—whatever became of such a marriage, it would have the same effect. The church would be too wise to allow you to come back. She knows when she cannot live down a scandal—and that is all I'm after, Father, to see that you don't come back. The church would know that you could never make your flock believe in you again—they are doubting

282

you now—how will they feel when you leave them to marry? They will not mind whether the marriage is valid or invalid—all they will know is that you left them for *her;* that you went to such lengths for a *girl.* If you did not love her you would not go to such lengths, no matter how you may try to wriggle out of it afterwards—and shall I tell you something, Father? You do love her. You will go to such lengths, and I do not think you will try to wriggle out of it afterwards." Malo waited, and when Father Keogh was silent he continued, "I said there were sins you could save me from, and now we are coming to those. If you went to the Jefe, Father—oh, I know you would never disclose a confessional secret, but supposing you were tempted to trick me—well, you would have to decide whether you prefer to see her alive or to give evidence against me after she is dead. And you would be wasting your time, for that would not be possible—she would be found dead in circumstances which could prove nothing but that she had taken her own life. You would be able to tell the Jefe the truth of course, but how much weight would it carry? We should be two jealous men with two different versions of one girl's death. Some letters of mine would be found in the Señorita's possession—young women always keep love letters—and they will show that I was crazily in love with her—so why should I do her harm? They will show also that she was in love with you, and that I knew of it and that my heart bled for her. They will show that I offered to help her if she could not face being married by the man she loved to someone she had no feelings for—there was no question of force, she came to me voluntarily. There were dozens of people to witness that, she ran out of the church and came straight to me. You will say that I kept her with me by threats—but how can that be, when she told the Jefe herself that she needed no help, and she turned her own mother away? You can imagine the threats, Father, but you could not prove them." Malo rose from his knees, "I am truly repentant, Father, and I want you to save my soul from further sins." He asked with interest, "Well, will you absolve me for that?"

Father Keogh answered, "When you said that the Jefe could not help you, you were right. He cannot pray for you. I can—and I will do so—but I cannot absolve you. You do not need me to tell you that you're not penitent—you know it as well as I do."

He had already begun the prayer when Malo said, "In case you are still unable to believe that the church has slipped up—why not talk to the girl? Find out for yourself how much she loves you. You may see her any time you like."

283

Immediately afterwards Father Keogh went up to Porfirio's bar. Malo had arrived a few minutes before him. He affected surprise at the sight of Father Keogh. "Well, we've missed you, Father. We thought you were neglecting us."

Father Keogh asked, "Will you let me see Locha alone, please?" Malo shook his head.

Outside the door Father Keogh tried again, "Are you sure you won't allow me to see her alone?"

"Quite sure," Malo said.

Below them Vito strummed the guitar and they heard Maria sing.

Locha lay white-faced and wretched across the bed. She raised herself up when she saw Father Keogh. He crossed over and sat beside her.

For a moment they both watched Malo. He showed no interest in them.

Father Keogh looked at Locha. She leaned against the wall with her knees drawn up. He noticed that her legs were bare. Her lips were open slightly and under pale lashes she looked at the priest.

It was close in the tiny room. Where the hair grew down to a peak Locha's forehead was damp. The pale strands curled up in the moisture and there was a faint line of it round her lips. There were circles of it under Father Keogh's eyes and it spread over the palms of his hands. Only Malo appeared to feel no heat. He kept his steady eyes upon them. Their insistence made words very difficult. "When you were a child I loved you, Locha—and to me you have never grown up."

Without moving her head she looked at Malo. Then she brought her eyes back to the priest. Her chin was uppermost and her throat ran down from it long and supple and palely skinned. Her breasts made no blatant outward thrust as Maria's were trained to make, but they made a soft and a sweet impression. The skin of her legs was as smooth as her arms. Her hair was tied round to hang down on one shoulder and on her knees she let three slim fingers lightly hold her wrist. Under her eyes there were faintly shadowed hollows and there were hollows in both her cheeks.

Father Keogh looked down at his hands. He wondered if it was the first time that he had noticed every line about her. Father Keogh asked her, "Locha, why are you here with Malo?" He was appalled at the fear which he saw in her eyes. She began to repeat in a parrot fashion that he remembered so well from her childhood, "I love him,

284

I want to stay with him—" He knew from the look on her face and the pathetic effort she was making to convince him that what Malo had told him was true. He sat looking down at her, tears in his own eyes.

Malo leaned forward easily, "Señorita, Father Keogh cannot tell you because it was something he has heard in the confessional, but he knows that you love him. I have told him myself."

Father Keogh was still looking down at her when she put herself into his arms. She sighed against him—as if it were an almost unbearable relief to be in his arms at last.

She looked into his deep and troubled eyes. "I did try to fight it. I promise I did—oh, I did, I really did—you must go away—you must go." She gave him no time to answer her. She drew her lips across his cheek and brought them tenderly back to lie quietly on his mouth. Then she touched him a little timidly, his forehead, his eyes, and his lips again. There was every caress in her fingertips. She had her arms round him, pressing herself tightly against him. He felt the bones in her body as well as the flesh. He raised his eyes slowly to look at Malo. Malo's expression remained unchanged. The two on the bed might not have existed for him.

Father Keogh looked down into Locha's face. "My child," he said, "my poor, poor child." She clung again to him, her chin driving into him as if it were not enough to feel him next to her, as if she felt unsafe outside him and must force her whole body inside his. "I know it's a sin—I know it is—don't be angry—don't hate me. I couldn't help it. You were always so wonderfully kind. No one has ever been more kind to me." He felt her kisses against him, unconscious kisses that came between her words. He tightened his arms and held her to him. But above her head he stared at Malo. "Oh, I love you so much. I love you, Father, not like a priest, like a man. I've wanted to touch you—I've longed to touch you." He felt her fingers. "I've had such wicked thoughts about you. I've even been jealous of Chela, Father. She sees you every day. I've hated your sister. I've hated my mother. I've hated anyone you've ever been nice to." He was listening to all her troubled words, but he did not look at her. He was holding Malo's eyes. "I've been so afraid for you. I don't remember being unafraid. I've been frozen with it. When I was little I prayed and prayed that you would be friendly with Malo like Father Gomez. I thought he wouldn't hurt you then. If you knew how I've suffered you couldn't be angry. Father, you

285

must understand." It was more of an order than an appeal to him. She repeated, "You *must* understand. You're you—and you feel like you and you look like you, you don't *look* like Father Gomez, you're you and I love you. I want you so much—you made me need you, you made me want you—you shouldn't have been so kind. I love you. I love you so much."

Father Keogh reminded her gently, "But there was a time, wasn't there, when you thought you could marry Dyke Brown?"

"Yes, there was. I really did think I loved him and I came back to prove it to myself and—well, you saw what happened," she said.

"What made you run away to the States in the first place?"

She was quieter now. He was stroking the head that was pressed against his breast. She could hear the beat of his heart and she listened to it, her eyes closed, a smile on her lips.

"Because Malo came back. I couldn't watch it all over again."

Father Keogh asked gently, "Those letters you wrote, Locha, you meant those for me?" When she nodded he said, "Why couldn't you tell me about it?"

"How could I? I knew what you'd say."

He was silent. His fingertips strayed to her lips. He felt her kiss them back. Then he made an effort to move her away. She fell away from him obedient and unresisting. She turned over on the bed, her face hidden. There was no sound to the sobs in the crook of her arm.

Malo opened the door for Father Keogh and followed him down the stairs.

In the bar he stood still for a moment. Then he pulled out a table and sat down. He sat with his head in his hands.

Vito's fingers slowed down on the old guitar. The Jeep slid off a stool and Porfirio's mouth hung open. Malo went to the bar and came back with a glass of brandy. "Here, Father, good for the heart."

He put the glass on the table and sat opposite the priest. Father Keogh uncovered his face to look at Malo.

"You're never driven to drink."

"I have no heart, my friend."

Father Keogh pushed the glass away. He lit a cigarette. "I'll leave this town," he said.

Malo said, "I am glad, Father."

Father Keogh stubbed out his cigarette. "Shall I *telephone* Father Lopez?"

"Yes, I think that would be quickest. The girl must stay here until you go of course."

286

The other three came to the table. They stood staring at Father Keogh. He paid no attention. He was looking at Malo.

Malo said, "If you are tempted to outsmart me, Father, I feel I should make something clear. When you have gone, I shall go to the girl. She is a noble child at heart, and you saw how she loves you. I think she would write a note—*Dear Father Keogh, I would rather die* than *allow you to make such a sacrifice*. That note could be found on her body."

"You've certainly thought of everything," Father Keogh said.

"I hope so," Malo said. Then he sat back and asked with interest, "What is it they do when a priest breaks his vows? Wouldn't they excommunicate him?"

"Possibly," Father Keogh said.

"Do you think they'll do that to you, my friend?"

"Possibly," Father Keogh said.

"How do you feel about that?"

"You know how I feel. You've been planning it."

"You will die by inches outside that church—it's what gives you your life. Without it you'll die very slowly, Father. It will not be a pleasant death."

"Surely you'd prefer that to seeing me killed outright?"

"So the flesh can catch out the best of us, Father? You know, somehow I never expected that it could catch out either you or me."

Before Father Keogh or Malo could reach the door the Jeep and Porfirio pushed before them. It took under half an hour for the news to reach every corner of the town.

Chapter 55

Father Keogh walked into the Hotel Martinez. He was preceded by Malo and followed by Vito. He asked to use the telephone. Sam came out of the bar. His face had lost most of its color. "For Chrissake, Mac, Salvadore stopped by and said he just heard—"

"Yes, it's true, Sam," Father Keogh said shortly, "I'm going away." Malo steered Father Keogh past him and picked up the telephone. He called Father Lopez's number himself. Father Keogh lit a cigarette.

Sam said, bewildered, "But, Mac, I don't get it—that kid was nuts over Pussyfoot."

"Not any more," Father Keogh said. Malo handed him the receiver and he spoke loudly into it. He guessed correctly, that Father Lopez would number amongst those with a mistrust of the telephone which makes them hold it away from their heads. He shouted, "Father Lopez, could you meet me as soon as possible at San Ignacio's stone? —Well, how soon could you make it—? I shouldn't ask you if it wasn't urgent. It's extremely important to me that you should be there. I need your help. What?" Father Lopez's mouth as well as his ear was a long way off the telephone. "It's in connection with the Señorita de Cortinez, you remember what I told you? May I rely on you, Father? I cannot stress the importance enough. Could you speak up, I can't hear you, Father." Father Lopez's mouth had come close to the receiver, but he was inaudible, biting his knuckles. When Father Keogh put down the receiver he said to Malo, "He cannot possibly be there until the day after tomorrow."

Malo said pleasantly, "That will do."

Sam caught Father Keogh's arm. "I just can't believe it, Mac. It's all around town that you're marrying the girl."

"Yes, I expect so," Father Keogh said.

"If you have to take a wife, Mac, for Chrissake don't pick one that works her way around until she gets to you. That kid's an all-time bitch. She had hot pants for Pussyfoot when she was young enough to have them taken down and her bottom smacked. Jeez! Mac, you don't know what you're buying, for Chrissake pull out while you can."

Father Keogh said, "I think you've misjudged her, Sam."

Malo added, "She came to me for help."

Sam said, "Yeah? I heard it called many things before, but I never heard it called help. It'd suit your book wouldn't it, Pussyfoot, if he gets himself hooked to the kid?" He pulled at Father Keogh's sleeve, his voice urgent, "For Chrissake, Mac, okay, so you got the itch— it ain't something no other priest never had, you bet they get it—you betcha sweet life they do, and you bet they work it out. I never went for this sublimation stuff—okay, Mac, work it out. Go some place, have yourself some fun, and then go confess to papa Lopez you been a bad boy and start afresh—honest to God, Mac, it ain't all that good, any guy's crazy to marry for it, let alone a priest."

Father Keogh said, "I'm afraid it's shocked you badly, Sam."

"Look, Mac, I don't go for church pap—I never went for it, but you did. How are you going to make out?"

Father Keogh said: "I'll make out."

"You're a real sucker for church pap, Mac—it's not going to come easy 'making out.' You doggone crazy mick—get a load of yourself! You'll never make out without church pap."

Father Keogh held out his hand. "Good-by, Sam—and thanks!"

Sam took it. "Well, it's like I said. I love you, Mac. I kind of hate to see you go—I kind of hate to think that life belt really slipped."

Father Keogh shut himself up in his house and refused to admit a single caller. All day long they appeared at his door, from the Jefe to the organito. Doña Marian called several times, and Sam tried three times within the hour.

Father Keogh wrote two letters. One was addressed to his Bishop, the other to Ellen-Dora. He told Ellen-Dora that if his actions should prove to be the end of him, he wished her to know that he had no alternative and that he could think of no other way out. He wrote a more lengthy letter to his Bishop.

To the Jefe, he wrote a short note:

You will have heard by now that I am leaving the town, and I want you to know that it is my own wish, so please put no obstacles in my way which might upset my plans.

Then he sent for Chela. He said to her carefully, "I want you to take this note to the Señor Sam." He placed it into the dark brown hands where the lines over the knuckles showed up black, and smiled at the disappointment which showed in the eyes that were swollen from crying. The note was sealed and its contents could not be relayed to friends en route. "Now, Chela, this note is very important and very secret. You must not give it yourself to the Señor Sam, you must go up to Saturnino's as if it was my ordinary list for the groceries. You will see that I have written my order on the back—and you must read it aloud in the shop in front of people. Saturnino will not have half the things in stock, he never has, so you will have to leave him the note to order from. I have written instructions to him to see that the note is sent down to the Hotel Martinez amongst the groceries for the Señor Sam. Here is some money for him to keep him quiet."

Chela's swollen eyes brightened. "Father, if you are ordering groceries, surely you mean to stay after all?"

Father Keogh shook his head. "No, Chela, I am leaving Quantana —and I am ordering these things for the new priest who will be taking my place—I shall be taking the Señorita de Cortinez with me. I can tell you that it is settled because I know you never gossip and would never pass it on." He looked at her between the eyes and kept his face straight.

Chela said without any alteration in the tone of her voice, "I could wish the Señorita was dead, Father—yes, I could, she has led you astray—I wish she could die this night. If the Bad One would kill her I would put flowers on his grave and pray for his soul all my life."

When she met Father Keogh's eyes she dropped her own and went out with the note. On her way to the store she crossed the market place. The Jeep followed, several paces behind. To everyone she met she whispered, "It is a secret, so do not shout it abroad—but there is no trick about this, the Father is going. He is taking the girl and will not change his mind—it is true what we heard, he has told me himself! He is ordering some things for the priest to come after him."

In Saturnino's store she read out her list. The Jeep was present amongst four or five people. To nearly every item on the list, Saturnino shook his head.

"Bless the Saints!" Chela exploded. "What are you, a grocer? or someone who has an empty store to sell? You must order these things from Huapan—the new Father who takes over will want something to eat."

She slapped the note on the counter and with it the money. Saturnino was puzzled at first. "There is no need to pay till I have the stuff." Then he read the list, picked up the money and flashed his teeth. "Tell the Father that these things shall be done."

Outside, the market place buzzed with the confirmation of Father Keogh's departure. Up to that moment Quantana had hoped.

The Jeep bore the news of the confirmation to Malo.

"Well it looks as if he does not intend to play any tricks—he is going all right. Everyone Chela spoke to, I questioned, and they all had the same to say, Anacleto, that she told them he was going and taking the girl with him. He had told her so himself and he was getting in stuff for the priest that comes after him—we'll fix him when he comes, eh, Anacleto? The new one won't stand a chance after this one has failed, the people will be through with priests. . . . No, Chela told them nothing else, and after that she just went to the grocer's. So it looks as if he'll be playing straight."

Malo said, "We need have no fears about Lopez. There's nothing that poor little lizard wouldn't do at the point of a gun. He'd marry the girl himself. But it's well to take precautions. Vito shall ride ahead." He turned to Vito. "Wait for Lopez at Ignacio's stone. If he's alone, keep him company until the others arrive, then ride straight back to me. If he has police with him ride back at once and meet the others—shoot the girl, but not the priest, I would rather he lived after that—then get into the blue caves behind the Arenales Hills, take the Jeep and Porfirio with you. If you are not back within half an hour of the appointed time, I will join you in the hills and we will get out of the country by plane. . . . Are you not glad that I saved what money I have left, my idiots?"

When Sam walked past Father Keogh's window, he whistled, and held up one thumb. Father Keogh went upstairs to pack.

Chela had not the heart to do it for him, but she stood by and watched him, weeping into something which struck him as suspiciously like one of his own handkerchiefs. When he packed his Roman collar into the suitcase, she sobbed out loud, "Oh, Father, you are packing it away as if you were not even sad to be saying good-by to it, upon my word, the devil must hide in that girl."

Malo had forbidden Domingo to drive them. He intended that Father Keogh should leave in Porfirio's cart. He wished the departure to be as slow and as humiliating as possible. He had apologized to Father Keogh when they discussed the arrangements, "The people will want a good view of you, right at the last, Father. I should not like to deny them that. It will be a sad day for them, Father, they are sorry to lose you, and a car would whisk you away too fast. We should not grudge them their last look at you."

"I understand," said Father Keogh bitterly. "You want to give me a 'good send-off.'"

"A car will meet you further out, of course, to take you on to Huapan—I will send the cart round to your house."

When it arrived, Father Keogh put his suitcase into it and drove round to Porfirio's bar. A crowd had collected on the Plaza and watched the cart draw up. It had nothing to say to him. There were no smiles, and no farewells for him, and the only hat that was raised was Sam's. He waved it and shouted, "So long, Mac."

Inside the bar Malo waited for him, and beside him, Locha stood. Porfirio and the Jeep lounged about. When she saw Father Keogh, Locha ran forward. Before she could speak, Father Keogh said brusquely, "Be quiet." He picked up his suitcase, but Malo stopped him.

"There is just one more thing, Father," and when Father Keogh put down his suitcase, he said, "I should like to see proof of the weakness of flesh."

"What more proof could I give you?"

"You could take her in your arms and you could let me see you kiss her."

The others crowded round.

Father Keogh said: "I see no point in demonstrating personal affection for the benefit of curious eyes."

There was a roar of applause from the Jeep and Porfirio.

"I've already explained the point," Malo said.

Locha put her arms round Father Keogh's neck. She put her lips against his, and whispered into them: "Father, pretend—pretend."

There was the usual elusive scent to her. But he recognized it then. It had the same curious fragrance as the little white flower she had given him on his first walk down the hill to Quantana. Her body was soft inside his arms. She felt as light and as fragile as the day he had carried her all the way home when the first Micky-Malo had died. There was no pressure on the lips he laid on hers, but she kissed him and forced them to open. It was his own arms that he felt tighten about her; his own head that he felt pressing down. He felt her warmth as his warmth and her lips as his lips. He could not tell the difference between them. He belonged to himself as little as he belonged to himself that night on his knees beside Father Gomez's bed.

The Jeep and Porfirio laughed out loud.

Malo stared expressionless at the two who stood before him. They were still in each other's arms. It was Locha who broke away. She picked up her suitcase herself. She was halfway to the door with it before Father Keogh took it from her.

He led Locha out to the cart. On the Plaza the crowd was thick— thick and resentful and silent. Quantana was still as the air is still before a thunderstorm. The trust he had fought so hard to win he saw dead on the face of the crowd. He saw fear, and despair, and misery.

He saw traces of a love that had not died, and now and again he saw resentment. But he saw very little hope.

Then he kept his own eyes on the ground and Locha kept her head down. The Jeep and Porfirio climbed into the cart. Malo followed to see them drive off. He leaned on the point of his shoulder in the doorway of the bar.

In the cart Father Keogh took Locha's hand, held it a moment, and put it back in her lap. Several times she tried to speak to him, but he interrupted her softly: "Be quiet." Then he smiled and said: "Keep your eyes closed." She turned her face into his shoulder and leaned against him. He put his arms about her and held her to him. He tightened the arm when the crowd booed.

They did not drive very far out of Quantana before they saw the car. A chauffeur in a peaked cap sat smoking behind the wheel. Porfirio drove the cart into the side of the road. He grinned at Father Keogh. "That wife of mine will not be such a fine lady now, for instance, she is to walk out and drive the cart back. It's a long time since she did what I told her to do."

It was not until she had climbed out of the cart and into the car that Locha recognized Dyke Brown. Father Keogh prepared to follow her. He carried both the suitcases. The Jeep and Porfirio went to follow him, but Father Keogh turned suddenly round upon them. He swung both the suitcases out. One caught the little Jeep in the face and sent him sprawling backwards. The other struck Porfirio square in the chest and his gun clattered down to the ground. The car started off at a pace that knocked Father Keogh onto his knees before them. Locha's scream was not heard in the noise of the shifting gears. All three men were in the dust when the car turned the bend of the mountain road and Porfirio fired hopelessly after it. There was nearly a head-on collision. The car that Malo had ordered from Huapan came speeding round the pass. Dyke had to swerve to avoid it. The driver drew up in a spray of dust. He heard the shots, put himself into reverse, turned, and drove hastily back towards Huapan after Dyke.

Father Keogh helped the Jeep to his feet. He was winded and his nose was bleeding. Porfirio's gun made a jab in Father Keogh's side.

"It's all right," Father Keogh told him. "I'll come back. I was always coming back." He held his handkerchief under the Jeep's nose, and asked him: "Has it stopped?" The Jeep shook his head, his eyes wide. He was frightened by the sight of his own blood. "Sit in the

293

cart," Father Keogh advised him. "Keep your head back and hold up your arms."

The Jeep slithered back to the cart again with his curious crippled movement. He sat with his hands above his head, and the blood from his nose shortly stopped.

Porfirio said: "I don't envy you, my friend."

Father Keogh paid no attention to him. He was opening his suitcase. He put on his Roman collar. Then he turned round. "I'm ready."

Porfirio pushed him savagely back to the cart and whipped up the mules.

Father Keogh forgot the two men. He was driving back to fight Malo again, but in the way that he held his shoulders—and in the way that he carried his head—there were no longer signs of strength. He felt a beaten man. It was not that he feared that he drove towards death, although he was expecting it. His fear was entirely of welcoming it. Within himself he felt already dead. He felt himself spiritually lifeless. Even in the humble standards he had set himself, he felt he had strived in vain. He had failed towards the innermost self which demands the highest in that self. That innermost self was dead. Yet it wanted to live—how it wanted to live. It longed for a second chance. It was driving back to claim it. A merciful God might grant that chance to a man who had dismally failed.

In the cart the Jeep raised his arms again, and held them above his head.

Father Keogh did not notice him; he was thinking that he had betrayed the voice of God that exists in every man. He had been a blindfold victim to the subtleties of sin. He had seen no defense against them; they had used every cunning ruse; they had set up a thousand excuses; they had disguised themselves as every well-meaning intention; they appeared as a lack of alternatives, as a means to meet an end, as the everyday failure to recognize the truth. They presented themselves as an honest endeavor and even as that God himself that exists in every man. They had withstood every form of detection; they hid in the face of a flower.

In his soul, in his heart, in his head, he believed he had failed. He had carried a fragment of God within him; it was only a tiny flame —too great a flame was too much to bear for the man who lives and breathes. Too great a flame the dead must carry; the dead have no breath to extinguish it; but if the living guard and tend that flame it will fire into something that the dead may carry on. He felt his

294

neglect of that flame; perhaps the devil sought out the unworthy—who was he to have lifted that precious torch and thought himself fit to carry it; who was he to have claimed that confidence? It would have been better to leave it where he found it to burn itself out unobserved by anyone else but himself, than to carry it aloft and loudly proclaim it, only to dim its light.

He saw in himself the able swimmer who runs to the scene of the rescue, who brushes aside the would-be saviors because he has more faith in himself, who takes so long to perfect his dive that he misses the drowning man. So he felt of his life in Quantana.

The air smelled thick and sweet about him. Even the awkward upward thrust of the organ cactus plant had a clamoring stately beauty. The dust on the road had an endearing familiarity as the worst of irritations can sometimes be forgiven when the irritation is about to pass. The sky spread blue and unrewarding, and from the hills the wind sent down a honey-sweet scent. The whole of life smelled appetizing. He remembered a man who was hanged. He had walked with that man to his death. He remembered those last few moments well. The man said to Father Keogh: "Even that wall smells good to me."

Father Keogh thought again of that defenseless flame within him. He had carried it proudly down Quantana's hill when he first arrived, but now he saw only the ashes left.

You know I don't go for that church pap.

Had he carried that flame to Sam? He had taught him to say: "I love you, Mac . . ." but not to say: "I love You, God." From the ever-open lips of Sam he had not induced one prayer.

You made *me need you—you* made *me want you—you were always so wonderfully kind.*

From a child that he loved he had provoked a love that he could never return or share, and she had not dared confess to him. "How could I? I knew what you'd say." He had inspired her love but he had given her little confidence in him. He had never proved a friend. What must he have made her feel towards the God of Love?

If I find in your church what you have found . . . you'll have beaten me, my friend.

God must have given him Malo, and how much of Malo had he given back to God? He had not induced in Malo one single Christian sentiment.

He came to another voice. He had missed the cry for help in it.

295

He had heard only the senseless chatter of it. He thought of his clumsy attempts to salve his own conscience by paying an outward Christian courtesy to that voice. He thought how obvious those attempts must have been and how they must have wounded.

Why, Father, I guess I must have bored you very much.

He felt an aching and a cruel remorse when he thought of Doña Marian.

There were no sins that he felt he had not committed. That kiss had been no pretense. His love for a child had turned into a sin, her body had made him betray it, and yet he loved only the child in it.

Chapter 56

Young Alejo the goatherd was the first to see the cart. He was on his way up the brown path to the mountain, his flock, multicolored, was bobbing before him. He turned to shield his eyes. On the road below him the cart moved slowly. The sun struck Father Keogh's black hair and the white Roman collar round his neck. The Jeep sat with his arms above his head.

Young Alejo went racing down the mountainside, his brown legs flying, his sandals kicking stones. He cannoned into Don Timoteo.

The old man took his shoulders. "Now then, young one, here's a fine thing. What would your father say?"

Alejo gabbled out his news: ". . . and I saw his white collar—he's come back a priest. I saw the white collar. He wears it again." Alejo made circles round his own neck with a quick brown hand. "And, Don Timoteo, Porfirio is driving, and the Jeep has his hands up. Perhaps the padre has a gun—the Jeep has his hands right over his head. The padre has beaten them. Isn't it fine?" He ducked beneath Don Timoteo's arm determined to take the news further. His footsteps rang hard as he ran up the street.

Doña Florencia appeared on her balcony. "Well, Don Timoteo, what has scared young Alejo?"

Don Timoteo called up the news. Salvadore and Don Miguel appeared on their balconies.

Alejo raced into the market place. He scattered the fruit from one tidy booth. Its owner cursed his clumsiness, but Alejo yelled his news. ". . . and the collar again—I saw it—and the Jeep has his arms above his head . . ."

He was nearly crushed as the crowd pressed round him. Don Federico lifted him onto a booth. His young voice rang proudly round the Plaza.

When Father Keogh reached the edge of the town he was greeted by a sea of faces. The crowd burst into cheers at the sight of the cart. The Jeep and Porfirio were surrounded.

Father Keogh could never forget the cheers nor the hands that stretched out to him nor the tears that were shed for him.

The Jefe fought his way to the side of the cart. "Well, Father, you have some explaining to do."

He took the reins from Porfirio. He gave the man a push and knocked him out of the cart. Porfirio fell into a collection of up-stretched arms that immediately tossed him up again.

A chorus of voices sang, "What a fine baby!"

"Who brought our priest back? Now there's a fine boy!"

Someone shouted, "He's not the only good boy to be thanked. It's unfair to spoil one without the other—give us the little one, Jefe."

The Jefe put one big hand on the back of the Jeep's collar and dropped him without comment into the waiting arms. He rose high in the air again at once.

Father Keogh was alarmed. "Jefe—they'll lynch them, won't they?"

"No, no," said the Jefe. "They are good-natured. It's a happy day for them. They will throw them about but that's all."

Father Keogh watched anxiously as Porfirio and the little Jeep were hurled across the crowd.

It was impossible to talk within the cart for the noise of the people who marched beside it. So many people had climbed into it that Father Keogh and the Jefe were in danger of falling out. No less than four men had their arms round Father Keogh to protect him from such a fate.

They grinned into his face and slapped his back. And shouted into his ears simultaneously, "I was the only one to say that you would be coming back."

"It was me who said you and the Jefe were up to something."

"This is the answer to my own special prayers."

It took them over twenty minutes to reach the police station. Father Keogh shielded his eyes. He saw Porfirio and the Jeep pitched backwards and forwards. Each time they were caught with a cheer. Outside Porfirio's bar the crowd took aim. It hurled the two men through the doorway as if it had been a goal.

Father Keogh himself was lifted down from the cart and placed gently inside the police station.

The Jefe closed the door, sat down and mopped his face. Then he said, "Well, Father?"

Father Keogh told his tale. The Jefe lit a cigar and kept quiet eyes on him. When he had finished he said, "And now that this fool of a girl has gone you will not refuse to testify?"

Father Keogh sighed, "No, I suppose not."

The Jefe leaned over and picked up a pad. He wrote vigorously on it himself. Outside on the Plaza the crowd was preparing to celebrate the Day-of-the-Holy-Father's-Second-Winnings. The fireworks had already started. The Jefe observed as he wrote, "I have always disliked the young."

Father Keogh turned back from the window. He had been trying to think how he could best assist Malo. How he could claim his second chance. He asked puzzled, "What's all this got to do with the young?"

The Jefe looked up and shouted at him, "All this is entirely to do with the young. That fool of a girl and her passion for you—a passion at that age is just self-importance—think where it might have landed us."

Father Keogh smiled at him. "What beats in the place of policemen's hearts?"

The Jefe banged down his pencil. "All right—so she falls for a priest! She can't have him! Too bad—when I was a boy I once fell for a nun. Does she think no one else ever fell for a priest? I have seen more than one pair of sheep's eyes made at you, but not all of them turned into tragedy queens. Not all of them think themselves so almighty important that their 'love' turns a town upside down."

Father Keogh laughed at him. "Jefe, I believe you're frustrated. You've been looking for the ideal female witness and you've never found her. It has made you a sour old man."

The Jefe said, "Listen, what your little love-martyr needed was a

298

beating right from the start, nothing more and nothing less, a beating, Father, right from the start."

"Well, I'm not sure I might not have administered it if I'd found out in time, but I didn't." Then Father Keogh added, "Jefe, she *was* young. She *did* lose her head. Who wouldn't in those circumstances? I nearly lost mine. But I don't think her passion was self-importance, I think it may have been a misguided devotion, but I believe it was devotion. It may have been youthful—I think that makes it more pathetic. She tried to bear the brunt of it herself. She tried to make good her mistakes. She did everything in her power to see that no one was hurt but herself—and the hurt to herself was considerable. That may have been foolish, but it was very courageous. Don't be hard on the child. She has suffered enough."

The Jefe beat his hand on his chest. "She's suffered! She's suffered! What about me?"

"Have you suffered, Jefe?"

The Jefe snapped angrily, "Yes." He put his head in his hands and his voice became quiet. "This morning I thought we had lost, Father."

They were silent until Father Keogh said, "Thank you, Jefe."

The Jefe said, "Okay. Sign this."

He pushed forward the pad he had written upon. It was a statement. It accused Malo of kidnaping the Señorita Dorotea Rosalia Teodora Maria-Cristina de Cortinez y Ketter, and of holding her to his person by force, of threatening the life of the said Señorita and of the Reverend Michael Patrick Keogh. Father Keogh read it through twice and signed.

"Right," said the Jefe. "We'll pick that lot up."

"May I see them?" Father Keogh asked. "Especially Anacleto."

"Sure," said the Jefe. "Do what you like as soon as I have them inside. I am sending you home under escort."

Father Keogh said, "Could I call at the Casa Grande first? I want to see Doña Marian."

"You may call nowhere until they're inside."

Chela had no greeting for him. Her eyes were still inflamed and red. But she had hot chocolate and tortillas waiting for him. "A nice old fright you gave me, Father. It's a shame when my stomach is poor."

Father Keogh smiled at her. "Chela, don't let anyone disturb me."

By the side of the bed he went down on his knees. This time his prayers came easily. He prayed for a second chance.

Chela interrupted him immediately. She burst in without a knock.

"Father, the Bad One has gone! He has left the town and the others with him. Everybody was so busy making happiness up on the Plaza that nobody saw them go. But there were horse marks up the mountainside. When the Jefe sent men down to take them to gaol, there was no one left but Porfirio's wife. The great God has answered my particular prayers, which is nice of Him, for you don't deserve it really, giving us all that fright."

Father Keogh went back to his own prayers. There seemed no limit to the depths of his failure. God's enemies had left. He was not fit to be entrusted with them, for God looks upon His enemy as a sadly misguided friend. He was not fit to serve God's friends. There was to be no second chance. His head was still bent and the moon was up when he heard Sam's voice downstairs.

Sam carried two bottles of brandy. "Mac, this time we're going to float that life belt." He jumped when the fireworks burst in the sky. "I never could stand firecrackers."

Father Keogh pushed a chair forward for him. "I can never thank you enough, Sam, so I'm not even going to try."

Sam put the bottles on the table, opened one of them, and poured out a couple of glasses. "For Pete's sake, Mac! That was some tough assignment you gave me."

Father Keogh said seriously, "Sam, I know. I assure you I know. But it was my only chance. And I knew you'd pull it off. I thought if you couldn't nobody could."

"Yeah! Well, I'll tell you—this Dyke Brown isn't so keen on the kid when I finally do get through to him. He was plenty sore at her still. Well, you couldn't blame him, could you? He didn't go for this chauffeur stuff at first. He says he kind of didn't like the idea of taking her hot from Pussyfoot—like if she'd rather have Pussyfoot she can go take a jump at herself with him. Then I have to tell him she gets tied up with Pussyfoot because she's scared of him—see I can't very well tell him the kid plumps for Pussyfoot because she's so nuts about you, that wouldn't've sounded too good to this guy either, that way he comes third on the list! Gee! Mac, did I get myself tied up! So I say Pussyfoot was so crazy about her he tells her if she goes through with this wedding, he'll plug everyone in sight. That gets him, and then when I tell him you're taking her out of town and I give him the dope on what you want him to do—he sounds like a kid out of high school he's so pleased to get his girl back. I guess he must be one hell of a nice guy."

300

Father Keogh raised his glass. "Here's to them, and here's to you, Sam—God bless you."

Sam replied, "Skoal! Say, Mac, that Chela shot her mouth off."

"I know," Father Keogh smiled. "I knew I could rely on you to keep yours shut, and Chela to open hers wide—dear Chela, I knew she would never give the note away, if I impressed her that that was important, but she can't resist gossip on small things." Then he asked suddenly, "Sam! How did you manage with Father Lopez? It must have been confusing for him."

Sam threw his head back and laughed. "Mac, you have to call that poor little guy. He won't know whether he's baptizing or burying folk—say, where does he keep his telephone, he sounded like he was talking from Heaven."

"He's nervous of it," Father Keogh chuckled.

"Oh, that poor little guy was so tied up! He keeps saying, 'Who are you? Father Keogh said it was important,' and I say, 'That's right, pal, Mac did say it was important but now he says it ain't important'—I have to call you 'Mac,' see, and that don't help him neither—but 'Fawther Kee-ogh' don't sound right from me," Sam drawled the words, exaggerating them. "But anyways, we finally get it sorted out, and he catches on that he don't have to go—but it's like I said, you should call him, Mac."

"I will," Father Keogh assured him. "Will you stay to dinner, Sam?"

"Mac, I'll stay to breakfast."

"That's fine," Father Keogh said.

Sam's voice became reproachful. "Mac, you had me so scared until I got your note I didn't have a fingernail left."

"I'm sorry, Sam," Father Keogh said. "But you see I couldn't risk giving Malo the slightest clue that I wasn't on the level with him."

Sam said, " 'Level!'—that 'level' had me rock bottom. I thought you was really going to marry that kid."

"You must know priests can't marry, Sam!"

Sam said, "Listen, bright—I figured it out you didn't aim to go on being a priest. You know me, I'm some dope, I see the way a thing looks and that's the way it looks to me."

"Would you really have minded, Sam?"

Sam spluttered, "Minded! Now see here, I'm a sinner, Mac, I don't have so many pals at court. If the only guy I have to put a word in for me gets the skids under him—I'll say I minded."

They were both laughing when Chela came in.

"Father, an Indio has come to the door."

"Oh, what does he want? Who is it?"

"It is not someone we know. It's a stranger, Father. I do not like the look of it."

"Well, what does he want?"

Chela's eyes were obstinate. "The Jefe has men out to search for the Bad One. He has not been caught yet, he is still somewhere about. It wouldn't be safe if you left the house."

Father Keogh repeated patiently, "Chela, what does this Indian want?"

Sam appeared behind him.

Chela answered reluctantly, "He is bound for Arenales. He was passing through Tephuango and somebody asked him to carry a message. But he's a stranger. It's not wise to trust him."

Father Keogh passed Chela and went to the door. The Indian awaited him patiently. He delivered his message in Spanish. A young woman had been taken ill in Tephuango. Her husband was afraid that she suffered from the evil eye. He requested the priest to visit her. The Indian repeated the message twice.

"The evil eye!" Chela squealed. "Then the Bad One has been seen there."

Father Keogh questioned the Indian carefully. It was hard to determine whether his liquid eyes concealed a final trap or whether they were the eyes of an indulgent God who denies no man a second chance to turn an enemy into a friend. Either way they represented a test. The Indian gave the names and particulars of the case concerned. Father Keogh knew the young woman and he trusted her husband.

Chela said, "Look, Father, so many times you have been there for nothing and the last time you went out and there no one was sick."

Father Keogh told Chela to give the Indian something to eat and thanked him for bringing the message. Then he said, "I'm sorry, Sam. I'm afraid our dinner party's off."

Sam replied anxiously, "There may be something in what Chela says, Mac, you never saw this Indio before and Pussyfoot's still at large."

Father Keogh went back to his room. He began to gather his medical equipment. "I shouldn't think he's hanging about within the Jefe's reach."

"You never know with Pussyfoot. He'd stop at nothing to get a last crack at you. Why can't you wait until he's driven him further afield?"

"My dear Sam, I can't refuse to go out on sick calls until I get news of Malo's whereabouts."

"It might not be a sick call, Mac."

"It's a risk I dare not take, Sam."

"Okay, I'm coming with you."

Father Keogh said: "No, you're not."

"Oh, so you *are* scared. You do have doubts."

"Well, you never know," Father Keogh admitted. "But I think this case is genuine."

Chela urged: "Go with him, Señor Sam. For myself I am going to the Jefe. I shall tell him where he's gone."

Sam said: "I'm going with him."

Nothing Father Keogh could say would dissuade him. Domingo was willing to drive them but Father Keogh refused the offer. He hired the car, but he drove himself.

Sam sat cuddling a bottle of brandy. "If the patient doesn't have a need of this—I do! I can't stand to see anyone sick."

There was no light in Tephuango except from the moon. The poverty-stricken huts looked less shabby beneath it.

Sam said: "Which one of these palaces is it?"

"Third from the end," Father Keogh said.

They stopped the car outside and walked into the hut. Sam still hugged the bottle of brandy. The fire in the center was out. They could see nothing until Father Keogh shone his torch. Then someone moaned in the corner.

"Sounds genuine," said Sam. "Gee, Mac! I hope there's no blood—do you want a hand?"

"Yes, I think I might. Could you manage the torch?"

Sam took the torch and they stepped round the fire to the corner. A figure lay wrapped in a petate.

Sam asked: "Why don't these guys send for the doctor when they're sick?"

"Because they're poor, and because they're always convinced that they're dying—they're worried about their souls."

He went down on one knee by the figure. When he moved aside the reed mat he recognized the Jeep. Then the torch failed and he heard a sharp thud and Sam cry out. He had heard nobody come up behind him. He sprang back to stumble against Sam at his feet. He felt for the torch but could not find it. He said anxiously: "Sam—what's happened? Sam—are you badly hurt?" He began to grope towards the

303

square of light that the doorway cut into the floor. He sensed Malo before he saw him. He called out: "Anacleto—how much is he hurt?"

Malo replied: "Not much."

When Father Keogh's eyes grew accustomed to the darkness he saw the black outline of Malo's figure. Vito and Porfirio came to the door. Porfirio was carrying a lamp. Father Keogh turned back towards Sam. Vito and Porfirio gripped his arms.

"Just let me see if he's hurt," Father Keogh said.

The Jeep wriggled free of his blanket. Malo came slowly towards Father Keogh. His face was no longer expressionless. Porfirio's lamp threw an odd yellow sheen across it. It seemed to awaken an inner light behind Malo's narrowed eyes. Father Keogh, looking at him, thought how sad it was that the light was not insane. There was nothing driving Malo that he could not have controlled himself.

Father Keogh asked him, "Won't this make it worse for you?" Malo made no reply. "You roused Chela's suspicions—she went to the Jefe. It's going to be difficult to make this look like an accident, isn't it? Or aren't you bothering about that sort of thing any more?"

The Jeep told him cheerfully, "Señor Frankenson has been a great help to us there. He will make it look more like an accident. The bottle he brought will be empty, you see. Señor Frankenson will be the one at the wheel when the car is found crashed, instead of Domingo. It will look very much better like that."

Porfirio said: "It's not kind to try and frighten the padre, Jeepo— you should explain that they'll both be dead first."

"Oh yes," the Jeep echoed, "they'll both be dead first."

Vito examined the butt of his gun; he slapped it against his palm.

Father Keogh addressed Malo. His voice was quiet. "Can't you leave Sam out?"

"I'm afraid he's a witness, my friend."

"I'll write a note in my own handwriting to say I took my own life for fear of you—or for any other reason you like to think up."

In the corner Sam rolled over and groaned. He sat up bewildered, calling: "Mac!" Then he crawled forward and found the bottle. He came up behind Vito, but the Jeep saw his arm swing. His shout turned Vito round. Father Keogh threw off Porfirio and the lamp struck the ground. It sent a thin acrid smoke up between them. Malo sprang at Father Keogh. When the priest raised his arms to fight him off, Vito fired his gun.

He meant to hit Father Keogh, but the bullet struck Malo instead.

304

It hit the hand that Malo had raised to strike the priest. It took three fingers off it, and left only the small finger and the thumb. It also embedded itself in the lung.

Sam's voice was agonized. "Mac?"

"He got Anacleto," Father Keogh said.

"For the love of Christ thank God!"

Malo lay on the floor. He lay as if none of his limbs belonged to him, but he kept his body straight. Father Keogh on his knees beside him thought how strange it seemed that Malo never lounged.

It was the Jeep who squeaked the question, "Is Anacleto dead?"

Father Keogh said: "No, but I think he's dying. Fetch the doctor—the car's outside."

Not one of the three men moved. Father Keogh looked up. "I said —fetch the doctor. He's dying."

There was a sudden stir behind his back. Sam called: "Let me alone, you sons of—!" Then his voice was cut short. Porfirio's dirty handkerchief was rammed inside his mouth and tied behind his head. Vito pulled Sam's coat down, with the sleeves they tied his arms behind his back. They threw him backwards and he fell on the ground trussed tightly, his face in the dirt.

Porfirio stood in the doorway. There were voices outside in the street. A few people had ventured out. Porfirio fired into the dust each side of them. The street was quickly cleared. Porfirio turned to Father Keogh. "When a man's dying it's too late for a doctor, what a dying man needs is a priest."

The Jeep backed after him keeping his gun on Father Keogh, and Vito backed after the Jeep.

Father Keogh called out: "Are you going to desert him?"

It was Malo who answered. "The rats are leaving—what did you expect of rats?"

Malo lay across the doorway. The moonlight crept over his face. It made it unnaturally white. They heard the car start up.

Father Keogh looked down at Malo. His chest was bleeding freely, and the blood trickled out of his mouth. But it was the shattered hand which hurt Father Keogh most. He had seen it lie motionless so many times. The blood round it raised the dirt and drove it forward in a narrow canal.

Father Keogh said: "When they've gone I'll free Sam. He shall go for the doctor. In the meantime I'll do what I can."

305

Malo's voice was still clear. "They were not all rats—there was old Uncle Joaquin, my friend."

Father Keogh had eased his handkerchief over the wound in the chest, and was raising the injured hand inch by inch when Vito returned to fire at him. He fired several times at Father Keogh. The bullets struck the shoulder, the stomach, and the chest. Then he flung the gun inside the hut.

Father Keogh was conscious not only of pain but a sharp surprise at it which quickly deadened, so that there was nothing left but pain.

They heard the car drive off.

Father Keogh felt the light of the moon across his face, but he found that he could no longer see. At first he thought his eyes were closed, and he felt for their lids with his fingertips. The lids were open, but the eyes remained sightless, and all hearing had gone from his ears. He heard only a senseless drumming in them. He was left with his fingertips. He felt forward with them guardedly towards the point where he knew Malo lay. He said: "Anacleto, can you hear me?" The voice was already a blind man's searching voice. . . .

Malo answered, "Yes."

But Father Keogh could not hear him. "Say an act of contrition, Anacleto. Say an act of contrition with me." In the corner Sam struggled to free himself. " 'Oh my God, I am heartily sorry for having offended thee.' "

Malo's voice was amused but not mocking. "I have no God to offend."

The anxious hands that traveled over him seemed to be begging more pitifully than the sightless black eyes. Father Keogh appealed to him. "Are you saying it? I can't seem to see or to hear any more. 'And I detest all my sins because I dread the loss of heaven and the pains of hell. . . .' "

"I dread neither heaven nor hell, my friend, those two are the same to me."

Father Keogh said: "Anacleto, if you're saying it, will you take my hand. If you're saying it—press it—let me feel you. Anacleto, press my hand."

He was conscious of an all-consuming pain such as he never dreamt existed. In his head he felt the words of the act of contrition receding further and further away from him. His dimming mind groped after them. If he lost them who could teach them to Malo? If he lost them who could save Malo?

306

Malo lay looking up at him; his eyes made a leisurely tour of the priest. When they returned to his face they remained on it. He saw that Father Keogh was crying and that it had nothing to do with his physical pain.

There was no longer any strength in his voice. "Oh, God, I have failed him. Oh, God, I have failed. Don't let him suffer because I have failed."

There had never before been a moment when Malo regretted causing pain. It was a sensation that brought him an agony of bewilderment more severe than the wounds that were nagging his body. It seemed to dissolve his remaining strength. He lay still with his eyes wide, and stared at the priest, at something he failed to understand. Then he moved his injured hand. He sent it out towards Vito's revolver. It lay on the floor two feet away from him.

Father Keogh rallied every available source of strength that was left within him to gather the cruelly retreating words. He failed to recapture some of them. He grasped what he could, and his voice regained strength. " 'Oh merciful Father whose love never fails, forgive me for I am truly sorry.' Anacleto—press my hand." It was a final and desperate appeal.

Malo's hand reached Vito's revolver. The mangled palm managed to grip it. There was no word for the pain that it cost him, that the cold metal caused to the finger stumps. He hit it down to the base of his wrist. With the remaining finger and thumb he managed to lift the gun.

Father Keogh's voice faltered: " 'Oh merciful Father whose love never fails . . .' Anacleto—press my hand."

Malo moved his good hand. It caught Father Keogh's sleeve. It felt its way down from the elbow with a deliberate care as if it feared that it might go astray. Then it found the priest's fingers—and pressed them.

Father Keogh smiled. He was hardly aware that he moved his lips. " 'To confess my sins, to do penance, and to amend my life . . .' "

Malo's injured hand brought the gun to the head of the priest. Malo's face was wet. There was fresh blood on his lower lip which his teeth had caused. He meant to pay the compliment that he only paid to cats, he meant to kill the priest outright. The thumb and the finger were forced into action. They managed to pull the trigger back.

But Sam's body rolled suddenly forward. It crashed into Malo's raised arm. The gun skidded. The bullet struck the wall of the hut.

Malo said: "What a God! No pity."

The hut became suddenly full of voices. Chela was crying, the Jefe was shouting. Someone was trying to relight the fire. The smoke drifted. Father Keogh believed that he lay in Ireland with the smell of burning turf in the air. Then he felt a pair of hands. They were neither gentle nor careful, but they loved him. In every rough gesture that hurt him he felt their love of him. Father Keogh recognized them. He said: "Sam, will you fetch me a priest."

Sam said: "Don't give me that dying stuff—listen, they shot the brandy up, how much more do you think a man can stand?"

Father Keogh said: "Father Lopez—Huapan. And Sam, you'll have to be quick."

"Listen, they have enough parsons up topside—what do you want to do to them, Mac, crowd them out? For Chrissake give the other guys a break."

Father Keogh's mind became suddenly clear. From the first word to the last he remembered the act of contrition, as if it had been written up before him in a black and impressive print. He lay smiling towards it. He said to Sam: "Is Anacleto dead?"

Sam said: "Jesus Christ who cares?"

"Sam, if he is will you look at him for me? If he looks peaceful—press my hand."

Sam shifted over to Malo. His eyes were wide open. They stared at the priest. Sam put a foot out and kicked him. "You goddamn son of a dirty bitch! You'd have plugged him, wouldn't you, when he was trying to save your goddamn soul. You goddamn dirty louse!" The body of Malo gave under his foot. It made no other movement. Sam said: "Yep! I guess he's burning." He went back and bent down to the priest. He met Father Keogh's black inquiring eyes. He shouted: "Pussyfoot looks a bloody sight too peaceful." Then he remembered and pressed the hand.

Father Keogh closed his eyes. His lips were moving. He was reciting the words that were written before him.

Sam asked the Jefe: "How much time do I have for that priest?"

The Jefe said: "No time. Stay with him. It's a question of minutes now."

Sam shouted: "Who says there's no time? If Mac wants a priest, he gets a priest."

He drove the Jefe's car. He wept behind the wheel. He said aloud: "For Chrissake—for Chrissake—" He raised his eyes to the heavens.

308

He said to them grimly: "Okay. I never said a prayer before—I shouldn't have done that to Pussyfoot—Pussyfoot had it coming to him—but you wouldn't get Mac dishing that stuff out. Okay—here's a prayer coming up. This is Sam Frankenson—praying!"

The Bishop received Father Keogh's letter.

> *I have enclosed a form of report much on the lines of the one submitted to your Lordship by Father Gomez, for the benefit of my successor. I am firmly convinced that if I am successful in my attempts to outwit Anacleto for the reasons your Lordship will find detailed in this report, he will not allow me to survive.*
>
> *I have laid my plans as carefully as possible with the help of my true friend Sam Frankenson, but I must repeat that if they succeed, I am certain, to use Father Gomez's own phrase, that I "shall not escape." Anacleto will forego all subtleties after this, and will stop at nothing to remove me from his path.*
>
> *It is a measure of my failure that my greatest grief is still a personal one; if I could have been certain that I had assisted but two of the people with whose spiritual care your Lordship entrusted me—if I could feel that I had bequeathed to my friend Sam even the possibility of acquainting himself with the limitless comfort of prayer, if I could feel that I had aroused in Anacleto one single moment's awakening to pity, I could die a happy man.*

The letter had crossed the Bishop's, informing Father Keogh of his transfer from Quantana.

In it the Bishop had written, "You may rest assured that in Father Marcelino Dominguez Lasques I have personally chosen someone whom I consider to be worthy of carrying on your work."